CARNAL URGES

OTHER BOOKS BY J.T. GEISSINGER

Queens and Monsters Series

Ruthless Creatures

Carnal Urges

Savage Hearts

Brutal Vows

Standalone

Pen Pal

CARNAL URGES

J.T. GEISSINGER

BRAMBLE
TOR PUBLISHING GROUP | NEW YORK

CARNAL URGES

Copyright © 2021 by J.T. Geissinger, Inc.

A Bramble Book
Published by Tom Doherty Associates / Tor Publishing Group
120 Broadway
New York, NY 10271

www.torpublishinggroup.com

Bramble™ is a trademark of Macmillan Publishing Group, LLC.

The Library of Congress Cataloging-in-Publication
Data is available upon request.

ISBN 978-1-250-34666-7 (trade paperback)
ISBN 978-1-250-34667-4 (ebook)

Our books may be purchased in bulk for promotional, educational, or business use. Please contact your local bookseller or the Macmillan Corporate and Premium Sales Department at 1-800-221-7945, extension 5442, or by email at MacmillanSpecialMarkets@macmillan.com.

Previously self-published by the author in 2021

First Bramble Trade Paperback Edition: 2025

Printed in the United States of America

0 9 8 7 6 5 4 3 2 1

For Jay. It's never not been you.

We are not mad, we are human and we want to love,
and someone must forgive us for the paths we take
to love, for the paths are many and dark and
we are ardent and cruel in our journey.

—LEONARD COHEN, FROM *A BALLET OF LEPERS*

ONE

SLOANE

I open my eyes to find a man leaning over me.

He's dressed in a black Armani suit. He has jet-black hair, a hard jaw, and the most beautiful blue eyes I've ever seen. They're surrounded by a thicket of lashes, long and curving, as dense and dark as his hair.

I'm intrigued by this handsome stranger for about two seconds, until I remember that he kidnapped me.

I should've known. The hotter a man is, the faster you should run away from him. A beautiful man is a bottomless pit your self-worth can disappear into and never be seen again.

His deep voice softened by a lilting Irish accent, my captor says, "You're awake."

"You sound disappointed."

The faintest of smiles curves his full lips. I'm amusing him. But the smile disappears as fast as it came, and he withdraws, settling his muscular frame in a chair opposite me.

He regards me with a look that could freeze molten lava. "Sit up. Let's talk."

I'm lying down. Sprawled on a cream-colored leather sofa in a narrow room with a rounded ceiling, my bare legs and feet chilled by the dry, cool air.

I have no recollection how I got here and no knowledge of where "here" is.

I remember only that I was going to visit my best friend, Natalie, in New York City, and the moment I stepped out of the car in the parking garage of her building, a half-dozen black SUVs with tinted windows roared up, and this blue-eyed devil jumped out of one of them and snatched me.

There was also gunfire. I do recall that. The burnt smell of gunpowder in the air, the deafening roar of the shots . . .

I sit up abruptly. The room starts to spin. There's a sharp ache in my right shoulder, as if I had been hit there. Fighting nausea, I take several deep breaths, one hand pressed to my churning stomach and the other to my clammy forehead.

I feel sick.

"That'll be the ketamine," says my captor, watching me.

His name swims into memory: Declan. He told me that right after he shoved me into his SUV. His name and that he was taking me to speak to his boss . . . in Boston.

Now I remember. I'm on an airplane headed to see the leader of the Irish mafia to answer some questions about how I might have started a war between his family and the Russians. And everyone else.

So much for my fun New York vacation.

I swallow several times, willing my queasy stomach to settle. "You drugged me?"

"We had to. You're surprisingly strong for someone who dresses like the Tooth Fairy."

The comparison irritates me. "Just because I'm girly doesn't mean I'm a little girl."

He lets his gaze drift over my outfit.

I'm wearing a hot-pink layered tulle miniskirt by Betsey Johnson that I paired with a short white denim jacket and a white tee underneath. I bedazzled the jacket with rhinestone butterflies because butterflies are beautiful, kickass symbols of hope, change, and self-transformation, and that's exactly the kind of positive fucking energy I'm all about.

Even if it is girly.

His tone dry, Declan says, "Evidently. That right hook of yours is impressive."

"What do you mean?"

"I mean what you did to Kieran's nose."

"I don't know a Kieran. Or his nose."

"You don't remember? You broke it."

"*Broke* it? No. I would've remembered breaking someone's nose."

When Declan stays silent and only sits there staring at me, my heart sinks. "The drugs?"

"Aye."

I look down at my right hand and am startled to see bruises on my knuckles. *I did break someone's nose. How could I not remember that?*

My voice climbs in panic. "Oh god. Am I brain damaged?"

He arches one dark eyebrow. "You mean more than you were before?"

"This isn't funny."

"How would you know? You're unironically wearing a child's Halloween costume. I'd say your sense of humor is as bad as your wardrobe."

I fight the unexpected urge to laugh. "Why am I barefoot? Where are my shoes?"

His silence is long and calculating.

"They're my only pair of Louis Vuitton. Do you have any idea how expensive those are? I had to save for months."

He tilts his head to one side and examines me with those piercing blue eyes for longer than is comfortable. "You're not afraid."

"You already told me you weren't going to hurt me."

He considers that for a moment, his brows drawn together thoughtfully. "Did I?"

"Yes. Back in the parking garage."

"I could change my mind."

"You won't."

"Why not?"

I shrug. "Because I'm charming. Everybody loves me."

His head tilt and frown are now accompanied by a derisive curl of his upper lip.

"It's true. I'm very likeable."

"I don't like you."

That makes me bristle, though I try not to show it. "I don't like you, either."

"I'm not the one claiming to be so charming."

"A good thing, too, because you're not."

We stare at each other. After a beat, he says, "I'm told my accent is charming."

That makes me chuckle. "It's *so* not."

When he looks dubious, I relent. "Even if it were, it's cancelled by the rest of your horrible personality. What did you want to talk about? Wait, I need to pee first. Where's the bathroom?"

When I stand, he leans forward, grasps my wrist, and pulls me back down to a sitting position. Without releasing my wrist, he growls, "You'll go to the bathroom when I say you can. Now stop running your bloody mouth and listen to me."

It's my turn to arch an eyebrow. "I listen better when I'm not being manhandled."

We do the staring thing again. I'll go blind before I'll blink first. It's a standoff, a silent push-pull with neither of us giving an inch, until finally, a muscle flexes in his jaw. Then he exhales and grudgingly releases my wrist.

Ha. Get used to losing, gangster. I smile at him and say pleasantly, "Thank you."

He's wearing the same look my older brother used to wear when we were kids and he was about to deck me for being annoying. Naturally, it makes me smile wider.

Men say they love a strong woman, right up until they meet one.

I fold my hands in my lap and wait for him to control his temper. He sits back in his chair, straightens his tie, grinds his molars for a while, then says, "Here are the rules."

Rules. For me? Hilarious. But I'm pretending to be cooperative, so I sit patiently and listen instead of laughing in his face.

"One: I don't tolerate disobedience. If I give you an order, you follow it."

Magic 8 Ball says: Outlook not so good.

"Two: you don't speak unless you're spoken to."

In what universe is that happening? Not this one.

"Three: I'm not Kieran. If you hit me, I hit back." His blue eyes glitter. His voice drops. "And it will hurt."

He's trying to scare me into obedience. That tactic never worked for my father, and it won't work for him. My voice drips with disdain. "What a gentleman."

"You lasses are the ones who're always crying about equal treatment. Except when it's inconvenient."

He's a first-class asshole, but also right. If I can't take it, I shouldn't dish it out.

Except I *can* take it and I *can* dish it out. Sooner or later, he'll find out exactly how well.

I didn't spend the last ten years sweating my ass off in self-defense classes so I could burst into tears at a threat from some random Irish gangster.

After a while when he doesn't continue, I say, "Are there more?"

He deadpans, "I figured three would be all your damaged brain could handle."

Boy, this one could really charm the birds right out of the trees. "So thoughtful."

"Like you said. I'm a gentleman."

He stands. Towering over me at his full height, he's suddenly imposing. I lean back and stare up at him, unsure what he's going to do next.

He looks satisfied by my alarmed expression. "The loo is at the back of the plane. You have two minutes. If you're not out by then, I'll break down the door."

"Why? Do you think I'll try to escape through the toilet?"

His lashes lower. I can tell he's annoyed again by the slow, aggravated breath he draws. He says softly, "Careful, lass. Your boyfriend, Stavros, might tolerate mouthy women, but I don't."

I suppose he mentioned Stavros to clue me in that he knows things about me, that he's done his homework on his captive, but it doesn't surprise me. Any kidnapper worth his salt would do the same.

But he's got one important fact wrong, and I'm a stickler for accuracy on this particular topic. "Stavros isn't my boyfriend."

Declan gives me the arched eyebrow again, wry and disdainful. "Excuse me?"

"I said he's not my boyfriend. I don't keep boyfriends."

"Due to your exhausting need to run your mouth, no doubt."

His testicles are at about eye level, but I resist the urge to acquaint them with my fist. There's always later.

"No, I meant that I don't *keep* them, like the way you keep chickens. Or how a man keeps a mistress. I don't have the patience for boyfriends. They're too high-maintenance. Way more trouble than they're worth."

He stares down at me with an expressionless face, but his eyes are doing something interesting. I can almost see the wheels turning inside his head.

"So you broke up."

"Are you even listening? He was never my 'boyfriend.' I don't do boyfriends."

His smile is faintly evil. "Good. Then I won't have to deal with him riding in on his white horse to try to rescue you."

I laugh at the mental image of Stavros on a horse. He's terrified of animals. "Oh, he'll totally try to rescue me."

When Declan narrows his eyes, I add, "If you could not hurt him, that would be great. I'd feel really guilty if he got hurt on my account."

The deafening silence that follows calls for an explanation. "I mean, of course you have to do your gangster thing, but Stavros is actually a nice guy. It's not his fault he'll try to rescue me. He won't be able to help himself."

"And why is that?"

"I told you. I'm charming. He was a goner from the day we met."

I have never been looked at the way Declan is looking at me right now. If an alien spacecraft landed on top of the plane and sucked us inside with a tractor beam, he couldn't look more confounded.

I have to admit it's pretty satisfying.

The sense of satisfaction evaporates when he wraps his big hands around my upper arms and hauls me upright.

He leans close to my face and says from between gritted teeth, "You're about as charming as herpes. Now go take a piss."

He pushes me away, drags his hands through his hair, and mutters a curse under his breath.

If the stick stuck up this guy's ass were any bigger, he'd be a tree.

I head toward the back of the plane, passing more plush leather sofas and chairs. The décor is elegant and understated, everything done in shades of champagne and gold. All the windows have little curtains drawn across them. The carpeting is soft and luxurious under my bare feet. It's like a miniature penthouse . . . complete with security.

Six buff gangsters in black suits glower at me as I approach.

They're seated on opposite sides of the aisle in captain's chairs with glossy wood tables between them. Two of them are playing cards. Two of them are drinking whiskey. A fifth has a magazine in his meaty hands, and the sixth looks like he wants to tear my head clear off my body.

He's the biggest one with the black eyes, a strip of medical tape across the swollen bridge of his nose, and spots of blood decorating the collar of his white dress shirt.

I almost feel bad that I did that to him, especially in front of all his buddies. No wonder he's looking at me like that. Beaten by a girl—his ego is a five-year-old having a screaming tantrum in the ice cream aisle.

But I might need an ally at some point in this adventure. A little groveling now could go a long way in the future.

I stop next to his chair and smile at him. "I'm sorry about your nose, Kieran."

A few of the men snort. A couple others exchange surprised glances.

Kieran's burning stare could melt steel. I've spent a lot of time around gangsters, however, so I'm immune to their tempers.

"If it makes a difference, I don't remember anything. That ketamine you guys gave me knocked me out pretty good. I'm usually not so nasty. Don't get me wrong, I'm all for violence when it's necessary, but I only go there as a last resort. When I'm conscious, that is."

I think for a moment as Kieran glares at me.

"To tell the truth, I probably would've tried to break your nose even if I wasn't on drugs. You were kidnapping me, after all. So there's that. But in any case, I promise I won't break anything else unless you make it necessary. In fact, I'll make you a deal: if you need me to get into the trunk of a car or the cargo hold of a ship or onto another airplane or whatever, just ask politely, and I'll be happy to oblige. This doesn't have to be acrimonious."

Kieran takes a moment to decide how to respond. Or maybe he's trying to figure out what acrimonious means. Either way, this guy isn't what you'd call a brilliant conversationalist. I'm going to have to do all the heavy lifting.

"What I mean is that we don't have to be hostile toward each other. You have a job to do. I get it. I won't try to make it harder than it has to be. Just communicate with me, okay? We'll be out of each other's hair in no time."

Silence. He blinks, once. I take it as a yes and beam at him.

"Cool. Thanks. And thank you for not hitting me back. Your boss tells me he doesn't have the same scruples."

From the other end of the plane, Declan thunders, *"Take your bloody piss!"*

Shaking my head, I say, "I feel sorry for his mother. She should've swallowed instead."

I go into the restroom, the sound of six gangsters' stunned silence echoing behind me as I close the door.

TWO

DECLAN

*K*idnapping a woman shouldn't be this aggravating.

Part of me is surprised we even managed to get her onto the plane. From the moment we grabbed her in that parking garage in Manhattan, she's been an absolute pain in the arse.

Most people—most sane people—do one of three things when subjected to a traumatic experience like kidnapping: they cry, they beg, or they shut down completely, paralyzed by fear. The rare person will fight for his life or try to escape. Few are that brave.

And then there's *this* barmy lass.

Chatty, cheerful, and calm, she acts as if she's starring in a biopic about a beloved historical figure who died at the height of her beauty while saving a group of starving orphans from a burning building or some such noble shite.

Her confidence is unshakable. I've never met anyone more completely self-assured.

Or one with so little reason to be.

She teaches *yoga,* for fuck's sake. In a tiny mountain lake town. The way she carries herself, you'd think she's the Queen of England.

How the hell does a twentysomething yoga instructor who barely scraped through college, has never had a long-term boyfriend, and looks like she buys her clothes at a Tinker Bell estate sale get so confident?

I don't know. I don't *want* to know.

I'm curious about her fighting skills, though. She might not remember clobbering Kieran, but I certainly do. In all our years working together, I've never seen anyone take him down.

I hate to admit it, but it was impressive.

I know from the background check I ran on her that she didn't serve in the military and has no formal combat or martial arts training. And there's no indication in the thousands of selfies on her Instagram page that she knows how to do anything other than eat kale, bend like a pretzel, and strike a pose in good lighting wearing tight, revealing athletic gear.

He was probably distracted by her tits.

Or maybe it was her legs.

Or maybe it was that cocky grin she likes to flash, right before she says something that makes you want to put your hands around her neck and squeeze, if only to get her to stop talking.

The sooner this is over, the better. I've known her for all of two hours—half of that while she was unconscious—and I'm ready to shoot myself in the face.

I take out my cell, dial the same number I've been dialing since we picked her up, and listen to it ring.

Once again, it goes to voicemail.

And once again, my sense that something is very wrong grows stronger.

THREE

SLOANE

*I*t comes back to me as I'm sitting on the toilet: I jumped out of a moving vehicle.

No wonder my shoulder is killing me.

I try to piece together the memory, but the images are dark and shifting. There's a vague recollection of running down a rainy street with Declan in pursuit, another of adopting a fighting stance in the middle of a circle of him and his thug buddies.

Then nothing.

My stomach is still unsettled, but it's my throbbing skull that really worries me. I hit my head on the cement when Declan dragged me out of the car in the parking garage. I think I might have already lost consciousness before the drug knocked me out.

A head injury, even a small one, can be big trouble.

Bigger trouble even than being kidnapped and taken to see the leader of the Irish mafia.

I finish up, wash my hands, and head back to where Declan's waiting at the front of the plane. He watches me approach, wearing an expression like he's suffering from hemorrhoids.

I sit on the sofa I woke up on and fold my legs comfortably underneath me. "Question: why did I jump out of the car?"

Frowning, Declan looks at my folded legs. "You got one look at the handcuffs Kieran was going to put on you and took a flying leap."

Yes, that would've done it. I'm the one who puts the handcuffs on men, not vice versa. "Was that before or after I broke his nose?"

His lashes lift, and now I'm being roasted by a pair of burning blue eyes. His voice is low and tight. "It must be that brain damage that's making you forget rule number two."

I think for a moment. "Which was number two?"

"Don't speak unless you're spoken to."

"Oh, right. Sorry. I'm not so good with rules."

"Or with following orders."

"I'm not trying to aggravate you on purpose." I pause. "Okay, maybe I am a little. But you did kidnap me."

He glances at my legs again. His expression is one of distaste. Offended by his look, I say, "What?"

"Don't sit like that."

"Like what?"

He makes a dismissive motion with his hand to indicate my posture. "Like you're on the ground in kindergarten class waiting for your teacher to start story time."

"Floor."

"Excuse me?"

"You mean floor, not ground. Ground is outside. Floor is in."

His glare is withering, but I don't wilt. I smile instead.

He says, "Whoever gave you the idea you're charming was an idiot."

"Oh, c'mon. Admit it. You're already a big fan."

His expression indicates he might throw up. Then he gets mad and snaps, "What kind of woman isn't afraid of her kidnappers?"

"One who's spent a lot of time around men in your line of work and knows how you operate."

"Meaning?"

"Meaning the mafia is more anal than the military when it comes to hierarchy and commands. You already told me you weren't going to hurt me. Which means when your boss ordered you to nab me and bring me to him for a chat, he also said to make sure I wasn't harmed on the way. Which means you'll go to extreme measures to make sure I don't have anything negative to tell him about the way you treated me during my trip. May I please have a glass of water? My mouth is as dry as a bone."

We stare at each other for what feels like an hour. He seems to enjoy trying to intimidate me and failing.

Finally, he speaks. Working at the knot in his tie, he says darkly, "That mouth is going to get you into trouble one day, Tinker Bell."

He whips off his tie and lunges at me.

A startled yelp is all I can manage before he's on me, pushing me flat to my back and wedging his knee between my legs. We grapple for a moment as I try to get him off me—it's impossible, this fucker is *strong*—until he manages to get both my arms over my head. Then there's a flash of metal and a *click*, and I'm handcuffed.

And furious.

I shout, "You son of a—"

Declan wraps his tie over my mouth and around my jaw and knots it against the back of my head.

Now I'm gagged.

Breathing hard through my nose, I glare up at him in outrage. It's of little satisfaction that he's breathing hard, too.

"That's better." *Now* he's smiling, the psychopath.

I try to yell *Pig!* but it comes out muffled. He gets the gist of it, anyway.

Clucking in mock dismay, he says, "Now, now, what kind of language is that for a charming young lady? Didn't they teach you in finishing school that swearing is unbecoming?"

One more rhetorical question, and I'll slice off your balls.

He's sickeningly pleased with himself, the ass. Meanwhile, I'm so mad, I'm almost vibrating.

And he still hasn't gotten off me.

His forearms are propped on either side of my head. Pelvis to chest, his body rests against mine. He's warm and heavy, smells faintly of peppermint and something spicy, and I hope that's a gun in his pants' pocket, because *holy* . . .

Our eyes lock. His smile dies. A flicker of something other than disdain appears in his cold blue eyes.

In one swift motion, he rolls off me and stands.

His shoulders stiff and his back to me, he drags a hand through his thick dark hair and snaps, "I wasn't ordered not to harm you, so don't fucking test me."

His voice is so rough and raspy, it sounds like he's been swallowing rocks. I'm not sure which one of us is more disoriented.

I sit up. He turns and scowls down at me like he's Lord Voldemort and I'm Harry Potter.

Why is this man so *crabby*?

I don't care. I just want to kick him in the shin. No—somewhere more tender.

Before I can shout more muffled curses at him through his necktie, he hauls me up by my wrists, spins me around, backs me up a few steps, then pushes me into the chair he was sitting in. He fastens the lap belt over me, cinching it tightly across my lap. Then he leans down into my face, all muscular and murdery.

He snaps, "You have a choice to make, lass. Either you sit here quietly until the end of the flight, or you continue to test my patience. If you decide to go with option number two, the consequences will be dire."

I must be psychically telegraphing that I doubt him, because he elaborates.

"I'll call the boys back here and let them watch while I tear that ridiculous tutu off you and spank your naked ass until it's red."

Sweet baby Jesus, I wish I knew Morse code. I would blink this asshole such a terrorist threat with my eyelids that he wouldn't be able to sleep for the rest of his life.

Whatever he sees in my eyes makes him smile. I hate it that he gets a charge out of infuriating me.

"So, which will it be? One or two?"

He cocks his eyebrow and waits for me to respond. Maintaining eye contact, I lift my bound hands and raise a single finger.

The middle one.

A muscle flexes in his jaw. He exhales slowly through his nose. He grinds his back teeth for a while, because apparently it's his thing, then he straightens and gazes down at me like I'm a turd on the bottom of his shoe.

When his cell phone rings, he whips it out of his pocket so fast, it's a blur.

Sounding tense, he orders whoever's calling, "Talk to me."

He listens intently, unmoving, his eyes narrowed, his gaze focused on a spot somewhere on the wall above my head. The hand not holding the phone clenches to a fist. Then he closes his eyes and mutters, *"Fuck."*

He listens a while longer, then disconnects. He lowers his arm to his side.

Then he stands there with his eyes closed, every muscle in his body tensed. His hand is gripped so hard around the phone, his knuckles are white.

When he finally opens his eyes and looks down at me, his eyes aren't blue anymore.

They're black.

I decide this is the wrong time to demonstrate that he should've cuffed my hands behind my back, not in front. All I need to do to ungag myself is to reach up and pull the tie out of my mouth and down my jaw.

But he doesn't seem in the mood for one-upmanship, so I wait.

He turns away abruptly and strides down the aisle toward his crew. He says a few words to them. Whatever his news is, it shocks them. They shift in their seats, muttering to each other and throwing me strange glances. Kieran looks especially unnerved.

I don't have time to wonder what's happening, because Declan is striding back to me, his eyes fierce, his jaw like stone.

He sweeps by and disappears into the galley behind the cockpit. In a moment, he reappears, holding a glass of water. He sits opposite me and holds out the glass without a word.

When I take it from him, he leans over and pries the tie out of my mouth, sliding it down my jaw until it drops to my chest and hangs there like a necklace. Or a noose.

Surprised at this reversal, I thank him.

He doesn't respond. He simply sits and stares at me, his expression dark. One index finger taps a slow, steady beat on the arm of the sofa.

I polish off the glass of water, aware of him watching my every move. Aware of him thinking as he gazes at me. His eyes are speculative. Calculating. Hard.

Whatever that phone call was about, it had something to do with me.

We sit in awkward silence until I'm so self-conscious, I have to force myself not to squirm in my seat.

Finally, he says, "Do you know how to use a gun?"

The question startles me. Judging by his expression, I was expecting him to lunge at me again. "Yes."

He doesn't look surprised. "And I assume from the way you handled yourself with Kieran, you know some form of self-defense?"

Where is he going with this? "Yes."

He mutters, "Good."

Good? What's going on here?

When he remains silent, brooding over whatever his call was about, I wiggle my fingers for permission to speak. He sends me a curt nod.

"What's happened?"

His cold blue gaze on me is steady. "There's been a change of plans."

My mouth is dry again, despite the water I drank. "So I'm not going to meet the head of your family?"

Something about the question amuses him, but in a dark way. His chuckle is totally devoid of humor. "You're meeting with him right now."

It takes a moment for it to dawn on me. Declan is the new boss of the Irish mafia.

Whoever the old boss was, he's dead.

And somehow, I'm the cause of it.

FOUR

SLOANE

It's raining in Boston when the plane touches down. I don't know what time it is, but I'm exhausted. Everything aches, including the soles of my feet, which are covered in tiny cuts and bruises.

Wherever I ran in my escape attempt before they finally got me onto the plane, it must've been far.

I wish I could recall, but there's a black hole in my memory. It matches the black holes of Declan's eyes every time they swing in my direction.

"Let's go," he says in a muted tone, reaching down to grasp my arm.

He pulls me to my feet, handling me more gently than before. The gentleness is confusing, considering he has even more reason to hate me now than he did earlier.

Not that he's confirmed anything, but I'm reading between the lines.

Unlike the gag, my handcuffs remain in place. Declan guides

me down the metal airstairs leading to the rain-swept tarmac, his hand wrapped firmly around my biceps. Both of us are getting wet in the cold, steady drizzle. My teeth start to chatter halfway down.

When we reach the bottom, I slip on the last step.

Before I do a face-plant onto the wet asphalt, he catches me and swings me up into his arms, as easily as if I weighed no more than a feather.

Startled, I inhale sharply. I look at him, handsome in profile and very grim, and start to open my mouth.

"Not a word," he warns, carrying me toward the waiting limo.

He's furious, of that I'm certain. I'm less certain now, however, that his anger is directed at me. His arms feel less like a cage and more like a kind of protection.

The way his gaze sweeps the area feels protective, too, as if he's expecting an armed gang to pounce from the shadows. If they are, he seems fully prepared to take them on.

Stavros and I were once caught in a gunfight. Well, technically, Stavros and his minions *started* a gunfight, and I was caught in it, but I digress. I remember very clearly how panicked he was, how even though he had a weapon and was doing his best to protect me, his hands shook and his voice came out high and he hyperventilated so badly, he almost passed out.

I can't picture Declan hyperventilating.

I can't picture him panicking.

I *can* picture irritating him to death, but that's a different story.

A uniformed driver opens the back door of the limo as we approach. Two other vehicles wait behind the limo, SUVs that I assume are for the rest of the crew.

Declan sets me on my feet and helps me into the car, sliding across the leather bench seat to sit beside me. The driver slams shut the door and jumps into the front, gunning the engine before peeling out so fast, I gasp.

"Here."

Declan holds out a hand towel he removed from a compartment near the door. When I take it from him, he says, "Wait."

He removes a small key from the inside pocket of his suit jacket and uncuffs me. He looks at the glinting circles of metal in his hands, then abruptly throws them against the smoked-glass partition that divides the back of the limo from the driver's seat. They bounce off and clatter to the floor. His suit jacket follows the cuffs, then he drops his head against the headrest and closes his eyes, muttering in Gaelic.

I sit holding the towel and stare at him, lost. "Are you okay?"

After a moment, he turns his head and peers at me.

"I mean, you just seem . . . oh, sorry. I forgot I'm not supposed to be talking."

I busy myself with drying my hair and face, blotting my mascara carefully so I don't wind up with raccoon eyes. I wipe the rain off my bare legs, too, wondering what I'm going to do for clothes for however long I'm going to be a captive.

All the while, I'm aware of him silently watching me. The air is thick with all the things he wants to say but doesn't.

We drive. He takes phone calls, one after another, speaking in Gaelic through each one. After maybe a dozen, he hangs up and turns to me.

"Don't try to run. It's safer for you with me than anywhere else right now."

"Trust me, my feet hurt too much to . . . What do you mean, it's safer with you?"

"Exactly what I said."

We gaze at each other as the limo speeds through the night. Wherever we're going, we're going there fast. "So all that stuff you threatened me with on the plane—"

He interrupts, "What kinds of guns have you handled?"

When I blink, he growls, "Answer the fucking question, please."

Please. Astonished, I open my mouth, then close it again. My second attempt is successful. "A .357 Desert Eagle. Glock G19. AK-47."

His brows lift. He's surprised by the AK.

"Stavros had rifles lying all over the place. He liked to shoot at fish in the lake."

"Of course he did. Fucking Russians." He shakes his head in disgust, then leans down and pulls a small black pistol from a holder around his ankle.

He hands it to me.

"If we're separated, use it on anyone who approaches you, even if they seem friendly. Even if it's a little old lady, shoot that bitch between the eyes."

I stare at him with my mouth hanging open and my eyes wide.

He sends me a mirthless smile. "At last. Silence."

I can't form words. This psychotic blue-eyed gangster has rendered me speechless.

When I finally manage to regain control of my tongue, I say, "How do you know I'm not going to shoot *you*?"

"Are you?"

I consider it. "Maybe."

"Decide. We don't have much time."

"You're insane, is that it?"

"Believe me, lass, I sometimes wonder."

Pulling a beefy silver semi-automatic handgun from his waistband at the small of his back, he continues. "Things are going to get bad. We're going to take fire. The car is armored, but if the tires are compromised, we have about eighty kilometers before they die."

He stops and looks at me, "That's roughly fifty miles."

I see. He doesn't think I'm brain damaged, he thinks I'm just plain stupid.

"I don't give a shit about the tires. Rewind to the part about things getting bad and start over. What the hell is going on?"

"I can't tell you."

"If you can hand me a loaded gun and tell me to shoot an old lady between the eyes, you can tell me what's happening. We're past the honeymoon stage. Besides, I can handle it, no matter how bad it is. Spill."

I could swear that flash in his eyes is admiration, but it's probably just an urge to wrap his hands around my neck and choke me.

And not in the good way.

"War is what's happening, Tinker Bell," he says ominously. "War and all the bloody business that goes along with it."

"Oh, swell. You're being cryptic. I just love an incomprehensible Irishman. They're my absolute favorite."

"Careful. You'll exhaust yourself using your entire vocabulary all at once."

"Can you tell from my tone how much I want to smash the butt of this gun into your face?"

"Can you tell from my face how much I want to smash the palm of my hand into your butt?"

"That was stupid."

"Says the girl who jumped from a speeding car."

"I would've jumped from a skyscraper if it meant I wouldn't have to be near you."

"If I'd known that, I would've taken you straight to the top of the Hancock Tower."

I roll my eyes. "Just tell me the truth. I swear I won't burst into tears. The last time that happened was before I'd even gotten my first period."

He pauses, his gaze assessing. "Tell me how it's possible that you're not scared of me, or of this situation, or of anything else as far as I can see, and I'll tell you what's happening."

I give it serious thought for a moment. "Honestly? I'm just badass like that."

After a short, disbelieving silence, Declan starts to laugh.

It's a deep, rich, sexy sound, beautifully masculine. I hate myself for liking it. And for noticing what nice white teeth he has. And how strong his jaw is. And is that a *dimple* in his cheek?

He stops laughing abruptly, looking as disturbed by the unexpected outburst as I am. Guess he wasn't expecting that, either.

"Got that out of your system?"

Glowering, he says, "Aye."

"Good. So who's going to be shooting at us?"

"MS-13."

More gangsters. I'm in up to my eyeballs. "Because . . . ?"

"They don't like me."

I stare at him with my lower lip pinched between my teeth.

He says drily, "Thank you for showing restraint. It must be incredibly difficult."

"You have no idea."

"There's another reason they're after me."

When he only sits there gazing at me in inscrutable silence, I prompt, "Anytime you feel like enlightening me, I'm all ears."

"You."

Surprised, I blink. "Me?"

"Aye. You."

"I don't know any Salvadorans. Of the mobster variety, that is."

"Did you think your abduction would go over well with your friend Mr. Portnov?"

He means Kage, my bestie's man, who also happens to be top dog of the Russian mafia.

From what Stavros once told me, MS-13 is the fastest-growing gang in the Boston area. Kage must've made some kind of deal with them to try to rescue me as soon as I got off the plane. But how would he know where Declan took me after the parking garage or where we might ultimately be headed?

Or even if I'm dead or alive, for that matter? Declan could've slit my throat the moment he nabbed me.

Then it hits me: Natalie doesn't know if I'm dead or alive, either.

I sit bolt upright on the seat and shout, "Oh my god, she'll be so worried! Give me your cell phone."

"I'm not giving you my cell phone."

"I have to let my girlfriend know I'm alive."

His pause seems loaded. "Ah."

"What do you mean, *ah*?"

"You and your girlfriend."

"What about us?"

"You're very . . . close."

"Of course we're close. She's been my best friend since . . ." I trail off, frowning at his expression. Then I sigh. "Oh, for fuck's sake."

"I'm not judging."

"Will you shut up already? We're not lesbians."

He looks unconvinced. "You did say you couldn't keep a boyfriend."

"No, I said I don't *keep* boyfriends. You totally missed the emphasis. Boyfriends are like koi fish: a time-consuming and boring hobby. I have no interest in that kind of commitment. Are you getting this?"

"You also seem like you really dislike the opposite sex."

I smile at him. "Only a deserving few."

He ignores that. "And there is the matter of the way you handle pressure."

"What about it?"

"You're almost as brave as a man."

"What a coincidence, I was just thinking that about you."

He exhales a short breath through his nose and shakes his head.

He doesn't know whether to laugh or clobber me. "You're really something else, lass."

"I keep telling you, gangster. I'm charming. By the time this is all over, you'll be head over heels in love with me."

Blue eyes burning, he opens his mouth to speak, but his words are lost in the sudden, deafening noise of a hailstorm of bullets bombarding the side of the car.

FIVE

SLOANE

*T*he first thing Declan does is throw himself on top of me.

It has the immediate effect of knocking all the breath from my lungs and the pistol from my hand. I lie flattened on the bench seat, stunned and wheezing, as Declan lies over me, an Irish gangster blanket weighing approximately ten tons.

"Sean is an excellent driver," he says calmly, looking toward the closed partition window. "So there's a chance we can outrun them. But if they've blocked off streets—like I would've done—they could be intentionally steering us toward a dead end."

He gazes down at me. "Which wouldn't be good."

The limo swerves wildly, fishtailing for a moment before straightening and continuing at breakneck speed. Another volley of gunfire rings out. Bullets pepper the rear window and ricochet off, leaving little round indents surrounded by spiderweb cracks.

Struggling for breath, I say faintly, "I have questions."

"What a surprise."

"How did you know they'd be waiting for us? What happened

to your boss? What happens if they steer us toward a dead end? And why the hell are you lying on top of me?"

He looks vaguely insulted. "To protect you, of course."

"You said this car was armored."

That stumps him for a moment. "Right. Sorry. Instincts."

He withdraws, sitting up and pulling me along with him. I retrieve my cute little pistol from the floor, stick it into the back waistband of my skirt, and turn to face him on the seat.

"What kind of kidnapper has protective instincts for his kidnappee?"

He snaps, "The stupid kind. I should open the door and throw you to the wolves."

I inspect his expression. "But you won't."

His answer is a dissatisfied grumble. Meanwhile, we're still speeding, the bullets are still flying, and I'm starting to have a good time.

"Ha! You see? I'm charming you already."

He closes his eyes and sighs. "Dear god, make it stop."

"Hold on, back up. What do you mean, 'throw you to the wolves'? Aren't these MS-13 guys supposed to be trying to rescue me? You know, from *you*?"

He scoffs. "If you had any brains, you'd be dangerous."

"Oh, you think you're better than them?"

"We're not even the same species, lass."

I make a face. "That sounds more than a little racist. You might want to check your prejudice, pal."

Outraged, he glares at me. Then he thunders, "I'm not talking about their fucking *race*! I'm talking about what they'd do to you if they got their hands on you, you bloody little gobshite! Them or any other family!" He mutters, "Thick as a plank, y'are."

His accent gets more pronounced when he's angry. It's almost hot.

"You're not making sense. Why would they 'do' anything to me if they're trying to help me?"

"*Help* you?" He laughs. "I thought you said you'd spent time with men in my line of work?"

Feeling defensive, I say, "They didn't raise me from birth. I've just dated a few. Okay, one. But yes, I did spend plenty of time with him, and with his buddies, and also some with my girlfriend's man, so I know the rules."

His blue eyes glitter in the dim light. "We're at war, lass. There are no rules. Especially when it comes to the woman who started the whole bloody mess in the first place. If they returned you to New York barely breathing, your Russian boss friend would consider it a solid."

His tone drops. "No matter how many times you were raped and beaten along the way."

I know he's serious, but this is also the man who threatened to rip off my skirt, spank my ass, and let his crew do the same to me—or worse—then turned around and handed me a gun. I'm not so sure his judgement can be trusted.

Besides, Nat would kill Kage if the men he sent to rescue me harmed me instead. He'd be castrated in ten seconds, which I'm sure he knows.

Onward.

"You keep blaming me for starting a war. Why?"

"Because you did."

"I think I would've remembered that."

"You don't remember jumping from the car or punching Kieran."

"I see. So I started this mafia war while under the influence of the drugs you gave me?"

He doesn't like my tone, which drips sarcasm. I can tell he's wishing he never took his tie off my mouth.

"I don't have the time or patience to paint a fucking picture for you."

"Calm down. You don't have to curse at me."

His blistering glare could peel paint from a wall. "I think you're lying about not having boyfriends. I think you've had plenty, and they all committed suicide."

"And I think it's scary that people like you are allowed to vote. You never answered my other questions."

"I'm too busy planning where I'm going to bury your body."

He's grinding his molars again. I'm really bad for his dental health. Pity, because those teeth of his are awfully nice.

"Did you have braces when you were young?"

"What the . . . ? Never mind. Jesus. Get down on the floor. If the car stops and I get out, stay inside. And for the love of all that's holy, *be quiet*."

He shoves me down onto the floor and holds me there with his hand wrapped firmly around the back of my neck. I look up at him, marveling that he actually thinks I'm going to obey a single one of those instructions.

How are men in charge of running everything? They're clueless.

"Hey. Gangster."

He closes his eyes, makes a growling noise, and tightens his hand on my neck.

"Oh, relax. I just wanted to ask if you think Reverse Stockholm syndrome is already a thing, or if you're about to invent it?"

"How many times did your parents beg you to run away from home?"

Good one. He's really getting the hang of this. "After the first few dozen, they got used to the idea that I don't respond well to demands."

When he opens his eyes to glare down at me, I smile. "Oh, come on. You're just mad because you're usually the one poking the bear."

He pauses his glaring to be surprised. "How did you know that?"

"I can spot a fellow smartass a mile away. It's one of my many talents. If you really want to be impressed, you should watch me play Texas Hold'em. I slay."

Gaze softening, he tilts his head and looks at me. Really *looks* at me, the way men rarely do, with genuine curiosity.

Most of them never get past my boobs.

But the look is gone in a flash as more bullets pummel the side of the car. It slips sideways, skidding. Then we hit something, hard, and come to a jolting stop. The only reason I don't smash through the rear window and go flying out like a missile is because Declan is somehow on top of me again, pinning me down with his substantial weight.

When the dust settles, I say breathlessly, "This is getting to be kind of a thing."

"You'll be running your mouth in your grave, won't you, lass?"

"I'm going to be cremated. There won't be any mouth to run."

"I'm sure you'll find a way around it."

His heartbeat thuds slow and steady against my breastbone. His face is so close, I can count every piece of dark stubble on his lovely square jaw. His peppermint-spice scent fills my nose, one of his big hands is protectively cradling my head, and I become the teeniest bit aware that my kidnapper is, in fact, attractive.

Not just handsome. Attractive. As in, my ovaries are very, very interested in that big pistol he's packing between his legs.

He was right. I am brain damaged.

He must hear my ovaries fangirling over him, because he turns his head a fraction of an inch and cocks an eyebrow at me.

"What, no smart comeback?"

"Um. No."

How are my hands clutching his waist? How is one of his thick thighs wedged between my legs? How did the temperature in this car suddenly rise by twenty degrees?

Declan's gaze drops to my mouth. A smoldering pause ensues.

Then, in a husky voice, he says, "I'll be back in a few minutes. Remember what I said: stay here."

He rolls off me, throws open one of the doors, slams it shut, and is gone.

"Back?" I shout into the emptiness. "Where the hell are you going?"

As if in answer, gunfire erupts outside.

I flinch when more bullets slam into the windows. Then I let out a little scream when someone jumps onto the roof. Then, aggravated with the flinching and screaming, I sit up, yank the gun out of my waistband, and huddle into the corner of the back seat holding it in both hands, my finger on the trigger.

Outside, World War III is in full swing.

Whoever's on the roof is thumping and bumping all around, stomping his feet like a bull and roaring like a lion. I wish I could see what's going on, but between the night, the tinted windows, and the pouring rain, all I see are the blur of swiftly moving figures and the bursts of bright white light when someone fires his gun.

It goes on for what seems like a hundred years before everything falls eerily silent.

When minutes tick by and nothing happens, a sense of dread creeps over me. I'm a sitting duck in here. A bunny rabbit waiting for the wolves to swarm in.

Declan said not to move, but . . . what if Declan's dead?

Then I suppose the gentlemen of MS-13 will be my new captors.

Out of the frying pan and into the fire, as it were.

I mutter, "Oh, screw this," quietly crack open the door, and peek out.

We're in an industrial area not far from the airport. Overhead, a jumbo jet flies low, headed to a distant runway with a muffled roar. Nearby, a manufacturing plant chugs smoke from tall cement stacks. Lined on either side of the street are large warehouses, their parking lots empty. Several yards behind me, a dozen or so vehicles block the road, muscle cars and motorcycles that must belong to the other gang.

Bodies litter the middle of the street.

Other than the landing jet and the distant sounds of traffic, I hear nothing. No voices. No footsteps. No cries for help.

It's creepy as hell.

"Going somewhere?"

Startled, I suck in a breath. Peeking around the door, I see Declan there, leaning against the side of the limo, arms folded over his chest. He stares down at me with half-lidded eyes.

I look him up and down. Unfortunately, he doesn't appear to be bleeding. "You're alive."

"You sound disappointed."

"Almost as disappointed as you were when I woke up on the plane."

He reaches down and pulls me out of the car. When I'm on my feet, he takes the pistol from my hand, bends to shove it back into the holster around his ankle, then straightens and looks at me.

"I wasn't disappointed. I was depressed."

"Gee, thanks. You're all heart."

Okay, not *all* heart. He's got another organ of substantial size, but I'm not thinking about that.

He leads me across the street with his hand wrapped around my upper arm, towing me along like luggage. When I start to limp, he stops short and looks at me.

"My feet hurt. It's no big—"

He picks me up again, hoisting me into his arms and continuing along as if he does this every day. Which maybe he does. I have no idea how often this man kidnaps people and carries them across rainy streets forested with dead bodies.

He sets me down next to a black Chevy Camaro, opens the passenger door, and pushes me in. He slams shut the door and trots around to the driver's side, sliding his big frame into the seat with surprising grace. He starts the car and guns the engine.

"Seat belt."

"We're stealing this car?"

"You have a talent for noticing the obvious."

"Good thing the guy left the keys in the ignition."

"It wouldn't have mattered if he didn't. I know how to hot-wire old cars."

"A skill you learned in prison, no doubt. Will you let me drive?"

When he cuts me a lethal look, I say, "A guy I knew in college had this awesome red Camaro that he used to let me—"

"Seat belt!"

"There's no need to shout."

He leans across me, grabs the seat belt, yanks it down, and clicks it into place. Then he grabs the steering wheel and grips it so hard, it's like he's wishing it were my neck. We take off, the Camaro's V-8 engine roaring.

As we're speeding down the street, two black SUVs round the corner and head toward us.

"Is that your men?"

"Aye."

"So it was only you and Sean against all those other guys? How is that possible? There were like a dozen of them. You didn't have enough rounds of ammo in your gun. Unless Sean had a high-capacity magazine in his or something. But still, you'd both have to be *really* good shots. Or really lucky. And where'd he go, anyway?"

He mutters, "Jesus, Mary, and Joseph."

"I'm trying to pay you a compliment here."

"No, you're trying to drive me mad."

"Okay, fine. I'll shut up."

He snorts.

"I'm serious. I'm going to be quiet from now on. But I'm warning you, you won't like it."

I find the lever on the side of the seat that lowers it back. Reclining, I try to get comfortable and close my eyes.

The car slows. Declan rolls down his window and shares a few curt words in Gaelic with one of his men from the SUVs. Then we continue on, driving fast but controlled to who knows where.

I try to ignore the pounding in my head. I'm more successful at ignoring my throbbing shoulder and aching feet, but my head is truly painful. I hope it's the aftereffects of the ketamine and not a concussion, because I seriously doubt Declan would agree to take me to a hospital to get my skull checked out for cracks.

"Feet off the dash."

I bite my tongue and slide my feet off the dashboard and onto the floor.

"Thank you."

I don't respond. I'm sure it's my imagination that makes me think I can feel him looking at me. Me and my legs.

After a long time, he says quietly, "You were right about something."

It takes every ounce of willpower at my disposal not to respond.

When I don't, he exhales a heavy breath. "I'm not going to hurt you. You have my word."

I resist the urge to sit bolt upright in my seat and shout *Ha!* and pretend to snore a little instead.

His low chuckle is somehow the sexiest thing I've ever heard.

I must fall asleep, because the next thing I know, Declan is lowering me from his strong arms onto a bed.

SIX

DECLAN

*I*t's a miracle this mouthy, overconfident little demon can look so sweet and innocent, but she manages it.

As I lower her onto the bed in the master bedroom, she blinks sleepily up at me. Her eyelids are heavy. Her cheeks are flushed. Her hair spills over the pillow, a mess of silky dark tresses I'd like to comb my fingers through—no. Christ. What am I thinking?

She'd bite them off.

Gazing up at me, she mumbles, "I want to tell you something, but I'm not talking to you. G'night, gangster."

Then she rolls over onto her side and promptly falls back asleep.

I stand at the edge of the bed and stare down at her, amazed. She didn't even ask where we are. Or where we're going. She also didn't bat an eyelash at all the corpses we left behind us.

I've never met anyone so resilient. So fearless. So damn . . .

Annoying.

Or so fit. She's got legs like a dancer's, long and lithe, and an arse I could bounce a quarter off. And those tits of hers—

Stop.

Frustrated with myself, I close my eyes and draw a deep breath.

I'm not normally distracted like this. Even around a woman with a tight little body like hers. *Especially* around a woman with such an extreme case of verbal diarrhea.

I like the quiet ones. The submissive ones. The ones who don't make me want to tear out my hair and set myself on fire. For every hour I spend in her company, my sympathy for her ex-boyfriend Stavros grows.

Ex-lover. Ex-whatever. I'm starting to think the man is a saint.

I kick off my shoes and head into the kitchen to pour myself a whiskey. I drink that one and pour another. Then I go to the wall of windows in the living room and stand looking at the incredible glittering view of Boston at night and swallow a scream.

I never wanted this.

This responsibility. This life.

I was always the man in the background. The one behind the curtain, cleaning up messes and bringing up the rear.

I have no appetite for fame. I prefer to operate in the shadows. Now I'll have every single head of organized crime around the world in my fucking face.

I'll have to negotiate with them. Make treaties with them. *Work* with them, when all I want to do is burn their brutal empires to the ground.

But as a wise man once told me long ago, the best way to kill a nest of snakes is from the inside. "Keep your friends close and your enemies closer" and all that shite.

The Russians. The Chinese. The Italians. The Armenians. The Mexicans . . . the list goes on. When I started this so long ago, I thought I'd be making the world a better place. I thought I'd be making innocent people safer.

But I've learned the hard way that as soon as one snake dies, another takes its place. There are always more bad guys. There's an endless, unlimited supply.

It makes me wonder if I've made any difference at all.

I pass a hand over my face, shake off the gloom, and go back to the kitchen to pour a glass of water. I leave it on the nightstand next to a quietly slumbering Sloane, then head to the shower.

After that, I dress in a fresh suit and put on a pot of strong black coffee.

I'll need it.

Because as soon as the sun comes up, a parade of visitors will arrive from all over to pay their respects to their new king.

SEVEN

SLOANE

*W*hen I wake, it takes a moment to orient myself to the strange room.

Everything is done in shades of gray and black. The furnishings are contemporary and masculine. An unlit fireplace dominates one side of the room. A sofa and chairs are clustered into a sitting area nearby. Heavy black drapes are drawn across the windows so the room is dark, but a pale glow from an open door across from me provides enough light to see my surroundings.

I sit up, shivering. I have no idea what time it is or how much time has passed, but I'm starving, and I have to pee.

The glass of water on the nightstand sits there like a dare.

Ignoring it because it's probably drugged, I swing my legs over the side of the king-size bed and pad across plush carpeting toward the open door. Inside it, I find a massive master bathroom. Automatic lights come on when I enter, illuminating acres of white marble and glass.

I use the toilet, then rummage around in the drawers under the sinks until I find a tube of toothpaste. I do the best I can to brush my teeth with my finger, then wash my face and attempt to tame my snarled hair with my hands.

It doesn't work. I look exactly like what I am: a kidnapping victim.

Except I hate that word. I've gone to great lengths to avoid having it pinned on me. Once you accept the victim label, it sticks.

Get it together, Sloane. Take a deep breath and remember who the fuck you are.

I close my eyes, center myself, and clear my mind.

I have no clean underwear.

I don't know why that's the first thought that floats into my consciousness, but it is. I breathe through a moment of pure anger at Declan. No clothes, no cell phone, no toiletries, no birth control pills—

Oh, shit. Without my pills, I'll start my period any minute. And I'll be damned if I'm going to ruin this skirt by getting blood all over it. It's rumpled and wrinkled, but nothing that can't be fixed.

I need a change of clothes.

Heading out of the bathroom, I find another door that leads to a walk-in closet. Lights blink on in here, too. The closet is filled with identical black suits hanging in a row, along with a row of identical white dress shirts. A few pairs of black jeans complete his entire wardrobe.

Opening a drawer in the square wood dresser in the middle of the room, I find perfectly folded white undershirts. Another drawer reveals perfectly folded cotton briefs, both black and white. In a third, I find black T-shirts, also folded like they're on display for sale in a store.

It appears Declan is a bit anal retentive about his clothing.

Which is fantastic considering I'll soon be bleeding all over it.

I strip out of my skirt, shirt, jacket, and panties, and step into a pair of white briefs. They're too big and fit like a diaper, but who cares. Next I pull one of the white dress shirts off its hanger. It drapes halfway down my thighs when I put it on. I roll up the sleeves and am just pushing the last button through its hole near the hem when a voice speaks from behind me.

"What are you doing?"

I resist the instinct to whirl around in surprise. Instead, I pause for a moment, then look over my shoulder.

Wearing one of his collection of identical black suits, Declan leans against the doorframe. His big arms are folded over his chest. His expression is guarded. His beautiful eyes are endlessly blue.

"I know your memory isn't so sharp because you're a senior citizen, so I'll remind you that I'm not talking to you."

He holds my gaze just long enough to make my heart skip a beat before he answers. "And I'll remind you that you're not in charge here."

Aren't I?

He must see the thought pass through my head, because his expression darkens. Unfolding his arms, he steps toward me.

I don't move as he approaches. I won't give him the satisfaction.

He stops a foot away, so close I can smell him. So close I can see that he hasn't shaved, and that his eyes are bloodshot, and that he's exhausted.

In a husky voice, he says, "No, you're not."

We stand like that for a moment, just looking at each other, until he grasps my shoulder and turns me to face him. His eyes take a road trip down my figure, lingering on my painted toenails, sweeping up my legs, snagging on the hem of his dress shirt where it meets my bare thighs.

He moistens his lips.

My heart skips another beat. Then another.

"You're wearing my shirt."

It's a statement, not a question, so I decide it doesn't require an answer.

After a crackling pause, he lifts a hand and takes the hem between two fingers. He rubs the material thoughtfully, a muscle sliding in his jaw.

Somebody turned up the temperature again. My hands are sweaty, so are my armpits, and the flush creeping over my cheeks makes them burn.

His voice an octave lower, he says, "What do you have on beneath?"

Breathe. Stay cool. He's just trying to intimidate you. "Your briefs."

"You're wearing my underwear?"

His gaze flashes up to mine. I never knew blue eyes could burn so hotly, but they do.

It's my turn to moisten my lips. He watches the movement of my tongue with the sharp gaze of a predator.

"In case you haven't noticed, I don't have any other clothes."

I was going for a tone of cool disinterest, but miss badly. I sound like I just ran a four-minute mile.

Declan's hand tightens around my shoulder. The pulse in the side of his neck throbs.

Holy shit, it's sweltering in here. I need to get out of this closet before I erupt into flames.

"I'll let you go when I'm ready," he murmurs.

My held breath comes out in a rush. "You don't get to start reading my mind. That isn't a thing that's going to happen, so forget it. Don't even try."

"Can't help it. You've got a face like an open book."

Unnerved by how throaty his voice is, how sweaty I am, and how my traitorous ovaries have decided to stage a coup on my entire nervous system, I shake my head. "No, I don't. I'm as cool as a cucumber. I'm an ice cube. I'm a cat."

"A cat?"

"You know. Aloof. Unreadable."

Maintaining eye contact with me, he slides his hand down my arm until it reaches my wrist. He encircles it with his giant paw, pressing his thumb against my pulse point.

After a moment, he says softly, "For such an aloof little cat, you've got quite the frantic heartbeat."

"It runs in my family." *Stop panting! Why the hell are you panting? You sound like a Labrador!*

Declan's thumb moves slowly back and forth over my throbbing, tattletale vein. His gaze drops to my mouth.

"Would you like to know what runs in my family, little cat?"

There's a voice between my legs screaming, *Boy, would I!* but with a valiant effort, I ignore it.

When I don't answer, Declan leans close to my ear and murmurs, "That's what I thought."

"I didn't say anything."

"Aye, lass, you did. Just not in words."

I want to scream. I want to punch him in the throat. I want to stomp on his toe and slap his arrogant face and slash every stupid black suit in his closet to shreds.

Instead, I muster my dignity and say calmly, "You wish."

He inhales against my neck, his nose skimming the sensitive spot underneath my ear. It makes goose bumps break out all along my arms.

Then he withdraws abruptly and releases my shoulder. He steps back, blinking, looking like he's not sure what just came over him, and also as if he'd like to give himself a black eye.

He digs into his jacket pocket and produces a cell phone. He thrusts it at me.

"Here."

He pauses for a rough throat clearing as I take the phone. "My number's programmed in. If you need something, text me. You can't dial out except for that number. There's no internet connection. Don't bother trying to contact anyone else."

He spins on his heel and strides out of the closet.

"Wait!" I run after him. He's already halfway across the room. "Declan!"

He stops at the door. Without turning around, he says gruffly, "What?"

"How long are you going to keep me here?"

"As long as it takes."

"As long as what takes?"

He's silent for a moment, debating with himself, then turns and faces me. His expression is grim. "I wasn't going to tell you this, but those MS-13 lads who shot at us? That wasn't a rescue attempt."

"What do you mean?"

"I mean they were trying to kill us. Both."

A chill runs down my spine. "Why would they try to kill me? You said Kage sent them."

"No, I said your abduction wouldn't go over well with him. And that was accurate. He did mobilize his own soldiers to form a rescue party. But somehow, the other syndicates discovered the identity of my cargo as well."

Cargo. I'm nothing more than a package to these people. "And?"

"I told you. We're at war. You're a valued member of the Bratva—"

"Whoa. Hold on. I'm not in the Russian mafia."

Declan gazes at me with dark, unreadable eyes. "You're loved by some who are."

Natalie. Stavros. Oh god. "So you're saying now I'm a gangster by default?"

"What you are is a target. Because of the shootings that happened at the annual Christmas Eve meeting of the families, Kazimir closed down all the ports, disrupted distribution pipelines, sabotaged shipments, and interrupted the flow of money. Every-one's hurting. If the other families get their hands on you, you'll be used as either a bargaining chip or . . ."

Payback.

He doesn't have to say it. I understand where this story leads.

Holding his gaze, I say, "And which will you use me for?"

"If I wanted you dead, you already would be."

"So it'll be a negotiation, then."

"I'm not negotiating with that piece of rubbish."

There's something hateful in his tone, something that hints at old vendettas and even older scars. He despises Kage, that much is clear, but also seems to think he's superior to him.

As if one racketeering, drug-smuggling, money-laundering criminal is better than another.

"If I'm not a bargaining chip to you, or a means for retaliation, what am I? Why am I here?"

"I already told you, lass. Right now, it's safer for you with me than anywhere else."

It hits me then: Declan saved my life.

If what he's saying is true and MS-13 had managed to get their hands on me . . . No. I won't think about that.

I also don't want to think about what it means that my kidnap-per has turned into my protector. My head isn't equipped to handle that particular mindfuck just yet.

There are a million different things I want to say, things that would make so much more sense, but what comes out of my mouth surprises us both.

"Thank you."

There isn't a word to describe his expression. Maybe boggled.

"What?"

"I said thank you. If what you just told me is true, you saved my life. I owe you one."

He stares at me like I'm an alien who just landed on his lawn and informed him I needed his kidneys or an entire race of intelligent beings in some distant galaxy would die.

I make my voice stronger. "I'm not saying that to make you angry."

"I know."

"Oh. Okay. So."

"So."

We stare at each other. I'm aware of every inch of skin on my body. My stomach takes the opportunity to emit a loud rumble into the awkward silence.

"You need food." Declan shakes his head as if the realization makes him irritated with himself for not thinking of it sooner.

"Yes. Please."

"Anything else?"

When I hesitate, he says, "I'll let your girlfriend know you're safe."

I don't understand this polite, protective kidnapper. What happened to the growling jerk? "Thank you. Again. But that's not what I was thinking."

He can see I'm uncomfortable. He lifts his brows, waiting.

"I need toiletries. Girl things."

"Just text me a list. I'll get whatever you need."

My surprise is so great, I can't hold it in. "You'll buy me tampons?"

His mouth does something strange. Is he trying not to smile?

"No. I'll send Kieran."

"Not Kieran."

"Why not?"

"I'm trying to get on his good side."

"Because?"

"There's nothing that hurts a man's pride like being seen as weak in front of his friends. I don't want to embarrass him more than I already have."

Declan does his head tilt thing that he does whenever he's really looking at me. His eyes are penetrating. Examining. *Knowing*.

It makes me flustered. "I might need to make him fall in love with me and break me out of here, okay? Jesus."

He chuckles, shaking his head. "Okay."

Then he sighs heavily, rakes a hand through his hair, and seems to gather himself. Standing taller and smoothing a hand over his tie, he squares his shoulders and sets his jaw.

It strikes me that he doesn't want to go back outside.

Not because he wants to stay with me, but because whatever or whoever is waiting for him, he's dreading it.

When he turns to go, I say impulsively, "Hey. Gangster."

He turns back, his smile faint. "Aye, lass?"

"You got this."

He frowns a little, not understanding.

"You heard me. Whatever you're about to go do, you're gonna do great. Just take a deep breath and remember who the fuck you are."

Looking stunned, he repeats faintly, "Remember . . . ?"

"That's what I always tell myself when I'm not feeling one hundred percent. Remember who you are."

I can tell he doesn't want to ask, but curiosity gets the better of him. "And who are you?"

"The only one of me who ever has been or ever will be. Same as you. In a word: irreplaceable."

His lips part. He gazes at me for a long, silent moment. "You were dropped on your head a lot as a baby. That's it, isn't it?"

I have to smile at the depth of his astonishment. "No. There was no dropping. I was the middle kid, so I was mostly just ignored. But I did learn to be my own cheerleader, and you know what? The more you try to believe in yourself, the more you actually do. Your mental self-talk is very powerful. You have to keep it positive. So just go out there, say to yourself, 'I got this,' and believe it. You'll be fine."

Now he looks angry. "You're giving me *a pep talk*?"

"You look like you could use one."

He says flatly, "You're not from this planet."

"Thank you."

Irritated by my smile, his old glare-that-could-melt-steel returns. Muttering something under his breath, he turns around, yanks open the door, and walks out, slamming the door shut behind him.

EIGHT

DECLAN

*N*ot even ten minutes later, the texts start.

I'm sorry I annoy you so much.

When I ignore that one, she sends another.

Okay, "sorry" might be a stretch. Here's the list of stuff
   I need.

She sends a list so long, I regret giving her the phone. The list
includes specific items of clothing, makeup, toiletries, and food. Organic food, to be exact, exotic things I've never heard of with names
like rambutan, cherimoya, and aguaje. Plus four different varieties
of kale.

There's a pause of no more than five minutes, then the texts
start up again with only a few moments lapsing between each
one.

Did you let Natalie know I'm okay yet? I'm worried
    about her.
Is Sean alive? I didn't see him get out of the limo. I'm
    worried about him, too.
Why is there no television in your bedroom?
There are suit makers other than Armani, you know.
Remember: you got this.

I finally have to turn off the ringer because everyone keeps looking at me strangely. I'm standing in a room full of thirty Irish mob-
sters who came to pay their respects, and my phone is blowing up
like some teenager's in the midst of an emotional meltdown.

I text back, YOU'RE NOT TALKING TO ME, REMEMBER?

She sends back a middle finger emoji.

I can't fucking believe this is my life.

NINE

SLOANE

Thirty minutes after Declan leaves, Kieran comes in, carrying a tray with food. He sets it on the coffee table and turns to leave. "Kieran?"

He stops in his tracks. He doesn't turn back to me. He simply exhales in dread.

"I just wanted to ask how you're feeling."

There's a pause, then he says in his thick Irish accent, "Come again?"

"Your nose. You okay?"

He turns just enough to scowl at me over his shoulder. "Stop acting the maggot."

Yikes. What a lovely visual. "I don't know how that translates to English, but I'm guessing it's not complimentary."

"Yer bang on."

"Um. Okay?"

"Not the full shilling, are ye, lass?"

Apparently, we're going to run through the entire gamut of obscure Irish slang before I can get a yes or a no. I need to move this along. "Arnica cream will help with the bruising. And remember, ice is your friend."

He stares at me like he's trying to decide between shoving my hand down a garbage disposal or running me over with the SUV.

When I send him a winning smile, he grumbles under his breath and walks out.

I test the door after he slams it shut behind him, but it's locked. No luck.

The tray he left is filled with an array of food that would appeal to any fifteen-year-old boy. There's a can of Coke, a bag of peanut M&M's, a bigger bag of beef jerky, a party-size bag of Lay's potato chips, and a jar of ranch dip.

Now I understand Declan's mood swings. He's in full-on sugar crash within an hour of every meal.

There's also—the horror—a bologna sandwich on white bread with a slice of that kind of American cheese that comes individually wrapped in plastic and will easily remain edible through the next ice age because of all the preservatives embedded in its shiny, nuclear-orange skin.

I pick the bologna off the sandwich and sniff it. There's not much to smell as it's covered in a thick layer of mayo. I wipe all the mayo on one of the napkins that came with the tray, then take a nibble of the meat.

It's so salty, my ankles are probably already swelling. How does this qualify as food?

I spit it out. Then I send Declan another text.

If you're trying to poison me, it's working.

He hasn't answered any of my other texts, so I'm not expecting anything this time, either. But within seconds, a response comes through.

Finally, some good news.

I answer back, smiling.

Oh, look, you found your sense of humor. Was your
    missing charm with it?

His answer comes zinging back so fast, I'm not sure how he
managed to type it.

Please don't interrupt me while I'm ignoring you.

That makes me laugh out loud.

Good one, geezer. How old are you, anyway?

Around other people—forty-two. Around you—it feels
    like forty-two hundred.

He's older than he looks. Smiling at the phone, I murmur, "Ouch.
Savage."

I debate sending something back, but decide to let him have
the last word. Maybe it will improve his disposition the next time
I see him.

Probably not, but I'll give it a shot.

In the cabinet under the sinks in his enormous bathroom, I
find aspirin, Neosporin, hydrogen peroxide, and bandages. I down
two of the aspirin with a gulp of water from the sink, then take a
shower. After locking the bathroom door first, of course.

When I'm finished with the shower, I towel dry my hair, put on
Declan's briefs and dress shirt again, and sit on the toilet to attend
to the soles of my feet. I disinfect them with the peroxide, dab on
the antibacterial cream, and stick a bandage on a few of the worst
cuts.

Then, with nothing left to do and no television to watch, I decide to try to get more sleep.

I've already rummaged through all his drawers. He keeps nothing personal in his personal space, which I find very interesting. No photos, no books, no jewelry, no notes. Not a single item in his bedroom could identify him as the occupant. Only his clothes, hanging meticulously in his closet and folded with such anal precision in the drawers, could identify the space as belonging to a male. All else is neutral.

Empty.

He could vanish without a trace at any moment, and no one would ever know he'd been here.

Which, perhaps, is the point.

But it makes me curious. About him and his life, about what would drive a man to be so absent in his own home. Maybe he's got a bunch of family photos in the living room, but somehow, I doubt it.

Somehow, I doubt he has a family.

Other than the mafia, that is. Besides his brothers-in-arms, Declan seems very much like a lone wolf.

I don't have much to go on, but I've always been intuitive about people. And if my intuition is right, the man keeping me under his roof has more than the normal number of secrets a man in his position would have.

I suspect his proverbial closet doesn't just have skeletons. It has entire graveyards.

Pulling down a corner of the black silk duvet, I crawl under the sheets and snuggle down, getting comfy. After I'm motionless for a few minutes, the automatic lights dim. I drift off to sleep to the sound of my rumbling stomach.

Sometime later, I wake to the sound of breathing beside me.

Without even opening my eyes, I know it's Declan. The peppermint-spice scent is a dead giveaway, as is the heat he's generating. The man's body temperature is set at permanent full blast.

After a moment, he says in a voice thick with fatigue, "The guest rooms are full. So is the sofa. And I can't sleep sitting up in a chair."

"I wasn't going to suggest you should."

We're quiet for a while, until he says, "You didn't eat your food."

"I didn't want to get diabetes."

A rustle on the pillow next to mine makes me open my eyes. He's lying on his back, but has turned his head and is looking at me.

He's taken off his suit jacket and shoes, but otherwise is fully clothed. His jaw is dark with scruff. His blue eyes are heavy lidded. He is very, very handsome.

"You're not worried about waking up next to me in bed?"

I yawn. "You don't like me. I don't like you. There's zero chance of accidental ravishment."

"Plenty of people have sex who don't like each other."

"Don't sound so put out. I'm not insulting your manhood. I'm sure you *could* ravish me if you wanted to, but I know you don't. Plus, you gave me your word you wouldn't hurt me. So I'm not going to worry about it."

I'm conveniently ignoring the little interlude in his closet earlier, because who the hell knows what that was about? Not me.

He turns his head and stares at the ceiling. After a while, he says, "You're not normal."

"Thank you."

"Christ. You think every insult is a compliment. Your ego is like Teflon."

"Teflon? No. Something way tougher than that."

"Seriously, how can you be so bloody blasé about everything? The only time I got a rise out of you was when I gagged you with my tie. But the minute I took it off, you thanked me and went right back to being . . . you."

He's starting to sound aggravated. What a shocker.

"'I make the best use of what's in my power, and take the rest as it happens.'"

There follows a long silence. It's not really silent, though. It's quite loud, actually, loud and cavernous, echoing with his disbelief.

"Did you . . . did you just quote Epictetus?"

"You know the Stoics?"

"You're fucking kidding me. You *did* quote Epictetus."

"It's a good thing I have that Teflon ego you accused me of, because my feelings would be really hurt right about now, gangster. The size of my intellect doesn't exist in inverse proportion to the size of my boobs."

His voice rises. "You almost flunked out of college. You failed English, for fuck's sake, and it's your native language!"

"English Comp," I correct. "And I failed it because it was too easy, like the rest of my classes."

Another silence. I think I'm going to break his brain.

"That makes no sense. You realize what you just said makes not one bloody bit of sense, right?"

"First, take a deep breath. Your blood pressure will thank you. Second, I'm the kind of person who needs a challenge. I get bored extremely easily." I pause. "I'd tell you that's typical of people with genius-level IQs, but it would probably just piss you off. So we'll pretend I said it's because I'm a Scorpio and leave it at that. Wait—how did you know I failed English?"

His sigh is heavy and communicates that he'd rather be strapped to a prison's electric chair with the warden's finger hovering over the *on* button than having this conversation.

"I ran a background check on you."

I'm intrigued. "Really? How fascinating. When? What else did it tell you? Oh—so you already *know* I have a genius IQ!"

He mutters, "What I wouldn't give for a massive heart attack right now."

"You're just mad because I'm smarter than you."

When he turns his head to glare at me, he finds me grinning at him. Which, of course, sets him off all over again.

"You are *not* fucking smarter than me."

"No? What's your IQ?"

"Higher than yours."

"Sure. That's what all the boys say. Wait, let me guess. One thirty."

He says angrily, "I tested above that when I was a wee chiseler."

"Whatever that is. One forty."

"Jesus, Mary, and Joseph."

"You keep calling for them, but I don't think they're listening. One fifty."

When he only lies there, seething, I say smugly, "Ah. Under one fifty. No wonder you're angry. I'm *way* more intelligent than—"

He rolls on top of me, clamps a hand over my mouth, and growls, "Introduce your top lip to your lower one for a change. And. Be. *Quiet.*"

The first thing that comes to mind is that he's on top of me again. We're setting records for the most amount of full-body contact between two people who aren't having sex.

The next thing that comes to mind is . . . nothing.

I'm too busy feeling. My brain has become nonoperational. I'm nothing but skin, bone, and tingling nerves.

There's something delicious about his weight. He's so solid. I've always liked a big man, but Declan is more than simply big. He's dense. Powerful. Hard.

Everywhere.

We make eye contact. I feel it in my guts.

After a moment, he says roughly, "You're the most irritating person I've ever met."

I smile. Because his hand is clamped over my mouth, he feels it.

He mutters something in Gaelic. It doesn't sound like a

compliment. "I'm going to remove my hand from your mouth. Will you be quiet?"

I nod, trying to appear serious.

"Do you promise?"

After a beat, I decide to be honest and shake my head.

"Then I won't move my hand."

I make big pleading eyes at him, blinking like a coy ingenue.

"No."

We seem to be at an impasse. So I do the only thing I can think of that might work. I dig my fingers into his ribs and tickle him.

He jerks, curses, and rolls off me, hollering. "What the bloody hell?"

Propping myself up on my elbows, I smile at his fury. "So the king of the jungle has a soft spot. Good to know."

Sitting on the other side of the bed, he stares at me like he's trying to will my head to explode.

"Don't worry. I won't tell anyone."

"This is karma, isn't it? I'm being punished for something I did in a former life."

"You believe in reincarnation? That's interesting. I've always thought—"

He thunders, "It was a figure of speech!"

"You know, I think your diet is having a negative effect on your mood. I'm betting you don't get enough roughage."

"Roughage?"

"Fiber."

"I know what it means, I just can't believe you said it!"

I purse my lips and consider him. "You could probably also use a good deep-tissue massage. You're very tense, in case you haven't noticed."

Glaring at me, he says flatly, "I wonder why."

"No, I think this predates me. You have an unhealthy lifestyle. Poor diet. Too much stress. Too little sleep. Any of this sound

familiar? You're headed straight for that heart attack you were wishing for earlier."

He stares at me for a beat, then leans over, props his elbows on
his knees, drops his head into his hands, and groans.

I watch him, alarmed. What if he *does* have a heart attack? God.
I'll be locked in here with his big dead corpse until Kieran decides
to do a status check on me, who knows how many days later.

I should go easy on him. Better yet . . .

I crawl across the mattress to where he's sitting, rise up on
my knees, and dig my thumbs into the rock-hard muscles of his
shoulders.

He stiffens.

"Just take a breath, gangster. I know what I'm doing. You can
thank me later."

Rigid and silent, he sits perfectly still on the edge of the bed as I
work my fingers across his trapezius and down to his scapula. When
I get to the rhomboid muscle, he flinches, sucking in a sharp breath.

I murmur, "Sorry. Better?"

Gentling the pressure, I move around the knot in slow circles
until I hear him exhale. When the muscle suddenly gives under my
fingers, relaxing, he softly moans.

It's a sound thick with pleasure. My pulse ticks up in response.

I move to his other shoulder and repeat the process, massaging
the corded muscles, working my fingers into their stony hardness
until I feel them soften. When I rub my thumbs lower down his
middle back and spine, he releases a breath so full of pent-up tension, I almost feel sorry for him.

"Here," I say softly. "What about this?"

I wrap both hands around the back of his thick neck and
squeeze.

It earns me another soft moan.

I decide I like that sound, and rub slow circles with my thumbs
around the base of his skull on either side of his spinal column, where

his head meets his neck. This time, he doesn't moan. He makes a sound like a drowsy bear, a low, masculine rumbling in his chest.

"Good?"

After a pause, he murmurs, "Good."

Why that should make me so pleased, I'm not sure. I keep going, working my fingers up the back of his head through his thick hair, massaging his skull—it's as big as the rest of him, this guy's got a *noggin*—until I reach his temples.

Then he freezes, stiffening all over again.

That's when I realize that I've leaned so far forward, I'm pressed up against his back.

This wouldn't be a problem, except that I'm not wearing a bra.

And my nipples are hard.

Which he has obviously noticed.

I pull away, my heart hammering. I sit back on my heels, my arms folded over my chest, waiting for him to do or say something. Waiting for him to tell me I'm annoying, or holler at me, or stalk out of the room and slam the door.

But he only sits there, silent.

Just as I'm about to scramble back across the bed and dive under the covers to hide in embarrassment, he says, "Thank you."

It's quiet. It's also sincere. I'm relieved, but also confused, because I have zero idea what he's thinking.

"You're welcome."

There's another crackling silence. "I'm sending you home as soon as I work out the logistics."

That surprises me. "But didn't you want to ask me questions? Isn't that why you went to all the trouble to get me here?"

"That was Diego's idea."

"Diego was your boss?"

"Aye."

"And now Diego's . . ." I hesitate to say "dead," but he gets it anyway.

"Aye."

"Right. I'm sorry for your loss."

He turns his head. "Why? You didn't know him."

"No, but I know you."

"What difference does that make?"

"I don't like to see anyone suffering, even if they're my kid-napper."

He's getting mad again. I can feel it. The atmosphere changes with his temper. It gets charged and ominous, the way it does with an approaching storm.

"Why does that make you angry? I'm not lying."

He says gruffly, "I know you're not. That's why it makes me angry."

"I don't understand."

"I wouldn't expect you to."

He stands, puts on his shoes and coat, crosses to the door, and lets himself out, shutting it quietly behind him.

TEN

DECLAN

When I return to the living room, Kieran takes one look at my face and snorts.

"She got to ye, too, eh?"

And how.

I know he means that she got to me in the way she has that makes a man want to throw himself into a pool of sharks to escape because a quick, violent death is preferable to the slow, agonizing one caused by spending time in her company.

But she got to me in another way. It's far worse. And far more dangerous than a pool of sharks.

She's kind.

She worries about other people. She notices their pain. She empathizes—even with her fucking kidnapper.

She's also funny. Funny, quick-witted, and smart. She knows Epictetus, for fuck's sake, and *nobody* knows him.

Worst of all, she's completely unflappable. It's like her superpower. She wakes up in bed with me beside her, and her reaction is a yawn.

A fucking *yawn*. Who *is* this woman?

Angry with myself for being intrigued, I make a list:

This is the woman who got four of my men killed.

This is the woman who started a war between all the families.

This is the woman who fucks members of the Russian mafia and is lifelong best friends with the girlfriend of the *head* of the Russian mafia.

The woman who can't shut her mouth for more than ten seconds at a time.

The woman who doesn't "keep" boyfriends.

The woman with gorgeous green eyes and legs that go on for days and a pair of full, lush tits that just beg to be squeezed, licked, and—

"Get me a whiskey," I snap at Kieran, sounding like I'm ordering him to get me a gun instead.

He ambles away, shaking his head.

Bloody hell. I'm unraveling.

When he returns with the drink, I gulp it down in one swallow. "Is Tommy back from the store?"

"Aye."

"Good. Make up another tray and bring it to her."

Kieran pulls a face. "Why me?"

"She likes you."

He couldn't be more shocked if I'd squared off and punched him in the gut. "Me? Ach! She banjaxed my nose!"

"She feels bad about it."

"Aye?" He pauses. "She told me that, too. I thought she was pullin' my leg. Havin' a wee laugh at me."

"No."

"Huh."

He rearranges a few things in his head, then shrugs. "Well, I am quite likeable."

Dear god, not him, too.

My scowl sends him hurrying away into the kitchen.

I try to turn my attention to all the things that need to be done, the phone calls and meetings and strategy planning. But all I can think about is the green-eyed demon in my bed, wearing my clothes, lying underneath my body, smiling at me.

Rubbing away the tension in my shoulders with surprisingly strong hands.

Saying softly, "Good?"

I have to get her out of this house before my dick makes me do something stupid.

In a life full of unforgivable sins, sleeping with the enemy would be the absolute worst.

ELEVEN

SLOANE

I'm trying to decide what smartass thing to text Declan when Kieran returns, carrying another tray.

He sets it on the coffee table next to the one with all the junk. When he straightens, he clears his throat. "Here's yer . . ." He glances at the tray, grimacing. "Food."

"Oh, great. Thank you. Mmm, wheatgrass. And you found the lacinato kale!"

"I can't take the credit. Tommy did the shopping."

"That's okay. You brought it in. I appreciate it."

He looks at me. He looks back at the tray. "Ye really gonna eat that?"

"It's super good. Full of vitamins. Want to try some?"

"Looks like lawn clippings."

"No, it's really yummy. I promise. You probably wouldn't like it raw, though. That takes a bit of getting used to. But I could cook you some. Sautéed with a little garlic and olive oil, it's divine."

He stares at me with a strange expression. I can't tell if he's horrified or stunned.

"Maybe Declan would let me use the kitchen. I love to cook. I could make some food for all you guys, the whole crew. When was the last time you had a home-cooked meal?"

Kieran opens his mouth, thinks a moment, then closes it.

"I knew it. Listen, see if you can get Declan to agree to let me into the kitchen, and I'll get you sorted, okay? And if he says no, just tell him that you and I have an agreement. You remember, from the plane? If you need me to do something, just ask me. Your boss likes to bark orders all over the place, and that's really not my thing, but you and I are copacetic."

"Copa . . ."

"It means we're friends."

He couldn't look more astonished if he tried. "We are?"

"Yes."

"Oh."

"Right. So if Declan says I can't go into the kitchen because there are knives in there and he thinks I'll attack him with a cleaver, you can just ask me to hand them over and there won't be any more knives. Or whatever. That's just an example. My point being that I'll honor *your* requests, because I know you'll put them to me politely. With respect. Right?"

"Uh . . . right."

He has no idea what's happening. Honestly, there's nothing more adorable than a befuddled man. Especially when they're huge and armed.

I smile, thank him again, and lead him to the door. He exits in a fog of uncertainty.

Twenty minutes later, just as I'm finishing up my meal, Declan storms in.

He snaps, "What have you done to Kieran?"

"Moi?" I say innocently.

"Aye, you."

"Whatever can you mean?"

He looks suspicious at my tone of wounded surprise. "I mean he came into this room working for me, and he went out of it working for you. He suddenly thinks he's your goddamn butler!"

"I prefer the term 'majordomo.'"

Declan narrows his eyes. "Don't push your luck, lass."

"Oh, don't get your panties in a bunch, gangster. I just told him I'd like to cook for him is all. Can you blame the guy for wanting to have a home-cooked meal?"

When he stands there silently, glaring at me in outrage, I add, "I think he needs someone to look after him. I'm guessing his blood pressure isn't what it should be, either."

I can almost see Declan's hair falling out, strand by strand.

I smile at him. "Any updates on the clothes I needed? I'd kill for a pair of lululemons right now."

He mutters, "You probably shouldn't mention the word 'kill' at the moment."

God, it's so satisfying getting under his skin. It might be my new favorite thing. My smile grows wider. "You know what I think?"

"Whatever you're going to say, don't."

"I think you just wanted an excuse to come back in here and see me."

"And I think calling you an idiot would be giving you far too much credit."

I laugh. "Good one. How long did it take you to figure out how to use the internet to look that up, Grandpa?"

"Your parents are brother and sister, aren't they?"

"Oh, look, we finally have something in common!"

His face turns red. His hands curl to fists at his sides. He stands there staring at me in unblinking, silent fury, breathing hard and gritting his teeth even harder.

I've finally done it. Declan is about to drop dead from rage.

I stand, wipe my hands on a napkin, and cross to him. Looking up into his angry face, I say, "I'd like to show you a trick that might help you cope when you're in stressful situations."

"And I'd like to show you the inside of a dungeon, but we can't always get what we want."

"Be quiet for a minute, gangster."

"You first."

That makes me roll my eyes. "I'm trying to be helpful here."

"I didn't need any help until I met you."

My smile is sweet. "You mean 'kidnapped' me. As I was saying, a trick."

I draw a slow breath for a count of four, hold it for a count of four, exhale for a count of four, then wait to draw another breath until I've counted to four.

He watches me with a look of disgust. "Congratulations. You know how to hold your breath. It will come in handy after I've put the cement shoes on your feet and thrown you into the harbor."

"No, silly, I'm breathing in squares! My dad taught me how to do it."

"Your father had to teach you how to breathe? What a surprise. Pity he didn't put a pillow over your face first."

I give him a smack on his rock-hard biceps. "Will you listen to me?"

"I am. That's the problem."

"Box breathing is something he learned in the navy. It's an excellent way to calm your nervous system and focus your mind. Try it. We can do it together."

"I'd rather be burned alive."

"Oh, come on! I swear, it works."

I lift my arms wide and make a big show of inhaling. Declan mutters some kind of voodoo curse. I hold the breath, making googly eyes at him, and he groans. When I exhale, I slowly drop my arms to the silent count in my head. He's looking at the ceiling, sighing.

"You're like cancer. Only not as fun."

I poke him in the chest with a finger. "Just try it. I didn't think you were the hyperventilating kind, but I'm starting to think I was wrong."

He lowers his head and gazes at me. "For your information, I'm familiar with box breathing."

That takes the wind out of my sails. "Oh." We stare at each other for a moment, until I brighten. "See, it worked!"

"What are you blabbering about now?"

"You're not mad anymore. You calmed down."

"How did it work? I wasn't the one doing all the heavy breathing."

"I know, but watching *me* do the box breathing calmed *you* down. That's how effective it is. It can even work on other people by osmosis!"

He stares at me for a beat, blue eyes feverish with the urge to commit homicide. His voice comes out thick. "I can honestly say, and I mean this with all sincerity, I've never met anyone quite like you, lass."

My smile could blind a man. "You're welcome. Oh, by the way, I was thinking."

"Did it hurt?"

"Look at you go with the snappy comebacks! I'm a good influence on you."

"If this is you being a *good* influence on me, I should kill myself immediately."

I wave that off. "I think I figured out why you keep saying I started a war. And you're wrong."

He stares at me for a moment. "I have a feeling I should be sitting down for this."

I gesture to the nearest chair. "Be my guest."

"You do recall this is my home, correct? You're *my* guest."

"I've been upgraded from captive to guest? Cool."

He scowls. "No. That's not what I—oh, fuck. Never mind."

He drops into the chair and sits there like he's in Death's waiting room, praying for his number to be called.

I sit across from him and fold my legs underneath me. When he directs his scowl at my folded legs, I simply smile. "As I was saying. This war you keep accusing me of starting. It all began with a dinner at La Cantina in Lake Tahoe, didn't it?"

He doesn't respond.

"Okay, maybe you didn't know that. Or you did, and you're just being your usual dazzlingly charming self. Either way, I remember Stavros telling me that a war was brewing. Well, technically, he didn't tell me, I overheard it. Okay, fine, I was eavesdropping on him and his crew, but the point is, this was only a few days after the gunfight at La Cantina where some Irish gangsters were killed. That part you obviously know about."

I pause, examining his expression. "Why are you so quiet?"

"I don't plan murder out loud."

"Ha. Back to the dead Irish gangsters. They came to our table during dinner and had words with Stavros. Don't ask me what was said, because it was all in Russian and Gaelic, but the whole kerfuffle started in the first place because one of the Irish guys slapped my ass when I was walking beside Stavros on the way to our table when we first came in. Stavros nearly blew a gasket, but I managed to get him to walk away. But all bets were off when Mr. Ass Slapper showed up again in the middle of dinner."

Declan leans forward and props his elbows on his knees. He steeples his fingers under his chin and says softly, "Did it ever occur to you that I know exactly what happened inside that restaurant?"

"How could you know if you weren't there?"

"I know everything."

I scoff. "So you're omniscient? Please."

"The point is that I know you were the reason it all went sideways in the first place. *You,* swinging that ass in that tiny white dress you were wearing. *You,* strutting around like you owned the place. *You,* flashing that smile at a man you passed by, even though you already had one on your arm."

Anger unfurls like a snake's coils inside my belly. I sit back in my chair and gaze at him.

"That's a nasty little manipulation called 'victim blaming.' Not that I'm a victim, but the premise holds, and it's utter bullshit."

His voice hardens. "Those dead men aren't bullshit."

"No, but you mansplaining their deaths as the inevitable fallout from seeing my ass and my smile is. Men pulling guns on each other because a woman smiled in the wrong direction is caused by their infantile egos, unchecked aggression, and overinflated sense of entitlement, *not* by her."

We glare at each other. Somewhere in the room, a clock ticks.

Or maybe that's the bomb he set for me.

Holding his hard gaze, I say more softly, "You know I'm right. And I understand the loss of your men must be hard for you. But people are responsible for their own actions. It's unfair—not to mention inaccurate—to pin this war on me."

He closes his eyes. He's silent for what seems like a very long time. I have no idea what he's thinking, until he says quietly, "Aye."

I nearly fall out of my chair.

When he opens his eyes and sees my face, his expression sours. "I could do without the bloody gloating."

"It's more like shock. But I'll try."

He stands and starts to pace. I watch him stalking back and forth in agitation and decide to let him work off steam without interruption. It looks like he's brewing something important in that giant noggin of his.

If I'm lucky, it might be to my benefit.

He pulls up short and stares at me down his nose. A ruthless dictator couldn't look more imperious. He commands, "Tell me everything you know about Kazimir Portnov."

"First: no. Second: why?"

"Because he's my enemy. And you're my captive. And you *know* him."

"Yes, I do know him. He's my friend."

When that makes Declan's eyes turn black, I say, "Okay, technically we're not *friends* friends. I only formally met him that one time at the doomed dinner. But my girlfriend is madly in love with the guy, and she's an extraordinarily good person. She's practically Mother Teresa. If she likes him, he can't be all that bad."

"Women in love are notoriously poor judges of character."

He says that so darkly, with such raw pain behind the words, it makes me stop and wonder. "Have experience in that department, do you?"

He blows right past that and demands, "How did your girl-friend meet him?"

I take a moment to compose myself, knowing that what I'm going to say won't go over well. And god only knows how Declan will react, considering the mood he's in. But it has to be said.

There are just some lines that can't be crossed.

I look him straight in his icy blue eyes. "I say this not out of disrespect for you, but out of love and loyalty for my friend. None of your fucking business."

When he opens his mouth—no doubt to holler a threat—I talk over him, my voice loud.

"I will never, ever, not in a million years betray Natalie. Do what you will to me. Beat me, starve me, keep me locked up in this room forever, I don't care. She's all the best parts of me, and a better person than I could ever dream of being, and I love her like a sister.

I take that back—I love her *more* than my sister. And not in a gay way, before you start in on that again. I just love her. Which means I've got her back. Which means I'm not telling you jack shit about her *or* her man, no matter how much you don't like it."

I stand with the intention of turning my back on him and walking away, but that plan goes out the window when the room slips sideways and starts to violently spin.

Then everything goes black, and I fall.

TWELVE

DECLAN

*I*t happens fast.

One moment, she's on her feet. The next, she crumples to the floor, her legs giving out like they've become boneless. Her expression changes in a flash from one of irritation to one of surprise.

Not fear. Not shock. Just simple surprise, as if she's thinking *This is new* right before she loses consciousness.

Instincts have me reacting without needing to think. I catch her and ease her onto the carpet. She's completely limp in my arms. Her mouth is slack. Her face is pale.

I noticed the color draining from her face a few minutes ago, but I attributed it to anger at me. It appears to be something much more sinister.

I should've known. This isn't a woman who gets upset from an argument. Or from anything else. Godzilla could come crashing through the door, and she'd probably tell him calmly to piss off, then go right back to whatever she was doing.

Making a deal with the devil for the souls of all who've displeased her or such.

"Lass. Lass, can you hear me?"

I hear how rough and anxious my voice is, but am too busy focusing on her to care. Leaning over her on my hands and knees, I brush a strand of dark hair off her face. She's unresponsive. I lightly slap her pale cheek.

Her eyes move restlessly under her lids. She exhales the faintest moan. Her lids flutter, then her lashes lift and she looks up at me. Her gaze is hazy and unfocused.

"Oh, wow," she whispers, sounding impressed. "So blue."

Something in her dazed expression sets off an alarm bell in the back of my mind. "Are you all right? Can you sit up?"

She blinks slowly. Then she smiles and reaches up to touch my face. She strokes her fingers gently down my cheek to my jaw, then sighs in pleasure. She closes her eyes again, smiling.

Something is very wrong.

"I'm going to move you, lass."

I pick her up, carry her across the room, and ease her onto the bed, adjusting her head on the pillow. When my fingers brush the back of her skull, she makes a small noise of discomfort.

Bloody hell. That's a big bump. Frowning, I run my fingertips gently over the swollen area.

She winces, then opens her eyes and pins me with a cold stare. "I know I'm irresistible, gangster, but quit fondling me." She pauses. "Why do you look worried?"

"You fainted."

That makes her laugh. "Please. I'd never do such a thing."

"What's the last thing you remember?"

She pauses again to think. "Telling you to suck my dick. Figuratively speaking."

"Anything after that? Like touching my face?"

She wrinkles her nose. It's almost adorable. "You drugged me again to get me to be quiet, didn't you?"

"Against my better judgement, no."

"There's no way I touched your face unless I was attempting to claw out your eyeballs."

When I stay silent, her eyes widen in alarm.

"No."

"Aye. Stroked your fingers down my cheek like it was made of mink." To see how she'll handle it, I slip in, "You also told me how handsome I am."

Her smile returns. "Now I *know* you're lying."

She doesn't think I'm handsome? That stings. I don't care about her opinion, of course, it's just that women are always telling me how good-looking I am.

Wait. I forgot. She's not a woman. She's a raging banshee who eats men's sanity for supper.

"Tell me how you came to be lying on the bed, then."

She looks around as if trying to remember. When her eyes meet mine again, I see her frustration.

"Fucking asphalt."

"Come again?"

"I hit my head on the ground in the parking garage when you pulled me out of the car and dropped me. Hit it really hard, in fact. I think I might've passed out before you even gave me the ketamine."

I don't like the sound of that, but she's wrong on one count. It seems oddly important to correct her. "I wasn't the one who pulled you out of the car."

"Yes, you did, I saw . . . Oh. Now that you mention it, I didn't see the face of the person who did it."

"It wasn't me."

"Who was it, then?"

"Why does it matter?"

"So I know who to be mad at."

Kieran was the one who pulled her out of Kazimir's Bentley and dropped her before throwing her into our SUV, but I'm not about to tell her that.

On the other hand, maybe she'll fire him from being her new best friend and things will go back to normal around here. He actually had the nerve to suggest I should let her into the kitchen to cook for us.

As if it wouldn't cause a mutiny if I tried to serve my men the rabbit food she eats.

But I decide the last thing anyone needs at the moment is this mouthy Tinker Bell banshee carrying a vendetta against him. We've got enough problems as it is.

"Forget it. But I'm going to bring the doctor in to have a look at you."

I help her sit up. The color is coming back to her cheeks, which is good, but she still looks a little shaky. I squash the ridiculous urge to give her a reassuring hug and step back instead.

She looks up at me, squinting. "Did you say 'doctor'?"

"Don't tell me your ears aren't working, either."

"They're working. I'm just surprised."

"By what?"

"That you'd do that for me."

The way she's looking at me is odd. She almost looks as if she's grateful. As if . . .

She likes me.

Which is pure fantasy on my part. The woman despises me. Perhaps I've hit my head on asphalt, too.

My voice comes out gruff. "You're no good to me dead."

"What difference does it make if I'm dead? You said you were working on getting me home. You don't need me anymore. Right?"

She sounds curious. Or is that suspicious? I can't tell. "I didn't say I didn't need you."

As soon as it's out, I'm fucking horrified. I know exactly how bad it sounded.

If I didn't, the look on Sloane's face would clue me in.

Green eyes as sharp as the edge of a blade, she says, "So you *do* need me? For what, exactly?"

I growl, "Target practice."

Her gaze is steady. Unblinking. Unnerving.

She says softly, "Gangster . . . do you have a crush on me?"

"No."

"Because no one would blame you if you did."

"Jesus. You're off in the head."

"And I did tell you this would happen."

I thunder, "It didn't happen! *Nothing has happened!*"

"No?"

She rises and approaches me. I take a step back, then curse myself silently and stand my ground as she nears.

When she stops, she's standing so close, I can smell the shampoo she used to wash her hair. *My* shampoo. That's my soap, too, scenting her skin. And my shirt she's wearing.

And my briefs, unless she took those off.

Fuck, did she take them off? Is she naked under my shirt?

Looking up into my face, she says, "I'll be the judge of that."

Then she stands on her toes and kisses me.

THIRTEEN

SLOANE

*I*t's like kissing a brick wall.

No, that's not right. Let me rephrase.

It's like kissing a frozen, angry brick wall that hated you and everything you stood for, had been nursing a lifelong grudge against you, and had made a vow of honor that it was going to kill you to avenge the murder of its father.

Declan's mouth is hard, cold, and unyielding. Somehow, his lips transmit that they'd rather be injected with the Ebola virus than suffer the absolute disgust of meeting mine.

He curls his hands around my shoulders and pushes me away. Holding me at arm's length, he glares at me like I'm a puppy who just shit on his favorite pair of shoes.

Thunderclouds gathered over his head, he says darkly, "Don't. Ever. Do that. Again."

"I won't. Apologies." My laugh is small and embarrassed. "Sometimes my self-confidence goes a little overboard."

"You *think*?"

"Um. Yes. It's not my fault, though."

"Don't elaborate. For the love of god, don't say another word."

"It's just that most men are sort of . . . easy. I guess you're not."

"No," he snarls, lip curled. "I'm *not*."

He's holding me away from him like I'm contagious. Like he's wishing there were an open window right behind me. Or a bottomless pit.

Needless to say, it's deflating. I'm obviously losing my edge. Or maybe it's my mind I'm losing. I could've sworn he looked at me with longing.

I turn away and sit on the edge of the bed, folding my hands between my knees and avoiding his eyes.

Without another word, Declan spins on his heel and walks out.

When he returns many hours later, he brings another man with him.

"The doctor," he announces, then leaves the two of us alone.

After the door slams shut behind Declan, the small man in the blue suit removes his hat and sets it on the coffee table. He sets his black bag beside the hat and removes a stethoscope.

"There's nothing wrong with my heart or lungs. It's my head we need to be worried about."

The doctor straightens and looks at me. He's about sixty, with white hair and a kind smile. "Just following orders to be thorough, dear. I'm sure you understand."

"Oh. Right. Where do you want me?"

He gestures to a chair, which I sit in. "So you're a mafia doctor? That must be an interesting line of work. How many gunshot wounds have you stitched up?"

The doctor turns and gazes at me, looking like he's enjoying some private joke.

"What?"

He says warmly, "Mr. O'Donnell warned me that you were chatty. There's nothing worse than a quiet woman, I told him, because it only means they're up to no good. He seemed to think you were up to no good regardless."

He puts the buds of the stethoscope in his ears. "Careful about getting on his bad side, miss. He's got a bit of a temper."

"His bad side?" My laugh is dry. "You say that like he has a good one."

"Draw a deep breath, please."

The doctor presses the end of the stethoscope against my back. I inhale, he listens, then moves it to the opposite side of my spine. I draw another breath, and he listens again.

"He does. He's one of the best men I've ever known."

I say drily, "You must not get out much."

He moves to my chest and listens to my heart. Then he produces a blood pressure cuff from his bag and wraps it around my arm.

As it's inflating, he asks me about my periods.

"They're regular. Like I said, it's my head that's the problem." Though my ovaries have been acting strange lately, I'm not about to tell Declan's doctor that.

When he's satisfied my blood pressure is normal, he shines a light into both my eyes.

"Ow. That's really bright."

"Your pupil response is normal. Where is this lump Mr. O'Donnell mentioned?"

"Here." I show him. When he touches it, I wince.

He makes a soft sound of sympathy. "Yes, I'd imagine that hurts. You've got quite a lot of swelling. Have you had any headaches?"

"Yes."

"Nausea?"

"No. Actually, I take that back. I felt sick on the plane when I woke up. But I figured it was from the ketamine Declan gave me."

If the doctor thinks it's strange that Declan administered me a drug that made me pass out, he doesn't mention it. That's probably the least strange thing he's seen treating one of Declan's patients.

"Are you seeing flashing lights? Any problems with your hearing?"

"No and no."

"Recent memory loss?"

"Yes . . . and apparently, I fainted. But I don't remember that."

"Ringing ears or double vision?"

"No to both. Am I dying or what?"

"You are, but it will take four or five more decades."

At least he has a sense of humor.

He packs up and puts his hat back on, preparing to leave.

"Seriously, though, what's the verdict?"

"A mild concussion. Nothing to worry about, but make sure you rest for a few days. If you experience any more symptoms, or if your headaches get worse, we'll need to get you a CT scan to ensure there's no bleeding on the brain. In the meantime, ice that lump. It will help the swelling and discomfort."

"Bleeding on the brain? That doesn't sound good."

"It isn't. So please tell Mr. O'Donnell immediately if you continue to feel unwell."

"I will. Thank you."

When he leaves, I feel restless and unsettled. So of course, I have to send Declan a text.

> The doctor said I'm dying.

I pace until his response comes back.

> So my luck has finally changed.
>
> Jerk. Will you please come in here and talk to me?
> Why?

I'm bored.

If only that were lethal.

Stop being mean to me!

Give me one good reason why.

I chew my lip before answering, I think I'm scared.

He doesn't answer. I don't know why I was expecting he would. I pace around the room, chewing my lip and imagining what death by brain bleed would look like, until the door opens and Declan walks in.

With his hand still on the knob, he says, "If that was a lie, I'll open that window and push you out."

Why does he have to be such an asshole? Such a *handsome* asshole, which is somehow even worse.

"I've never been sick a day in my life, and now my brain is bleeding, and my memory is going, and I'm fainting like one of those stupid goats, and my head hurts like someone's been jackhammering it, and I'm probably going to die with only *you* for company. Can you blame me for being upset?"

His eyes are narrowed, doubtful, arctic blue.

I throw my hands in the air. "I'm not invincible!"

"So that deal you made with the devil for the power to kill with run-on sentences didn't include immortality?"

I stare at him with my heart beating hard and anger working its way up my throat. "You know what? Forget it. Go back to your fulfilling mobster lifestyle of kidnapping innocent people and murdering your enemies and generally making the world a much shittier place, and forget I said a damn thing."

I turn and walk as far away from him as I can go, to the wall of windows on the opposite side of the room. Then I stand with my back to him and my arms wrapped around myself, trying for the first time since I was a fat little kid getting bullied on the playground to hold back tears.

I hate him for this. *Nobody* makes me cry.

When I hear the door close, I release a breath and bow my head, closing my eyes and cursing myself for showing weakness.

"It's just that you don't seem like you have a vulnerable bone in your body, lass."

The voice is warm, soft, and comes from directly behind me. The bastard snuck up on me while I was busy feeling sorry for myself.

"Go away."

"That's not what you wanted two minutes ago."

"Two minutes ago, I didn't hate your guts."

"No? I feel sorry for the people whose guts you do hate if this is what you *not* hating them looks like."

I groan and bang my forehead against the window a few times.

He pulls me away from the glass and says softly, "Stop. You'll hurt your head."

"It's already hurt, thanks to you."

"I told you I wasn't the one who dropped you."

"Stop talking. You're making my headache worse."

His hands had been around my upper arms, but now they slide up to my shoulders and rest lightly there. He's quiet behind me, as if he's mulling something over.

"If you're about to strangle me, just get it over with."

"The thought had occurred to me."

I'd tell you to go to hell, but it wouldn't be a burn, considering that's your hometown.

After a long moment when I'm silent, he says, "You're too quiet for my comfort. What's going on in that head of yours?"

"Your funeral."

I'm surprised when he starts to laugh. He laughs and laughs, like he hasn't enjoyed himself this much in a long time.

I look up at him over my shoulder. "You're bipolar. Right? That's the root cause of all your mystifying behavior. Bipolar disorder."

"No."

"Too bad. If you'd said yes, I would've been nicer to you."

"Why's that?"

"Because mental health problems aren't a choice. You, on the other hand, are deliberately an asshole."

His smile is so bright, it's almost blinding. "You bring out the best in me, lass."

"Oh, go jump off a bridge." I turn back to the window.

We stand there like that for a while, looking out at the view of Boston far below. It's late afternoon, and I have no idea how long I've been here. One day? Two? Or the ten thousand it feels like?

When I glance at Declan's reflection in the glass, he's gazing at his hands resting on my shoulders as if he doesn't remember how they got there.

I wish I didn't find him attractive. I hate him, but I can't deny he's hot. Between those blue eyes and that strong jaw and that damn Irish accent . . .

"Why such a heavy sigh?" he murmurs.

"You're still alive and breathing."

"Not so long ago, you were thanking me for saving your life."

"I know. I wish I could go back in time and kick my own ass."

He's laughing again. Silently, trying to hold it in, but I can see his shoulders shaking in his reflection in the glass. For some reason, that makes me even more depressed.

"Please go away. I promise I won't bother you anymore. No more texts. No more talking. Just leave me alone."

I sound sad and pathetic. This man is draining the badass right out of me.

He knows it, too, because his voice grows soft. "I'll go if you answer a question."

"How would I like to kill you? Something slow and painful that involves flesh-eating bacteria."

Ignoring that, he continues in his gentle tone. "Why did you get involved with the Russian mafia?"

I consider not answering him. Because fuck him, that's why. But ultimately, I decide to tell him the truth. I'm suddenly too tired to fight. "I didn't know I was."

In the short pause that follows, Declan's hands tighten on my shoulders. He wants more.

If it will get rid of him, he can have it.

"When I met Stavros, he was just a cute guy who used to take my beginner's class a few times a week. He said he worked in tech. Which was true, he does own a software company. What I *didn't* know was that software was developed for illegal online gaming.

"But I guessed something was up when I saw his house on the lake. He has an estate right next to Zuckerberg's with three hundred feet of private beach. The place is probably worth fifty million dollars. Then there was the private jet, and the passports from various countries, and his little buddies who all spoke Russian. So, you know, one plus one equals two. He never told me, and I never asked, but it didn't matter. He was already past his expiration date by then."

Declan digests all that in silence. "Because boyfriends are like koi fish: a time-consuming and boring hobby."

"Exactly."

"So when did you finally confirm he was in the mafia?"

"Not until that night at La Cantina when the Irish guys were talking shit and the bullets started to fly."

He turns me to face him. It's so abrupt and unexpected, I'm startled.

Staring down at me with blistering intensity, he says, "You didn't know he was in the mafia when you got together?"

"No."

"And when you found out, you left him?"

"Don't make it sound noble. I wasn't a conscientious objector to his lifestyle or anything. The reason I left him is because I got bored."

Declan is incredulous. "He's a billionaire. A powerful, rich, good-looking young billionaire. With *billions*."

"I'm familiar with the word. You don't have to keep repeating it. And I have no idea how much money he has. I didn't conduct a forensic accounting."

"Trust me on this."

"Okay. And?"

"And you got bored."

"Money isn't what makes a man interesting. It's not even on the list. Stop making that face at me."

"Let me get this straight. You dated Stavros because *you thought he was cute?*"

"How is it possible that you can make that sound like a moral failing?"

"I just don't get it." He shakes his head. "He's fucking *rich*."

"So are you, by the looks of it. It doesn't make you interesting, either."

Judging by his expression, he can't decide if he's more surprised or offended.

"You're telling me I'm not interesting?"

"You're about as interesting as a koi fish. An old one. With digestive issues and a malfunctioning swim bladder."

Now he's outraged. His face is turning red.

God, that feels good.

Just to twist the knife deeper, I add, "Plus, you don't even know how to kiss."

His eyes flare. His jaw clenches. He growls, "Believe me, I know how to fucking kiss."

"Sure you do. If it's opposite day."

When I smile at his obvious fury, he mutters, "Bloody little smartass."

Then he grabs my face in both hands and crushes his mouth to mine.

FOURTEEN

DECLAN

I know it's a bad idea, but the woman has an uncanny knack for knowing exactly what to say to push my buttons.

The FBI should hire her for their terrorist interrogation team. There's not a man on earth whose will to live she couldn't break.

Holding her head and ignoring her little cry of surprise, I drink deep from her mouth. Her sweet, soft, warm mouth.

Her delicious, feminine, incredible mouth, whose appeal is surpassed only by the feel of her lush tits pressed against my chest. And the small tremor that runs through her as I deepen the kiss. And maybe the way the tension in her body starts to melt until she's leaning into me, giving me her weight and letting her head fall back as my tongue slides against hers.

When she slips her arms up around my neck and sighs in pleasure, a growl of victory rumbles through my chest.

Can't kiss, my arse.

I wind an arm around her back, the other around her waist, and pull her closer. She fits perfectly against my body, soft everywhere

I'm hard. Pliant everywhere my fingers dig. And curved in all the right places.

The urge to push her down to the floor and fuck her until she's screaming my name is so strong, it shakes me to my core.

I pull away, breathing hard.

She's breathing hard, too. We stand there for a silent moment, faces inches apart, hearts pounding, until she licks her lips and says in a husky whisper, "Five out of ten."

"Bollocks. That was the best kiss you've ever had, and you know it."

"I think you can do better."

She pulls my head down and fits her mouth against mine.

This time, the kiss is slower. Softer, but somehow deeper. It goes on and on, getting hotter and hungrier, until she's squirming against me and my dick is a throbbing steel bar.

I flex my pelvis into hers. She moans softly in the back of her throat. When I break away this time, I'm panting and more than a little dizzy.

She opens her eyes and gazes up at me. Cheeks flushed, lips wet, she looks incredible. Satan did a good job when he created her.

"Six," she breathes. "C'mon, gangster. Don't tell me that's all you've got."

"That was a fucking ten. And you're not in charge here."

She says teasingly, "You keep saying that, but I'm not sure if it's me you're trying to convince or yourself."

I fist a hand into her hair, sink the other into a plush ass cheek, and hold her head steady as I kiss her again.

I don't stop until she's grinding her pelvis against mine and mewling like a kitten.

"*Ten*," I growl against her mouth.

Without opening her eyes, she says faintly, "Seven and a half. And that's being generous."

When I let loose a blistering string of curses in Gaelic, she laughs. It's low, pleased, and as maddening as it is sexy.

My heartbeat flying, I put my mouth next to her ear. "You like to live dangerously, don't you, lass?"

"'Live dangerously and you live right.'"

I pull away and gaze at her, astonished. "Goethe? Now you're quoting fucking *Goethe*?"

She smiles. "Just because I'm cute doesn't mean my brain is tiny."

Then she pushes me away, props her hands on her hips, and sends me a look of icy disdain that would make any queen proud. "Oh. I just remembered."

"What?"

"I hate you."

We stare at each other. She's saved from strangulation when my cell phone rings. When I see the number on the screen, I thrust the phone at her and snap, "You have thirty seconds."

Then I whirl around and walk away, blowing out a hard breath and dragging a shaking hand through my hair. Trying to pull myself together.

I should've never taken that gag off her mouth.

"Hello? Nat! Oh my god, I was so worried about you."

Behind me, Sloane pauses, listening. Then she laughs. "Me? Don't be ridiculous! You know I always land on my feet."

Another pause. "Yes, I'm sure it looked bad. But security cameras make everything look worse. It was much less dramatic in real . . . yes, I did hit my head. Yes, everyone was shooting at each other, but . . . oh, babe. I'm fine. I promise."

She listens for a while, then says firmly, "Natalie. Take a breath. I haven't been beaten. I haven't been dismembered. I haven't been buried in a shallow grave."

I look at her over my shoulder with what I hope are evil, slitted eyes that transmit *Yet*.

She makes a face and waves a dismissive hand in the air like I'm being silly.

"No, no, I'm being treated very well. *No,* he doesn't have a gun pointed at my head right now. Actually . . ."

A new look comes into her eyes. It's crafty and confident and worries me.

"Well, if you must know, he's halfway in love with me already."

My mouth drops open.

She's laughing into the phone. "Right? Poor guy. He was a goner from the first time we met."

I know she's just trying to aggravate me, but that's exactly what she said about Stavros. I think I'm going to break something. Maybe her knees.

I stride toward her, holding out my hand for the phone, but she backs away, waving me off like I'm an annoying fly.

"No, tell Kage not to do that. It's not necessary."

I stop a foot away and glare down at her, breathing fire from my nose. I'd grab the phone, but the mention of Kage makes me hesitate. I want to hear where this conversation is going. What he has planned.

She gazes calmly up at me, staring straight into my eyes when she says, "Declan would never hurt me, that's why. Even if he wanted to. Which he usually does. How do I know?" Her smile is soft. "Because he gave me his word."

I mouth *I lied.*

She sticks out her tongue.

"Now, listen, Nat. I need you to do something for me. Tell your man to call off the cavalry. Tell him that Declan wants to have a sit-down and work this whole war thing out. Tell him that—"

I grab the phone from her, cover the receiver with my hand, and snap, "What the hell do you think you're doing?"

She meets my furious gaze with a level one of her own. "Saving your ass, gangster."

"It doesn't need saving."

"You might change your mind when you hear that Kage put out a thirty-million-dollar bounty on your head for kidnapping me. Whichever one of the families kills you first gets the money, plus their access to shipping and distribution restored." Her smile is smug. "There's another thirty mil for whoever returns me safely to New York. So now *you're* the only one with a target on his back. Funny how fast this game can change, isn't it?"

When I only stare at her, infuriated by her hubris, she says politely, "I'll be rubbing this in later, but for now, may I get back to my call, please?"

I put the phone to my ear. Looking into Sloane's eyes as I speak, I say, "Tell Kazimir that if he doesn't cancel both bounties within the hour, Sloane's mutilated body will be dumped on his doorstep by midnight."

I disconnect and glare at her.

She folds her arms over her chest and glares back. "That wasn't smart."

Seething, I say softly, "You have no idea what kind of game is being played here, lass. None at all. You're absolutely fucking clueless. And to tell you the truth, I'm sick of listening to you run that bloody mouth."

I slip the phone into my coat pocket. When I start to work at the knot in my tie, she backs up, shaking her head.

"Don't you dare try to gag me, gangster."

I whip it off and stalk toward her.

"I'm warning you!" she shouts, stumbling backward. "I'll kick your ass!"

I lunge.

She yelps and whirls around to run away, but I'm too close. I grab her by the scruff of her neck and yank her against my chest.

I'm rewarded for that move by her heel smashing down onto the top of my foot.

It's a hard strike. A good one. But it takes a hell of a lot more than that to stop me when I've lost my temper.

And I've finally lost it. Honestly, it's a miracle I've held on to it this long.

I shove her face-down onto the bed. Twisting like a caged animal, she kicks and screams as I straddle her waist. She's furious she can't budge me. When I pin her arms behind her back, she kicks up with her heel and catches me right in the kidney.

I forget about wanting to stuff the tie down her throat and tie it around her wrists instead.

The punishment I'm about to administer doesn't require silence.

She's shouting. Bucking like a wild bull, trying to throw me off. I realize she hates to not be the one in control almost as much as she hates to show anything remotely close to weakness.

It gives me a profound sense of satisfaction that I'm subjecting her to both.

"Fuck you and your laughing!" she hollers.

"Come on, hellcat. Weren't you supposed to be kicking my ass? So far, I give you a five out of ten."

"Prick!"

"Don't tell me that's all you've got. I think you can do better."

Frustrated that I'm throwing her words back at her, she lets loose a scream. She screams louder when I laugh again.

I sit on the edge of the bed and drag her onto my lap, holding her down with one hand gripped around the back of her neck, the other around her hip.

It's not easy. She's fighting me hard. And she's stronger than she looks. I have to give her credit for that. But she can't match my strength, no matter how hard she fights.

I yank down her underwear—*my* underwear—to the middle of her thighs and rain down a series of sharp, stinging blows with my open hand on her bare arse.

She sucks in a breath, back stiffening.

"You deserve every one of those," I say through gritted teeth. "And every one that's coming."

I spank her again and again until my palm is hot and her bottom is bright red. I'm so intent on what I'm doing, I don't notice until I stop that she's no longer struggling. She lies still, her cheek pressed to the mattress, her eyes closed. She's breathing as hard as I am.

Trembling, too. Her entire body is trembling.

And my dick is as hard as a rock.

After a moment, she whispers brokenly, "Three out of ten."

It's a dare.

My breath leaves my chest in a ragged rush. I stare down at her naked arse—firm, round, cherry red—and am almost overcome by a savagely powerful need to take it.

To release my aching cock from my trousers and shove it deep inside her.

To hold her down and fuck her hard while I bite her neck.

To listen to her cry out as I come inside her, pulling her hair.

To punish her, dominate her, make her submit to me.

To make her mine.

Her eyes drift open. She looks up at me. Whatever she sees on my face sends a shiver through her body.

I growl, "Not a fucking word."

She swallows. Licks her lips. Tries to do box breathing to calm herself and fails.

I like her like this.

Obedient and mercifully silent, obviously turned on. That she's allowing me to keep her on my lap without struggling or trying to get away tells me that she enjoyed that spanking, just as much as her erratic breathing and flushed face do.

Or maybe it's how hard she's trembling. Or that wild look in her eyes, like she's unsure what I'm going to do next and can't decide if she likes not knowing or hates it.

Watching her face closely, I say, "I've got a question for you, hellcat. And if there's been any time since we met that you need to tell me the truth, it's now."

She squeezes her eyes shut.

"No, don't hide from me. Open your eyes."

She turns her face to the bedsheets.

I drop my voice and say her name. It's a warning, and she knows it.

Her voice muffled by the sheets, she says, "Please don't make me say it."

"You don't know what I was going to ask."

After a pause, she speaks in a miserable whisper. "Yes, I do. And we both know the answer. And I couldn't bear it if you made me say it out loud. I'll hate myself forever. Please don't make me say it, Declan. Please."

Ah, fuck. What that does to me.

It's like she plugged me into a socket. Electricity jolts through my body. Adrenaline floods my veins. I break out in a sweat, and my heartbeat goes arrhythmic. My dick aches, my balls are tight, and holy fuck, I want this woman so much, my mouth waters.

And all it would take is to force her to admit she wants me to keep going.

Which she does . . . but also doesn't.

I exhale slowly, gathering my self-control.

I flip her over, settle her between my spread thighs, and grasp her jaw in my hand.

I kiss her. Deeply.

She responds, sagging against the arm I've got wound around her back and making a soft, feminine sound of pleasure deep in her throat.

Then I push her off my lap, stand, and walk out of the room.

In a life full of difficult moments, this one makes the top five.

FIFTEEN

SLOANE

*S*o here I am, sprawled on the carpet with my hands tied behind my back, stunned, panting, and humiliated.

And soaking wet.

Because although *I* hate Declan, my coochie thinks that bastard is divine.

To top it all off, he handled me like I was as weak as a limp noodle. All those years of self-defense training, all the hours I've sweated through advanced yoga poses, contorting my body in near-impossible ways, honing my core strength and toning my muscles, and that bossy Irishman wrangled me into submission in ten seconds flat like I was a bleating baby cow in its rodeo debut.

Then he spanked me, kissed me, and—for the final indignity—shoved me onto the floor and swaggered out.

The arrogant son of a bitch. First, he almost made me cry. Then, he almost made me come. As soon as I get the chance, I'm going to kill him.

Slowly.

Muttering curses, I sit up and get to work on the necktie binding my hands. After a few minutes of struggling, the knots loosen, and I get free.

The first thing I do is head straight to the drawer in the dresser in his closet where I saw a cigarette lighter when I was snooping earlier. I return to the bedroom and light his tie on fire.

Watching it burn is right up there with the top five most satisfying moments of my life.

When there's nothing left but a smoldering scorch mark on the carpet and the acrid scent of burnt silk in the air, I toss the lighter onto the bed, sit cross-legged on the floor in front of the windows, slow my breathing, and meditate for twenty minutes.

And when I say "meditate," I mean mentally run through all the ways I'd love to see Declan die.

Take a deep breath and remember who the fuck you are.

He'll never get a rise out of me again. Every time I see him from now on, I'll be a rock. I'll be a cat, aloof and disinterested. Armed with sharp teeth and claws.

"Fucker," I mutter under my breath. "Egotistical, overbearing, bad-tempered jerk."

Take a deep breath. Remember who you are.

Another twenty minutes of affirmations produces as little positive effect on my mental state as the meditation did. I move on to yoga, but quickly discover that all the Feathered Peacock poses in the world can't rid me of the brain stain that is Declan O'Donnell.

So be it.

I've survived bullies before.

I've survived humiliation before.

I'll survive him.

Hours later, another one of the goon squad arrives, carrying a tray of food. He's got dark blond hair, hazel eyes, broad shoulders, a cleft chin, and a spiderweb tattoo on one side of his neck.

His hands are the size of anvils. His jawline could cut steel. I instantly nickname him Thor.

I'm beginning to think Declan hires these guys based on their level of hotness. Birds of a feather and all that.

"Where's Kieran?"

Thor doesn't spare me a glance as he sets the tray down and picks up the old one. "Don't bother tryin' to chat me up, lass. I've been told not to talk to you."

Like Kieran, he pronounces "you" like "ye." Declan must've put something funny in the last food delivery, because I'm starting to think Irish accents are the sexiest of them all.

Or maybe that's my brain bleed talking.

I don my brightest smile. "Oh, that's okay. I don't want to get you in trouble. I just wanted to know your name so I could tell Declan what a good job you did, but I understand you're under orders. Mum's the word."

He straightens and glowers at me.

I make a zipper motion across my lips. "Seriously. No talking, I promise. Except if you could just tell me if Kieran's okay, that would be great. We're friends, you know. You and I could be friends, too, if you wanted, but I know that probably goes against your whole badass gangster vibe to befriend a helpless captive and whatnot. Has anyone ever told you that you bear a striking resemblance to Thor, the Norse god of thunder?"

He pauses before saying, "Usually I get Captain America."

I gasp. "Oh my god, you're so right! It's that jaw. Very heroic."

He looks momentarily pleased, before he remembers he's not supposed to be talking to me. The glower makes a reappearance.

"Right. Sorry. My bad. If you could just tell Kieran I was asking after him, I'd really appreciate it. I feel so bad about his nose."

"Don't. It's an improvement." The faint approximation of a smile curves the corners of his mouth. "All the lads thought it was dead sound, lass. Wicked craic." His smile vanishes. "Don't tell Declan I said that, if you please."

"I won't. You can count on me. If he asks about you, I'll tell him you were a mute asshole. That should make him happy."

He lowers his head and examines my face for a moment. Then he nods and turns back to the door. Just as he's about to leave, he turns back to me.

"The name's Spider."

"Your mother named you *Spider*? I don't think so. What's your real name?"

He considers me in silence for a while, then says grudgingly, "Homer. And if you repeat that, I'll—"

"Homer? Very cool! I wish I were named after an ancient Greek poet, but I'm embarrassed to admit my mom wanted a name that would fit either a boy or a girl and found Sloane on some random baby name website. At least your mother had real inspiration. I think mine was drunk on rosé."

When I notice how strangely he's looking at me, I get worried. "Did I say something wrong?"

"Most people from this country think of the cartoon character Homer Simpson when I tell them my name."

"Oh. Well, I'm not most people, now, am I?"

When I grin, he chuckles softly, shaking his head. "I hear you offered to cook Kieran a meal."

"Yes. But not only him. I offered to cook for all of you. I'm a very good chef, if I do say so myself. It's too bad you and Kieran aren't supposed to be talking to me, because you could lobby Declan to let me into the kitchen. It would be good therapy for us both. I'm already getting bored. Imagine how much I'll annoy him in another few days when I'm really climbing the walls!"

He opens his mouth, remembers he shouldn't be having this conversation, and shuts it again.

"Oops. That's my fault. I don't want to get you in trouble, so you should probably go. When I see Declan next, I'll pretend to be crying and blame it on you."

"Decent of you. Thanks."

"You're welcome."

"By the way, what's that stench?"

"I used Declan's cigarette lighter to burn one of his ties."

We gaze at each other in silence for a moment. He says gently, "Why don't you give me the lighter, lass?"

"Ooh, good idea! You can tell him you took it away from me and I started sobbing. He'll probably give you a raise."

I retrieve the lighter from the bed and set it on the tray of empty dishes Homer's holding. Then I smile at him. "It's been nice meeting you. You and Kieran are both very sweet. I can't believe you work for such a douche."

He suddenly turns deadly serious. "It's my honor to work for him. He's one of the best men I've ever known."

Another one who's drunk the Kool-Aid. The doctor said the same thing. "I think we'll have to agree to disagree. But it was still nice to meet you. Please give Kieran my best."

Homer can't decide how to respond, so he leaves without saying anything.

He returns in short order with bags and bags of clothes. He sets the bags inside the door, turns to me, lowers his voice, says, "Kieran says hullo, and we're working on the cooking thing," then leaves again.

If only the lord of the manor were as nice as his minions.

I dig through the clothes, delighted to find almost everything I asked for. I contemplate texting Declan a list of things I'd like from Louis Vuitton and Cartier, just to see what he'd do, but decide I'd rather be shot dead than communicate with him. So I dress, eat the food Homer brought, and meditate again.

By the time all that's finished, it's twilight beyond the wall of windows, and I'm tired.

Unusually tired. Unless I'd had a big night out with Nat, I'm always brimming with energy. Right now, I feel like someone sucked all my energy out with a vacuum.

That's probably what Declan was doing right before I woke up next to him in bed.

I walk around the room three times, inspecting everything again, hoping to find any clue about its occupant I might have missed, but have no luck. I also don't find anything I can use as a weapon. Not that I think Declan is going to hurt me, but there's no telling when the desire to stab him will present itself.

I'm about to give up and go to sleep when the man himself returns.

I didn't think it was possible for him to look angrier than the last time I saw him, but I was wrong.

He closes the door behind him with such force, I jump. Then he stands there, staring at me with glittering icicle eyes, trying to kill me with a look.

"What did I do now?"

"What exactly did you say to Spider?"

I pretend innocence. "Was that the tall blond guy? I didn't say anything to him."

"No?"

Uh-oh. He knows something. Shit, I wonder if there are cameras in here? "I simply thanked him for bringing me food."

"And what did he say?"

"Only that he wasn't supposed to talk to me."

Declan moves toward me, one step at a time, never taking his blistering gaze from my face. I resist the urge to back up and square my shoulders instead.

His voice low, he says, "He *wasn't* supposed to talk to you. That was a direct order. Yet somehow he left this room with little red hearts in his eyes and the strange urge to conspire with Kieran to get me to let you cook for them."

"Oh. Really? That *is* strange."

He keeps moving slowly closer, a panther stalking its prey.

I clear my throat. "Actually, he was quite intimidating. He's really got that whole strong-silent-type thing down."

"So you're saying he was silent? He didn't speak a word?"

I lift my chin and meet his challenging stare. "Yes. That's what I'm saying."

Declan stops only inches away. He's so close, I feel the anger coming off him in heated waves. He gazes down at me, grinding his jaw.

"Why would you lie for him?"

Either there are cameras in here, or Spider confessed. Trying to bullshit him clearly isn't going to work, so I tell the truth instead. "I don't want him to get in trouble."

Declan draws a slow breath through flared nostrils. He's trying very hard not to grab me around the throat. "Why would you care if he gets in trouble?"

"I don't want him to get in trouble because of *me*. Also, he seems nice."

He repeats flatly, "Nice."

"Yes."

"He's killed six men within the past seventy-two hours."

"Oh. Hmm. That does seem like a high number for such a short period of time. But he is a gangster, so I guess it comes with the territory. Is there a quota they need to meet or something?"

He does the slow-breathing thing again. When he seems confident that he's controlled the urge to break my neck, he says, "You've bewitched two of my men. One whose nose you broke. The other one you only spent minutes with. Kieran fancies himself your butler, and Spider fancies himself in love. I won't be able to send anyone else in here for fear they'll come out trying to kill me."

I have to suppress my smile. If he sees it, he could explode. "Just because you're immune to my charms doesn't mean everyone else is."

His voice deadly soft and his eyes burning, he says, "Aye, your infamous 'charm.' That must be the influence your crazy ex Stavros was operating under when he attempted to shoot his way into the building."

I arch my brows. "Stavros tried to rescue me? Already?"

"Aye."

My heart skips a beat. "Oh god. Is he okay? You didn't kill him, did you?"

"Why do you care one way or another? He bored you so much, you broke up with him."

"That doesn't mean I want him dead! And I asked you not to hurt him, remember?"

"I remember. Which is the only reason he's still alive."

I exhale a relieved breath and press my hand over my heart. "Whew! What did you do with him?"

"Put him on a slow boat to China."

I can't tell if that's the truth or if he's being sarcastic, but I know he didn't hurt Stavros. I can tell by his expression that he's disappointed in himself about it.

"Thank you. I appreciate it. Sincerely."

When he only stands staring at me with those blistering eyes, I feel defensive.

"What now?"

"You're strange. And powerful. And aggravating beyond belief. I can't decide if I should muzzle you for the remainder of your stay or unleash you on my enemies. I think you'd have them all eating out of your hand within an afternoon."

After a moment, I say, "Funny, but that almost sounded like a compliment."

"It wasn't. I don't like you."

"I don't like you, either."

The space between us crackles with heat. His gaze is palpable, as if there's a current of electricity attached to it, shooting into my body, straight down between my legs.

He looks at my mouth and moistens his lips.

That's the last thing I remember before I wake up in the hospital.

SIXTEEN

DECLAN

*I*t's a subdural hematoma. Small, but dangerous. The mortality rate on these types of brain injuries is high. If the blood clot doesn't resolve on its own in forty-eight hours, she'll need surgery to relieve the pressure inside the skull and repair the injured vessels."

"What's the mortality rate?"

"The frequency of death in a certain population over a specific period of time."

I have to physically restrain myself from pulling out my gun and shooting this idiot doctor in the face. "I meant what's the mortality rate for subdural hematomas?"

"Oh, sorry. Fifty to ninety percent."

That stuns me. "You're telling me that most people with this condition die?"

"At least half of them, yes."

When I stare at him in horror, he quickly backtracks.

"But most of these injuries are seen in the elderly or in patients who've been in car accidents or other highly traumatic events.

Considering the age and overall health of this patient, her chances are much better than average."

I hear myself growl, "They better be. If she dies, so do you."

Because he knows who I am, he goes white. I jerk my chin at Kieran, who ushers the doctor out of the room before he can lose control of his bowels.

When the door closes, I tell Kieran, "Lock this whole fucking hospital down. Post men at all the exits and entrances and outside her room. Vet every person who wants to access this floor, including staff. Call O'Malley at the precinct and tell him we're in charge of Mass General until further notice. I don't want police interference, and I definitely don't want anyone trying to kidnap my captive."

"Aye, boss."

He turns to leave.

"And Kieran?"

He turns back to me, waiting.

"I'm putting you in charge of this because I think that's what she'd want. Don't disappoint me."

He vows, "I won't, boss. Nobody will get near our lass."

Our lass. Christ, now she's the team mascot?

Kieran sees my face and does the smart thing and leaves.

When I'm alone in the empty room, I take a moment to compose myself. Then I enter the adjoining room where Sloane is.

Pale but alert, she's sitting up in bed, playing with the TV remote control, clicking through channels. When she sees me, however, she stops.

"Oh god. It's bad, isn't it?"

"Aye. Subdural hematoma. There's at least a fifty percent chance you'll die."

After a beat, she says, "Gee, don't sugarcoat it."

"Would you want me to?"

"No. But you don't have to look so happy about it, either."

I sit in the chair next to the bed, drag a hand through my hair, and sigh. "I'm not happy about it."

"So that's your sad face?"

"This is my my-captive-is-a-pain-in-my-fucking-arse face."

"Ah, yes, now I recognize it. You could star in a hemorrhoid-cream commercial with that mug."

We gaze at each other. I'm trying not to feel admiration at how she's taking the news, but I should've known better. She's not one to break down and cry, even when she could be dying.

"Is there anyone you want me to call?"

Without missing a beat, she says, "Oprah Winfrey. I've always wanted to meet her. I feel like we'd hit it off, she'd invite me to all the cool parties at her Montecito mansion, and that's where I'd meet my future husband, the crown prince of Monaco. Or Morocco. I can't remember which was the cute one."

I fight a smile. "I'll get right on that. Anyone else?"

She sighs, settles back against the pillows, and shakes her head. "No. My mom passed away years ago, and I only talk to my dad on holidays. His new wife doesn't really like me. You probably already knew that, considering you're omniscient and all, but if anything happens to me, please let Natalie know. I don't want to worry her by telling her I'm here, but she'll freak out if she doesn't hear from me again soon. She's probably already freaking out now. She's very emotional, you know. She's the sensitive one."

She trails off, chewing her lip and frowning.

"She's lucky to have you as a friend. You're very loyal."

Sloane looks like I just informed her I sold her to a circus. "I'm sorry, it must be my janky brain, but I thought I heard you say something nice to me."

Now I can't help my smile. "It was definitely your janky brain."

"That's what I thought."

I stand and take off my jacket. I throw it over the back of the chair, then sit down again and pick up the celebrity gossip magazine from the small table beside the bed. I settle in the chair, get comfortable, and start to read.

"Um. What are you doing?"

I don't look up from the magazine when I answer. "What does it look like I'm doing?"

"Sitting. Reading. Staying."

I say drily, "Your powers of observation are astonishing."

Silence follows, but I know it will be short. And I'm right.

"Declan?"

"Aye, lass?"

"Don't you have important gangster things you should be out doing? Murdering your enemies and whatnot? Skulking around dark alleyways?"

"Aye, lass." I turn the page.

"So . . ."

"If anyone's going to kill you, it's going to be me. I don't trust that idiotic fifteen-year-old doctor."

"Are you talking about the *brain surgeon*?"

"Aye. Looks like he got his medical license from a Cracker Jack box."

Sloane starts to laugh. The sound is soft and surprisingly sweet. Even more surprising is how much I like hearing it.

"Are you sure you're only forty-two? Cracker Jacks are like from my dad's era."

I lower the magazine and look at her. "You remembered how old I said I was."

"I remember everything you've said."

When I raise my brows, her pale cheeks flush with color.

"Oh, shut up."

"You first."

She sighs in aggravation and rolls onto her side, her back facing me. I go back to my magazine.

After a five-minute pause where I can almost hear her internal struggle, she rolls over and pronounces, "This is very strange. You know that, right?"

I respond without looking up from the magazine, because I know it annoys her. "Which part?"

"All the parts. The whole thing! Me, you, kidnapping, car chases, hematomas, imminent death, hello?"

"It's probably best not to get too excited, lass. We don't want you bursting any more brain vessels."

"Are you . . . are you *laughing* at me?"

I say mildly, "Why, would your Teflon ego be hurt if I were?"

Another five minutes of silent seething passes before she can't stand it anymore. She sits up in bed. "Declan!"

I glance at her. "Mmm?"

"What the hell are you doing?"

Holding her gaze, I say, "Protecting you. Go to sleep."

She opens her mouth, but closes it when—a miracle—she can't find anything to say. Lying back against the pillows, she pulls the sheets up under her nose and looks at me with wide eyes.

It's disarmingly adorable. I wonder if she practices this stuff in front of a mirror.

"Declan?"

"For fuck's sake, lass, just ask the question. Don't say my name every time first."

She mutters, "So many rules."

I snap the magazine instead of her neck and go back to reading.

"I was just wondering if you could tell me a story."

I cut my gaze to hers.

Her voice comes out small. "To help me sleep."

When I narrow my eyes in suspicion, she says, "Please?"

"Whatever kind of game this is, I'm not playing."

After a moment, she whispers, "Okay," and rolls onto her side again, tucking her legs up to her chin so she's in a ball. A small, pathetic-looking ball.

I toss the magazine to the bedside table, wishing I hadn't given up on religion years ago. Now would be a good time to pray for god to kill me and save me from this misery.

Heaving a sigh, I begin. "Once upon a time, in a land far away, there lived . . ." I glance at the back of her head. "A princess."

Sloane turns slightly, listening. I continue.

"A terribly homely princess, with buck teeth, facial hair, and a large hump on her back. She looked like a wee camel, in fact."

She mutters, "Walt Disney, you're not."

"Am I telling this, or are you going to keep interrupting me?"

A grumble of discontent is my answer.

"As I was saying. The wee camel princess was homely, but she had an interesting personality that drew people to her. They had a hard time getting past her hideous looks, but once they did, they discovered she had a magical talent for . . . are you ready?"

She says flatly, "I can hardly contain my excitement."

"Talking to animals."

After a long pause, curiosity gets the better of her. "What kinds of animals?"

"All of them. But mainly dogs. The wee camel princess could make any dog, no matter how rabid or feral, fall in love with her and do her bidding."

"Ah. I see where this is going. The princess will fall in love with Lassie and create a new race of half-camel, half-dog babies called campups who turn on humans and kill them all. The end."

"No, but if that idea were made into a movie, I'd watch it. Especially if the campups were genetically modified so their left paw-arms were laser cannons they could operate by thought. May I proceed?"

She sighs heavily. I take it as an affirmative.

"One day the homely princess was going to visit her good friend Neddie, when suddenly she was abducted by the biggest, strongest, handsomest dog she had ever seen. He was the king of all the dogs— the top dog, so to speak—and famous for his bravery. Also for his intelligence. It was far superior to the wee camel princess's intelligence. Which was rather pathetic, despite her delusions otherwise."

"You're so lacking in imagination, there's a hole in your head where your brain should be."

Holding back a chuckle, I go on. "So the brave, strong, handsome, warrior-king dog—"

She mutters, "Unbelievable."

"—locks the wee camel princess up in his castle. His plan was to interrogate her for information on his sworn enemy, who she had befriended. What he didn't know, however, is how messy camels are. And stinky. Within days, the whole place reeked of regurgitated, half-digested grass. The castle smelled like a giant trash bin on a hot summer day. Oh, and greasy fur. And dung."

"Charming. Was this camel princess's name Slang, by any chance? Slung? Slune?"

Her tone is so sour, I have a hard time holding back a laugh. "No. Her name was Drone."

"*Drone.* Because she talked so much. You missed your true calling in comedy, gangster."

"I am quite funny, aren't I?"

"You'd be a lot funnier with a broken nose."

A nurse enters the room. Sloane quips, "Oh, good, maybe she brought an enema we can use to flush that stick out of your ass."

I have to cover my mouth with a hand to keep from laughing.

The nurse introduces herself as Nancy and says she's going to take Sloane's blood pressure. Then she turns to me with a tentative smile. "And you must be the father."

Sloane bursts into raucous laughter. Rolling over to gloat at me, she says, "Burn! Yes, that's my dad, Father Time, over there. He's not nearly as young and handsome as he thinks he is."

The nurse's smile falters. "I meant the father of the baby."

I fall still. My stomach clenches into a knot. It suddenly becomes very hard to breathe.

Sloane's still laughing. "Good one, gangster. How much did you pay her to say that?"

When she sees the expression on my face, her laughter dies.

Wide-eyed, she looks back at the nurse. Her face turns pale. Her voice comes out strangled. "Wait. What . . . what *baby*?"

At least the nurse has the good manners to look apologetic when she answers.

"The doctor didn't tell you? You're pregnant."

SEVENTEEN

DECLAN

*I*t's so silent in the room for a moment, I can hear someone's heart monitor beeping in another room down the hall. Then Sloane says flatly, "That's impossible. I've been on the pill for ten years. You've got the wrong person."

By this time, Nancy is looking extremely uncomfortable. She takes a single step backward toward the door. "Sorry. Maybe I'm mistaken. I'll just send the doctor back in—"

"Stop."

Though my tone is deadly soft, it does the trick. Nancy freezes in her tracks, swallowing.

Like the idiot doctor, she also knows who I am. Word gets around fast when a new king ascends the throne. "You ran a pregnancy test with the blood samples taken when she checked in?"

The nurse looks back and forth between me and Sloane, obviously wondering what kind of mess she just stepped into. "Yes. The doctor thought it was prudent considering—"

"No," interrupts Sloane, her voice loud. "I had my period last month. I've taken the pill every day since then. No missed days. I'm very careful. I'm not pregnant."

"The pill doesn't have a perfect success rate. And you can get pregnant during your period."

Sloane says, "And you can get the hell out of my room with that bullshit before I give you two black eyes, Nancy."

I stand. Nancy skitters back a few steps. I tell her to stop again, and she looks like she's going to faint.

"Listen, I'm just the messenger. The doctor can give you more information than I can."

I demand, "What's the accuracy on those blood tests?"

"Ninety-nine percent."

Fuck. "And how soon can it detect pregnancy after a missed period?"

"Within days."

I look at Sloane, red-faced and infuriated on the bed. "Have you missed a period?"

Her lips thin.

"Answer the goddamn question."

She admits grudgingly, "I was supposed to get it a few days ago. Or right now. My days are all mixed up."

When I pass a hand over my face, groaning, she insists, "I'm not pregnant! I know my body! Nothing has changed!"

"Typically, you won't start to feel symptoms until about week five or six."

Sloane's look could melt the skin right off poor Nancy's face. "That's a lot longer than it will take you to feel the symptoms of the kick I'm about to knock your teeth out with."

I snap, "Sloane, shut it. Nancy, get out."

Nancy spins around and runs out. When she's gone, Sloane turns to me, insistent. "I'm not. I'm *not,* Declan."

"Aye. Except it sounds like you are." Agitated, I start to pace.

"Well then, I'll just have to deal with it."

When I whirl on her, bristling, she lifts her brows.

"What's that look for?"

I growl, "You *are not* getting an abortion."

She examines my face in silence for a while. When she finally speaks, her voice is tranquil. "I didn't say I was. But if I were, it would be none of your damn business."

I lose my cool and shout, "Of course it's my business! You're my fucking captive!"

When her hair settles back around her face, she folds her hands in her lap. "I see you have strong feelings on the subject. I'd like to point out, however, that regardless of how I got to be here, it's curious that you'd care one way or the other. After all, you're not the father. Not that there is a father, because I'm not pregnant, but if I were, you wouldn't be him."

"Jesus Christ, do you think I'm an imbecile? I know I'm not the bloody father!"

She narrows her eyes. "Exactly. You're not the father, you're going to be sending me home soon, and I'll be out of your hair forever. So what are you getting so excited about?"

I flail around for something that would explain my bizarre emotional turmoil over this news. All I can come up with is, "I don't believe in abortion."

"Congratulations. Still not your business."

I start to pace again. Sloane watches me with eyes as sharp as a hawk's.

"If you're thinking that you're going to keep me chained up in your home indefinitely to block my reproductive rights, I'll tell you right now that won't work."

I wasn't thinking that, but it does make me curious. "Why not?"

"Kieran and Homer would never let you do that to me."

I gape at her, astounded. "Spider told you his real name?"

"Of course. Why is that so shocking?"

"He doesn't tell anyone his real name. I didn't know it until we'd known each other for more than ten years. And he was only in the room with you for three minutes."

She gives me a look. "The wee homely camel princess is good at getting dogs to do her bidding, remember?"

When I glare at her, seething, she sighs.

"Can we please not fight? I've got a splitting headache, my brain might be about to kill me, and I might be—but I'm not—with child. I don't have the energy for verbal combat."

She slumps back against the pillows and pulls the covers over her face.

I pace for a while longer. My mind is the smoking aftermath of a nuclear bomb.

Pregnant. The woman I kidnapped is pregnant with a Bratva baby? Holy fuck. And I thought things were bad before.

From under the covers, Sloane says, "If I ask you a personal question, will you answer?"

"No."

Naturally, she ignores that. "Did you have a girlfriend who terminated her pregnancy against your wishes?"

I drop into the chair beside her bed and exhale. "No."

"Oh. Okay. Sorry, that was none of my business. It's just that the topic seems like a trigger point for you."

"If I tell you it's because I believe all life is sacred, you'll laugh at me."

"Of course I'll laugh at you. Would you like to know why?"

"No."

"Because you kill people for a living."

I don't know why I bother answering her questions. All she does is ignore me. I grumble, "That's not all I do."

She flips the covers off her face and stares at me with her brows drawn together. "Oh, I'm sorry. I forgot extortion, racketeering, gunrunning, human trafficking—"

"No bloody human trafficking!"

"—drug smuggling, forgery, tax fraud, stock manipulation, corruption of public officials—"

"Where are you getting this information? Google?"

"Are you saying you don't do those things?"

I say through gritted teeth, "You have no idea what I do, lass."

"Don't glower at me. And why are *you* so upset? I'm the one with the brain damage and the maybe-baby." Her eyes go wide. "Oh god."

Alarmed by her expression, I say, "What now?"

"The ketamine you gave me . . ." She stares at me in horror.

My stomach rolls over. My voice comes out gruff. "It was only one dose. One low dose."

"It was enough to make me lose my memory. Imagine what it could do to a fetus!"

"That could've been the fall."

She says sarcastically, "The drop, you mean. And it might not have been."

When I don't say anything, she covers her eyes with a hand and whimpers.

I stand, take her hand away from her face, and lean over her, gazing down into her worried eyes. "The baby will be fine," I say with more conviction than I feel. "You're young, strong, and healthy. You're both going to be okay."

I don't add *Unless you die from that brain clot,* because that would just be rude.

She stares up at me, panicking, but managing to despise me nonetheless. "Declan, if it turns out that this kid that I'm not having has anything less than a genius IQ, I'll kill you. And I don't mean that figuratively."

Bypassing the threat on my life, which I'm sure she's sincere about, I smile. "Deal."

"Why are you smiling? I just said I'd kill you!"

"Exactly."

"I don't get it."

"If you want to slit my throat, you must be feeling better."

She purses her lips, considering me. "It wouldn't be throat slitting. Too bloody."

"Gun?"

She wrinkles her nose. "Too messy."

"Ah, I remember. Something slow and painful involving flesh-eating bacteria."

She nods. "So I could sit in a chair in the corner and watch as you're consumed inch by inch over the course of days. No, weeks. Months." She smiles. "In agony."

I chuckle. "You actually like that idea. What a little monster. And you look so sweet."

After an odd pause, her voice comes out tentative. "You think I look sweet?"

"No. I think you look like a camel. You're revolting."

We stare into each other's eyes. I become aware of her breathing, the flush creeping over her cheeks, and that I've leaned closer, so close, our noses are only inches apart.

She says softly, "You don't think I look like a camel."

I have to moisten my lips before I answer, my mouth is so dry. "A hyena. A warthog. A kakapo."

"I don't know that last one."

"It's a giant flightless parrot."

"A parrot? So it's cute."

I shake my head slowly, fighting the urge to lean closer and press my mouth to hers. My voice is husky when I answer. "No. It's disgusting."

After a moment, she whispers, "Liar."

She pushes me away and rolls over onto her side again.

I straighten and blow out a slow, silent breath. I pass a hand through my hair. Then I take my cell phone from my pocket and send a text to Spider.

I'm coming there now. Make sure he's ready to talk.

With one last glance at Sloane, I leave the room, nodding at the armed men in black suits Kieran has installed on either side of the door while I've been inside.

I head out for a chat with Stavros.

I wonder if Sloane would ever forgive me if I went back on my word and killed him.

Only one way to find out.

EIGHTEEN

SLOANE

The instant the door closes behind Declan, I push the call button for the nurse.

Sixty seconds later, Nancy arrives, looking like she'd rather be eating a bowl of razor blades than visiting me.

"Hi, Nancy. I apologize for being a witch to you earlier, but I'm not feeling that great at the moment. Aside from my brain bleeding all over itself, I've been kidnapped."

She blinks. "Uh . . ."

"You don't have to do anything about it. I'm not asking for help. I know you'd get into big trouble with the Irish mafia if they found out you called the police, so don't do that, okay? I don't want your entire family getting killed on my behalf."

"O . . . kay."

"Great. Thanks. So listen, I was wondering if you could tell me what would cause a false-positive pregnancy test?"

After she uncrosses her eyes, she says, "It's extremely rare for a blood test to return a false positive."

"But if it did, what would cause it?"

She thinks for a moment. "There are several conditions that raise the level of proteins in the blood. Recent miscarriage or abortion. Ectopic pregnancy, where a fertilized egg implants in the fallopian tubes. Some medications. Certain health conditions."

"Like what?"

"I'd have to look it up for a complete list, but off the top of my head . . . kidney disease. Rheumatoid factors. Cancer."

"What kinds of cancer?"

"Ovarian, primarily."

Oh god. That's what my mother died of. A pang of panic makes my heartbeat surge, but I breathe through it. "What about exposure to the drug ketamine?"

"That's an anesthetic. It wouldn't affect the test results."

"Anything else you can think of?"

"No."

"Okay. Thanks for the info. I appreciate it. Since I'm here, can we check for tumors on my ovaries? And let's also do all the other blood tests I need to look for kidney disease and whatever else."

"Why don't we do another pregnancy test first?"

"I know I'm not pregnant."

I can tell she's thinking I'm in total denial, but she wisely doesn't mention that.

"All right. I'll order the tests."

"Thank you."

She stares at me for a moment, troubled. Pointing her thumb over her shoulder toward the door, she says, "So . . ."

"The head of the Irish mafia kidnapped me. Yeah."

"But . . ."

I wave a hand in the air. "I'm fine. Don't worry about me. He got the worse end of the deal. We'll probably be back here in a week when he has the massive coronary he's got brewing. Hey, would it be possible for me to get a protein smoothie? Oh, and could I also ask you to please call Lakeside Yoga in King's Beach, Tahoe, and tell them that Sloane has the flu and will be out for a while? If they ask who you are, just say Riley. That's my little sister."

I smile at her. She blinks a few more times, looking totally confused, before turning and walking out.

I slide down in bed, pull the covers over my face, close my eyes, and start silently repeating positive affirmations.

I'm not pregnant.

I'm not pregnant.

I'm not . . . Wait. That's a negative phrasing, not a positive one. We need to keep it positive. Try again.

I am free from a baby.

I am baby-less.

I am without child.

I am non-pregnant.

I am a total fucking moron.

Groaning, I flip the covers off my face and stare at the ceiling. I spend a while counting the cracks in the ceiling tiles, until I realize this is the perfect scenario for Declan to unburden himself of me.

He doesn't have to take me back to New York where he snatched me from. He doesn't have to make arrangements for travel or avoiding whoever might be trying to rescue me. He could simply leave me in the hospital and walk out.

Like he did only minutes ago.

Right after Nancy announced I was pregnant.

My heart starts to pound. My mouth goes dry. There's an awful tightness in the pit of my stomach.

Okay, what is this feeling? Let's name this feeling to defuse its power.

Right now, I'm feeling . . . strange.

Too vague. Try again.

I'm feeling . . . unwell.

Could be that blood clot in your head. Let's talk about your emotional state, not your physical one, Sloane.

I hate it when you get snippy with me.

And I hate it when you talk back to your inner voices like you're a crazy person. WHAT ARE YOU FEELING?

Aloud, I blurt, "Hurt."

As soon as I say it, I know it's true. Then the disbelief comes.

I've lost my mind. My feelings are hurt because my kidnapper left when he heard about the baby.

The non-baby that I am definitely not having.

I leap from bed, run to the door, and yank it open. I don't know what I had planned, I'm acting on sheer instinct, but as soon as the door flies open, four huge men in black suits jump from their places flanking either side of the door to create an impenetrable bristling gangster wall in front of me.

One of them is Kieran.

Why seeing him causes such relief to flood my body, I don't want to know.

He takes one look at my face and slams into scary high-alert mode. Yanking a gun from his waistband, he peers behind me into the room, hackles raised and growling.

"What's the craic? Are ye all right, lass?"

"Yes, I'm all right. I just . . . um. I was . . . thirsty."

Kieran relaxes his shoulders and exhales a breath. Then he turns to the man beside him.

"Go fetch a wee glass of water for the lass, and be quick about it." He puts the gun back into its holster and turns to me, smiling. "Boy's a dear, you had me soilin' my kex with that puss of yours."

I don't think I'll ever understand a word the man says, but I know on a cellular level that he was worried about me, that he was ready to shoot any intruder who might be in my room, and that

Declan not only hasn't abandoned me in this hospital, he's left me with my own personal protection unit in his absence.

I refuse to name this feeling. It might be the final straw that breaks my brain.

"Best get back in bed, lass," says Kieran with a chin jerk. "Declan'll go mad as a box of frogs if he finds ye worse off when he gets back."

Instead of answering, I give Kieran a hug.

When I release him, everyone is staring wide-eyed at me like I farted in church.

I say sincerely, "Thank you, Kieran. And all you guys, too. I feel so much better knowing you're out here. I really appreciate you watching out for me. I'm sure there's probably lots of other stuff you'd all rather be doing . . ."

I inhale an unsteady breath. No one says anything. The gangster who Kieran sent to get the water returns and hands me a paper cup.

I stare at it in my hand, surprised to see it shaking.

"In ye go now, lass," says Kieran gently. "Rest, aye?"

"Okay. Aye."

He winks at me. For some bizarre reason, it makes me emotional.

Looking at my bodyguards, I say in a strangled voice, "I just want you all to know that I think Irish gangsters are *much* cooler than Russian ones. Except for Declan. But you guys are just the best."

I go inside, close the door, chug the water, then lie face-down on the bed, breathing deeply into the pillow until Nancy arrives again.

"If it's all right with you, I'll draw more blood now so we can get those tests going, then we can head over to Radiology to get an ultrasound to look inside your uterus and ovaries."

"Brilliant. Let's do this."

I sit quietly while she draws six small vials of blood. It seems like an awful lot, but I don't mention it. "How long until we get the blood test results back?"

"For you, about an hour."

I'm getting pushed to the head of the line. No doubt thanks to her terror of Declan annihilating her entire family tree. "I appreciate it. Thank you, Nancy."

She pauses what she's doing to glance up at me. Sending a furtive look toward the door, she murmurs, "Are you sure you're okay?"

"Of course. Being kidnapped isn't the worst thing I've been through. And they're only men. It's not like they're hard to handle. I've known Chihuahuas who were way scarier."

"I haven't. Those guys are terrifying. And their boss . . ." She shudders.

Curiosity rears its ugly head. "Have you lived in Boston your whole life?"

She nods.

"So the Irish mafia here is pretty powerful, huh?"

"They run the city. It's been that way as long as I can remember. Even the cops are on their payroll."

I can tell she's warming up to me, so I make a small, encouraging noise to indicate I'm listening.

"I mean, we've got the Italians, too. And the Russians. And lots of others, but the Irish have a stronger presence in Boston than in any other city in America. Things used to be more stable, but over the past few years, turf wars have broken out. The top Mob bosses keep getting killed. There was a murder just this week, as a matter of fact."

"I heard about that. Diego, was it?"

"Yes."

"Strange name for an Irishman."

"Oh, he wasn't Irish. He was Mexican-American. It was all over the streets when his boss got shot and he took over. They said it was a sign of the times, a Latino guy taking the helm. The Mob going more international or whatever."

The Russians had an ethnic Ukrainian as their last leader, so I guess it's not so odd that the Irish would have a Mexican-American. "So what happened to this Diego?"

"The papers said his body was found at the dump. They still haven't found his head."

How gruesome. I wonder how close he and Declan were? "Do they have any idea who did it?"

She gives me a look. "It wasn't one of his friends, that's for sure."

Of course. It was one of his enemies. Like maybe the Italians.

Or the Russians.

Or Kage.

No wonder Declan looks at me with so much . . . whatever it is. I'm Natalie's best friend. I said I was friends with Kage. I dated Stavros. Even if he admits I didn't start a war, he still thinks I'm his enemy.

An enemy he's going to an awful lot of trouble to protect.

The question is: why?

"Excuse me?"

Startled from my thoughts, I realize I spoke that last part out loud. "Nothing. Sorry. I'm just all up in my head. Things are a bit complicated at the moment."

Nancy sidesteps that minefield and says she'll get me a wheel-chair for our trip to Radiology, which is on the second floor.

"Do I look that bad?"

"No." She pauses. "But . . ." She clears her throat. "If you were to fall and hurt yourself, I'd have to explain to Mr. O'Donnell how I let that happen. And he left rather specific instructions that you were to be well taken care of." She pauses again. "To be perfectly honest, he told Dr. Callahan that if you died, he would, too. I'm guessing the same standard applies to me."

Declan threatened the doctor's life? I can't decide if that's awful or sweet.

"Gotcha. No worries. He's not going to kill anyone. He just likes to throw that around to scare people."

Nancy looks doubtful. "I don't mean to contradict you, but he didn't earn his position with Boy Scout badges."

She leaves me to mull that over while she gets the wheelchair. When she returns, Kieran is all in a huff.

"What's this, then?" he growls, crowding in the doorway with the rest of the gang. He eyes the wheelchair suspiciously, like it's wired with explosives.

"I'm going down to the radiation department to get more tests."

His brows draw together. He doesn't like the idea. "Declan said nothin' about lettin' ye outta the room."

"Why don't you come with? We'll make it a field trip."

"Or ye can just wait till he gets back."

To ask permission, he means. As if.

I say blithely, "Oh, I'll leave it up to you. He said he wanted me to get all the tests I needed done as soon as possible to make sure this brain bleed thing isn't going to kill me, but if you think it's best for me not to, that's fine."

I wait, smiling expectantly.

Two minutes later, all six of us are crowded into the hospital elevator, headed down.

When the doors open on the second floor, Kieran and his men exit first, weapons drawn. They conduct a sweep of the corridor before they let Nancy and me off the elevator. Then they walk on either side of us like the president's personal field agents, glaring daggers at anyone who dares to look our way.

I hate to admit I love the drama of it. I feel like a celebrity. It's a good thing I'm not, because I'd be a horrible diva. Two flights on a private jet—one of them while in captivity—and I don't think I'll ever be able to fly economy again.

The ultrasound goes without a hitch. There are no tumors or cysts on my ovaries, and my uterus is as barren as the Sahara. I leave smiling.

The smiling ends when we're back in my room and Nancy tells me the results of the blood tests.

NINETEEN

DECLAN

The warehouse is near the docks. It's cold, dank, and smells like rancid seawater and rotting wood. But it's not close to any other buildings, which makes it a convenient spot for interrogations.

Screams get lost here. Blood washes easily off the cement, into the sewer, and out to sea.

"Hullo, Stavros."

He's tied to a metal chair with a black cloth hood over his head. Normally, I'd have him on his knees—freezing-cold cement is hell on the knees—but he was already like this when I got here.

The hooded head lifts. A voice with a slight Russian accent says, "Who's there?"

"Sloane's new best friend."

After a short pause, he curses viciously in Russian.

Amused, I turn to Spider, standing beside me. "I bet he thinks I don't understand his language."

Spider chuckles. "I bet he thinks a lot of things that aren't true. Stupid people are like that."

"What have you done with her? If you've hurt her, I'll fucking kill you!"

His angry shouts echo off the walls. He struggles against his bindings. His breathing is rough and fast.

"Relax. She's still in one piece. But keep it up, and I'll bring you one of her fingers for every time you shout at me."

Streaming through the hood, his breath sends white clouds into the frigid air. His voice lower but still shaking with fury, he says, "You'll regret this."

I'm intrigued. From Sloane's description of him as boring, I was expecting less energy. "Why? Is your master, Kazimir, coming to rescue you? You're not high up enough on the totem pole, boyo."

"I'm talking about kidnapping my woman."

Hearing him call her that sets my teeth on edge. "*Your* woman? You seem to be operating under the misconception that she gives a shite about you."

Or that she could belong to anyone. No man could ever really own her. Like all unbroken spirits, she can't be claimed.

Stavros is undeterred by my sarcasm. "You have no idea how she feels about me."

"I know she thinks you're as interesting as curdled milk."

"She wouldn't tell *you* the truth!"

"She might. Under pressure."

The insinuation that I've tortured her for information doesn't faze him. He shakes his head vehemently.

"You don't know her. Sloane's not like other people. She won't give anything she doesn't want to give, no matter what it costs."

I'm starting to get aggravated by his confidence. Could she have lied to me about her feelings for him?

"Everyone has a breaking point. You, for instance. How many fingers of yours will I have to remove before you tell me everything I want to know about your boss?"

His reply is instant. "None. I'll tell you anything. I'll tell you everything about him that I know."

Spider is astonished. "This is the loyalty you show your king?"

"I don't care about him. I only care that you don't harm Sloane. If you let her go, I'll do whatever you ask. I'll spy on him if you want me to."

Disgusted, Spider spits on the cement. "Unfuckingbelievable. For a woman."

I turn and give him a cold stare. In Gaelic, I say tightly, "That's a mighty high horse you rode in on. Have you already forgotten how easily the same woman tested your loyalty, *Homer*?"

He freezes. A look of guilt comes into his eyes.

"Take off his hood. And get me a chair."

I turn back to Stavros and watch as Spider pulls the hood from his head. Stavros sees me standing in front of him and gives me a quick once-over.

I'm satisfied to see him swallow in fear.

Spider places a chair in front of me and stands back. I turn the chair around, straddle it, and sit facing Stavros with my forearms resting on top, my hands dangling loosely over the edges.

Then I tell Spider to leave us alone.

When the echo of his footsteps has faded, I say to Stavros, "You're in love with her."

The question catches him off guard. I can tell he's trying to guess what angle I'm playing. He debates with himself for a moment, then says simply, "Yes."

"So much so that you'd betray Kazimir without a thought."

"Yes."

Interesting. "How long were the two of you together?"

He's starting to look confused. Maybe he expected I'd be slicing off body parts by now, not engaging in polite conversation.

"Three months."

That's all? When I raise my brows, he says defensively, "Fourteen weeks, to be exact. And two days."

Jesus. I'm sure if I asked him how many hours and minutes, he'd know.

He blurts, "Tell me if she's all right."

Holding his gaze, I say quietly, "You're in no position to be making demands."

"Please. I have to know. It's killing me. I've been going out of my mind."

His dark eyes plead with me. I experience a strong urge to gouge them out. Instead of doing that, I say, "She's fine."

His exhalation is huge and relieved. He says a prayer of thanks to the Virgin Mary in Russian. Now I'd like to pour gasoline over this kid and light him on fire.

My ego decides it's time to fuck with me and reminds me that Stavros isn't a kid. He's a man, full-grown. And, like Sloane, at least a decade younger than I am. He's young, strong, good-looking, and madly in love with my captive.

Maybe her perfume is laced with oxytocin. It would explain a lot.

"What is it you love so much about her?"

"Everything."

"Name one thing."

He's even more confused by my challenging tone. If I'm being honest, it's confusing me, too.

"Is this some kind of game?"

"Indulge me."

After a moment of closely inspecting my expression, his changes to one of horror. His voice comes out choked. "You have feelings for her."

I scoff. "Aye. Many feelings. Annoyance. Aggravation. Exasperation. I could go on."

When he only keeps staring at me with that look of dismay, I decide to prod him a little. "I admit, her tits are bloody amazing. And that arse . . . well. You know."

My smile suggests I've seen quite a lot of her perfect arse. Suggests that I've taken it. As I knew it would, the idea drives him insane.

"Fuck you!"

"No, thanks. Back to Sloane."

He seethes for a while, debating whether to scream more obscenities at me or obey.

"I won't talk to you about her."

I remove my gun from my waistband, lean forward, and shove it against his kneecap. "How about now?"

He's sweating. The veins in his neck stand out. He licks his lips nervously, takes a breath, then shakes his head.

His courage surprises me. Deeply. After twenty years in the syndicate, I'm rarely surprised. "You'd give up your boss for nothing, but you won't talk to me about a woman you're not even with anymore?"

"Not for nothing. For her. I wouldn't expect you to understand."

He's so frightened, he's almost shitting himself. But he's also defiant. Willing to get his kneecap blown off to defend her honor.

Goddammit. I *refuse* to like this kid.

I lean closer and shove the gun into his crotch. He emits a small cry of terror.

"Let's try this again. What is it you love so much about her?"

He spends a few moments hyperventilating and convulsively swallowing the excess saliva in his mouth. I give him some leeway to pull himself together and wait calmly until he manages to speak.

"S-she's the smartest person I've ever met."

Fuck. I was hoping he'd say something shallow about her body so I could shoot his dick off. I say drily, "She agrees with you. What else?"

"She isn't afraid of anything. She's thoughtful and kind. And funny. You don't expect a girl so hot to be funny, but she is."

"But *irritating*, though, right? Didn't she irritate you something brutal?"

He looks appalled by the suggestion. "No. She's not irritating. She's a goddess."

I'm beginning to see why Sloane got bored of him. His earnestness is tiresome. This kid is as dry as unbuttered toast. She's so far above his head, they're not even in the same atmosphere.

I shove the gun back into my waistband and consider him.

Apparently, he thinks I'm plotting his murder. He turns a shade paler and starts to shake.

"I'm not going to kill you, Stavros."

"You're not?"

"No. It would be too depressing."

"I don't understand."

"That's because life hasn't sucked all the joy out of you yet." I stand and start to pace in front of the chair. "But I can't let you go, either. Not only did you have the extremely stupid idea to try to shoot your way into my building with your pathetic rescue attempt, you also shot two of my men at La Cantina in Tahoe."

"I've never shot anyone."

I stop short and look at him.

"I haven't. Unless you count fish."

"So those two men killed themselves?"

"No. Alexei shot the two who came to our table. Kazimir shot the other two."

I already knew about Kazimir. But the intel I have is that Stavros was the shooter at the table. Then again, he and his dead friend Alexei look very much alike. Tall, slim, dark-haired, the same tattoos on their knuckles. Almost like brothers.

He says, "I don't care if you don't believe me. It's the truth. I actually hate guns. I'm more of a computer nerd."

"Let me get this straight. You've never shot anyone before, but you decided it would be a brilliant idea to come to Boston to try to rescue a woman you dated for a few months from a man who *has* shot people before. Many of them. For far less stupid things."

"I didn't have a choice."

"We always have a choice."

"The heart leads where it will."

"What is that supposed to mean? You're her puppet?"

He smiles wistfully. "No. I'm just in love. It doesn't matter if I live or die, as long as I'm near her."

I glare at him. "Are you *trying* to get killed here? You have a death wish, is that it?"

"I wouldn't expect someone like you to understand."

I growl, "Don't get snippy with me, boyo. I can shoot plenty of things off your body and still keep you alive."

A sudden vivid image of him on top of Sloane, thrusting between her spread thighs as she moans and arches beneath him, sucks the breath out of my lungs. In its place comes poison.

The poison of pure jealousy.

He sees the look on my face and swallows again.

I return to my pacing. Back and forth I go, thinking. Stavros sits silently, watching me with trepidation.

Like Sloane, he's not at all what I expected. He's not a hardened killer. He's not loyal to anything but romantic notions of true love. He's young and idealistic, brave and intelligent, and—if I'm honest with myself—is probably a better person than I am.

A person who'd make a good father.

I turn to him and demand, "So you want to marry her?"

He blinks in surprise. "I don't understand—"

"Answer the bloody question."

"All right. Yes, I want to marry her."

"And children? You want those with her, too?"

His eyes shining with emotion, he says roughly, "As many as

she'd agree to, yes. I've always wanted to be a father. And she'd make a wonderful mother. I'd give it all up if she asked me to. The life. The money. Anything. The only thing that matters to me is her."

Fuck. This isn't how I wanted this interrogation to go.

I drag a hand through my hair, exhale hard, and close my eyes. When I open them, Stavros is staring at me like he's been washed overboard in a raging storm, and I'm the life jacket someone's about to throw him.

Which I am.

Trying not to sound as depressed as I feel, I say, "All right, boyo. It's your lucky day. Let's make a deal."

TWENTY

SLOANE

W ait, Nancy. Start over. What is it called again?"

"Immunoglobulin A deficiency. IgA for short. It's a ge-netic condition passed down from your parents."

Breathe in for a count of four. Hold for a count of four. Exhale for a count of four. "But I don't feel sick. Other than this stupid brain clot, I feel fine. I'm in perfect health. I have no symptoms of illness."

"Most people with the condition have no symptoms."

"Is there a cure?"

"No."

Great. I have an incurable disease. At least a pregnancy would be over in nine months. "So what is it, exactly? What am I dealing with?"

"IgA is an antibody that's part of your immune system. When you're lacking it, you're more prone to getting infections. The condi-tion also seems to play a role in asthma, allergies, and autoimmune disorders."

Confused, I frown at her. "I don't get infections. And I don't have asthma, allergies, or an autoimmune disorder. Or any other disorder that I'm aware of, except an unusual affinity for kale."

She says casually, "Oh, only one in four people who have an IgA deficiency develop any health issues. It's a silent condition that doesn't cause any problems for most."

I can't be hearing this right. Didn't she just tell me I had an incurable disease? "It doesn't cause problems for most people?"

"Correct."

"But if it does cause problems, I'm looking at stuff like . . . allergies?"

"Possibly, yes. Or more frequent colds, things like that. And, as in the case of your false-positive pregnancy test, it can interfere with certain blood tests."

"That's it?"

"That's it."

My voice rises. "So it's not going to kill me?"

Nancy is shocked. "Goodness, no."

Exasperated, I throw my hands in the air. "Do you think you could've started with that?"

"I'm sorry, I thought I did."

"No, Nancy. No, you did not. You were all 'incurable' this and 'genetic condition' that. I thought I had cancer!"

"You don't have cancer." She pauses. "At least not at the moment."

"Okay, we really need to work on your bedside manner."

"I'm simply trying to be medically accurate. At this moment, you don't have cancer."

"But if I did, it wouldn't be caused by the IgA thing, right?"

"Right."

When I don't respond and only sit staring at her, she turns and quietly leaves the room.

I lie down on the bed, my central nervous system in overdrive. Between the brain bleed, the pregnancy scare, and Nancy's inept delivery of the news about the IgA, I've got an excess of adrenaline flooding my system. Still, I somehow manage to fall asleep.

When I wake hours later, sunshine is streaming through the windows, and Declan is sitting in the chair beside my bed.

Staring at me with a strange, unwavering intensity.

Yawning, I prop myself up against the pillows and squint at him. "You okay?"

He makes a noise of disbelief and shakes his head.

"What?"

"You're the one in the hospital bed, and you're asking me if *I'm* okay."

"Because you're the one with a face like someone just told you your grandma died. What's up?"

"It's almost time for your next CT scan."

"Nice try. What's wrong, Declan?"

He closes his eyes and rests his head against the back of the chair. "Nothing's wrong, lass."

"Then why are you hiding from me?"

"I'm not hiding from you. I'm sitting three feet away."

"Don't be a jackass. You know what I'm saying."

He sighs heavily. "I never know what you're saying. All I hear is an awful noise that does my head in."

Worried, I stare at him. Though he won't admit it, I know something's wrong. He seems different. Depressed. Not his usual hair-trigger-temper, rigged-to-explode self.

"How long have you been sitting there?"

"Dunno. A few hours."

"Were you able to sleep at all?"

"No."

"Do you want to switch?" When he cracks open an eye to look at me questioningly, I point to the bed. "I can take the chair for a while if you'd like to get some rest."

He opens the other eye and lifts his head. Now I've got two icy blue orbs glaring at me with piercing animosity.

Bizarrely, that makes me feel better. I smile. "Ah, look. The charmer has returned. Is it hard, living with all those different mean personalities in one body? Must get tense in there. Like an overcrowded prison."

"Why the bloody hell are you worried about me? *I'm your kidnapper.*"

He seems really invested in the answer, so I think about it for a moment while he busies himself with trying to burn my face off with his stare. "Hmm. It's not because I like you, because we've already established I don't."

He reminds me scathingly, "The feeling is mutual."

"Exactly. How could you like someone who looks like a camel and smells like regurgitated grass? Unless you're one of those weirdos who are into animals. You know. Sexually."

I send him a look that implies I wouldn't put bestiality past him. He sends me a look back that could liquefy steel.

"Listen, if it makes you feel better, let's just say I worry about you because it's in my best interest. If you die of a heart attack or take a bullet or whatever, what's going to happen to me?"

Without missing a beat, he says sourly, "You'd take over my position, no doubt. Wouldn't be hard, considering you've already recruited half my army to join your ranks."

"Oh, come on. Kieran and Spider can't be half your army."

"No, but there are three more men posted outside that door who mysteriously joined your fan club in my absence. I'm sure it would be easy for you to convert the rest."

"What do you mean?"

"Something about a moving little speech you made regarding Irish gangsters being better than Russian ones? And an emotional hug for Kieran?"

I say sheepishly, "Oh. That."

"Aye. That. They found it quite captivating. They're also impressed with how you're handling the whole situation."

"By situation, are you referring to my brain clot or you?"

"I'm not a situation."

I laugh at that. "Believe me, gangster, you're a situation with a capital *S*. You could turn Gandhi into a serial killer."

He gazes at me for a moment, then his voice comes warm and low. "As could you, lass. As could you."

"Look at us, finding so much in common. Pretty soon we'll have something to talk about other than your inexplicable mood changes."

A muscle flexes in his jaw. I can tell he's fighting hard not to smile, and I chide, "C'mon, show me those pearly whites. They're literally the only good thing about your face."

"God, I miss when you were asleep. It was so peaceful."

"Hey, can we ask Kieran to do a food run for us? I asked Nancy to get me a protein smoothie, but she spaced."

He says drily, "Does the infamous Tinker Bell charm not work on other women?"

"Don't be ridiculous. Of course it does. Nancy's just freaked out that she's going to do something wrong and you'll kill her." When he doesn't respond to that, I add, "Could be the threat you made on the doctor's life. Just guessing."

One of Declan's dark eyebrows forms into a dangerous-looking arch. "Did she tell you that or did he?"

"Pfft. Like I'd tell you. I don't want to be the cause of any attacks on my medical team."

"You make it sound like I'm a rabid wolf."

"I was thinking something less macho. Like a squirrel. With plague fleas."

When I grin at his scowl, he stands and stares down at me. "You know what you need?"

"Yes. A hundred million dollars and a button on my bedside table that gives you a shock every time you ask me a stupid rhetorical question."

He says darkly, "No. A spanking."

My breath catches. My stomach flips. I stare up at him, my mouth suddenly dry and my heartbeat galloping.

He reaches out and takes my chin firmly in his hand. He runs his thumb over my lips. Eyes hot, he murmurs, "You like that idea."

I manage to eke out a no that doesn't convince either of us.

In a throaty, sexy-as-hell voice, Declan says, "Aye, lass. You like it as much as I do. You like being forced to give up control. Because it never happens."

I'm bacon sizzling on a griddle. I'm a stick of butter melting under the summer sun. I'm a five-alarm fire that's about to burn down the entire goddamn building.

"Look at you tremble," he whispers, fingers tightening on my face. "Look at those eyes."

Whatever he sees, he's fascinated by it.

I'm sweating. It's almost impossible to swallow or breathe. I feel frozen, pinned like a deer in headlights, too stunned to move, too hypnotized to run and save myself.

I don't want to save myself.

In this moment, all I want is to let him run me over.

To let him break me, savage me, tear me apart.

I've never felt like this before in my life.

Blue eyes glittering, he licks his lips. When he bends toward me, I almost moan in relief. I need his mouth on mine like I need oxygen.

"Oh. Pardon me."

The doctor stands in the open doorway, looking nervously back and forth between us. When we don't say anything, he coughs discreetly into his hand.

"I had you scheduled for another CT scan, but I can certainly come back at a better time."

When he turns to leave, Declan says, "No. We'll do it now."

His voice is rough. His jaw is hard. He straightens and cuts his burning gaze back to mine. He holds my chin for a moment longer, then drops his hand to his side.

I nearly topple off the bed onto the floor, but manage to keep myself upright.

"Be good," he commands, his tone warning. Then he turns on his heel and walks out.

The doctor looks at me with raised brows. There's a high possibility I'm going to punch him in the throat.

The entire time I'm having the CT scan done, all I can think about is Declan's expression when he had his hand around my jaw.

I've never seen a man look so hungry.

Or so at war with himself.

The scan shows improvement of the blood clot, which makes Dr. Callahan glow with relief. I'm taken back to my room and given a meal of Jell-O, applesauce, and white rice. I tell the nurse's assistant who brings it that I still have my teeth and my colon and ask her to take the tray away.

Then I wait for Declan to return.

He never does.

For the rest of that day, I'm left alone with only the occasional visit from Nancy checking my vitals to keep me company. I try to distract myself from thoughts of Declan by reading, napping, and watching TV, but nothing helps. He's installed himself inside my head like a tumor.

The next morning, there's another CT scan. The results are so good, the doctor says I can go home.

Home. Like I know where that is anymore. My apartment in
Tahoe? In New York City with Natalie? At Declan's impersonal bachelor pad?

He kidnapped me and cut me off from my life, leaving me
drifting aimlessly in an inflatable raft with no paddles. I don't feel
like myself anymore. I have a curious sense that all it would take is
one big wave to come crashing over me, and I'll sink.

When I'm released from the hospital that evening, it's Kieran
who drives me. I ask where his boss is, but all I get is a shrug.

Something about that shrug unsettles me. The feeling grows
stronger as we take a turn off the highway and start to drive in the
opposite direction from where Declan lives in the city center.

Looking at the suburbs passing by, I say, "Where are we going?"

When he answers, his voice is grim. "Yer bein' picked up by yer
mate."

I turn to him, heart pounding. "My mate? You mean Natalie?
What's happening?"

"Yer goin' home, lass. That's all I know."

I stare at his tense profile, feeling like someone pulled a rug out
from under me. "So Declan's making you take out the trash, huh?
You're the lucky one who gets to clean up the mess he made?"

He glances at me and says gently, "Don't be sore. I could tell he
wasn't happy about it."

"*Wasn't happy?* Well, god forbid the grand pooh-bah isn't happy.
Is that even a thing that ever happens, him being happy? I thought
resting bitch face was the default mode for his entire personality!"

I realize my voice is too high. I also realize I'm shaking.

I'm so angry, I'm about to explode.

I'm being discarded. Without so much as a goodbye, *Declan is
discarding me.*

Kieran wisely remains silent. For the next thirty minutes, I seethe
next to him in the passenger seat as we drive farther on, out of the

suburbs and into the country, until finally we pull to a stop off the side of a dirt road.

Kieran puts the SUV into park but leaves the engine running. Without a word, he gets out and goes around to the back. He opens the rear door, removes several bags, slams the door shut, and walks down the dark road.

As soon as he's out of range of the headlights, another pair of headlights turns on a few hundred feet away. I now see we've parked on one side of a wooden bridge that connects the dirt road. A stream runs beneath the bridge. A car waits on the other side.

My hand tightens around the door handle. My heart throbs like a jungle drum inside my chest.

Kieran returns. He settles himself into the driver's seat. Without looking at me, he says, "Off you go."

"What was in those bags?"

"Yer clothes."

The clothes Declan bought me, he means. The clothes I asked him for, he bought me, and I barely got to wear before I went into the hospital.

I can't imagine why he bothered.

My voice heated, I say, "I want you to tell him something for me. Tell him—"

"You can tell him yerself," Kieran says quietly, nodding at my window.

When I look over, I see a figure materialize out of the shadows of the trees lining the road. The figure is tall, broad-shouldered, and wearing a black suit. A lit cigarette burns orange against the night, glowing brighter when the figure lifts it to his lips for a drag.

It's Declan. Without even being able to see his face, I know it's him.

What is this feeling?

Don't name it. Don't you dare.

I open the door and hop out. Before I close it, I say, "It was nice knowing you, Kieran. Thank you for taking care of me. Tell Spider I said goodbye. I hope you both have a good life."

He looks at me and smiles. He says something in Gaelic that I choose to believe is a farewell.

I close the door and walk toward Declan. When I'm a few feet away, I stop. Neither one of us speaks for a moment. Then I say, "I didn't know you smoke."

"I quit a while ago. I've recently taken it up again." His voice is quiet. Steady. As unreadable as his eyes.

"So this is goodbye."

He takes a long drag on his cigarette. "Aye."

"Great. I can't wait to never see you again."

Smoke billows out his nostrils like a dragon. He gazes at me, silent, cool as a cat.

I hate cats.

"Okay. Good talk, as always, gangster. I guess I'll see you around."

When I turn to leave, he says, "Wait."

He moves closer. Pulling a cell phone from his coat pocket, he says gruffly, "Here."

"What's this?"

"A cell phone."

"You have no idea how much I'd like to put out that cigarette on your eyeball."

"*Your* cell phone, lass. The one I gave you that has my number programmed in."

I take it from him, suddenly unsure. "Why are you giving this to me?"

There's an odd pause. He glances away. "You never know when you might need to hurl scathing insults at someone. Might as well be me. Considering you're so good at it."

I peer at him through the shadows. There's something strange in his voice. Something that's making my heart trip all over itself.

"Who's waiting for me on the other side of that bridge, Declan?"

He smokes. Tilts his head back and blows perfect smoke rings into the air. His silence is infuriating.

"Answer me, dammit."

As if on cue, the driver's door of the other car opens. Someone gets out and lifts a hand over their eyes, shading it from the SUV's headlights, and I'm introduced for the second time in five minutes to a skill I never knew I had: identifying people solely by their silhouette.

"Stavros?" I whisper in horror. I whirl on Declan and demand, "You called *Stavros* to pick me up? Isn't he your *enemy*?"

Gazing at me with those unreadable eyes, he says, "The word has gained a new flexibility for me of late. And who better than the father of your child to rescue you from the nightmare you've been living?"

The father of your child.

Oh my god. He left the hospital without talking to the doctor about my other test results. He doesn't know about the IgA.

He doesn't know I'm not pregnant.

I can't recall the last time I was this angry. Honestly, I think I never have been.

I step toward him, shaking all over. "You arrogant, idiotic man. You think you know what's best for everyone, but you don't even know what's best for yourself."

He's frowning at me. Scowling, actually. "What are you talking about?"

"I'm talking about you being so sure of your own infallibility that you're blind. But here's something I'll leave you with. I haven't been with Stavros since the beginning of January. We're almost in March now. What makes you think I haven't been with anyone else in between?"

He falls so still, he's not even breathing. His lips part. He stares at me, shock registering all over his face.

I say softly, "You might want to verify the identity of the baby daddy the next time you decide to play matchmaker, gangster. See you around."

I turn and run away as fast as I can, telling myself as I get closer to where Stavros waits for me that the water in my eyes and the pain in my chest have everything to do with overwhelming relief and nothing at all to do with the man I'm leaving behind me.

TWENTY-ONE

SLOANE

On the drive to the private jet terminal at the airport, Stavros is silent, but he holds my hand.

I let him. I think it's because once the anger drained away, I was left numb.

Numb is better than angry. Numb doesn't demand answers. Numb is a welcome relief from too many intense emotions.

Numb is my new best friend.

As soon as we're on his jet and the airstairs fold up behind us, Stavros turns and grabs me in a crushing bear hug. He whispers the pet name that used to drive me up a wall: *mamochka*. Then he sinks to his knees and buries his face between my thighs.

It's not a sexual thing. He's just hiding.

Looking down at his dark head, I say quietly, "What did you promise him?"

"Nothing."

He doesn't look up when he speaks. That's how I know he's lying.

I sink a hand into his hair and tug. Finally, he glances up at me, biting his lip. His hands tighten around the backs of my thighs. He looks about ten years old.

"Whatever it was, Kage will find out. And when he does, he'll kill you."

"I don't care. I saved you. That's all that matters to me. That you're safe."

My smile must look very sad, because Stavros's brows draw together. I murmur, "Sweet boy. What makes you think I needed saving?"

He says angrily, "He took you. He *took* you."

"I know what he did."

The anger fades. Gazing up at me with pleading eyes, he swallows, his Adam's apple bobbing. "I thought if I . . . if you . . . that maybe we . . ."

I sigh, stroking his hair. "Oh, Stavi."

That's all I have to say before he goes back to hiding his face between my legs. "Come on," I say, smoothing a hand over his hair. "Get up. We have to talk."

His voice turns petulant. "I don't want to talk. I know what you're going to say."

"Stavi—"

"No!"

I used to hate it when he'd get like this, stubborn as a child denied his favorite toy. I also hate the only thing that can budge him.

"If you're good, I'll let you do it."

He goes still. His voice comes out small. "You will?"

"Yes. Get up."

In one swift unbending of limbs, he's standing, looking down at me with his heart in his eyes.

No, not his heart. The organ he's looking at me with is farther south than that.

I point to the nearest chair. "Sit."

He obeys without hesitation. I sit across from him in another one of the cream-colored leather captain's chairs. The jet's engines roar to life. "Buckle up."

He fastens the safety belt over his lap, then sits there staring at me, fidgeting.

"Tell me what you promised him."

"I can't."

"When Kage finds out, I'm the only one who might be able to help you."

"He won't find out."

He gazes longingly at my shoes. I have to force myself not to heave a sigh.

"Stavi, look at me."

It takes a moment for him to tear his gaze away from my feet.

I make my face and voice very stern. "Tell me."

Frantic, he licks his lips. "I . . . I . . ." He pauses, then it comes out in a burst. "I told him I'd wear a wire anytime I'm with Kazimir and that he could tap my phone and my email to monitor our communications."

I'm so horrified, I'm unable to speak for a full minute.

In the interim, Stavros starts to grovel.

"I'm sorry, I'm sorry, I know I shouldn't have, but I was so worried about you, and he said he wouldn't let you go unless we made a deal, so I had to, I *had* to!"

I hold up a hand to stop the torrent. Stavros falls silent, panting and white-knuckling the arms of his chair.

A wire. A deal. Those two details stick out in my head like neon flashing lights. They sound official. Like terms a prosecutor would use. Or the police.

Then something else occurs to me. With trepidation, I look at the front of Stavros's white button-down dress shirt.

He shakes his head.

Relieved I'm not being recorded, I sit back in the chair and blow out a hard breath. I debate telling Stavros that Declan was going to let me go without his help, but decide against it. The less said about him, the better.

Besides, Stavros is already distracted again by my feet.

I slip off my shoe, stand, and hand it to him. Then I lock myself in the bathroom so I don't have to listen to the sniffs and moans as Stavros jerks himself to release with his nose buried in my footwear.

I take my time using the toilet, washing my hands, and splashing water on my face. When I exit the bathroom ten minutes later, Stavros is flattened against one of the windows, staring wide-eyed and white-faced at something on the tarmac below.

"What's wrong?"

"It's *him*," he says, his voice strangled. "The Irishman!"

My heart jumps into my throat. I run to the nearest window and look out. Sure enough, there stands Declan on the tarmac near the front of the plane.

He's got a rocket launcher slung over one shoulder.

Stavros screams, *"He's going to kill us!"*

"No, he's not. He just likes to make a grand entrance. Go tell the pilot to cut the engines."

As a hyperventilating Stavros scrambles down the aisle toward the cockpit, the cell phone Declan gave me buzzes. I turn away from the window and pull it from the back pocket of my jeans. Though I might be having a heart attack, I make myself sound bored when I answer.

"Gino's Pizza, may I take your order?"

Over the line comes the growl of an infuriated grizzly bear. "Aye, I'll give you a bloody order. Get your arse off that plane before I blow your little boy toy to smithereens."

"Nobody says smithereens anymore, gangster. In case you haven't heard, it's the twenty-first century."

"You have five seconds. Four. Three."

"I'm sorry, which personality am I speaking to now? Because it's definitely not the one who told me goodbye half an hour ago."

"Half an hour ago, I didn't know you weren't pregnant."

I pause for a moment. "You called the doctor?"

"I called the doctor. I knew something was up when you said I was blind. And you don't have nearly as good a poker face as you think."

"What is that supposed to mean?"

"You were upset that I was letting you go."

"You're high."

"I must be if I'm coming after you again. Now get off that fucking plane before I lose my temper and do something I'll regret."

I stand there with my hands shaking, my knees quaking, and my heart beating outside my chest. I don't know exactly if it's anger, adrenaline, or a fucked-up kind of elation I'm feeling, but in any case, I'm definitely not in the mood to be bossed around.

So I say coldly and deliberately into the phone, "No."

I hang up. Then I go to the window and flip him the bird.

I see the fury in his eyes all the way from where he's standing. He's got a red glow around his head.

I'm sure it matches mine.

I withdraw and start to pace angrily up and down the aisle, until Stavros emerges in a panic from the cockpit with a cell phone against his ear, blabbering frantically.

"No—she won't—I can't—she won't listen to *me*! I don't know *how* to open the door!"

Of course Declan would have Stavros's cell phone number. Of course he would.

I say loudly, "He's not going to shoot that thing. Hang up, and let's get going."

"I'm trying to save your life!"

Not this again.

I stride down the aisle to Stavros, snatch the phone from his hand, and put it to my ear. I snap, "Your deal with Stavi is off. He won't be spying on anyone for you. And you'll be keeping your word not to hurt him."

Declan's laugh is dark and perversely pleased. "I should've known you'd get him talking."

"Yes, you should have. You continue to underestimate me."

"A mistake I won't repeat. Get off the plane. Now. Or my promise not to hurt your poor lapdog 'Stavi' expires."

This time, he's the one who hangs up.

I stand shaking in hot fury, debating with myself, and conclude there's no way out of this. If I don't do as he asks, I have no doubt he'll hurt Stavros. Now that he knows Stavros isn't the father of my nonexistent unborn baby, there's no reason to keep him alive.

The son of a bitch has me checkmated.

I give Stavros back his phone and tell him to instruct the pilot to open the cabin door and lower the airstairs.

He's horrified by the suggestion. "No! I can't do that!"

"You can, and you will. I'm not asking."

He gestures wildly toward the windows. "He's an animal!"

"Yes, but a reasonable one. Do I look hurt to you?"

After a moment, he says reluctantly, "No."

"That's because I know how to handle him."

He looks at me strangely. "I don't think you do. I've never seen you like this."

"Like what?"

"Emotional."

It unnerves me that he's right. When I brush past him, headed toward the cockpit to talk to the pilot myself, he grabs my arm and pleads with me.

"You don't understand! He asked me all these questions about you. About us. He wanted to know everything. I think he's obsessed with you!"

"The only person he's obsessed with is himself. Let me go."

"*Mamochka,* please!"

I turn back to him, frame his face in my hands, and say, "Stop."

He stands in front of me with his head hanging down and closes his eyes.

We're silent for a moment, until I say, "I love what you did for me. You were very brave. Now I'm going to do the same for you. And you're going to let me."

He inhales and exhales deeply. Then, reluctantly, he nods.

"Good. Now, listen. When this is all over, I'll help you find the girl you need, okay? We both know it's not me. But your match is out there, and I'll make sure she's good enough for you. In the meantime, you won't make any more deals with anyone to spy on Kazimir. And if anyone asks you to, you'll tell me. Understood?"

He nods again.

"Okay. Now give me a hug."

He wraps his arms around me and sighs.

I pat his back, wondering where I'm going to find a girl who wants to play mommy to a grown man with a raging women's shoe fetish and an addiction to livestreaming himself playing *World of Warcraft* in his underwear.

Then I remember he's super rich and know I'll have plenty of takers.

The pilot opens the cabin door. The airstairs unfold. I say good-bye to Stavros, kiss his forehead, and descend. Seething, Declan waits for me at the bottom, the rocket launcher discarded at his feet.

As soon as I step foot onto the tarmac, he picks me up, throws me over his shoulder, and stalks off toward the waiting SUV.

TWENTY-TWO

SLOANE

I'm tossed into the back seat like luggage. Declan leans into my face and orders, "Stay."

He slams the door, runs around to the other side, gets in, and barks at Kieran in the driver's seat to get going.

"Hi, Kieran. Long time no see," I say calmly, ignoring Declan doing an excellent impersonation of an erupting volcano on the seat beside me.

Kieran suppresses a chuckle. "Hullo, lass." He puts the car into drive, and we pull away.

Then I hear an alarming metallic clinking. I look over at Declan just in time to see him pull a pair of handcuffs out of a pocket on the back of the driver's seat. In a burst of panic, I fumble for the door handle, but the door is locked.

"Those child locks are a real pain, aren't they? Pity the car we used in New York to pick you up didn't have them. I won't make that mistake again, either."

"You smug son of a bitch."

Smiling dangerously, he dangles the handcuffs from a fingertip. "Hold out your wrists."

"Go to hell."

"Been there every day since we met. Do it."

"No."

"This is the last time I'll ask nice."

My laugh sounds mad and scary. "That's you asking nice? Such great manners. By the way, it should be 'nicely.' So much for that high IQ you keep bragging about."

Six seconds of thundering silence pass before anything happens. I know because I count.

Then Declan says, "I have one word for you: Stavi."

I clench my hands to fists.

He turns his palm upward, waiting.

"I'll get you back for this. I swear, I will."

His dangerous smile deepens.

I moisten my lips, do a round of utterly ineffective box breathing, then hold out my left hand.

Never taking his gaze from mine, he encircles my wrist with cold metal. An involuntary shiver runs through my body. It makes his dangerous smile grow hot.

He cuffs my other wrist, closing his hands around the metal so I'm bound by both.

Trying hard to keep my voice calm, I say, "I've never seen you look so happy, gangster."

"And I've never seen you look so nervous. What awful thing do you imagine I'm going to do to you?"

He's trying to intimidate me. I refuse to give him the satisfaction of an answer and remain silent.

He pulls me close, fists a hand into my hair, and puts his mouth next to my ear. His voice husky, he says, "Whatever it is, you're right."

Heart, calm down. This isn't the time to explode. That goes for you, too, ovaries.

"Being in your presence is awful enough."

He inhales against my neck, sending a cascade of shivers down my spine. "Why didn't you tell me about the other tests?"

"I was too busy being worried that you were okay, which, in retrospect, is one of the stupidest things I've ever done. Or thought. Or heard of."

"And why were you worried about me, hellcat? Tell the truth."

God, his voice is hot. And his body is hot. As are the air, my skin, and my panties. I've got a conflagration in my underpants that could turn the entire East Coast into a pile of smoking ashes.

I say hoarsely, "Because I hate you, and I want to be there when you finally get shot through the heart by one of your enemies."

"But I already have, lass," he murmurs, his lips moving against my skin. "I already have."

He pulls my head back and kisses me.

And just like that, I'm gone.

All the fight drains out of me. The will to resist him vanishes in a snap. I sag against him and let him drink deep from my mouth, not caring about the little sounds of pleasure I'm making or that Kieran is witnessing all this or anything else.

I simply surrender.

To his mouth.

To the kiss.

To him.

When the kiss finally ends and I return from outer space, I'm curled in his lap like a kitten, my legs thrown over one of his muscular thighs and my bound arms wound around his broad shoulders. His arms hold me tight as a visc.

I'm panting. Trembling. I don't think I've ever felt so alive.

"So fucking sweet," he says, breathing raggedly. "I want more of that sweet side. Give it to me."

I whisper, "Okay."

He takes my mouth again. I sink, then sink further until I'm completely lost, floating lazily on waves of delicious heat, as thick and sugary as cotton candy. He moans into my mouth, and I shudder.

He grasps my jaw and bites my lips. When I whimper, he slides his hand down to my neck. His big hand wraps almost all the way around it.

I might gasp. I might groan or shift against him. I'm not sure what I do, but it makes him even hotter, greedier, and ten times more intense.

"Look at me."

My lids drift open. He stares down at me with eyes like fire.

"You're my captive."

I nod, my head fuzzy. He wants something, but I don't know what it is. I can't think. I can barely even breathe. I've got Red Bull and heroin scorching through my veins.

"You're going to stay with me. And do what I tell you to do this time. And be good. Obedient."

That makes me smile. I like him when he's delusional.

"Say yes."

"Yes. For tonight."

"We'll talk about timing later. Why are you only wearing one shoe?"

"It's a long story."

His mouth claims mine again, seeking, pulling, demanding. He kisses me like he's on death row, about to be executed, and I'm his last meal. I've never been so savored. So devoured.

Or so turned on. I think if he even breathed on my nipple, I'd come.

But he doesn't go anywhere near my breasts. He simply kisses me, over and over, all the way back to the city. Every once in a while, he stops to murmur something to me in Gaelic, his mouth pressed close to my ear so only I can hear. By the time we pull into the parking garage of his building, I'm out of my mind with need.

For the elevator ride to the top floor, I'm thrown over his shoulder again.

With any other man, being treated like luggage would make me crazy. I'd never accept it. I'd kick him in the face and make him lick my foot.

But there's something incredibly hot about the way Declan's big hand is splayed possessively over the back of my thigh, and how easily he can carry my weight, and how he didn't ask permission to manhandle me. He just did. Like it wasn't up to me. Like he's calling all the shots from here on out, whether I like it or not.

God help me, I like it.

A lot.

The elevator doors slide open. He walks us inside his home. The automatic lights come on, illuminating our way down the corridor to the master bedroom. Neither of us speaks a word.

He flips me over and tosses me onto the bed. I bounce, breathless, and stare up at him with wide eyes, my heartbeat flying, my bound arms raised over my head.

He gazes down at me with a hard jaw and half-lidded eyes, working at the knot in his tie.

"You need food. And a shower."

I take a moment to catch my breath. "That wasn't what I was expecting you'd say."

"I'm going to bathe you. Then feed you. Then fuck you, in that order. No, close your mouth. No talking."

Trembling, I bite my lip and stare up at him. He smiles.

First, he discards his tie to the floor. Next, he shrugs off his suit jacket and tosses it aside. He unbuttons his white dress shirt, his strong fingers working deftly until they reach the bottom button.

Then he pulls the shirt off and stands there with it dangling from one hand as I struggle to draw another breath.

The man is art.

Hot-as-fuck, tattooed, muscular art.

Had I known what he looked like under his tailored Armani suits, I might have been nicer to him sooner. I'm lucky I wasn't standing up for this, because I'd definitely have melted into a puddle at his feet.

"Are you drooling?" he says, his smile growing wider.

He's relishing my obvious lust and astonishment, but I ignore him.

He's covered in ink, from his shoulders all the way down both arms and all over his chest and washboard abs. There are roses and skulls and angel's wings, crosses and sunbeams shining through clouds. I glimpse other Biblical stuff, including a line from scripture, inked in heavy black serif right over his heart: *Vengeance Is Mine.*

And he's ripped as hell, like all he does is eat lean protein and work out twelve hours a day. His shoulders are wide, his lats taper to his waist in a perfect V, and why am I only now just noticing that even his *hands* are gorgeous?

Someone should sculpt this person. This kind of masculine beauty should be on display in a museum.

Please, God, let him have a good dick. Nothing skinny or crooked or short. Do me this one favor, and I'll start going to church again.

I stop praying when Declan leans over me and plants his hands on the mattress on either side of my head.

"My turn."

He hooks a finger into the open collar of my blouse. His expression turns thoughtful. "I just remembered . . . you didn't ask for any bras on that clothing list you gave me."

"Yes, I did. You just didn't buy them."

"Must've slipped my mind. Speak again, and I'll spank you."

He stares deep into my eyes as I suffer through a moment of existential angst trying to decide if I should obey him and be quiet or burst out singing the national anthem. Which will earn me an orgasm first?

He smiles again. "Ah, such a tough decision. I'll wait."

I smile back. "It wasn't all that tough."

He flashes a grin, then rolls me onto my belly and spanks me, the blows hard, his palm stinging me right through my jeans. When he finishes, we're both panting.

But I'm the only one who starts begging.

"More. Please. With my pants down. Pretty pretty please."

"I appreciate the 'please,' but next time add a 'sir.'"

I flash murder eyes at him over my shoulder. "You're on drugs."

"No, I'm your captor. And this is my game you agreed to play, remember?"

Without waiting for a response, he flips me back over, takes the front of my blouse in both hands, and rips it wide open. Buttons fly everywhere. I gasp in surprise.

Nothing else happens for a while, because Declan is too busy looking at me.

It's excruciating, lying there helplessly, not knowing what he's thinking as he silently takes me in. I'm naked from the waist up, my shirt in tatters, my arms thrown overhead and my chest heaving.

The air is cool on my bare skin. My face is hot. I can't seem to draw a deep enough breath.

When he finally touches me, I'm so wound up, I jerk.

"Easy," he murmurs, sliding his hands along the curve of my waist. He's bent over me, one knee on the bed, eyes ravenous. He slides his hands up my rib cage and under my breasts, cupping them and squeezing.

I arch into his hands. My lids slide shut. When I feel his hot mouth close around my rigid nipple, I moan softly. A flush of heat between my legs makes me rub my thighs restlessly together.

"Aye, lass," he whispers against my flesh. "Give me that sweetness. Give me everything you've got to give."

He goes back and forth between my hard nipples, licking and sucking, worshipping me with his mouth. Just when I think I can't stand another minute without begging again, he kisses a soft trail down my stomach to my belly button. He swirls his tongue around, dipping it in and out, then flicks open the button on my jeans.

When I whimper, he chuckles.

He pulls down the zipper so slowly, I almost scream. He nuzzles his nose into the flesh above my panties. He licks and bites me there while at the same time rhythmically pinching my nipples. Then he takes the hem of my panties between his teeth and tugs on it, dragging it against my swollen clit.

I arch against the bed, sink my fingers into his hair, and moan.

He rises to push my arms back. He pins my handcuffed wrists in one of his big hands and gazes down at me, blue eyes burning hot. "Hands above your head. Don't move unless I give you permission."

"I'm sensing a theme here," I say, panting.

"Aye. And you just bought yourself another spanking."

"Oh, darn."

"And another." He smiles. "But I won't let you come during either of them."

My eyes widen in horror. His smile turns into a low, satisfied chuckle.

He peels my jeans off my legs, angrily flinging them away like he never wants to see them again. Then he stares at me lying there shaking and licks his lips.

I ache to feel his tongue between my legs. I ache to feel him inside me. My skin burns, my heart pounds, and I'm more frightened than I can ever remember being, because this is never how it is for me.

I'm not the girl who gets butterflies. I'm not the girl who swoons or begs. I'm the one who moves on before things get complicated, who keeps moving on relentlessly without looking back, like a shark that has to keep swimming forward its whole life or it will die.

I'm the one who doesn't fall. Who doesn't feel. Who doesn't get attached.

Ever.

To make matters worse, Declan sees me struggling.

He lies on top of me, settles his weight between my spread legs, and cradles my head in his hands. Looking into my eyes, he says in a husky voice, "You're safe with me. You can let your guard down. I'll catch you if you need to fall."

That hurts like a knife plunged into my heart.

I turn my head, suck in a hard breath, and close my eyes.

He puts his mouth near my ear and whispers, "You can't hide from me. I see you. I see all the strange and wonderful things you are, little lion."

My voice choked with emotion, I say, "I'm not little. And I'm not yours."

"Aye, you are, if only for tonight. We'll deal with everything else in the morning."

He kisses me then, hard and demanding. It feels like he's staking a claim.

When I'm sure I can't contain the emotion building in my chest one second longer, he breaks the kiss, picks me up, and carries me into the bathroom.

TWENTY-THREE

DECLAN

I set her down next to the shower, tell her to stay where I've put her, then get a pair of scissors from one of the drawers under the sink. I use them to cut the remains of her shredded shirt from around her wrists and the handcuffs, put the scissors aside and pull off her panties, then turn on the shower.

I strip.

She watches me remove the rest of my clothing with a wild look in her eyes. The pulse in the side of her throat hammers. She looks like she might bolt any second.

But she remains still and silent. Beautiful and bound. My brave hellcat Venus in chains.

My dick is so hard for her.

She looks at it with wide, greedy eyes. "Thank god."

"For what?"

"Never mind."

I pull her against my chest and kiss her, wrapping a hand around her throat and fisting the other in her hair. The shiver of pleasure that runs through her body makes me feel ravenous.

I say, "Here are the rules."

Her laugh is throaty and scornful. She stops laughing when I slap her bare arse.

"The rules," I begin again, relishing the small, involuntary moan that slipped from her lips when I spanked her. "Number one: total obedience, or you'll be punished. And not in the good way."

Her eyes are machetes. Revving chain saws. Sharpened swords held aloft with a battle cry. I wouldn't expect anything less.

"Number two: total honesty. If I ask you if you like something I'm doing, I expect an honest answer. If you don't like it, if you're uncomfortable or unsure, tell me. This isn't about me. It's about us. It has to work for both of us, or it isn't a turn-on for me. I don't want to do anything you don't like."

The fury in her eyes cools. It's replaced with a sweet sort of hesitancy, like she hopes I'm telling the truth but can't decide if I am or not.

My voice softer, I say, "Number three: total trust."

She swallows. A panicked look replaces the hesitant one.

"I know that will be the hardest for you. Even more than you hate to be told what to do, you hate being vulnerable. Correct?"

After a moment, she nods.

She looks truly frightened now, the first time I've seen this from her. Kidnap her in a blaze of gunfire or tell her there's a good chance she could die from a brain clot, no big deal. But ask her to open her heart, even for a night, and she reacts like a cornered wolf.

I wrap my arms around her and hold her tight. "It's the same for me. The exact same. That's why you have my word I'll earn that trust and never break it."

"You can't promise that. You can't say 'never' and mean it."

Stroking her hair away from her face, I say, "I can. And I do. But if you can't trust me, I understand. All this will end now if you want it to."

I lower my head and kiss her gently. "You're the one in control here, lass. We'd just be pretending otherwise for a while."

She searches my face for any sign of dishonesty. "Trust, huh?"

"Aye."

"And honesty?"

"Aye."

"Okay. You go first. Do you really think I look like a camel?"

"No. I think you look like Rockefeller Center at Christmas, Japan in cherry blossom season, and the thousand vivid shades of green in the wild moors of Northern Ireland, all rolled into one."

Her lips part. Her eyes shine. Her throat works as she swallows. Then she says in a choked voice, "Finally, you're making some sense," and rises up on her toes to kiss me.

All of who I am meets her in that kiss.

Everything inside me expands at the same time it unravels, leaving me bigger than before, but also more exposed. I'm thousands of acres of unplanted farmland, and she's the plow that's upturned me and tilled new seeds into my dusty soil.

My heart and body aching, I lead her into the shower.

Turning her so her back is to the spray, I grab the shampoo bottle and pour a dollop into my hand. "Tilt your head back. Hands on my chest."

She complies without hesitation, flattening her palms over my chest and closing her eyes as she lets the water run through her hair.

When it's all wet, I move the showerhead to one side. Then I work the shampoo through her hair, massaging her scalp. She leans into me, sighing.

I bend my head and whisper into her ear, "Good girl."

She makes a little noise of frustration. I know what she wants.

"You can speak."

"Thank you. God, I can't believe I said that. I'm *never* submissive. This is so weird."

Watching her face, I move one hand between her legs and slide my soapy fingers through her folds. When she gasps, I say, "So weird you want me to stop?"

"If you do, I'll kill you."

"That's what I thought. Now be quiet. Get out of your head. Just let your body feel this."

I slide my thumb back and forth over her clit and kiss her. She shudders and digs her fingernails into my chest. When I pinch her clit between two fingers, she makes a desperate little noise deep in her throat.

I want so badly to pick her up, pin her against the shower wall, and fuck her. Hard. But I manage to control myself and rinse the shampoo from her hair instead.

When I do finally shove my dick inside her, I want her so wound up, she'll come in instant convulsions, screaming my name.

I don't know how much time I have before she decides this wicked game we're playing is too much and shuts down completely.

I grab a bar of soap, turn her around, pull her back against me, and start to wash her body. Neck, chest, breasts, belly. Arms, underarms, hips. With an arm wound around her waist, I wash her arse, kissing her neck as I knead my fingers into her luscious flesh. She drops her head back against my shoulder and exhales a slow, ragged breath.

"Sweet girl," I growl against her throat. "My pretty captive. You're going to let me do anything I want to this gorgeous body. I'll taste you and tease you and fuck you. I'll spank you and give you my marks. I'll make you get on your knees and take my cock down your throat. I'll bind you and blindfold you, probably gag you with my tie, too. And I'll make you come, over and over. I'll make you glad you let yourself submit. Are you ready?"

Her breathing is shallow and uneven. Her nipples are taut. She's a live wire in my arms, thrumming with electricity, every nerve alight, attuned to me. I feel the fight inside her, feel her struggle to let go and give in to me because I've asked her to, and fire floods my veins.

She whispers, "Yes. Please be careful. I think you could break me if you're not."

Then she exhales and relaxes against me, surrendering.

A surge of exhilaration makes my heartbeat take off at a thundering gallop. I wrap a hand around her throat. "You're perfect. Nothing is more perfect than you are, right now. Give me your mouth."

She turns her head and lets me ravage her mouth until she's shaking.

I quickly wash my own body, then rinse the soap from us both. Then I bend her over the tile bench that runs along one side of the shower wall and spank her.

My hand wrapped firmly around the back of her neck, I spank her arse until it's bright red, every so often stopping to fondle her drenched pussy and rub my fingertips over her swollen clit.

She takes it silently, head hanging down and legs shaking, until finally she lets out a long, low moan.

She's close to orgasm. My cock throbs with the need to take her.

Breathing hard, I say, "I might need to reconsider the order of events. How hungry are you?"

Her only response is a whimper.

I grab the showerhead from the wall and set the spray to pulse. Then I put it between her legs, take her jaw in my hand and turn her face toward me, and command, "Suck."

The crown of my cock nudges her lips. She opens her mouth without hesitation. I flex my hips forward, sliding into wet heat. She starts to suckle me.

Her mouth is heaven.

With every thrust of my hips, she opens her throat wide and takes my shaft all the way in. When I withdraw, she swirls her tongue around the head and licks the slit. I watch her suck me, pleasure pulsing in my cock, pressure building in my balls, until she moans again, her whole body shuddering.

I move the pulsing spray away from her pussy. Panting, I say, "Don't come. Not yet."

She looks up at me with hazy, unfocused eyes, licking her lips.

I've never seen anything so beautiful.

I turn off the water, grab a towel, pull her upright, and dry her off. She stands silent as I finish, then watches, blinking slowly, as I dry myself. She looks like she's in a trance.

I pick her up and carry her to the bed. "Arms over your head. Spread your legs."

She complies instantly.

Bloody hell, that makes me even harder.

Standing at the edge of the bed, I stare at her naked body and slowly stroke my shaft. Lying very still, she watches as I kneel between her spread legs.

When I apply my mouth to her pussy, she arches off the bed and groans brokenly. When I reach up and pinch her rigid nipples, she shivers. I gently suck her clit, and she breathes my name.

The way she responds to me makes me feel like a king, an animal, and a lovestruck teenager, all at once. The feeling is instantly addictive.

I want more.

I finger fuck her and lick her delicious wet cunt until she's writhing against my face and almost sobbing with the effort not to come.

"Such a good girl." I yank open the drawer in the nightstand. I dig out a condom from its box, tear off the wrapper, roll it onto my throbbing cock with shaking hands.

Then I roll her onto her belly and spank her again.

She jerks, moaning with every stinging strike of my open palm, her hips rocking, until she starts to beg. "Please! Please! Declan, god, please *I'm so close—*"

"You know what to say."

"What? No, I don't."

My voice dark, I say, "Aye. You know what to call me. Say it."

She's silent. Out of her body and back up into her head.

Defying me.

I reach under and pinch her clit, tugging gently at the engorged little bud. *"Say it."*

She sucks in a breath, holds it for a split second, then lets it out in a rush. Along with it goes her resistance. She blurts, "Sir, please let me come."

Good god, the rush of adrenaline that courses through my body should kill me.

I roll her onto her back, take my jutting cock in one hand, and rub it up and down through her soaked folds. Looking into her eyes, I growl, "Who do you belong to?"

"You."

It's barely even a whisper, but I heard it. So did my cock. A surge of electricity shoots from my balls to the crown.

I grab her hips and shove my dick deep inside her.

We groan at the same time. Then Sloane starts to buck frantically underneath me, fucking herself onto my cock, desperate for release. I give her my weight, fist a hand in her hair, and close the other around her throat.

Into her ear, I say gruffly, "Don't forget it, beautiful captive. You're mine. *Now, come.*"

Her entire body jerks. She cries out. Arching against me as I drive into her over and over, her pussy clenching around my cock, she sobs my name. I test one of her hard nipples with my teeth, and she screams it.

My body reacts to that like I've been struck by lightning.

There's scorching heat and a crackling current, a sense of danger rippling beneath the awe. Though we agreed this thing between us is a short-term negotiation, it has the raw and uncontrollable power of nature sizzling through it, a blinding white burn of energy that's as beautiful as it is perilous.

A force powerful enough to end your life.

I kiss her breasts to smother my moan of despair. I know she'll be able to walk away from this raging storm unscathed, but I doubt I'll be so lucky.

If I'm being honest with myself, I knew it from day one.

I crush my mouth to hers and kiss her as I climax, tumbling off a cliff of pure pleasure, falling down toward the crashing waves and rocky shore far below, where I shatter into a million tiny pieces, all of them hers.

TWENTY-FOUR

SLOANE

*I*t's a long while before I come back to myself.

When I do, Declan is still on top of me, still inside me, and speaking in Gaelic, his voice a guttural rasp next to my ear.

We're both panting. Shaking. Covered in sweat. My trembling legs are wrapped around his waist, his big rough hand around my throat.

It feels as if we've just survived a bombing.

He softly kisses both my cheeks. The corners of my mouth. My jaw, neck, and shoulders. Propping himself up on his elbows, he tangles both hands into my damp hair and holds my head as he looks into my eyes.

"Hullo."

Feeling strangely shy, I murmur, "Hi."

Has he always been this beautiful? Have those blue eyes always had that tender shine? I can't remember. Time seems split into before this moment and after, like we've broken the laws of physics and arrived here in our own little bubble, shipwrecked on an island where nothing ever existed before.

Where no one ever existed but the two of us.

His voice thick, he says, "I didn't mean for that to happen."

My laugh is weak. "You could've fooled me."

"I meant I planned on feeding you first."

"It's okay. You couldn't help it. I know I'm irresistible."

He starts to laugh this lovely, husky laugh that makes me feel warm all over. He withdraws and rolls onto his back, taking me with him, tucks my head into the space between his shoulder and neck, then winds his arms around me and holds me tight.

His sigh is deep and full of satisfaction.

I ask tentatively, "Is it okay if I talk now? Um . . . sir?"

He peppers sweet kisses all over my forehead. "You're the most amazing woman who ever lived."

"I'm so glad you're finally getting caught up with the program, gangster."

He reaches down and smartly swats my ass.

"Excuse me. *Sir.*"

"That's better."

He's trying to be stern, but I hear the pleasure in his voice. I hear the warmth and softness underneath. It makes something hard in the middle of my chest feel squishy.

"Aye, you can talk now. Try not to slice me up with that razor-blade tongue."

"I'll do my best." Hiding my face in his neck, I close my eyes. "Are we still doing the honesty thing? Because I might have something to put out there."

Hearing the emotion in my voice, he stills beneath me. He waits patiently until I gather enough courage to say, "I'm no virgin. I'm sure that's obvious. There have been a lot of men."

"There's no need to confess a number. I'd never ask."

"I wasn't going to."

He exhales in relief. "Thank god."

"May I continue?"

"Aye. I think."

"Don't be so worried. I'm about to give you a compliment."

"Ah. In that case, please proceed."

My arms are draped over his head, and I'm still bound at the wrists by the handcuffs, so instead of giving him a sharp thump on the chest, the best I can do is tug on a lock of his hair.

"As I was saying." I clear my throat. "I, um . . . Jesus. Okay, here's the thing: have you ever been to the Grand Canyon?"

There's a baffled pause. "Are you about to compare my manhood to a mule's?"

"What the hell?"

"I understand they use mules to take tourists down the trails into the Grand Canyon. And, as everyone knows, mules are very well-endowed."

"If you'd stop trying to pat yourself on the back over the size of your dick for a second, I'll get to the point."

He presses his lips to the top of my head and squeezes me. I know he's trying not to laugh, the bastard.

"Again, *as I was saying*. The Grand Canyon. It's vast. So big you can't imagine it until you're standing at the edge of one of the rocky red cliffs, looking down. It's not only deep, though, it's wide, so wide you can't see the other side. And long, too, like three hundred miles or something. There's a river that snakes through the bottom, and incredible rock formations everywhere, and in the canyon walls, individual sedimentary layers where nearly two billion years of Earth's history are exposed. It's been inhabited by Native Americans for thousands of years, and many of the tribes consider it a holy site. Because it looks and feels holy. Sacred and awe-inspiring, like a natural temple cut right into the earth.

"And it sort of has its own atmosphere. Gusts of hot wind come up out of nowhere, blasting through your hair and blowing grit into your eyes. But there can also be fog, and crazy thunderstorms, and below-freezing temperatures and even snow, all depending on if you're near the rim or the canyon floor and what time of year you visit. There are about a hundred different animal species, and all these different ecological zones, and it's all just sitting out there, self-contained, smack in the middle of this vast expanse of nothingness. It's unexpected. Wild and strange. And so beautiful, it makes your chest ache."

When I don't go on, Declan says, "I'm afraid you've lost me."

I exhale a hard breath and muster my courage. "That's what this feels like to me. Standing stunned and overwhelmed at the edge of the Grand Canyon, staring at all the impossible beauty with my eyes nearly blinded and my mouth hanging open in awe."

Silence.

Long, stony silence, unbroken only by the sound of my own crashing heartbeat in my ears.

Just as I'm about to try to cover that horrible mistake with a laugh and an *Only kidding!* Declan rolls us back over, throws a heavy leg over both of mine, and kisses me so passionately, my mind goes blank for a moment.

He pulls away, breathing raggedly. "Why aren't you kissing me back?"

"I'm trying to figure out what's happening."

"What's happening is that you're breaking my bloody heart. Now fucking *kiss me*."

I do, mainly because I'm still in obedient mode and there's no telling how much longer it will be before the sand in that hourglass will run out.

When we come up for air, Declan stares down at me with an expression like he's in excruciating pain. It's not exactly comforting.

"Maybe you could say something nice right now so I could stop feeling like such a gigantic idiot."

"You're not an idiot, lass. I'm the idiot."

"That's close to nice. Try again."

He drops his head to my shoulder and hides his face in the crook of my neck.

"Oh my god. You can't even come up with anything to say to me after I vomited my heart all over the place? Let me up. I'm leaving."

Squirming with humiliation, I try to rise, but I'm flattened beneath his enormous weight.

He grasps my jaw and holds my head steady, then says gruffly into my ear, "What you just said is the best thing anyone has ever said to me. In my life. The bloody best thing. And I know I'll be thinking about it for the rest of my days, long after you've forgotten me. You're young and beautiful, and you've got dozens of men in your future who'll fall madly in love with you—"

"Hundreds. At least."

"—and I'll be nothing but a distant memory for you. But I'll still be trying to scrub your face and your taste and your sweet voice from my mind fifty years from now, because I already know nothing else will ever be able to compare to you. Nothing and no one will ever come close."

My heart swells. I inhale slowly, feeling his words sink down through my flesh and settle into the marrow of my bones. When I speak, my voice comes out shaky. "I'm not sure you have fifty years left, geezer."

"Not if I spend much more time in your company, hellcat."

He takes my face in his hands and kisses me deeply, letting me feel everything he's feeling. Then he rolls over again so he's lying on his back, and I'm cradled in his strong arms with my cheek pressed to his chest, listening to his pounding heart.

We lie like that for a long time, until the emotion expanding inside my body becomes too unbearable.

"One last nugget of honesty."

He groans. "I don't know if I can take it."

"You're stronger than you think. So here it is. I'll never forget you. And I'll never call any other man 'sir.' Even if someone asks me to—which they won't, I'm much too terrifying—that word will always be reserved for you and only you. You're welcome."

His exhalation is a big, sudden burst of air. "Holy fuck. I don't know whether to laugh, kiss you, or jump out the nearest window."

"You can decide later. For now, why don't you just make me something to eat? I could really murder a salad."

"No sane person craves salad."

"Who said I was sane? Clearly, I'm not. I'm lying here with the elderly gangster who kidnapped me and whose idea of romance is calling me a camel."

"How many times did you use the thesaurus to look up alternatives for the word 'old'?"

"None. I just sat there looking at you when I woke up on your jet after you first kidnapped me and made a list in my head."

"Very funny. Forty-two isn't old."

"Not if you're a tortoise. Or a giant sequoia. Or one of those glass sponges in the East China Sea that can live to be like ten thousand. But in human years, you're already more than half-dead."

He laughs. "We just made love, and you're telling me I'm more than half-dead? And you accuse me of not being romantic."

Made love.

Not fucked or had sex or any of the other less charming options. Made love.

I won't name this emotion. I doubt there's a word for it, anyway.

Declan removes my handcuffs long enough to dress me in one of his white button-down shirts, then recuffs me and drags on a pair of black jeans. Barefoot and bare chested, he leads me into the kitchen. He sets me on a stool at the huge marble island and kisses my forehead.

Then he sets about rummaging through his huge refrigerator for something to feed me.

I watch him, marveling at the masterpiece of architecture that is his back. "How often do you work out?"

"Every day. Ham?" He holds up a plastic bag of deli meat.

"Is it salad flavored?"

"No."

"Exactly."

He peers at me over his shoulder. "Are you a vegan?"

"What did that background check you ran on me tell you?"

"Many different things, none of which concerned your diet. Are you?"

"No. I just really love veggies. I used to eat a lot of junk, but I cleaned up my diet. I feel much better now. Didn't you buy a bunch of green stuff for me when I first got here?"

Declan turns back to the fridge, replaces the ham in the drawer he removed it from, and opens another drawer. Staring down into it, he sighs. "Aye. I was hoping it somehow disappeared while you were in the hospital."

"I could make you something, if you want. I promise you'll think it's good."

When he looks at me over his shoulder again, his expression is doubtful.

"Okay, maybe not good. Edible, at least. I'll sprinkle it with lots of M&M's and Lay's potato chips. That should make you happy."

"I don't eat that stuff. I keep it for Kieran. He has a sweet tooth. And a salty tooth. A fried tooth, too. Basically anything a doctor wouldn't want you to eat, he loves it."

"No wonder he looked at the tray he brought me like he was about to throw up."

Declan chuckles. "Didn't stop him from trying to convince me I should unleash you in the kitchen to cook up a batch of rabbit food for him and the boys."

"Such is my power. Speaking of the boys, where is everyone?"

He turns from the fridge with a bunch of vegetables in baggies. He lets the door swing shut and sets everything down on the counter across from me. Removing a cutting board and a knife from a drawer, he says, "Downstairs."

"What's downstairs?"

He pauses with the knife in midair over a cucumber. "The entrance to the building."

Right. Kieran's a bodyguard. He's on bodyguard duty. "Does he ever go home?"

"The men work in shifts. I don't keep them chained to my side." With a sly grin, he slices into a cucumber.

"Ah. I see what you did there. Clever gangster."

"I am." His grin fades, leaving a dissatisfied look in its place. His voice lowers. "Except when it comes to you."

I say softly, "Yeah, I know the feeling."

Our eyes meet. There's something so raw in his gaze. Raw and unhappy.

"What are you thinking right now?"

"I'm thinking . . ." He pauses long enough to look down at the knife in his hand as if he doesn't know how it got there. He resumes slicing the cucumber. "It's nice having a woman in my home. Not that I've forgotten you're really Dearg Due, but I'll call you a woman for simplicity's sake."

"What's a Dearg Due? Something super cute, I bet."

"She's an Irish female demon that seduces men and drains them of their blood."

"Blood? Yuck. I'd rather drain them of their will to live."

When he glances up at me, I'm grinning. "Go ahead. That's a gimme."

When he fails to take the bait and insult me, I know something's wrong. I mentally rewind to what he said a minute ago about having a woman in his home.

Does that mean he doesn't usually have women here? Though I give him an awful lot of shit about being old, that's baloney. The man is as hot as they come. Handsome, virile, and downright sexy. With a fatty in his pants, to boot. There's no way he isn't swimming in women.

What is that awful twisting in the pit of my stomach?

Don't tell me it's jealousy. I'll never be able to look myself in the eye in a mirror again.

"Are we still doing the honesty thing?"

"You know we are. But if you're about to lay another of your Grand Canyon speeches on me, let me know and I'll set the knife down first. I don't want to accidentally kill myself when I fall on it, sobbing." He goes back to slicing.

"Ha. You're not the sobbing kind. I bet if you tried to cry, it would just look like you were constipated. You know. Like usual."

Now he's trying not to laugh, which makes me feel better. I don't like it when he's unhappy.

Man, I'd like to kick myself in the face.

"Okay. All joking aside." I take a breath and look down at my hands. "I know I keep saying I don't like you. I don't want to, and I shouldn't, but I do. I mean, when you're not being an asshole."

He doesn't say anything. I don't dare look up. I just take another breath and continue.

"I'm telling you that because I never like men. That sounded wrong. I'm not a man-hater. I think men are pleasant distractions. If the rest of my life is the main course, men are desserts. Enjoyable, forgettable treats. That's a deliberate choice, based on some bad stuff that happened to me, and it's served me well for a long time. It's protected me. Until you."

When I glance up, he's staring at me in total stillness, a look of intense concentration on his face. That muscle in his jaw flexes. He grips the knife like he's about to plunge it into someone's chest.

Holding his gaze, I say quietly, "I think you and I are the same. I think we both have secrets, and those secrets made us who we are. I think that's why this feels different to me. And why it's so dangerous. So I'm going to say this with the full knowledge that it might sound ridiculous, but I want you to promise me that you won't keep me here too long."

His voice gruff, Declan says, "Why not?"

"Because you feel like quicksand to me, and I'm already sinking."

He slowly sets down the knife. "I thought I felt like the Grand Canyon."

"You feel like both. Which is worse. You're a Grand Canyon filled with quicksand."

After a tense moment, he says, "So now you know how I feel. Except the quicksand in my Grand Canyon is laced with poison and swimming with man-eating sharks."

My hands are trembling. There's a good chance I'm about to fall off this stool. I moisten my lips and whisper, "Then maybe you should let me go right now. It's probably best for both of us."

Blue eyes glittering, he says in a throaty purr, "I'm not letting you go anywhere."

The way he's looking at me makes my heart pound and my stomach clench. I feel trapped. Panicked. Gripped by a sudden and overwhelming urge to bolt, like a mouse that knows there's a hungry cat creeping up behind it.

So I do the only thing I can think of.

I jump off the stool and run.

TWENTY-FIVE

—————

SLOANE

*D*eclan catches me before I've gone twenty feet.

He tackles me from behind. We crash to the living room carpet. He rolls on top of me.

Then he kisses me, hard and hungrily, his mouth fused to mine.

The fear I feel is overpowering. He's only kissing me, not killing me, but it feels like I'm fighting for my very life.

It feels like I'm drowning.

I gasp, twisting my head away and squirming underneath him. "Get off me!"

"You're forgetting who's in charge here," he growls, pulling my head back so my throat is exposed. He bites my neck, chuckling when I scream in frustration.

"You said I was in charge!"

"I lied. Submit, captive."

"Go to hell!"

"Submit."

"No! Stop saying that!"

My bound arms are pinned between our bodies. He reaches down, grasps the short chain that links the handcuffs, and yanks my arms over my head. Then he gives me all his weight, flattening me.

This time when he kisses me, I taste victory on his lips.

Victory and something darker.

He breaks away, panting. "Don't run away from me. You're braver than that."

I'm not, though. I always thought I was tough, but he's proven I'm nothing more than a big fat coward. I'm so scared he'll see more than I want him to see that I can't even look at him.

Into my ear, he says, "Cat's already out of the bag. You can't hide from me anymore."

"I take it all back! I was lying!"

That infuriates him.

With a snarl that's more than a little scary, he makes me look at him, his hand gripped around my jaw. "Bollocks. You were telling the truth, maybe for the first fucking time. Weren't you?"

When I don't respond, he insists, *"Weren't you?"*

Shaking all over, I close my eyes and whisper, "Stop. Please. This was a mistake."

"No, lass, it wasn't. I'm betting this is the first real thing either of us has had."

He takes my mouth again. When I try to break away, he doesn't let me. He doesn't let me move my arms, or end the kiss, or wriggle out from underneath him. He doesn't try to command me this time, either, he simply *forces* me to submit.

I fight him, but he's too strong. Or I'm too weak. Either way, in a few moments, all the fight is drained out of me. I lie limply underneath him, sucking in short, hard breaths through my nose as I'm washed over a cliff and out to sea.

He reaches down and rips open his zipper. His hard cock springs out from his jeans. He fists it in his hand, rubbing it back and forth through my wetness.

"Open your eyes."

When I do, I find him staring down at me in blistering intensity, his face hard and beautiful. "Yes or no. I'm a lot of bad things, but a man who takes a woman against her will isn't one of them."

Yet he could. Easily. He could simply shove inside me and ignore my protests, knowing there was no one who could stop him.

That he doesn't makes it all somehow so much worse.

"My gentleman gangster," I whisper brokenly, and spread my thighs.

He thrusts. Then he's in, and I'm moaning.

He leans over, bites my hard nipple right through the fabric of the shirt, and fucks me like he's possessed. Like he's starving.

This time, it isn't making love. It's a primal thing, raw and animalistic. He grunts as he drives into me, harsh, ragged sounds that rise from deep within his chest. He's taking me, and I'm allowing myself to be had.

I wish I didn't love it so much. I'm afraid this kind of surrender can be addictive.

He withdraws, flips me over, drags me up onto my knees, then fucks me from behind, his strong fingers digging into my hips and his heavy balls slapping against my pussy.

He pulls my hair.

Spanks my ass.

Reaches around between my legs and fondles my clit as he thrusts, sliding his fingers through my folds.

The carpet burning my knees, I moan and cry out deliriously.

He rasps, "Come on your master's cock. My beautiful captive, be a good girl and come for me."

His words work like magic. Within seconds, I'm convulsing around his erection, bucking back against it and calling out his name.

Had anyone told me a month ago that a man would handcuff me, get me to orgasm on command, and use the words "master" and "captive" to refer to our relationship, I would have laughed until I peed myself.

But here we are.

And holy hell, what a wonderful place it is to be.

Hands around my hips, Declan sits back on the balls of his feet, taking me with him so I'm upright. He rips open the front of the button-down shirt he dressed me in and starts to fondle my naked breasts with one hand, flattening the other over my belly and holding me against his body. I lean back against his chest, close my eyes, and sigh.

"I want you to come again," he says roughly, rolling my nipple between two fingers. "Like this."

He lightly slaps me between the legs.

I jerk, gasping. My eyes fly open wide.

"Harder or softer?" he growls, nipping at my neck.

My pulse is flying. My thighs tremble. I don't know what's up or down. "Harder. And faster."

His groan is soft and filled with pleasure. I think he was hoping I'd say that.

The next slap stings, but also sends a shockwave of pleasure throughout my body. He does it again and again, holding me steady with an arm around my waist, until I'm shaking and so wet, it's slipping down my thighs.

"How close are you?"

"There," I gasp. "I'm right there."

"Give me your mouth."

I tip my head back and am immediately rewarded with a deep, hot kiss. Declan's fingers delve between my legs, exploring every inch, sliding around where he's buried inside me. When they brush my exquisitely sensitive clit, I whimper into his mouth.

"Ready?" he whispers.

"Yes, sir. Thank you, sir."

His exhalation is ragged. "Goddamn, woman. Goddamn."

Then he slaps my throbbing pussy, and I come.

Sobbing and jerking in his arms, I come so hard, I lose myself. The entire time, he whispers praises into my ear, words in English and Gaelic that melt like butter over my heated skin.

Then he's jerking, too, hips thrusting erratically, broken moans falling from his lips. I feel him throbbing inside me, feel a spreading warmth as his hand closes around my throat.

He spills himself inside me with a roar.

As we fall limp and spent to the carpet and he gathers me into his arms, I wonder how this dark fairy tale will end.

Because it will end. It has to. The only question is who will be left standing when the castle walls come crashing down—the princess? The dark knight?

Or maybe no one at all.

Back in the kitchen, neither of us speaks. Declan finishes making the salad, puts everything into a big bowl, grabs a fork, then leads me over to the dining table.

He sits in a chair and pulls me down gently to the floor.

Appalled, I stare up at him. "I'm not kneeling at your feet."

Eyes shining, he says, "Strange, but it looks like you are."

He waits for me to decide what I'm going to do about it. I simmer for a few moments, debating, observing from a safe distance as my ego throws a hissy fit.

He says gently, "I just want to feed you."

"Like an owner feeds his dog scraps under the table?"

"No, lass. Like a man feeds his lover. If you don't like it, get up."

He proceeds to spear a bunch of salad onto the fork. Then he holds the fork to my lips, cradling my jaw in his other hand as he gazes down at me with feverish eyes.

Oh, that look. It makes me shiver. I've never been looked at like that by a man. The need in his eyes is so hot, it could burn us both to the ground.

I whisper, "This is a dangerous game we're playing."

"You don't know the half of it."

Those are his skeletons I hear behind his words. His ghosts rattling their chains. What the hell am I getting myself into?

"Promise me you'll—"

"Aye. I promise."

"You don't know what I was going to ask."

"It doesn't matter. Ask me for anything. To be careful with you, to be honest with you, to bring you someone's head on a plate. I'll say aye. You're not the only one in chains here. Now open those pretty lips and let me feed you. You'll need your energy. I'll want to fuck you again soon."

He nudges my lips with the fork.

Staring up at him in a weird combination of terror, fascination, and awe, I open my mouth and let him slide the food in.

Watching me chew, he caresses my cheek. He murmurs, "Your face is red."

"Humiliation does that to me."

"You're not being humiliated. You're being worshipped. You're just too proud to know the difference."

"Usually when I'm being worshipped by a man, he's the one in this position."

"I'm not your usual man. This isn't your usual situation. None of the old rules apply."

I glance down, avoiding his eyes. He allows it for a moment, until he gets impatient.

"Talk to me."

"I don't like to think of myself as someone who's irrational."

He knows exactly what I mean. "You can be a feminist and still want to be dominated by a man in bed."

"Gloria Steinem would be so disappointed in me."

"Gloria Steinem got married, lass. The woman who popularized the phrase 'A woman needs a man like a fish needs a bicycle' eventually wanted a husband. It's biological. Evolutionary. Even the strongest woman needs a man."

I wrinkle my nose. "Barf."

He chuckles. "The opposite is also true. Even the strongest man needs a woman. We're made for each other."

"How do gay people fit into that gendered philosophy?"

"They're made for each other, too. It's not about tab A fits into slot B. It's about who you are as a human. What turns you on. What you need. Everyone has a match. A fit. Yin to yang, light to darkness. It's when we fight it and judge it that we run into problems. Open your mouth."

He's nudging my lips with another forkful of salad. I'm too caught up in the conversation to protest. Around a mouthful of salad, I say, "How is it possible that despite your rather caveman approach to things, you almost sound liberated?"

"Maybe I am. Is that so hard to fathom?"

"This from the man who ordered me off a plane with a rocket launcher. Where did you get that thing, anyway?"

"I keep an arsenal of weapons in the back of every SUV. You never know when you might need the odd machine gun or hand grenade."

I say drily, "Right. How silly of me. One needs to be prepared. What a Boy Scout."

He chuckles again. "Believe it or not, I was. Ireland's version, anyway. I was involved with Scouting Ireland almost until I went into the military."

Surprised by that tidbit of information, I raise my brows. "You were in the military?"

He pauses to take a bite of the salad for himself. It seems deliberate. Like an avoidance tactic. After he swallows, he simply says, "Aye."

He's not meeting my eyes.

"Declan."

His wary gaze flashes up to meet mine.

"We can do Don't Ask–Don't Tell if you want. We don't have to share our sad stories. It's probably safer that way."

"Safer?"

I'm flustered by his penetrating look. It seems to say he knows I'm trying desperately to protect myself from him. "I meant smarter."

Examining my expression, he sweeps his thumb over my lips. "Don't hide. When I said you were safe with me, I meant it."

"Okay, but only if you don't hide from me."

He caresses my face a moment longer. "The difference is, you haven't said I'm safe with you. Which is good, because we both know I'm not."

"So this total trust thing only works one way? From me to you?"

His brows pull together. "Do you want me to trust you?"

"Could you?"

Our gazes are locked together. The air between us turns crackling.

His voice low and rough, he says, "If you gave yourself to me and meant it. If I knew you'd be loyal to me the way you are with your girlfriend, Natalie. Then aye. I could trust you. But if I did, it would be with everything, including my life. I don't do half measures. I wouldn't hold back. And there's a lot of ugliness my trust would expose you to. There are many things you'd discover that might make you regret ever meeting me at all.

"So before you ask for my trust, think carefully. Because if I give it to you, it means I'm yours. And you're mine. For good. There's never any getting out of that, even if you asked me to. Even if it got to be too much and you wanted to run away."

His voice drops. His gaze drills into mine. "Because I take the words 'until death do us part' literally."

I don't know how we got here. One minute we're chatting about feminism, and the next we're falling down a rabbit hole of marriage vows and death pacts.

"Okay. Wow. That's a lot."

"I don't see you running away, though."

There's a challenge in his tone. A challenge in his eyes. A look that says I should decide right now how this is going to go.

My heart hammering, I moisten my lips. "No. I'm not running. But I'm not promising I won't want to."

He smiles. "Good enough for now. If you change your mind, let me know."

"And you'll let me go when I ask you to?"

"If," he corrects. "If you ask me to."

"You seem pretty sure of yourself there. I do have a life to get back to, you know."

He gazes at me for a beat. Then he takes another bite of the salad, thinking. When he swallows, he looks back at me with something in his eyes I've never seen before.

Pain.

"I'm a lot older than you, as you keep pointing out. I've traveled more roads, many of them dark. I've learned that no matter how well you think you know yourself, you can still be surprised. You can't control what moves you. The only thing in your control is the choice over whether or not you surrender to it.

"I think you realize, deep down, that you can trust me. The only thing you're really on the fence about is if you're willing to trust yourself. Because up till now, you haven't met a man who knew how to handle you. Who could see what you are behind that ivory tower you've built around your heart. But I see you. And I know you're scared seven shades of shite to let me in.

"I can't convince you to. That's a leap you have to make yourself. And I can promise you that it'll be messy. You, me, what that would mean to everyone else . . . messy. But worth it, at least in my opinion. Because this half-dead gangster of yours has seen a lot in his time, but nothing as fine as this."

When I only sit there swallowing around the lump in my throat, he says, "Now let's finish this horrible bowl of rabbit food and go to bed."

"Okay."

He looks at me with an arched eyebrow.

"I mean . . . yes, sir."

When he leans down and kisses me tenderly, I realize exactly how much trouble I'm really in, and how right he was about the ivory tower I've built to keep my heart safe.

A heart that's safe would never ache with so much longing.

TWENTY-SIX

SLOANE

*D*eclan removes my handcuffs before we get into bed. He removes the shirt he put on me, too, then gets undressed himself and pulls me down on top of him. He settles us under the covers and presses a kiss to my forehead, ordering me to go to sleep.

"How can you sleep with me on top of you? Aren't I heavy?"

"Aye. Camels weigh a bloody ton."

"Ha."

"Stop worrying about me, and do as I tell you."

We lie there in the dark, my head on his chest, listening to each other breathing, until the whirlwind in my head makes me sigh. "I don't think I'm tired."

"I'm sure you have some kind of ridiculous breathing trick that will help."

"I usually do a flow visualization when I have trouble falling asleep, but there's something I'm freaking out about, so I know it won't help."

Declan had been rubbing his hand up and down my spine, but he stops. "What is it?"

"We haven't had the STD talk. And we didn't use a condom last time."

He says immediately, "I'm clean."

"Good. Me, too."

"I can get tested if you don't believe me."

"No, I trust you."

That hangs there in the air like a party piñata stuffed with candy surrounded by a bunch of grinning five-year-old kids holding bats. I close my eyes, cursing myself.

Then Declan says quietly, "Thank you."

At least he's not gloating.

After I blow out a hard breath, he changes the subject. "What's a flow visualization?"

"It's a relaxation practice. When I'm stressed out, I picture myself sitting underneath a big oak tree beside a stream in the country. The weather is warm, and there's a gentle breeze. I'm wearing some kind of super cool *Lord of the Rings* fairy queen costume, and my hair looks great."

Declan snorts. I ignore him.

"Whatever worried thought comes to mind, I just mentally put the thought on a leaf in the stream and watch it flow away until it disappears around a bend. Money? It goes on a leaf and drifts away. My future? I put the words on a leaf. My boss at work? She goes on a leaf. In miniature. It's fun to watch her screaming and stamping her foot, two inches tall, then disappear. Sometimes I make a big fish come up and swallow her."

After a thoughtful pause, Declan says, "What do you worry about your future?"

I answer without thinking. "The usual stuff. Cancer. Bankruptcy. Dying alone."

He sounds disturbed. "That's a heavy list for someone who isn't even thirty. You should be worried about what you're going to do next weekend, not about dying alone."

"Everyone dies alone. I just want to do it with dignity. But there's nothing dignified about being so sick you can't wipe your own ass or so weak you can't tell the nurse you're in such agony you don't want to live another minute."

Declan rolls me onto my back, props himself up on an elbow, and looks at me. Even in the dark room, I see the soft shine of his blue eyes.

"You're talking about your mother."

"How did you know that?"

When he doesn't answer, I say, "Oh. Right. The background check you ran on me."

"Aye."

"It must've been pretty extensive."

"Aye."

I study his face. In the shadows, he looks very serious, his expression intent. Hesitant, unsure if he'll tell me the truth, I say, "Was it through a detective agency, something like that?"

"No. Through the NSA."

"What's that?"

"The National Security Agency."

When I only lie there looking at him with a frown, he elaborates.

"It's the intelligence agency of the U.S. Department of State."

"Wait. You mean the people who spy on us? Who record our phone calls and emails and stuff for the government?"

"Aye, though I'm sure they'd tell you they don't do that."

"I read an article about them not long ago. They're like Big Brother!"

"No, lass, they're much worse. They make Big Brother look like Ronald McDonald."

"Oh my god. And they have information about me?"

"They have information about everyone. No, don't try to sit up. Stay right there."

"You want me to remain flat after I found out the government has been spying on me?"

"You're not special. They spy on everybody."

I stare at him, horrified. "So you know someone who works there who gave you all this information?"

"Aye. I know your credit card balances, your medical history, your educational background, your driving record, that you have no criminal record but you did once talk yourself out of a DUI, everywhere you've lived and traveled your entire life, what you buy from Instagram ads, how much money you have in your bank accounts, and, basically, everything else."

He pauses for a beat. "Including that you had a negative STD test on your visit to your gynecologist last month."

I clap a hand over my eyes. "Wow, this honesty-and-trust thing is fucking awful."

"We haven't even really gotten started yet."

"I feel sick."

"I did warn you."

"You should probably stop talking now."

He takes my wrist and pins my arm next to my side. "Let's get back to your worries."

"Let's not and say we did."

Blowing right past that, he says, "I'll give you money if you need it."

I turn my head on the pillow and look at him. "Excuse me?"

"You heard what I said."

"I also heard you say you knew how much money I have in my bank accounts."

"I do."

"So then you know I've been saving."

In his pause, I sense that he's trying to word something so as not to be insulting. He fails miserably.

"Considering the amount in question, I'd guess you were saving for a weekend cruise to Tijuana. On one of those cheap cruise lines. Where everyone ends up getting diarrhea from tainted drinking water."

"That's not very nice."

"I apologize."

"Not everyone is rich."

"No. Especially not you."

Insulted, I glare at him.

"Don't take it personally. It's not about your character. I'm only saying you don't have much money, which I'd be happy to rectify."

"Say the word 'money' to me again. I dare you."

"I can see this is a point of pride for you. Let's move on. What have you been saving for?"

"The laser beam that will blow you into a million tiny gangster pieces."

He tries very hard not to laugh as I lie there staring murder at him.

"Seriously. Tell me."

"Why? So you can mock me with your superior finances?"

"No, so I can be amazed by how cool it is."

I say grudgingly, "It *is* cool."

"I know it will be. So tell me."

Sighing heavily, I turn my head and stare at the ceiling. After a short debate with myself, I relent.

"I'm going to open my own yoga studio. But for kids. Girls, to be exact. It'll be called Fit for a Queen, and we'll hand out tiaras at the start of every class, and teach the kids how to feel empowered and proud of their bodies, instead of ashamed. There won't be any scales. There won't be any mirrors. There won't be any asshole helicopter moms in the back of the room watching and wringing their hands over how fat little Abby and Eva are.

"But there will be lots of hugs and encouragement. There will be lots of positive affirmations. There will be lots of tools they can learn to use to help themselves survive in a world that only values what they look like. Because there are way too many little girls who're being taught to smother their fire and stamp out their light so they can seem smaller to people who are scared of how big they really are. Or how big they could be, if only someone believed in them."

In the wake of that passionate speech, total silence.

I refuse to break it first. I lie there with my heart pounding, waiting for him to say something, until, finally, he does.

"That's beautiful, Sloane. That's bloody beautiful."

The quiet wonder in his voice makes my chest tight. My throat gets tight, too. "Thank you."

He pulls me in to his side, tucking me close. The arm he wraps around me feels possessive.

I whisper into his chest, "You said you'd promise me anything I asked. Was that true?"

"Aye."

"I only have one thing."

"Which is?"

"Please don't hurt Stavros. No matter how this turns out, leave him out of it. He doesn't deserve to get hurt because of me."

His chest expands with his slow inhalation. His voice comes out rough. "You're very protective of him."

"He's a friend."

"He's an ex-lover."

"He needs someone to look out for him."

"We're talking about a wealthy, grown man, not a child."

"Oh, please. You've met him. You know what I mean."

After a pause, Declan says grudgingly, "Aye."

"So do you promise?"

Though I can't see his face, I feel his confusion. "If you care for him so much, why aren't you still with him? He's in love with you."

"No, he's in love with my shoes."

"I have no idea what that means."

"It means he loves what I give him, not me. He doesn't even know me. He'll be head-over-heels for the next girl who meets his needs, trust me. My point is that I couldn't live with myself if he were to get hurt because of something I did. Or didn't do. Something related to us."

When he doesn't answer me, I say, "Please, Declan. It would mean a lot to me."

"Are you this worried about all your exes?"

"No. Are you jealous?"

"Not of him."

It sounds like he's hedging the truth. "Of what, then?"

After a long moment, he answers reluctantly. "He didn't have to force you. You chose him."

I can tell he didn't want to admit that, and it makes my heart ache that he did. I say gently, "You didn't force me."

"I kidnapped you. I took you against your will."

"Let's not get hung up on how this all started. Things could be worse. It's not like we met in prison."

He's silent, thinking. When he doesn't talk for too long, I say, "Spit it out."

"The way your mind works continues to amaze me. Or maybe 'confuse' is the right word. I've never known anyone so able to accept things as they are without a shred of denial."

"I wasn't always this pragmatic. Life kicked my ass pretty good when I was a kid. Lucky for me, too, because it brought out the fighter in me. If I was never knocked down, I'd never have discovered the strength it took to stand back up. And to keep getting up after every future kick, knowing that I could."

He murmurs, "'Out of suffering have emerged the strongest souls.'"

"And 'the most massive characters are seared with scars.'"

His heavy exhalation sounds depressed. "Fuck."

"What's wrong?"

"You know Khalil Gibran."

"I love him. Have you read *The Prophet*?"

"It's only my favorite book."

"Why does that make you depressed?"

His voice gains a rough edge. "Because you're a twenty-eight-year-old girl I fucking *abducted,* a girl who's best friends with the girlfriend of my worst enemy, a girl who frets over her ex-lover—also my enemy—who was born more than a decade after me in a different country than me and has lived an entirely different life than me, and who somehow fucking knows obscure ancient Stoic philosophers and obscure twentieth-century Lebanese poets, and who wants to cook healthy meals for her kidnappers and teach them stress-reduction techniques. You don't make *sense.*"

Into his angry silence, I say softly, "For you, you mean."

A growling sound is my only answer.

"If it makes you feel any better, you don't make any sense for me, either. You're too old and too grouchy and *way* too bossy. Plus, you're right. Kidnapping is a terrible way to start a relationship. It's completely fucked up. We're totally doomed, I get it. But you know what else?"

"No. What?"

"I don't care about any of that, because the way you look at me makes me feel like I could fly."

His entire body goes still. The breath he eventually releases is slow and ragged. "I thought you were scared of me. Of this."

"I am. I hate that I am, too. I want to be that aloof, disinterested cat. But the reality is that I'm not. And it's awful. It could also maybe be amazing, I don't know. I also hope we don't have to keep talking about it, because that's pretty awful, too. But I don't want to have one of those situations where some stupid misunderstanding could be cleared up with a simple conversation, because I hate that shit. It's lame. Do you agree?"

"Aye."

"Okay. So here's the bottom line. We both think this is impossible but also awesome. We both think it's fantastic and also sucks. We both have massive trust issues and friends who will hate this and really problematic personal histories that will most likely cause all kinds of issues going forward, but for right now, it's on."

"It?"

"Us."

"Just like that?"

"Yeah. I just decided. That ivory tower–dark roads speech you made really resonated. But you still have to promise me about Stavros. That's nonnegotiable."

He grasps my jaw and tilts my head up so I'm looking into his eyes. His beautiful, blue, shining eyes. His voice thick, he says, "I promise."

"Thank you."

"But I do have a question."

"What's that?"

"If you're not my captive, then what are you?"

I think about it for a moment. "I don't love labels, but if you need to call me something, you can just call me your queen."

His kiss is rough and deep. He rolls on top of me, giving me his warmth and weight, and kisses me until I can hardly breathe anymore. He pulls away, panting, his stiff cock trapped between us.

"This is gonna be complicated, baby. You ready for that?"

Baby. Oh, what that does to me. How it makes everything inside me glow. I grin up at him. "The more complicated, the better. At least I know I won't get bored."

He growls, "You're damn right you won't," and crushes his mouth to mine.

Then he fucks me with so much passion and possession, there can be no mistaking that when he said I was his, he meant it. I fall asleep sweaty and sated in his arms.

When I wake in the morning, I'm sore and starving. Declan is gone, but my period has arrived, staining the sheets beneath me red.

Oddly, the bloody stain is in the shape of a heart.

I hope that isn't a bad omen.

TWENTY-SEVEN

DECLAN

A re you insane?"

"No."

"Yes, you are. You've lost your goddamn mind. She's a fucking civilian!"

"I know what she is. Lower your voice. You're being conspicuous."

The soccer mom loading her kids into the minivan parked next to us gives me another sidelong glance. She glances at Grayson in the front seat, his hands gripped tightly around the steering wheel, forearm tats showing under his rolled-up sleeves, and tells her pigtailed daughter to hurry up and get inside their car.

She probably thinks we're pedophiles.

The reality is worse than that.

For the past ten years on the same day at the same time every week, Grayson and I have been meeting somewhere in town in his car. Today, our meeting is in a lot on the third floor of the parking garage near the movie complex.

He always drives an older-model beige Chevy Impala. I always sit in the back, and he sits up front. He never turns to look at me when I enter the car. I never say goodbye when I leave.

Sometimes I have the depressing thought we'll still be doing the same thing when we're old men, thirty years from now.

But I doubt I'll live another two. This life I lead isn't made for longevity.

Though that's what I thought over twenty years ago when I first started out, back when the Grayson in my life was a grizzled old handler named Howard who used to tell rambling nonsensical anecdotes about the 1984 Olympics. He died of cirrhosis.

Helluva way to go. I'd take a bullet over that misery any day.

In a lower, more controlled tone, Grayson says, "I never would've approved of the idea of picking her up in the first place, but you didn't tell me."

"It was Diego's idea. He didn't tell you because he knew you wouldn't have approved. I agreed with that decision."

"Great. So you've gone rogue now, too?"

"Don't be so bloody dramatic. Your permission isn't required."

"But my knowledge is. You have to keep me in the loop, Dec."

"I don't have to do anything, Gray. Which you know."

He stares at me in the rearview mirror, his dark eyes made even darker with fury.

Our tempers are one of the few things we have in common. He's even more prone to angry outbursts than I am.

The only son of a third-generation beat cop, he always knew he'd go into law enforcement. It's the family business. But I suspect he wishes he'd followed in his father's footsteps and joined Boston PD instead of the FBI, so he wouldn't have to deal with me.

I'm making him old before his time.

"So what's the plan? You'll question her, then send her back to Kazimir? And what do you think will happen to her when he finds out she's been questioned about him? Because I can guarantee you, it won't be good."

"I'm not sending her back to anywhere. She's going to stay with me."

His silence echoes with disbelief. In the rearview mirror, I see him blinking, trying to decide if he heard me right.

"You're making this poor girl your *slave*?"

The word conjures images of Sloane naked and handcuffed on her knees with my hard dick in her mouth. Heat floods my groin. I make a mental note to reproduce that fantasy at home, tonight.

I say mildly, "What a charming opinion you have of me."

"I know you. My opinion is based on fact."

"Then it will disappoint you to hear that I'm not making her a slave. I'm just making her mine. Period."

More blinking. He's so confused, it's like I'm speaking Portuguese.

"What's the angle?"

"There is no angle."

"There's always an angle. You don't have girlfriends. You don't have a personal life. You only have the job, which is how you've always wanted it. Which is why you're so good at it. You're unencumbered. Undistracted. *Alone*."

"People can change."

"Is that a fucking joke? Are you joking with me right now?"

I say through gritted teeth, "This is getting tiresome. Listen to the words coming out of my mouth. I'm keeping her. She's mine. Get it on the books, get the word out, and get everyone on board."

"Whoa, whoa, whoa. Hold on a second. Are you saying you want to make her an asset?"

"Potentially. She's definitely got what it takes."

He's incredulous. "You're willing to blow your cover for a piece of ass?"

"Call her that again, and you'll be dead within ten seconds."

We stare at each other, the mirror reflecting two sets of angry eyes. One blue, one brown, both stubborn as hell.

After a tense moment, he says, "That's the first time you've ever threatened me."

"And if you disrespect her again, the threat will be followed by a bullet."

He shakes his head in disbelief. "Jesus Christ. I'd ask you if her pussy is lined with gold, but I don't want to get shot."

I growl, "That was too close for comfort and your last hall pass."

He puts his hands in the air, surrendering. "Fine. I'll run it up the flagpole. But you might want to take a minute to consider what *she'd* want. Because I can guaran-goddamn-tee you if I could go back in time and choose whether or not to take on this job, I wouldn't."

"I love you, too."

He mutters, "Quit busting my balls, man."

"You have the list?"

Grayson digs in his shirt pocket. He has a fondness for red-and-black-plaid shirts. I think he fancies they make him look like a lumberjack. Though he does have the over-muscled forearms and broad back of someone who swings an axe for a living, I'll give him that.

Without turning around, he hands a folded piece of paper over his shoulder.

"Try to keep it low profile. I can't explain too many bodies at once."

"You know I will."

He scoffs. "I know you'll do whatever the fuck you want, is what I know."

Something in his tone makes me pause to look at him more closely.

He needs a haircut. And a shave. He was never exactly clean-cut before, but now he looks like he's been sleeping on someone's couch for a month. And that beard of his has gone beyond lumberjack territory and straight into antisocial mountain man who shoots bears for fun.

"How's the wife, Gray?"

His shocked gaze flashes to mine in the mirror. "Is this you asking me a personal question?"

"You're thirty percent more of an asshole than usual. Everything okay at home?"

He scowls. "Why does it have to be a problem at home?"

"Because I'm smarter than you are. What's happened?"

He looks out the window and exhales a hard breath through his nostrils. "She left me for her fucking tennis coach."

"I'm sorry to hear that. Would you like me to kill him?"

"Jesus. Don't tempt me."

"It's on the table. Think about it."

"Absolutely not." He pauses. "Unless I change my mind. Which I won't."

"Understood. But when you come to your senses, just text me his name and address, and I'll take care of it."

He seems touched. "Thank you, Declan. That's the nicest and the most fucked-up thing anyone has ever said to me. It almost makes up for when you threatened to kill me for insulting your new girlfriend a few minutes back."

"Don't mention it."

I open the door and get out. Walking toward the elevators, I call Kieran. He picks up on the second ring.

"Howya, boss."

"Did the delivery come yet?"

"Aye."

"You brought it up?"

"Aye. She answered the door in one of them skimpy workout thingies. Like a full-body leotard, except with the middle missing. Nearly gave me a bloody heart attack."

I clench my teeth, aggravated at the thought of Kieran seeing Sloane in yoga wear. Though knowing her, she was probably doing all her ridiculous bending and stretching right in front of the bedroom windows for all of Boston to see.

"How did she seem?"

"Whaddya mean?"

"I mean did she seem happy? Sad? What was her mood?"

I hear the shrug in his voice. "The usual. Wonder Woman meets Lucy Ricardo."

"Lucy Ricardo?"

"The wacky wife from that old black-and-white sitcom on the telly, *I Love Lucy*."

I won't tell Sloane he said that. She'd take it as a huge compliment and adopt Kieran as her loyal sidekick.

I forgot. She already has.

"I'll be back in a few hours. Got a few loose ends to clean up before the move."

"Copy that. Everything's ready at the new digs. Is it okay if I eat this muffin the wee lass baked me? I thought I'd better check with ye first."

"She baked you *muffins*?"

"Aye. For me and Spider. Haven't a baldy notion what's in 'em, but they're awful green and lumpy. Looks like she grabbed a fistful of dirt and rolled it in some grass."

Had I known she'd go straight into the kitchen and start cooking the shite she eats when I left the bedroom door unlocked this morning, I might have double bolted it instead. "Sounds manky."

"Looks it, too. But she said it had lots of roughage and would be good for me, so I feel like I should give it a go."

Roughage. Christ. Smiling, I say, "Aye, you can eat it. Don't come crying to me when you have to purge your guts into the porcelain throne."

I hang up, take the elevator down two floors, and get into the Escalade I parked next to the back exit of the garage. I drive across town to the Old North Church, the site where the lanterns hung in the belfry alerted Boston patriots that the British were coming by sea at the start of the American Revolution. I park in the lot and go inside through a small door in the side chapel, then make my way through the nave, passing row after row of empty pews, until I get to the confessional booth.

I open the door and sit down on the narrow bench, closing the door behind me. "Bless me, Father, for I have sinned. It's been eleventy-seven years since my last confession."

An exasperated sigh comes through the carved wooden privacy screen to my left. "For feck's sake, lad. You don't have to make a mockery of the blessed sacrament."

Like me, Father O'Toole still has his Irish accent from when he first landed on Boston soil, decades ago. Some things die hard.

"How are you, padre?"

"Don't give me that padre shite," he says crossly. "It's still Father O'Toole to you, boyo, no matter how high and mighty you fancy yourself. And I'm the same as I was the last time you asked. A sinner livin' on borrowed time."

"Aren't we all?"

"Some of us more than others. Then there's you."

I smile at the dour tone of his voice. "Aye. Then there's me. Still saying a prayer for my salvation every night?"

He snorts. "That ship sailed years ago, sonny, which we both know. The only O'Donnells I pray for nowadays are your mum and da, God bless their souls."

He pauses. His voice drops an octave. "The old girl'd be awful proud of you, you know. Even though you're damned for eternity for all the blood you've shed."

"Just had to add that last bit in, didn't you?"

"I'm a priest. Guilting sinners goes with the territory."

"I've always wanted to ask. Why should I be damned if the only people I kill are evil? You'd think it could be looked upon as a public service."

"Ach. Pure ego, that is. God doesn't need a helping hand dispensing His justice, lad."

"I disagree."

"Of course you do. What have you got for me today?"

"A name. I need you to pass it along."

"To whom?"

"Whomever your contact is in the Russian Orthodox church."

"Ach. The Russians again. Bloody communists."

"They're more capitalists than communists nowadays."

"What's the name?"

"Mikhail Antonov."

His pause is thoughtful. "Why does that sound familiar?"

"He's the head of the local Bratva."

Silence. After he wraps his head around what I'm up to, he warns, "That's a big bite to chew, lad."

"Aye."

"It'll attract a lot of attention."

"Exactly."

"And it'll be expensive."

"It always is." I open the door to the confessional. "Thank you, Father."

"Leave your donation in the usual place, son."

"I will."

Buttoning my jacket, I exit the church the same way I entered it: damned. Then I head to the home address of the second name on Grayson's list. This one's much more personal than the one I gave Father O'Toole, and I want to take care of it myself.

"An eye for an eye" is a crude concept, but so effective in my line of work.

TWENTY-EIGHT

SLOANE

I'm putting dishes into the dishwasher when a low voice from behind me says, "Making yourself at home, I see."

I turn to find Declan standing at the corner of the kitchen. He's been gone all day without leaving a note or texting me where he was going or when he'd be back, and I'm annoyed with myself for wishing that he would have.

Or is that normal? I don't know. I've never visited Emotionville before. So far, it's quite confusing.

I wish I had a map.

"You left the bedroom door unlocked, so I figured I was allowed to venture out. Was I wrong?"

Working at the knot in his tie, he lets his gaze drift over my body. I'm wearing yoga pants and a sleeveless stretchy crop top, and my feet are bare. By the hungry look in his eyes, you'd think I was stark naked.

"It wasn't wrong," he says, voice husky. "But don't get too comfortable here. We're moving."

That surprises me. "Moving? Why? Where?"

He steps closer, pulling the tie off. When he drops it on the counter and opens the top two buttons on the collar of his white dress shirt, I get distracted from the moving bomb he just dropped.

Alarmed, I say, "Is that blood on your collar?"

"Aye."

"Is it yours?"

"No."

His expression is closed off. Or it could be simply calm, I can't tell.

"Are you okay?"

"Better now. Come here."

Holding out a hand, he waits for me to cross to him. I do, wondering whose blood is all over his shirt and relieved it's not his.

When I'm close enough, he reaches out and grabs me, pulling me into a hard hug. He buries his face in my neck and inhales deeply.

Standing on my toes with my arms wrapped around his shoulders, I whisper, "Thank you for the roses."

"You're welcome."

"And the diamond bracelet. It's crazy beautiful."

"Not as crazy beautiful as you. Why aren't you wearing it?"

"I thought you might like to be the one to put it on."

That pleases him. He murmurs, "Good girl. Maybe next I'll buy you a diamond collar."

He reaches down and squeezes my ass. Then he kisses my neck, sucking and biting my skin. When I shiver, he backs me up against the counter and takes my mouth, kissing me so savagely, it leaves me breathless.

His erection leaves no doubt as to where this is headed.

When he shoves up my shirt and leans down to suck on my nipple, I say, "I started my period."

"How nice for you."

He pulls the shirt off over my head, tosses it aside, takes my breasts in his big rough hands, and goes back to sucking on a nipple.

I groan in pleasure, arching into his greedy mouth. "I mean, I have a tampon in."

"Noted. Now be quiet."

Apparently, he doesn't care about the tampon, but sex on my period just isn't my thing. The few times I've tried it, it's been so messy, I couldn't concentrate on anything other than how I was going to get all the blood out of the sheets.

"I'll be quiet after I say this one thing. Sex when I'm on my period doesn't make me feel sexy."

He stops and looks at me.

"Sorry. Just being honest."

"Don't apologize. Thank you for telling me. Hold out your hands." He steps back, waiting.

My pulse starts to fly. I don't know what he's planning, but I can tell he's not in the mood for any sass.

I hold my hands out in front of me, unsurprised to see them shaking. The amount of adrenaline coursing through my veins right now might electrocute me.

He takes his tie from where he left it on the counter and winds it around my wrists, knotting it at the ends. Then he pushes me down until I'm kneeling on the floor in front of him.

He unzips his trousers, takes his hard cock in his hand, and fists the other into my hair at the scruff of my neck.

Gazing down at me with burning eyes, he growls, "I've been obsessing about that mouth of yours all day, baby. Suck me off. If you're good and don't spill a drop, I'll make you come. If not, you'll be punished."

A thrill runs through my body at his dominant, dirty words.

This is heaven. I've died and gone to heaven.

Encircling his shaft with my bound hands, I swirl my tongue

around the engorged head, loving the faintly salty taste of his skin. I close my eyes and take him into my mouth, shivering in pleasure when I hear his low moan.

He cradles my head in both hands and flexes his pelvis, slowly sliding his hard cock down my throat. I take and take until my mouth is stretched open wide, and he's all the way in.

"Bloody hell," he whispers raggedly. "My sweet girl. You're gorgeous."

I swallow around the length of him, and he moans again.

Setting a slow, steady pace, I take him in and out of my mouth, sucking and licking the crown and stroking his rigid shaft, sliding my tongue along the throbbing vein that runs under the length of it. I suck and swirl and stroke, my head bobbing and my nipples aching, so turned on, I think I might be able to come from the friction of my panties against my clit alone.

He rasps, "Stop rubbing your thighs together. You'll come when I let you."

I whimper in need. It makes his fingers tighten against my head.

He fucks my mouth until he's panting. Low, helpless groans work from deep within his chest. He wraps a trembling hand around my throat.

"Ah, fuck. I'm close, baby. Are you ready?"

When I make a small sound of agreement, he starts to thrust harder and faster until he's moaning lustily, his head thrown back and his eyes closed.

He climaxes with a shout, spilling himself onto my tongue in short bursts, every one of which I swallow as I stare up at him in a lust-filled haze.

I know I'm the one kneeling, but damn do I feel powerful right now. He needed this so much, he didn't even take the time to remove his jacket or undo his belt.

He's still for a few moments, breathing hard, until he opens his eyes and looks down at me, cleaning him off with my tongue.

"Was I good . . . sir?"

He smiles.

Then he lifts me up by my armpits, turns me around to the big marble island, bends me over it, and yanks down my yoga pants and panties to the middle of my thighs.

Standing to one side of me, he slides his left hand under my hips and between my legs. He strokes my throbbing clit between his thumb and forefinger.

I gasp in pleasure.

Keeping his left hand between my legs, he runs his right hand all over my exposed bottom, his jaw gritted as he stares at it.

The slap on my ass is hard and unexpected. Feeling my flesh jiggle, I suck in a breath. Heat blooms over my bare skin. He continues to lazily stroke my clit, gazing down at me with hooded eyes, a muscle flexing in his jaw.

I say breathlessly, "Are you angry with me?"

"No."

He spanks me again, harder. I jerk and moan. He tugs on my clit, and my legs start to shake.

"Am I being punished?"

"No."

He spanks my bare ass again, a single, stinging blow that makes me yelp. By now, I'm panting. And confused.

"Are you going to let me come?"

"Aye. As soon as you stop talking."

I bite my lip and close my eyes, resting my cheek on the cool marble. I'm going out of my mind with anticipation, shivering all over, my hips rocking against his fingers as he continues to fondle my clit.

"Good girl," he says roughly, then lets loose a volley of fast slaps on my tender backside, raining them down on one cheek, then the other as he works his left hand between my legs.

I try very hard not to make a sound, but I can't help how hard

I'm breathing. I keep my eyes squeezed shut as the pleasure builds. Heat ripples through my lower body in waves, intensifying with each stinging blow and stroke of his fingers. Soon, I'm biting my lower lip with the effort to keep from moaning.

When I can't bear it anymore and I sob his name, he commands, "Come."

He spanks me straight through my orgasm.

I buck and cry out, convulsing helplessly. He's growling something in Gaelic that sounds filthy, but I can't concentrate on anything else but the pleasure exploding through my body. The carnal pleasure he's orchestrating using only his hands.

When I finally return to myself, I'm weak, shaking all over, and feeling emotionally raw.

Declan slides his hand out from between my legs and licks his fingers. He smooths his other hand over my heated bottom. He leans down and kisses my cheek, brushing my hair from my face, and says gruffly, "Who do you belong to?"

"You."

"Who's your master?"

"You."

His voice softens. "And who thinks you're the most precious angel in the world?"

I swallow, suddenly fighting tears. His voice is so warm and full of feeling, and all at once, I'm overwhelmed. With a hitch in my voice, I whisper, "Y-you."

His lips brush my ear. "Aye, baby. And all I am is yours now, so take care of this monster you've enslaved."

He pulls me up and into his arms, throwing my bound wrists over his head and crushing me against his body.

We cling to each other silently, both of us breathing hard. I don't know why I feel such an ache inside my chest, but it's made a little easier because I know he feels it, too.

He kisses me.

It's deep and lingering, hot and slow. I sag against him, delirious with afterglow and emotion, and let him take everything he so desperately needs from my lips.

I'm aware on some semiconscious level that we both know despite me calling him master, he isn't in charge here, and never has been.

Instead of making me feel smug, like it would with any other man, it gives me a profound sense of humility and gratitude.

I make a silent vow that I'll never hurt him, even if it comes down to a choice between that and hurting myself.

When he breaks the kiss, I say, "I'm worried about you."

"Don't be."

"You seem upset."

"Tough day at the office."

His voice has a trace of sarcasm. Instinctively, I know he's talking about that blood on his collar and whatever happened to get it there.

"Do you want to tell me about it?"

He gazes down at me, stroking his hand over my hair. His expression is faintly amused. "Do you really want to hear?"

"If it will make you feel better, yes."

He slowly shakes his head, then kisses me gently. "Just hearing you say that makes me feel better. Now let's get you dressed. We're out of here in thirty minutes."

He bends to pull my panties and yoga pants back up my legs. I let him, resting my hands on his shoulders. When he's got everything back in place, he tenderly kisses each of my breasts, then takes my face in his hands and kisses my mouth.

Gazing deep into my eyes, he says, "If you answer the door half-naked again, I won't be pleased."

"Oh. You talked to Kieran?"

"Aye. And I could hear his hard-on through the phone. You're not a child, so I'll never tell you how to dress, but I am a jealous man. I don't share. And I'm not Stavros. If it were me that night at La Cantina and another man slapped your arse as we walked by, he'd be dead before he drew another breath. Not because of my ego, but because anyone who disrespects you will pay a price. And if they disrespect you in front of me, the price will be especially severe."

He's intense and deadly serious.

It's a testament to how fucked up our situation is that I think his words are deeply romantic.

"I hear you," I say softly, smiling. "And I promise to put on a robe before I answer the door again if I'm in workout clothes. But you also should consider that I have a tendency to cause trouble wherever I go, and maybe dial back the Tarzan overprotective tendencies. It'll be better for your blood pressure."

He quirks his lips. "Aye, you are a bloody troublemaker, that's for sure."

I tease, "But you knew that going in."

"It was the Tinker Bell tutu that gave it away."

His grin is sudden and blindingly beautiful. The man is so handsome, it hurts.

"Can I ask why we're moving?"

"Every gangster and his brother knows where I live now. It's not safe here anymore. If it were only me, I'd take my time relocating, but I've recently acquired some precious cargo I won't take any chances with."

"Aw. How sweet. Call me cargo again and see how long it takes before your nose gets broken. You can ask Kieran, he'll tell you."

Amused by my tart tone, he exhales a short breath through his nose. Then he slaps my ass, grinning.

"Get a coat and shoes on."

I bat my lashes at him and hold up my hands. "I'll put a shirt on, too, if you'd just untie me. Sir."

He murmurs, "Bloody little smartass," and undoes the knot in the tie.

Then he gives me a quick, hard kiss and turns away. His tie dangling from his fingers, he walks into the living room, picks up a remote control from the big glass coffee table, clicks the television on, and switches to a news station.

As I turn to leave the kitchen, headed to the bedroom to get dressed, a male reporter speaks in somber tones about the gruesome discovery of another headless body at the city dump, this one believed to be the man known to authorities as the leader of the local clique of the transnational gang MS-13.

I freeze. Goose bumps form all over my arms.

MS-13 was the gang who chased us from the airport. The gang Declan said would've killed us if they'd caught us.

Were they also the gang responsible for murdering his boss, Diego, and leaving his beheaded body at the landfill?

I think of the tattoo Declan has inked over his heart, and the goose bumps on my arms spread over my entire body. *Vengeance Is Mine,* it reads.

Maybe that's not only part of a passage from Biblical scripture.

Maybe it's more like a mission statement.

When I turn back to look at him, he's standing motionless in the middle of the living room, watching the news report with a grim, satisfied smile.

TWENTY-NINE

SLOANE

*W*e leave the high-rise in the middle of a caravan of a dozen black SUVs.

At the exit of the parking garage, half of them turn left. The other half turn right. At the next block, the same thing happens, until we're accompanied by only two other cars as we speed out of town.

It's an evasive technique. I get it. I also get the tension in the car. Both Declan, beside me, and Kieran, driving, are wound tight as springs. I know they're on the lookout for anyone who might try to jump us in a surprise attack or follow us to our new destination.

What I don't get is how wound up I am, too.

Not for me. For Declan. For what might happen to him. He could be arrested. He could be shot. He could be taken prisoner and tortured by a rival gang. And I'd be helpless to do anything about any of it.

I hate being helpless.

I hate being nervous, too.

In fact, I'm finding quite a few things to hate in this new land-scape called "caring," most of which have to do with the changes in myself.

How can you be a badass when you're constantly worried about someone else?

Declan notices my anxiety and squeezes my hand.

"We'll be there soon."

"How far is it?"

"We'll take a helicopter from the airport. From there, it's a one-hour flight."

"To?"

"Martha's Vineyard."

He watches my face closely as I digest that information, his fingers tight around mine.

"How long have you had a home on Martha's Vineyard?"

"A few days."

I arch my brows, surprised. "Days?"

His tone dry, he says, "I didn't know how many of your ex-lovers would attempt to shoot their way into my building."

"You move pretty fast, don't you?"

"Once I'm motivated, at the speed of light," he murmurs, his gaze locked to mine.

"And now you're motivated?"

"You know I am."

"By me?"

"Don't be coy."

"But I'm so cute when I'm being coy."

He reaches up and caresses my cheek. "Are you worried?"

"Hell, yes."

"About what?"

"That you'll die of your advanced age, and I'll have to find a Re-altor on short notice to unload this lover's pied-à-terre you bought."

Knowing I didn't want to admit I was worried about what might happen to him, he chuckles. "It's hardly a pied-à-terre."

"What do you mean?"

"I mean it's a ten-thousand-square-foot estate on six acres."

My lips part, but no sound comes out.

He smiles at my shock. "On the beach. With its own helipad. The Obamas have a place nearby."

Overwhelmed, I say faintly, "Oh, good. We can have cocktails together, talk about world peace."

"I doubt it."

"Why not?"

"You're registered to vote as a Libertarian. They'd probably think you're a nutcase."

I cover my face with my hands. "Man, that background check was really something else."

He says softly, "Aye. It revealed someone fascinating. A woman who marches to the beat of her own drum."

I drop my hands and look at him. "You're saying I'm eccentric."

"I'm saying you're an individual, above all else."

"No, above all else, I'm smarter than you, remember?"

"You're also crazy about me."

Flustered by the burn in his eyes, I glance away. "Or maybe just crazy."

He leans over and kisses my flushed cheek. Into my ear, he murmurs, "You're worried I'll get hurt. Which means you're crazy about me. Admit it. I want to hear you say the words."

"If you're going to be smug about it, I'll remind you that I worry about Stavros, too."

"Like someone worries about the family pet. He's no more than a gerbil to you. I, on the other hand, am—"

"An egomaniacal monster?" I smile. "Agreed."

He settles his hand around my throat and says in a husky voice, "A monster who wants you to tell him how you feel about him."

I glance at Kieran in the driver's seat. "Now?"

"Now. That Grand Canyon speech of yours has made me greedy for more."

"I can't replicate that. It was extemporaneous."

"God, how I love it when you use all your big words."

"Don't be an ass."

"Think of one that describes how you feel about me. Just give me one, baby."

His breath is hot on my neck. His hand is tight around my throat. His voice is low and rough, and all of it turns me on like a light switch has been thrown inside my body.

I close my eyes and search for the perfect word to describe how he makes me feel. "Intoxicated."

He takes my mouth, kissing me hungrily. We go over a bump in the road and break apart, but our faces are still close together. Our eyes are locked.

He says, "You're not the only one."

"I know."

"Have you ever been here before?"

"To Martha's Vineyard? No."

"Don't hide. You know what I'm asking."

His eyes are so intense. I feel exposed. Naked. And disoriented, like I'm tumbling down into a deep, dark hole. "You know I haven't."

"Say it."

"You really like to get right into it at the weirdest times, don't you? We're not even alone."

"Say it."

I can tell he won't be satisfied until I give him what he wants. So I lean close to his ear and obey him.

"No, I've never been here before. I've never felt like this about anyone. I've never lost myself, or wanted to lose myself like I want to lose myself in you. And I've never trusted a man, including my father. So if you break my heart, gangster, just know that you'll be the first and last to do it. Nobody before you has ever been able to even scratch it, and nobody will be able to pick up the shattered pieces behind you if you leave."

He exhales hard. He takes my face in his hands. His eyes are bright and exultant, brilliantly blue.

He pronounces gruffly, "I'll never leave. Because you're going to be my wife."

"Holy shit."

"Is that a yes?"

"No."

"Then make it a yes."

"I'm not wife material."

"I wasn't asking."

"I see. So you'll kidnap me into marriage?"

"Why are you getting angry?"

"Because your arrogance is larger than the entire known universe."

"It's the next logical step."

"Sure, if we'd been together more than four seconds."

"I won't live long, Sloane. I don't have the luxury of taking things slowly."

That puts the brakes on the conversation faster than anything else he could've said. Shocked, I say, "Are you sick?"

"No. I'm the new head of an international criminal empire. My expected lifespan has just been drastically reduced. My predecessor didn't make it a year in his position. How much longer do you think I'll get?"

Panic forms a cold, hard ball in the pit of my stomach. "Longer than that, if you're careful."

"I'm not careful. It's not in my nature to be. I'm lucky I've lasted this long, in fact. But the clock is ticking, and it's getting loud."

I can't decide if I should be horrified or if I should hit myself over the head. What he's saying makes total sense, and of course I knew all of it, but hearing him say it out loud right after he dropped a bombshell proposal is way too much.

I sit up straighter, shaking his hands off my face. "Let me get this straight. You think it would be a good idea for me to marry you—let's not even get started on all the hilarious issues about how we met, and the *vast* expanse of time since that happened— knowing full well that in a few short months or years, I'd be a widow?"

His brows draw together. His lips thin. He goes into his classic glower mode as fast as two fingers snapping. "You'd be my sole heir. You'd get everything I own—"

I cut him off with an acid laugh. "Oh, we're talking about money again! You seem to be under the impression that the only thing women care about is cash, which is less than charming. But I can assure you, *I don't give a shit* about how much money you have or would leave to me in the event of your untimely death."

My sarcasm makes his patience snap. "I know you don't care about the bloody money! But it might make your life easier once I'm gone!"

My heart pounds. My hands shake. I want so badly to sock him right in the nose. I manage to keep my voice steady, though everything inside me is churning.

"The only thing that would make any of this easier is if you weren't who you are. But that's impossible. So let's not entertain hypotheticals about futures that can never happen."

Nostrils flared and lips thinned, Declan looks like a bull with a rider on its back about to explode from a holding gate.

"And don't glare at me, either. If you want to drop me off on the next corner, that's fine."

As it turns out, that was the exact wrong thing to say. He regards me with entire cities burning to the ground in his eyes.

Pulling me close with a hand wrapped around the back of my neck, he growls, "I'm not dropping you anywhere, hellcat."

I flatten my hands over his chest and push. It's useless. I might as well be trying to move a mountain. "I hate that nickname, by the way."

"No, you don't. You fucking love it. And you hate that you love it. Get used to being seen, and being with a man who won't let you hide, and who won't cower when you lash that barbed tongue of yours."

He crushes his mouth to mine.

I'm starting to get that this is going to be what's politely called a volatile relationship.

I break away. He allows it, but only just. I fold my arms across my chest and stare straight ahead out the windshield, trying to get my ragged breathing under control.

He says darkly, "Why don't you try some box breathing? I've heard it's helpful in stressful situations."

From the corner of my eye, I see Kieran glance back at me in the rearview mirror. If he's worried his boss is about to get his eyes scratched out, he's right.

The remainder of the ride to the airport is spent in silence. Thick, tense, burning silence. The left side of my face is peeling off in layers due to Declan's blistering stare.

We come to a screeching stop at the heliport. I'm removed from the car by a tense Declan and led across the tarmac to a big black helicopter that looks like it was made to transport military troops. He opens the passenger door, settles me into the seat, buckles me in, and kisses me. Hard.

Then he says gruffly, "Please don't freeze me out. Be angry all you want, but don't shut down on me. I need you right now. I won't be able to think straight if you don't communicate with me."

I'm such a wuss. That softens me up like microwaved butter.

"Okay," I say, looking into his searching eyes. "But just because I'm not freezing you out doesn't mean I'm not breaking vases inside my head."

He kisses me again, this time more softly. "I know," he murmurs against my mouth. "I wouldn't expect anything less."

Then he slams shut my door, trots around to the other side, and gets in the pilot's seat. He buckles himself in and starts flipping switches. He gestures to a pair of green headphones resting on a stick on the dashboard, or whatever the console of a helicopter is called.

"Put those on."

"Don't tell me *you're* flying this thing."

"Of course I am."

Of course he is. Why am I even surprised?

Looking over at me, he smiles. "I told you I was in the military."

"You didn't say you were Tom Cruise in *Top Gun*."

"Didn't I? Must've forgotten to mention it. Now put on your headphones."

He dons his own pair of headphones and hits a switch that starts the engines. Above us, huge black blades begin to move in slow circles, quickly picking up speed.

I watch him go through the preflight checks with a deep sense of awe. I thought he was pretty macho before, but *this* . . .

Well, this wins the macho war. My ovaries are screaming in glee like a bunch of playground kids on sugar highs.

We lift off, rising into the twilight sky in a roar and a blast of wind that scatters the leaves on the tarmac and sends dust blasting out in a wave. Above us, the rotors beat a thundering *whump whump whump* that matches the pounding of my heart. When I look over at Declan, he's staring straight ahead, concentrating on the flight path.

He's grinning.

The ache in my cheeks means I'm grinning, too.

He glances over. "Tell me what you're thinking, baby."

"I'm thinking we're a couple of lunatics."

That makes him chuckle. "Aye. But my crazy matches your crazy. That's why it works."

I look down at the diamond tennis bracelet he clasped around my wrist before we left. It glitters, catching the waning light and sending a shower of colorful sparks across the windows.

For a moment, I'm blinded. Then the sparks clear, and I lift my gaze to the horizon. It stretches off across the city and out to the sapphire bay. The Atlantic is a rippling ribbon of dark blue far beyond.

I wish Nat were here to see this.

I miss my best friend with a fierce, sudden ache. An ache that worsens when I consider that she lives in New York now. There won't be any more girls' nights out at Downrigger's on the lake, giggling over cocktails and scarfing down shrimp enchiladas. There won't be any spontaneous shopping trips, or coffee runs, or movie nights.

There won't be any anything, because she's in love with Kage.

Which wouldn't have been a problem before, but Kage and Declan are mortal enemies. Which means that if I stay with Declan . . .

There won't be any more me and Nat.

Out of nowhere, it hits me with a force like a wrecking ball. A sledgehammer slams into my chest. I can barely draw a breath.

If I'm really going to be with Declan, it won't simply be an "issue" we'll all have to work through. Neither Kage nor Declan will allow us girls to hang out like it was business as usual. My friendship with Nat will be over.

In fact, I might never see her again.

Impossible. I won't let that happen. She won't let it happen, either. We'll figure out a way.

I look over at Declan, so calm and confident as he handles the helicopter, and remember his strange smile when the TV reporter was talking about the body found at the dump. I remember the vengeance tattoo on his chest. I remember the elation in his eyes when he asked me who I belonged to, and I answered, "You." The elation and the triumph.

Like he'd won.

Because he had.

This man who calls himself a monster kidnapped me and claimed me. He took me to his bed. He saved me from a rival gang, protected me while I was in the hospital, gave me a choice between yes and no, gave me things I didn't even know I needed.

Gave me a promise that he'd do anything I asked.

I told him the only thing I wanted was for him to not hurt Stavros, but now I'm thinking there will be more items to add to that list.

Starting with a promise that he won't ever go after Kage.

And I've got to get Nat to make Kage promise the same thing.

In the middle of a war, no less.

I wonder if Declan knew all this when he said it was going to be messy.

THIRTY

SLOANE

S o what do you think?"

I'm standing in the middle of a master bedroom larger than my entire apartment, staring through floor-to-ceiling windows at rolling sand dunes and the restless sea beyond. It's dark outside, but a bright moon floods the beach with ghostly light and reflects off the water. Waves crash onto the shore with repeated, muffled booms.

I say quietly, "I think it's the most beautiful home I've ever seen."

Declan comes up silently from behind and wraps his strong arms around me. He kisses the side of my neck, tickling my skin with his beard. In a husky voice, he says, "I'm glad you like it."

My laugh is faint. "I mean, it's a little on the small side. And who could sleep with all the racket from the ocean? That's so not relaxing."

He chuckles. "Everything you need is already here. Clothes. Toiletries. Rabbit food. Anything else you want, just tell me."

I close my eyes and draw a steadying breath. Every minute I

spend with this man challenges my equilibrium. "Thank you. I'm . . . overwhelmed."

He pulls my head back and takes my mouth, kissing me hungrily, his arm like a vise. When I tremble, he kisses me harder. I lean into him with a sigh, and he wraps a hand around my throat.

"I'm gonna give you everything, baby. Everything in the whole world."

His voice is hot and rough. He spins me around and grabs my ass, pulling me against his chest. Then he kisses me again, this time with more intention. As he walks me backward toward the bed, his erection digs into my hip.

I break the kiss, laughing. "We just had sex two hours ago."

"I'm gonna tie you up and make you come on my face. Are you complaining?"

"Your face? You know I said I had a tampon in."

"It won't be in the way of my tongue."

Thrilled by the need in his voice, I say, "That's very dirty, sir. And very hot."

"I love the way you taste. A little cotton plug won't stop me from putting my mouth on you."

We stop at the edge of the bed. He pulls off the jacket I'm wearing and tosses it aside. My shirt follows. He strips me out of the rest of my clothes and pushes me to a sitting position on the lovely white silk duvet.

Unlike his bachelor pad, this home is done entirely in shades of white and champagne, with touches of aqua and blush in the artwork and accessories. All the fixtures and finishes are in subtle, burnished gold. It's a very beachy house, and a feminine one.

Maybe Martha Stewart needed a quick extra dozen million or two.

Declan takes my chin firmly in his hand. Staring up at him with a hammering heartbeat, I lick my lips, my nipples tightening. Heat pulses between my legs.

He doesn't speak as he unbuckles his belt with his free hand, sliding it through the belt loops until he's standing there with it dangling by his side.

"Say it again."

His voice has changed. I recognize it, this dominant tone. I know what he wants.

"Sir."

"Ask me to spank you."

"Please spank me, sir."

"Are you sore from earlier from my hand?"

"Yes, sir. It doesn't matter. I want more."

"And you're going to get more, baby. You'll get as much as you can take."

His eyes are so needy and dark, so frighteningly beautiful. My pulse goes from skipping to pounding painfully. He leans down and kisses me ferociously, his fingers twisted in my hair.

Then he pushes me flat to my back with his big hand splayed over my chest, kneels on the floor between my legs, and spreads me open with his thumbs.

His leather belt rests over my naked hip and belly, the loveliest of warnings.

He puts his mouth on my clit and gently sucks. His mouth is hot, wet, and wonderful.

When I moan, he pulls away and slaps my inner thigh. Pleasure ripples through my pussy. My clit throbs.

Eyes closed, I whisper, "Please, sir. Please."

"You want more of that?"

"More of everything. More of you."

"I'll need you to be good, baby. I'll need you to be quiet."

"I will. I promise."

He slaps my thigh again, making me jerk. I say breathlessly, "I mean, I promise, *sir*."

He smooths his hand over the sting on my skin. His breathing has changed. It's as ragged as mine is.

"I don't think you will, angel. I think you need a little help."

I hear the slither of fabric, and soon enough, Declan's hands are at my face.

He winds his tie around my jaw and knots it, gagging me.

I whimper, writhing against the bed. He leans next to my ear.

"Hush. You're mine. I'll take care of you. Ready?"

I whimper again, and he kisses my cheek. "Remember, you're being worshipped. All of it is in service to you, because I know what you need."

He straightens, rolls me onto my belly, and whips my bare ass with his belt.

It's a single blow, and shocking. The snap of pain is white-hot. My eyes fly open and my back arches. I holler a muffled curse at him through his tie.

He pushes me down with a hand in the middle of my back. "If you want me to stop, nod."

I stay frozen, my heart pounding. Heat blooms in a pulsing stripe over my skin where the belt struck. My mind is utter chaos. An explosion at a fireworks factory. I can't think straight or catch my breath.

All I know is that I don't want him to stop. I want him to do it again. And again.

And again.

Trembling all over, I shake my head.

Declan exhales. "I'll do a few more, then stop and check in with you. Don't come. Ready?"

I curl my hands into the duvet and nod.

The blows come fast and hard. The sound it makes in the quiet room is as shocking as the sensation. When it's over, my ass is on fire, I'm hyperventilating and shaking like mad, and also very close to orgasm.

Declan rolls me to my back and shoves his face between my legs, sucking my clit like it's oxygen.

My mind blinks offline.

I dig my hands into his hair and buck my hips, grinding against his mouth, not caring if I'll suffocate him, not caring about anything but chasing the burn and relieving the agonizing ache.

I need to come so bad, I'm almost sobbing.

He pulls away, panting. "Such a bad girl," he says, sounding thrilled by my reaction. "You deserve another spanking."

Opening my eyes, I stare up at him. I put my hand between my legs and stroke my shaking fingers over my wet, swollen clit.

He slaps my hand away, rolls me onto my belly again, then gives me another five hard blows with the belt.

It's almost unbearable, both in how much it hurts and how much it makes my entire pussy pulse and tingle. It's glorious and dirty, and I know I'll be so bruised, I might not be able to sit for days, but holy fuck, how I love it.

I can't help myself. I start to desperately grind against the bed.

"*No*, baby," says Declan, chuckling darkly. "So sweet. So needy. But not yet."

He smooths a hand over my burning ass, stroking the curves of it and crooning. Then he flips me onto my back again and straddles me, gathering my wrists in his hands.

He winds his belt around my wrists, tucks the ends under, and pins my arms overhead. Leaning down into my face, he stares deep into my eyes. His own are feverish.

"I'm gonna lick your pussy until you're crying for me to let you orgasm. But I won't let you. You can't until I say you can. Understood?"

I know this delay is part of it, part of how he'll make the sensation that much more intense for me. The longer I can hold back, the better the climax will ultimately be.

I'd still like to kick him in the nuts.

Seeing the fury and uncontrolled lust in my eyes, he smiles. Then he straightens, unzips his trousers, and takes out his stiff cock. He strokes it lazily, gazing down at me.

He keeps stroking it as he moves backward and kneels between my legs, then starts licking me again, his jutting cock thick and hard in his fist.

I want to suck on it. I want him to fuck me with it. I want him to make me choke on it while he spanks me with his belt. I'm out of my mind with need and euphoria, riding a cresting wave of pleasure as his tongue flicks and licks and he jerks himself off on his knees between my spread thighs.

The light in the room glows brighter. The crashing of the waves outside grows louder. My eyes roll back into my head.

Uh-oh. I'll be punished for this.

If I'm lucky.

With a full body jerk and a scream muffled by his silk tie, I orgasm hard. My pussy contracts and convulses. My body bows against the bed.

As if from far away, I hear Declan curse. I feel a tug and a pull, and the tampon is gone. He falls on top of me, biting the soft flesh under my nipple and shoving his cock deep inside my body with an animal's territorial roar.

With a hand around my throat, he thrusts hard and fast as I come, and come, and come, bucking wildly underneath him.

"Baby. Ah, fuck, baby. I love the way you feel."

He's panting, pistoning into me, fucking me as I ride out the most intense climax I've ever had. The muscles in my ass cramp from clenching. The line between pain and pleasure blurs as he bites my nipples and squeezes my throat until I'm gasping.

He shudders. Moans long and low next to my ear. With one final thrust, he spills himself inside me, speaking in passionate, garbled Gaelic as he does.

"Tá tú mianach, cailín milis. Mianach."

He tucks his face into my neck and whispers my name like a prayer.

I wonder how I ever thought I'd known happiness before.

When we've finally both caught our breath and stopped shaking, Declan withdraws from me carefully, unwinds his necktie from around my jaw, and kisses me gently. Then he tells me not to move.

I lie staring at the ceiling as he goes into the bathroom, picking up the discarded tampon along the way. I hear water running. After a while, he returns, minus his clothing. In his left hand is a towel. In his right is a wet washcloth.

I close my eyes as he silently cleans me between my legs and dries me with the towel.

When I hear the sound of a paper wrapper tearing, I say, "I'm not going to let you put that in."

He says softly, "Show me how."

"God, no."

"Total trust, remember?"

"Nice try, Casanova. Even my gynecologist doesn't have those privileges, and I've been spreading my legs for him for years."

He chuckles and relents. "Give me your wrists."

I lower my arms from above my head, and he unfastens his belt, releasing me. He rubs my wrists, then kisses both my palms, one at a time. It's a sweet gesture, a nurturing one, and it makes me feel treasured.

Gazing at me with soft eyes, he murmurs, "You're so beautiful, lass."

I smile at him. "So beautifully sore."

"I'll get you aspirin. And some cream."

He goes into the bathroom again, giving me time to insert the tampon he left beside me on the bed. I grimace when I see what's become of the poor duvet underneath me and roll over, kicking it to one side. I flip it over on itself and push it off to the floor.

When Declan returns, holding a glass of water in one hand and a bottle of lotion in the other, he sees me lying there on top of the sheets, the duvet discarded. He quirks an eyebrow.

"It looked like a crime scene."

"It's only blood."

His tone is entirely nonchalant. I think of the blood on the collar of his shirt, realizing he's numb to the sight of it because he's seen it so much. Like an emergency room doctor.

Or someone who kills people for a living.

He sets everything on the nightstand, helps me to a sitting position, drops two aspirin into my palm, and hands me the glass. I'm so thirsty, I drink the entire thing.

He takes the glass away and gently pushes me back down again, rolling me onto my belly. Resting my cheek on the pillow, I close my eyes as he lightly rubs lotion into my burning skin.

"You have the most perfect arse I've seen in my life."

Sated and drowsy, my limbs heavy and my heart full, I have just enough strength to laugh. "Right? It should really be memorialized in plaster. No, something longer lasting. Cast in bronze."

His chuckle is low. "Someday you'll tell me how you got that self-confidence."

"You have self-confidence, too."

"It can't hold a candle to yours."

"Like your IQ."

"I'll let that go for now, considering the state of your arse, but I won't forget it."

We're quiet for a while as he continues to carefully spread the lotion all over my throbbing cheeks. It's strange that hands used to such rough business as his can be so tender.

"Declan?"

"Aye?"

"I don't want you to die."

The hand rubbing my ass cheek stills, then slides down to my upper thigh and squeezes.

He says quietly, "I can't promise I won't."

"Have you ever thought about quitting?"

His pause is so long, I start to get nervous. But I don't move an inch. I simply wait, my heartbeat picking up speed.

"A man can't quit the thing that makes him who he is."

"A gangster isn't who you are. It's what you do. There's a difference."

There's another long pause, this one charged with tension. It's like he's fighting with himself over what to say. When he speaks again, his voice is so low, I have to strain to hear it.

"Tell me I can trust you with my life and mean it, and I'll tell you if I've ever thought about quitting. And what would happen if I did."

I turn my face to the pillow and exhale the breath I've been holding. "Tell me I won't have to choose between you and Nat and mean it, and I'll say you can trust me with your life."

"It's not only her you'd be choosing. It's everything and everyone else."

I whisper, "I know."

"I'd never ask you to make that choice, lass." He pauses. "But she might."

"No fucking way she would."

"The Irish Mob killed Kazimir's entire family. Did you know that?"

Stunned, I look over my shoulder at him. "What?"

He nods. "His parents were murdered over a missed protection payment. And both his young sisters, too." He looks away. His voice lowers. "They had other things done to them before they died. Worse things. They sent Kazimir the pictures."

I think I might be sick. "Do you know the people who did that?"

"They're dead. Kazimir killed them all."

"Oh god."

"It was a long time ago. I'd just barely joined the ranks. I didn't personally know the men involved, but it makes no difference to Kazimir. The Irish murdered his family. His hatred for us runs deep."

"But all you guys cooperate with each other in business."

"Sometimes. Other times, we kill each other. If he had the chance, he wouldn't hesitate to kill me."

I roll onto my side and prop myself up on an elbow. "And you wouldn't hesitate to kill him."

His face darkens. I take that as a yes.

"You can't hurt him, Declan."

He looks at me for a moment, eyes flinty, then says, "Lass."

"Don't say that like I'm being absurd. You're the one who said you'd promise me anything."

"And you're the one who hasn't said I can trust you with my life."

Anger makes my cheeks flush. "So it's tit for tat?"

"No. Trust can't be negotiated."

Despite trying to keep it calm, my voice rises. "Natalie's my best friend. She's in love with him. If anything happens to him, it will kill her."

He exhales a short, derisive burst of air through his nose. "Then she signed up for the wrong relationship. He's got as many targets on his back as I do."

"He could have one less."

"You have no idea what you're asking."

"I know exactly what I'm asking, and the answer is a simple yes or no."

"Then the answer is no."

It's cold, hard, and leaves me breathless.

Examining my expression with icy eyes, he says, "We're enemies. We're killers. Where did you think that story would end?"

In heartbreak, obviously, for everyone involved.

I roll over, away from him, curling into a ball against the pain.

THIRTY-ONE

SLOANE

After a moment, Declan rises from the bed. He returns soon with a blanket that he drapes over me, tucking it around my body. He leans over and kisses my temple, then goes into the master closet. When he emerges, he's dressed in jeans, a leather jacket, and combat boots, all of them black.

He leaves the room without a word, turning off the lights and closing the door quietly behind him.

I say drily to the empty room, "So much for the after-sex cuddling."

I suffer through a moment of self-loathing for craving after-sex cuddling—a first—then throw off the blanket and get out of bed.

This house doesn't have the automatic lights like the other place did, but I have enough from the glowing moon to navigate the room. I find the light switch on the wall in the master closet and flick it on.

Looking around, I laugh out loud.

I've never seen a closet with French doors before, but this one has a set that leads to a Juliet balcony outside. A gold-and-crystal chandelier glitters overhead. One entire wall is lined all the way to the ceiling with lighted shelves displaying shoes and handbags.

Mine, presumably.

Another wall has drawer after gold-knobbed drawer beneath hanging racks of long-sleeved shirts, dresses, slacks, and coats. The third wall is filled with Declan's black suits and white dress shirts. A giant square dresser sits in the middle of it all, topped in cream marble with a display of white orchid plants in moss-filled glass.

This closet is as big as a retail clothing shop in a mall.

I go hunting through drawers until I find a lovely selection of La Perla lingerie in silk-lined dividers. I pause, staring at an exquisite pair of violet silk-and-tulle Brazilian-cut panties.

The price tag is still attached. The panties, one of maybe fifty pairs in the drawer, cost $240.

No wonder Declan made fun of my savings account.

I rip off the price tag, find a matching violet bra, and try them on in front of the full-length mirror.

Turning slowly back and forth as I admire my reflection, I realize I'll never be able to wear my three-pack-for-thirty-bucks cotton Hanes again.

I hunt through more drawers. I find a lifetime supply of lulu-lemons, along with jeans, sweaters, T-shirts, and everything else. I dress in a pair of $1,300 Dolce & Gabbana jeans and a black cashmere sweater so soft, it almost makes me cry, trying all the while to stay angry at Declan.

When I pull open one of the top drawers in the big center island, I stop short, sucking in a breath.

Apparently, his shopping spree also included a stop at Tiffany's.

I close the drawer, wait for the blinding sparkle of diamonds to fade from my vision, then leave the closet and its temptations behind. I head out barefoot to the kitchen.

Declan isn't there. He's not in the living room or media room, either. It takes me twenty minutes to go through the entire house, until finally I determine that I'm alone.

Except for the shadowy figures moving around the perimeter of the yard, that is.

The ones carrying the big rifles.

I slide open a glass door in the enclosed breakfast room off the kitchen. Salt air swirls in. The cold sea breeze stirs my hair. I stick my head out and call, "Hey! Hello? Over here!"

I wave an arm at the dark figure prowling along a tall hedge of privet. He pauses for a moment, looking in my direction, then lifts a hand to his ear.

"For fuck's sake, you don't have to get permission, Spider," I mutter, watching him speak into his wrist.

But I guess he did, because he starts to swagger my way.

When he reaches the flagstone patio outside the doors and enters the pool of light from the sconces mounted on the walls, I smile at him.

"Captain America! How are you?"

He tries not to smile at me, but it doesn't work. "Hullo, madam."

"Oh god," I say, appalled. "Please tell me Declan didn't say you have to call me that now."

Spider slings the rifle over his massive shoulder and grins. "Nah. Just thought I'd give you a wee fright. Knew I couldn't do it any other way, so . . ." He shrugs.

He's in a good mood. I wonder if he likes it better here at the beach than in the city?

"Well, I'm happy to see you, anyway. Is Kieran skulking around somewhere, too?"

"Aye. That was him in my ear. He says hullo. He's up front at the gates. Another thirty of us are spread out all over the property."

"Thirty?"

He shrugs again. "Big place. Big pores. Lots of places rats can sneak in."

"I don't like the sound of that."

"Don't worry. We've got it locked up tighter than a nun's snatch. Uh, excuse the language."

"Snatch isn't a bad word. Bureaucracy is. By any chance, do you know where Declan went?"

He makes a face and shifts his weight from foot to foot.

"You can't tell me. Sorry, I forgot we weren't supposed to talk."

Looking apologetic, he says, "It's just, you know, business."

I wave a hand in the air dismissively. "Oh, I know. Man stuff. The code and whatnot. By the way, I hope I didn't get you in trouble last time. I didn't tell Declan we talked, but he knew somehow."

He says solemnly, "He always knows everything."

I resist the urge to roll my eyes heavenward. "Is there anything I can get you? Coffee? Brandy? It's chilly out here."

When he hesitates, I say, "There's no way in hell he'll know. He's not even here."

After a moment of internal debate, he says gruffly, "Coffee would be quare."

"I don't speak Irish. Is that a yes?"

"Aye. Thank you."

"What about the other guys? I'll put a pot on, how about that? Whoever wants one can just tap on the door."

I don't give him time to answer, I simply smile and slide shut the door, then go into the kitchen and rummage around in the huge pantry for a coffeemaker. I can't find one, until I discover it's built right into the wall in a little niche next to the fridge.

It takes me another ten minutes to figure out how to load the beans I found in the pantry into the damn thing and get it working. By the time I go back to the slider with a cup of hot coffee for

Spider, three more hulking men in black carrying rifles are milling around just outside the pool of light on the patio.

"Hi, guys! I'll just go back and get the pot. Hold on a sec."

I give Spider his mug, then return to the kitchen and get a few more mugs and the pot of brewed coffee. Then it's back to the breakfast room, where I distribute the other mugs and fill them, feeling a little like Florence Nightingale without all the gore.

Deciding the guys need a little sustenance, I find tea biscuits and chocolate-chip cookies in the pantry and arrange them on a plate that I bring out. Soon there are a dozen men on the patio, and my mood has improved.

There's nothing like having a bunch of hunky men around to lift your spirits.

"Does anybody feel like playing cards?"

When that bright suggestion is met with blank looks and total silence, I say somberly, "Oh, that's right. I heard Irishmen are the *worst* at cards. Now, who told me that? I can't remember. Anyway, I'll leave you to it! Have a great night, guys. And thank you for doing such a good job protecting the place. I really appreciate it."

I turn back to the door. A gruff voice says, "Whoever said Irishmen can't play cards was a bloody eejit."

Grumbles of agreement greet me as I turn around again, smiling. "I thought so, too. Maybe somebody could teach me how to play poker? I've always wanted to learn."

An hour later, I've got two dozen men crowded around the kitchen table, and I'm three hundred dollars richer.

Wide-eyed, I stare at the pile of money in front of me. "Wow, beginner's luck is a real thing!"

"So is sandbagging. And disobeying orders."

At the sound of Declan's voice, every man in the room freezes.

I look up to find him staring at me from behind the circle of men with his arms crossed over his chest. The men part silently, moving aside so there's a clear path between me and Declan. Someone audibly gulps.

My ass stinging, I put my feet up on the table, smile at Declan, and say calmly, "Honey. You're home."

A muscle in his jaw flexes. He looks at each man in the room, one by one, his expression stony. Everyone shrinks.

"It's not their fault. I invited them in."

Ignoring me, he says something to the men in Gaelic, his voice steady and low.

Several of the men swallow. One or two fidget nervously. A few go white.

I stand and fold my arms to mimic Declan's posture. "I said, it's not their fault."

"I heard what you said. Spider, you go first."

Without a second's hesitation, Spider steps up to the table. He removes a huge knife from a sheath he's wearing under his coat. He leans over the table, flattens his left hand on the surface, and presses the knife to his pinkie.

I jump up, screaming. "No! Stop! Spider, *stop!*"

By the time I crash into him, blood is already welling from his skin.

I knock him off balance just enough to get his grip on the knife to slip. It clatters to the floor. On my hands and knees, I scramble for it. When I get it, I jump up and whirl around, livid.

At the top of my lungs, I shout at Declan, *"What the actual fuck, gangster?"*

He remains as calm and cold as an iceberg. "Give him back the knife."

"The hell I will."

His voice hardens. "Sloane. Do it."

"You want this knife? Come and get it. I'll bury it in your fucking skull, you savage. *That man is your friend.*"

Breathing hard, I stare at him. No one else in the room moves a muscle or makes a sound.

He says, "You misunderstand. I don't have friends. Spider works for me. He disobeyed my orders. And in our world, disobedience comes with consequences."

From the corner of my eye, I see one of the men curl his hand into a fist.

Two of the fingers on that fist are missing.

A blinding flash of fury engulfs me. I'm sick, too, and horrified, but mostly furious. My voice shaking, I say, "Then let me pay the consequences for them. This was my idea. Punish me instead."

The silence is profound. It's like the vast, echoing silence of a cathedral, one that's been abandoned to ghosts for a hundred years.

"Please, Declan. Please."

His eyes burn. His nostrils flare. When he draws a slow breath, I think he's considering it.

So I do the only thing I can think of that will tip him over the edge.

I sink to my knees on the floor.

In front of everyone.

I feel their shock. Feel it expand when I lean over and flatten my shaking hand against the lovely limestone tile. Feel it explode into panic when I grip the knife in my other hand and grit my teeth in determination.

I never realized how small a pinkie finger is. Maybe I won't even miss it.

Wondering if Declan keeps all his severed trophy fingers in a jar in a drawer in his desk, I take a breath and press down.

THIRTY-TWO

SLOANE

*T*here's a flash of black in my peripheral vision, then Declan kicks the knife away.

He grabs me and drags me to my feet. He throws his arms around me and crushes me against his chest, cursing.

"Bloody stubborn woman," he rasps, giving me a hard shake. "Jesus, Mary, and fucking Joseph, you're bloody mad!"

He takes my face in his hands and kisses me ravenously. I let him, curling my shaking hands into his jacket and trying to remain standing, though my legs are shaking, too.

When we come up for air, the kitchen is empty except for the two of us.

"Goddammit, Sloane. *Goddammit.*"

He slides his hands into my hair and grips my skull. He gives me another shake, his chest heaving. Then he presses his forehead to mine and closes his eyes, exhaling hard.

"Don't you ever fucking scare me like that again."

I can't help it. I start to weakly laugh.

"I'm bloody serious!"

"You're bloody nuts."

"*I'm* nuts? You were about to cut off your finger for a man you barely know!"

"It's the principle."

He's outraged. "The *principle*?"

"Yes. The principle. I only have a few of them, but they're airtight. One is that I don't cause other people's suffering if I can help it. Another is that I own my shit. I don't blame anyone else but me for what goes wrong in my life. Put those two together, and you've got me kneeling on the kitchen floor threatening my pinkie finger with a knife."

He kisses me again. It's frantic. "Fucking mad," he mutters to himself. "Bloody hell."

"You're the one with the multiple personalities. You walked in the door like the Terminator."

He winds his arms around me and pulls me close. His heart beats frantically against his breastbone. His hand wrapped around my head trembles. He rocks me slightly, catching his breath.

"I just can't leave you alone. Ever. That's the only solution."

My voice muffled against his chest, I say, "Don't worry. I won't speak to any of your men ever again. Lesson learned."

"I doubt you'll have a choice in the matter, considering they'll all be laying wreaths of roses at your feet every day from now on."

"I like the sound of that. Where did you go?"

"Give me a minute. I'm still in cardiac arrest."

He picks me up in his arms and carries me out of the kitchen and back to the bedroom. He sets me down next to the bed and strips off all my clothing, does the same to himself, then pushes me onto the bed and crawls in next to me. He drags the sheets and blanket over us, pulls me into his side, and holds me so tightly, it's like he's afraid I'm going to disappear in a puff of smoke.

After a while, I say, "I'm sorry I said that thing about burying the knife in your skull. I didn't mean it."

"You did."

"Okay, that's true. But I would've regretted it if I did. I would've cried really hard at your funeral. And I shouldn't have said it in front of your men. I apologize. But I can't guarantee I won't push you into traffic if you hurt one of those guys. They adore you. And it really wasn't their fault."

"The infamous Tinker Bell charm."

"Exactly."

"You should give them back the money you stole from them."

"I didn't steal it. I won it, fair and square."

"Aye? So you told them you 'slay' at poker, the same way you told me?"

"Of course not. It's all part of the game."

His sigh is heavy. "You're lethal, lass."

"I enjoy throwing on my crown to show people who they're dealing with. Where did you go?"

"For a walk."

Not altogether convinced, I repeat, "A walk."

"On the beach."

He went for a midnight stroll on the beach in combat boots? "Was there a baby seal you needed to club?"

"I needed to clear my head. And to give you some space. You were upset about how the conversation ended."

When I don't say anything, he adds, "I'm putting you in my will."

"Oh, no. Not the money thing again."

"Aye, the money thing again. You said something about your girlfriend that stuck with me."

"What?"

"That it would kill her if anything happened to Kazimir."

Caressing my cheek, he gently kisses me. His voice turns husky. "It made me think about how you'd react if something happened to me."

"I'd be too preoccupied sorting through all the diamonds in the closet to really pay much attention."

"Bollocks."

"You're trying to get me to tell you how I feel about you again, aren't you?"

"Aye."

"Will you use it against me when you start talking your craziness about marriage?"

"Aye."

"Then I won't tell you."

"I want to hear it. I *need* to hear it. You said you were intoxicated, but I'm beyond that. I'm addicted. If you don't give me another fix, I'll go mad."

His kisses are tender and quick, gentle pecks peppered over my lips, cheeks, and chin. He's bribing me.

"Fine. You have beautiful hands."

He pauses the kisses, lifting his head to look at me. He arches a brow.

"For god's sake, Declan, you know I'm no good at this."

"You're better than you think."

I exhale a hard breath, take his hand, and press it over my pounding heart. "Here. Just feel that. That's how I feel about you, you bossy ass."

He looks at his hand. He spreads his fingers wide and presses down. He closes his eyes. After a moment, he says with quiet wonder, "Our heartbeats are in sync."

Those few words fill me with a kind of fear I've never known. It's dread, pure and cold, and it sinks all the way through me, straight down into my bones.

Once it's started, a thing as powerful as two hearts beating in time together is impossible to stop.

Help. I've fallen and I can't get up.

"Don't look so scared."

"You said total honesty. My face is just going along with the plan."

He says drily, "I also said total obedience."

"Two out of three isn't bad."

His gaze sharpens. "Is that your way of telling me you trust me?"

My laugh is soft but exasperated. "Isn't it obvious? Any other man who tried to make me call him sir would already be a eunuch."

He cups my jaw in his big hand. "And what about me?" he says, all sudden fierceness and fiery eyes. "Can I trust you in return?"

"Dial it down, intenso. Why does everything have to be so life or death?"

"Don't change the subject."

"I'm not even sure what you're asking. It sounds like a hell of a lot more than the normal definition of trust. Do you need a heart transplant you're not telling me about, and you want me to be the donor?"

"I *will* need a heart transplant by the time this is all over."

"Great. That's very illuminating, thank you."

He glares at me. I want to harm him with a stick. "How about if you tell me what your definition of trust is? Let's start there."

He ticks off a list like he's got it tattooed on his brain. "No lies. No hiding. Complete loyalty. Complete dedication. Your life before mine, and vice versa. Everything I have is yours, and vice versa."

"Sounds like joining a cult."

"I wasn't finished."

"Jesus."

"We always have each other's back. We always keep our promises. And secrets are a thing of the past."

His voice dropped on the last one. Dropped lower and gained weight, like a sinking ship taking on water.

Looking at him closely, I say, "You have a lot of secrets, don't you?"

"You know I do."

"And you want to tell them to me?"

"I want you to understand who I am."

"I think I already do."

"No, lass. Your understanding is the outer layer of an onion. The dry, thin skin. To get to who I really am will take a bit of concentrated peeling."

"I have no idea where you're getting your metaphors, but I'd like to point out that trust is something that evolves over time. It's organic. It's based on experience."

"Wrong. Trust is a decision. You can make it between breaths." He pauses for effect before he delivers his killing blow. "Like you did with me in the shower."

I hate it when people have excellent memories.

"Hold on. Let me uncross my eyeballs. Are you saying that if I told you right now that you could trust me, that would be it? You would?"

"Aye."

"And you'd tell me all your onion peel stories?"

"Aye."

"Pardon the insult, but that seems extremely naïve for a man in your position."

"It would be, if I didn't already know you'd never say I could trust you if I couldn't."

Dammit. This relationship will never work if he's going to be right all the time. "I propose a compromise."

"I don't like compromises."

"What a colossal surprise. As I was saying, I think there's a middle ground somewhere between the two extremes. Why don't you tell me one secret, and we'll go from there?"

When he only stares at me, lips flattened, I say, "A small one. Like why you never wear a color other than black. Think of it like trust with training wheels."

After a moment where he practices his glower, he says darkly, "There will come a time, lass, and very soon, when I'll need to know one way or the other."

He rolls onto his back and stares at the ceiling. Then he rises, gets dressed, and leaves the room.

When he still hasn't returned three days later, I'm in a panic unlike anything I've ever known.

Because according to the news, the boss of every mafia syndicate in the country is being murdered, one by one.

THIRTY-THREE

DECLAN

It's late when I enter the house. Nearly three. I expect to find Sloane asleep in bed, but instead, she's in the media room, curled up on the sofa with a glass of red wine. Two wine bottles sit on the coffee table, one of them empty, the other a quarter full.

The television is tuned to a twenty-four-hour news station.

She doesn't notice me. I stand watching her from the door as she gulps from the wineglass and gnaws at her thumbnail. She looks exhausted. Strung out. Frantic with worry.

I feel a twinge of guilt, but am still glad I didn't call.

Not that it was easy.

She hasn't been off my mind for a second since I left. If I didn't already know I was obsessed, three days apart drove the point home with the subtlety of a hatchet.

Grabbing the remote, she starts clicking through channels, jumping from station to station, pausing mere seconds between each. Looking for something.

I know what.

"Try CNN. They love the bloody stuff."

Sloane jumps to her feet, dropping the glass of Cabernet to the floor. It spills all over the cream-colored carpet, leaving a pattern like the spray of a slit jugular vein.

Curling her hands to fists, she stares at me with wide, unblinking eyes.

"You're alive."

"Ah, those astonishing powers of observation."

Her eyes flash. "Don't you dare be nonchalant with me. Don't you dare be glib." She points a shaking finger at the sofa. "I've been sitting here for three fucking days, listening to reports about murdered gangsters. Three. *Days*. Do you have any idea what I've been through? Why didn't you call? Where the hell have you been?"

With every question, her voice rises. She's mad as hell.

That shouldn't make me happy, but it does. It makes me so happy, I could float.

"Working." I glance at the television, then back at her.

I know she understands when her face drains of color.

"You . . . *you* . . ."

I say softly, "'The supreme art of war is to subdue the enemy without fighting.'"

Closing her eyes, she shakes her head. "And now you're quoting Sun Tzu," she says bitterly. "Like that makes any sense at all."

"Just testing that superior IQ of yours. You passed. This time."

Her lids fly open. She impales me with a look of such fury, I almost smile.

"What the fuck, Declan?"

I lean against the wall and fold my arms over my chest. "You're cursing an unusual amount, lass, even for you. What's that about?" I let my smile unfurl, like a snake's coils. "Don't tell me you missed me."

The air around her head shimmers with a rage bordering on

insanity. I expect her eyes to pop from her head. She looks like she's channeling the ghost of Charles Manson.

She walks to where I'm standing and slaps me across the face.

When my head stops spinning, I look at her and grin.

"How dare you smile at me, you son of a bitch."

"Is that a rhetorical question? I thought you didn't like those."

"I've been sitting here thinking you were dead!"

"No, not me. Just the heads of all the other syndicates. Except Kazimir. I kept him alive because you asked me to."

She sucks in a breath so hard it's like she's trying not to drown. Her face screws up and turns red.

I think because she doesn't know what else to do, she slaps me again.

I grab her and kiss her, hard.

She bursts into tears. "You asshole! I hate you! I hate you!"

"I know, baby," I say, chuckling and holding her tight. "You hate my bloody guts. Except you don't. You're crazy about me. You're so in love with me, you cried because I'm alive."

Sobbing into my shoulder, she pounds a fist on my chest.

I whisper into her ear, "Sweet girl. My fierce little lion queen. Give me your mouth."

She sniffles and whimpers as I kiss her, clinging to me like she'll never let go.

I've never been happier in my entire life than right now, in this moment.

Until she pushes me away, that is.

She turns and walks away with her hands on her head, growling in aggravation.

I watch her walk slow circles around the room, inhaling deep breaths, then blowing them out slowly. She wipes her cheeks with shaking hands and walks more circles. When she's regained self-control, she stops and looks at me.

"Thank you for Kazimir. And fuck you for leaving me hanging. Don't ever do that to me again."

"I won't."

"Good. Jesus Christ, I think I'm having a stroke. What happens now?"

"Now I wait until your girlfriend's man calls me for a sit-down to discuss a cease-fire."

"How do you know he'll call?"

"That's the only way he'll be able to get me in a room so he can try to kill me."

After a beat, she says, "It's always going to be like this, isn't it?"

"Aye. That's the life. War. Death. Kill or be killed. Now you see why I'm in such a good mood most of the time."

She stares at me beseechingly. "Don't be sarcastic. I can't handle sarcastic right now. Just give it to me straight. *Is* he going to kill you?"

I cluck my tongue. "O ye of little faith."

"Quote the Bible to me again and see what happens to your two front teeth."

"He's not going to kill me."

She peers at me, unconvinced.

"I'm going to give him a good reason not to."

"Such as?"

"That Natalie would never forgive him if he murdered the love of your life."

She closes one eye and wrinkles her nose, trying to work it out. "Why would Natalie think you're the love of my life?"

"You're going to tell her I am."

Her face smooths out. She arches her eyebrows. "I'm sorry. I must've heard you incorrectly. Did you just suggest I tell my best friend that you"—she looks me up and down—"are the love of my life?"

"You heard me."

"So you want me to lie to her."

I tilt my head and gaze at her through half-lidded eyes.

"Sorry, gangster. Smolder all you want, but *she's* the love of my life."

I'm gone for three days, and she forgets who she's dealing with. "I see. So you'd like Kazimir to cut off my balls and choke me to death with them?"

When she blanches, I smile. "That's his specialty. Russians are so dramatic."

"You're blackmailing me. This is emotional blackmail!"

"It is. I'm not a good person. Whoops."

She props her hands on her hips and looks at me down her nose, like I'm a peasant with oozing sores. "Well, too bad. I won't do it. If you can't survive on your own without my help, you're not the gangster I thought you were."

Oh, how I'd like to spank that fine arse of hers until she's squealing.

She'd love it, though, so I don't.

I shrug and leave the room.

She follows on my heels. "What does that shrug mean? Where are you going?"

"To bed."

I head to the bedroom, her anger at my back like a toxic cloud. In the master bathroom, I kick off my boots, strip out of my clothes, and step into the shower.

I stand under the hot spray with my eyes closed for several moments, letting hot water slide over my skin. Sloane stands outside the door, seething at me through the glass.

"I won't tell her you're the love of my life."

"I heard you."

"And I know you don't need me to, either. You just *want* me to. This is only you trying to get me to say how I feel about you again."

"If that's what you think."

"It is what I think."

"Right. That's it, then."

"It is."

Ignoring her, I pick up the bar of soap and lather my chest. I take my time washing myself, soaping my arms, chest, and abs. Then I rinse, turn around, and tip my head back into the spray.

I can feel her greedy gaze on my body.

She mutters, "Show-off."

"Get your arse in here, woman."

"Pfft."

"*Now.*"

"Pardon me, but I'm not a terrier. You don't get to bark orders—"

Her snippy tirade ends as I open the door and drag her, fully clothed, into the shower.

I press her against the wall, pin her wrists above her head, and take her mouth. The kiss is hard and hungry.

She's just as starving as I am. She kisses me back like it's her last two minutes on earth.

Then it's a frantic race to get her out of her clothes. They're half wet and stick to her skin, but it doesn't slow us down.

"Tampon?"

"No. Period's done."

I lift her up and press her back against the wall. She wraps her legs around my waist and reaches down between us to guide me in.

"Fuck, baby. Hurry."

"Yes—oh—there—"

I shove inside with a chest-deep grunt that echoes off the tile walls. She arches back with a soft moan. Her fingernails dig into my shoulders.

I fuck her, holding her up against the shower wall, water spraying everywhere, until she cries out.

"God, I'm there. I'm there already, Declan—*oh*—"

Her pussy clenches convulsively around my cock. It feels like being milked by a fist.

I kiss her as I come, my tongue down her throat and my hands under her arse, my thighs burning and my heart on fire.

It doesn't matter if she won't say I'm the love of her life. It doesn't matter if she never tells me how she feels at all.

No words can compete with this.

When we're both breathing hard and twitching, coming down from the high, she drops her head and hides her face in my shoulder.

She whispers, "You might be a distant second to Nat. Very distant. Jerk."

My chest expands. I start to laugh, just to have somewhere for all the emotion to go.

Withdrawing from her body, I set her on her feet and take her face in my hands. My voice husky with pleasure, I say, "Good enough."

Then I kiss her, holding her close, filled with joy when I feel how hard her heart beats against my chest.

It's beating at the same pace as mine.

THIRTY-FOUR

DECLAN

*L*ater in bed, we lie together silently, watching the sun come up. We're on our sides, her back to my front, my arm underneath her neck, her head resting on my pillow. My knees are drawn up behind hers.

I once paid three hundred thousand dollars for a wristwatch. I remember it now and smile at how I thought a hunk of metal was worth something.

But I had nothing of real value to compare it to.

Now I do.

Sloane says, "You always wear black because it hides blood the best."

I wonder what's behind that, the training-wheel-trust question she suggested from days ago, before I left. *"Why don't you tell me one secret, and we'll go from there. Like why you always wear black."*

"Aye."

"I used to do the same thing."

"What do you mean?"

She inhales slowly, lets the breath out. "I used to cut myself. I didn't heal well. If I wore white, there would be little flecks of blood everywhere. I looked like an assault victim."

That stuns me. "You? Cut yourself? Why?"

"Pain needs an outlet."

I wait, knowing there will be more, not wanting to disrupt her thoughts before she puts them into words.

"I was this really chubby kid. My parents called me chunky monkey. Thought it was cute, my little belly roll, until I turned ten. Then my mother decided it was a bad reflection on her parenting. My dad thought it was a lack of willpower. A character flaw. They both hated it. And the bigger I got, the more disappointed they were in me, as if my flesh equaled my value. I took up too much space. Even without saying a word, I was too loud. Too obvious. Too overpowering. I had to be gotten under control."

I listen, riveted, trying to imagine this lion I know as a cub.

"The summer between fifth and sixth grades, they made me go to fat camp."

"Fat camp?"

"It's exactly as bad as it sounds. Six weeks of body shaming disguised as education. That's where I learned I wasn't okay as I was. I was defective. In order to be okay, in order to be acceptable to society, I had to change. I had to shrink. I couldn't be allowed to go on in my sad state, thinking my body was fine. Man, what that shit does to a little kid's brain."

"I don't like your parents."

I say it with too much force. Sloane laughs.

"The weird thing is? I know they had good intentions. They didn't want my life to be hard, and they thought it would be really hard if I stayed fat. But they never gave me a choice about it. So off I went to fat camp to be humiliated and demoralized on a daily basis. I think they hired the counselors based on lack of a soul. The lady in charge of me made Kathy Bates in *Misery* look like Mary Poppins."

She stops, sighing.

"What's the name of this fat camp?"

"You're not going to burn it down."

"That's what you think."

"That's sweet. But it's closed now, anyway. The state finally stepped in when they had too many reports about the beatings."

"Beatings?" I repeat loudly.

"Oh, not me. I got really good at hiding."

Sick but mesmerized, I say, "Where would you hide?"

"Right out in the open. I got so good at being what they wanted, their eyes would gloss right over me like I wasn't there. I lost more than thirty pounds in those six weeks, along with all my childhood." Her voice hardens. "And nobody ever saw the real me again."

I feel an almost overpowering need to break something. That counselor's nose.

"When I came home, my parents were ecstatic. They didn't notice my new silences. They didn't notice how I always looked at the floor. All they saw was my thin new body. Success. I really fucking hated them for that. So, to get back at them, I gained all the weight I'd lost, plus some. Then my mother got cancer and died. My dad remarried a lady who hated the sight of me. Everything was about as shitty as it could be, until my dad's best friend from the navy came to visit when I was fourteen, and I got an education in what the word 'victim' really meant."

I realize I'm squeezing her arm too hard. I relax my hand and kiss her shoulder, half of me waiting for her to continue, half of me wanting her to stop.

I already know where this is going.

"His name was Lance. To this day, if I hear that name, I want to throw up. Lance with the buzz cut and too much Polo cologne.

Lance with a smile like a shark's. My father worshipped him, my stepmother flirted with him, and I stayed as far away as I could because of the way his eyes followed me everywhere, like one of those haunted-house paintings at Disneyland."

She stops abruptly.

My voice low, I say, "What did he do to you?"

"Everything," she says with no emotion, as if it happened to someone else. "Everything that a grown man could do to a helpless young girl."

I have to close my eyes and breathe slowly and deliberately so I don't scream out loud. "Did you tell your father?"

"Yes."

"What did he do?"

"Do?" She laughs. "Nothing. He didn't believe me. He thought I was making it up. Looking for attention. Like a pathetic fat girl would."

I'm breathless with fury. Glowing white-hot with it. I need to put my hands around her father's throat and squeeze until I see the life fade from his eyes.

"Lance left in a week. Five weeks later, I found out I was pregnant."

I curse violently in Gaelic. Sloane sighs.

"If that makes you angry, you might not want to hear the rest."

Through gritted teeth, I say, "Tell me."

"I decided I wanted to keep the baby. I kept the pregnancy a secret from my dad, but I didn't know how I was supposed to handle being a teenage mom with no money. But ultimately, I didn't have to know. This guy at school who was always harassing me for being a 'fat fuck' pushed me down the stairs on the quad. I miscarried at thirteen weeks."

I can't speak. For a long, frozen moment, I'm blank, unable to process what she's telling me.

Her voice soft, she says, "That's how I knew I wasn't pregnant at the hospital. When there's a baby growing inside you, all kinds of things change."

"Sloane. Jesus. Fuck."

"I know. It's not pretty. It wasn't pretty for me for a few years there after that. I was depressed. I had terrible anxiety. I felt like I was going out of my head. I started cutting myself, wearing all black. I shaved my hair to a mohawk. Pierced my nose and a few other things. I shut down. But underneath that, I was so. Fucking. Angry. So angry, I wanted to die."

She rolls over and gazes at me with clear eyes. Her voice is calm. "Do you want to know what saved me?"

"What?"

"Natalie. My best friend. My only friend. I wanted to kill myself so many times during those years. The only reason I didn't is because of her. Over and over again, she saved my life. You know what else?"

"I don't know if I can take it."

"She never knew about the pregnancy. Except for the nurse who gave me the test at Planned Parenthood, no one knew. I was too ashamed. You're the only living soul I've ever told. I want you to understand what that means."

My pulse throbbing and my voice hoarse, I say, "It means I can trust you."

"No," she says softly, eyes shining. "It means you can't. If it comes down to a choice between the two of you, I can't honestly say what I'll do."

I close my eyes and drag a breath into my lungs. "I said I wouldn't make you choose."

"You did. And I believe you. But now you've upped the ante. Now, you and Kage are the last men standing."

"I wanted to end a war."

"And you may have. But you've also backed him into a corner. What choice does he have but to retaliate?"

"Surrender."

She says drily, "I take it you've never met the man."

"I've met him. Don't sound so bloody impressed."

"This is going to offend you, but I think the two of you are very much alike."

"You're right. I'm offended."

She settles her head on my chest and sighs. "Okay."

I'm nervous when she doesn't say anything else. I want to get her talking again. "How did you go from the girl who got pushed down the stairs to who you are now?"

"I eventually realized it wasn't that I wanted to die. It's that I wanted to escape my feelings. I wanted out. Life was too painful to live as it was. So I decided I needed to change it. My life, I mean. I needed to make it so that nothing bad could ever happen to me again. Which is magical thinking, of course. We can't control when bad things happen. But we can control how we react.

"I vowed I wouldn't be a victim ever again. I started taking care of myself. I got into yoga, fixed my shitty diet, read everything I could get my hands on about self-care. I built up my self-esteem like it was a house, brick by brick. Before I went off to college at eighteen, I did everything I could to be mentally and physically tough. It was either that or kill myself, so I figured it was worth a try. After a while, it worked. I dropped a bunch of weight, got strong, learned how to give zero fucks about what anyone else thought. I learned how to listen to myself. How to protect myself, because no one else would."

Picturing her as a teenager, a girl in pain determined to save herself, my admiration for her grows even deeper. "That's when you decided men were desserts."

"And nothing more," she says firmly. "Especially since they only paid me attention when I was fat and a source of ridicule and an easy target, or when I was in shape and a source of lust. I couldn't trust them."

I tuck her head into my neck, kiss her temple, and murmur, "I'm sorry."

"For what?"

"What I said to you in the hospital. How I acted like what to do about a pregnancy was my choice, not yours."

She's quiet for a moment. "Thank you."

"Fuck, don't thank me. I'm an idiot."

A seagull flies low over the waves, his wingtips skimming the water. Another one makes a wide, lazy circle overhead, crying a lonely seabird cry.

Watching them, it dawns on me what a terrible thing I've done by bringing Sloane here. By making her my captive, then earning her trust. I'm like one of those clueless conservationists who think keeping a tiger in captivity is safer for it than living out in the wild.

A cage is no place for a wild thing, no matter how gilded the bars.

To make things worse, I keep demanding she tell me I can trust her. Like she really wants to make some fucked-up pledge of allegiance to the man who snatched her from a parking garage. Like that would make any kind of bloody sense!

How am I only just realizing this?

My voice rough, I say, "You told me you didn't want me to keep you too long. Do you still feel that way?"

In her silence, I feel her attention sharpen. "Why?"

I have to swallow several times before I can force the words out. "I'll take you home if you want me to."

Her voice rises. "Take me home?"

"Let you go. Today, if that's what you want."

She exhales a hard little breath, full of disappointment. "See, I knew I shouldn't have told you that story."

"I'm not saying that because of the story. Ah, fuck, maybe I am. It doesn't matter. What matters is that I want you to know you always have a choice with me. A choice in everything. I haven't demonstrated that so far. I don't want to be like all the other men in your life. Taking. Hurting you. Letting you down."

"No one's hurt me in a long time," she says quietly, her breath warm against my chest.

But you could.

She doesn't say it, but I hear it all the same. She's already told me as much. I'm caught again between wanting to do the right thing and wanting to do the selfish thing, which is keeping her by my side forever, no matter what she has to say about it.

I wish that last tiny shred of humanity inside me would just fucking die already. Things would be so much easier.

But I meant what I said. She has a choice. I'm a soulless Neanderthal, but for her, I'll make an exception.

"I'll take you back to New York if—"

"Say another word and lose your testicles."

The anger's back. I hear it in her voice, feel it in the new tension in her body. I like my balls where they are, so I only kiss her temple again and remain silent.

She does box breathing for a while. Eventually, the tension drains from her limbs. We lie together silently until I think she's about to drift off to sleep.

Then my cell rings. It's on the bathroom counter.

Sloane lifts her head and looks at me with big eyes. "Is that him?"

"I doubt Kazimir would call this soon. Stay here."

I roll out of bed and cross to the bathroom. When I pick up the phone and look at the readout, it's Kieran's number I see.

I poke my head out the bathroom door, look at Sloane sitting up in bed, her eyes worried, and shake my head.

She collapses back against the mattress, releasing a big gust of air.

I answer Kieran's call, then listen to him absently as I take a piss. He's got logistics to go over. Plans that have to be made. A hundred different decisions await me, and it isn't even seven a.m. yet.

Wanting to get back to bed as quickly as possible, I give him ten minutes of my time. I hang up, splash water on my face, brush my teeth, then head back into the bedroom, stopping short when I see the empty bed.

Sloane's gone.

THIRTY-FIVE

SLOANE

I have no idea how long Declan will be on the phone. I can't tell what he's saying, either, because it's all in Gaelic. So I decide I need some fresh air and get dressed.

When I walk out the bedroom door, he's still in the bathroom, talking.

Ignoring my rumbling stomach as I pass through the kitchen, I pull open the glass door of the breakfast room and step outside. The air is brisk and fresh. Cold on my face, but not cold enough to send me back in. Wrapping my arms around myself, I walk over the patio and across the wide expanse of lawn until it gives way to sand.

At the end of the yard by the tall hedge of privets, Spider stands sentry.

Our eyes meet.

I raise a hand in greeting, then look away.

I haven't spoken to him since the incident in the kitchen. I haven't spoken to any of the men who prowl the grounds, not even when Declan was gone. I've stayed inside, locked out of sight, feeling foolish and angry with myself for what happened. That I risked their jobs and their pinkies like that. That I made them disobey orders because I was bored.

I wish it wasn't in my nature to play with fire. I know the only thing that happens is that someone gets burned.

The sun is a distant ball on the horizon, shimmering pale as it rises above a restless sea. The ocean is choppy this morning. Dark and white-capped from the stiff onshore breeze.

I head straight toward the water.

I want to feel it on my toes. Feel how different it might be from the crystalline water of Lake Tahoe, the water I spent all my summers in from the time I learned how to swim at five years old. Water so pure, I could see all the way down to the bottom as I peered over the side of my dad's little fishing boat.

Hopefully, the sea air will blow through my head and erase all these memories that are rising like ghosts from their graves since I told Declan my story.

The origin story of a warrior who doesn't feel so strong anymore.

Is this what love is? Weakness? I felt so much more powerful before I ever set eyes on Declan's face. Now I feel as raw and unsteady as a newborn foal.

Like I used to, all those years ago before I remade myself into something harder.

There's a yacht moored far offshore. A sleek white thing, glinting in the sun like a newly minted coin. Several other smaller craft bob on the water down the coastline. A trio of sailboats flit over the waves to the south. North? I'm not sure which direction I'm facing. Now that I think of it, how do I know I'm really on Martha's Vineyard at all?

My entire reality is based on what Declan has told me since he ripped me away from safe moorings in New York.

You could be anywhere. He drugged you, remember? You could be hallucinating all of this. You could be on the moon.

Exhausted, my heart as heavy as my legs, I walk over the rolling dunes down to where the sand is damp and firm underfoot. The sneakers I plucked from the closet are too nice to get wet, so I take them off and hold them as I meander down the beach. I dodge incoming waves as they crash and reach frothy fingers toward my feet.

I don't know how long I meander, picking up shells, but suddenly, a cold prickle raises the hair on the back of my neck.

It isn't the wind, of that I'm sure.

Frowning, I stop and look around.

The beach is deserted in both directions. Aside from the house I just left, there are no other structures within sight. The only thing I see that could be considered out of place is Spider, sprinting toward me from his post at the hedge of privet.

He's waving his rifle in the air. Hollering words that are swallowed by the wind.

Four more armed men in black suits appear behind him, running toward me.

On instinct, I whirl around.

My brain registers eight of them, sleek black figures rising from the sea with scuba tanks strapped to their backs and weapons in their gloved hands, before the one closest to me grabs me and drags me into the water.

"She's awake."

"You sure those handcuffs are enough? I think we should put the leg chains on, too."

"I bet you do. How's the nose feeling, Cliff?"

"Fuck you."

The voices are male, coming from somewhere nearby. They are the first thing I'm aware of. Next, the headache makes itself known, throbbing steadily behind my eyes to the beat of my heart. There's a sour taste in my mouth, my head weighs a thousand pounds, and my right hand feels like I've been smashing it against a wall for hours.

I'm also wet. My clothes, my hair, all of me. I lick my lips and taste salt. Seawater.

A door opens and closes. I open my eyes and look around.

I'm in a square gray room. A single fluorescent bulb flickers on the ceiling. The floor is bare cement, and the only furniture is the metal chair I'm sitting on and a dented metal table pushed against the wall to my left.

On the wall directly in front of me looms a large panel of sleek black glass.

Looking at my reflection in the two-way mirror, I realize I'm chained to the chair.

My wrists are bound behind my back by handcuffs. The handcuffs must be attached to the chair, and the chair must be bolted to the floor, because despite several vigorous attempts, nothing budges.

"Don't bother. You're not going anywhere."

I look over my right shoulder.

A man leans casually against the wall in the corner, his arms folded over his chest, one leg kicked up against the wall. He's about thirty-five. He's wearing an untucked red-and-black flannel shirt, faded jeans that are molded to his muscular thighs, and a pair of work boots. His hair is thick, wavy, brown, and looks like it hasn't seen a comb in ages. His eyes are brown, too. So is his beard.

He looks like the Marlboro Man, big and outdoorsy. There's a pale circle of skin on his tanned left ring finger where a wedding band used to be.

In a deep voice with a Boston accent, he says, "Good morning, Sloane."

"You need a haircut. Was your ex the one who made the appointments for you?"

Surprise registers in his eyes for a split second, then recedes as he draws a curtain of practiced blankness over his gaze. "I'll be the one asking the questions."

He pushes off the wall and comes to stand in front of me, his back to the panel of black glass. Crossing his arms again, he looks down his nose at me, projecting power and danger from every pore.

Dear god, how many times am I going to be kidnapped by alpha males this month? It's getting ridiculous.

Looking at his muscular forearms, I say, "I like your tats. Very Celtic. Did you know those spiral knots near your wrist represent a person's journey through life and into the spirit world, or did you just think they looked pretty?"

He tilts his head to one side.

I smile at him. "I've done a lot of reading about spiritual journeys."

Nothing happens for a while, until he says, "I'd like to talk about your boyfriend."

At least he's getting straight to it. I thought we might be here forever.

"Let me just stop you right there. I don't keep boyfriends. They're way too high-maintenance. Too much of a commitment. May I please have a glass of water? Even better, orange juice. Fresh squeezed if you have it."

He frowns. "I don't think you understand what's happening here."

"Oh, for fuck's sake, dude, don't let the D cups fool you. I know exactly what's happening."

I can't tell by his expression if he's amused or annoyed, but I know he's intrigued, because he says, "Which is?"

"You want that five hundred bucks I owe from last year."

He blinks. I don't think he means to. It makes me smile again, this time wider.

"Honestly, I'm impressed. You guys must've gotten a sweet

budget increase from the new administration. I'd love to hear how you're going after the corporations who owe lots of back taxes. The big fish must get an entire squadron of Navy SEALs coming after them, am I right?"

He leans down into my face, planting his hands on his massive thighs. When we're eye to eye, he says softly, "I'm not with the IRS, sweetheart. And this isn't a fucking joke. You're in big trouble."

"Wouldn't be the first time. Won't be the last. Do you like blondes? I know a girl who works at my yoga studio who'd go crazy for your whole Grizzly Adams vibe. Though she's got one of those annoyingly high baby-talk voices, but if you can look past that, she's really sweet. You look like you could use someone to look after you."

When he only stares at me with thinned lips and flared nostrils, I add, "Was it ketamine you gave me? Because I know how that messes up my memory, and I can't remember anything between when the creatures from the black lagoon pulled me into the water and now. I'd love to know how I didn't drown. By the way, props for ingenuity. James Bond would be proud."

After a beat, Mountain Man straightens. He throws a look over his shoulder toward the glass, then slowly walks behind my chair and stops there.

His voice carrying an overt warning, he says, "Declan O'Donnell."

"Nice to meet you, Declan."

I look directly at the glass when I say that, smiling my shit-eating smile.

I hope whoever's watching me behind that two-way mirror is having a meltdown. People hate it when you're not terrified like they're trying to make you be.

Mountain Man rests his hands on the back of my chair and leans close to my ear. In a low voice, he says, "Don't play me for a fucking fool, Sloane."

"Me? Play you for a fool? I would never. You seem much too intelligent. The plaid shirt's a dead giveaway."

I can almost hear his blood pressure rising.

"You think you're very smart, don't you?"

"I'm demonstrably smart. Would you like to give me an IQ test? Ten bucks says I'll beat yours by at least thirty points."

He gives up trying to intimidate me from behind and stalks around to stand in front of me again. He pronounces, "Laugh it up if you like, but if you don't cooperate with me, you're gonna stay in this room for the rest of your life with no contact with the outside world and nothing but a bucket to shit in."

"I see. So much for the Bill of Rights and those pesky sixth and eighth amendments."

He narrows his eyes at my tone of contempt. He grinds his jaw for a while. It reminds me of Declan. I miss him with a sharp, sudden ache.

"Declan O'Donnell," says Mountain Man again. "Tell me about him."

"Never heard of him. So how long have you been in the FBI? Or is it the CIA? I bet they have really good health benefits. Looks like their dress code has gotten a little lax, but I really only know anything about the federal government from the movies. Have you seen the Jason Bourne franchise? Love that guy. So intense."

"How did you meet him?"

"Who? Oh, the Declan guy again? I already told you, I have no idea who that is."

Mountain Man snaps, "We've been watching you. We know you're involved with him. We picked you up on his property."

"Listen, I'm just on vacation. I took a drive into the ritzy part of town and decided to take a walk on somebody's beach. Is that against the law here? We do it all the time in California. Then again, it is a very progressive state."

"We have pictures of you together," he says hotly, trying not to lose his patience.

I shrug. "Wasn't me."

There follows a long, stony silence. I take the opportunity to examine his forearm tattoos more closely.

"What is that, a Druid? Kind of looks like Gandalf from *Lord of the Rings*."

The door opens. Another man walks in.

This one is in a dark suit, a striped tie, and cuff links. He's got a full head of pewter hair and a face like a slab of granite. His oxfords could blind me with their shine.

"Oh, look, Mountain Man, senior management has arrived. Guess you weren't doing such a stellar job interrogating your prisoner."

Closing the door behind him with brisk efficiency, the new guy takes a moment to assess me. Then he presents me with a smile as friendly as a rabid dog baring its teeth.

"Hello, Miss Keller."

He has no discernable accent, but he does have the strangest way of drawing out the syllables so that it seems like he's testing a new language. As if he's a copy of a human, not a real one, an alien trying to fit in.

"Oh wow, I totally just got a flashback from the scene in *The Matrix* where Agent Smith questions Neo about his involvement with Morpheus. You sound exactly like him. Look like him, too. Except you're a lot older. And we need to get you a pair of dark sunglasses to cover those beady eyes."

Mountain Man and the suit share a look. The suit says, "I'll take over from here, Grayson."

"Grayson? Wow, that's a *very* cool name. I bet you were super popular in high school."

Grayson does something strange with his mouth. I think he's trying not to smile, but I could be imagining things.

He exits the room, leaving me alone with the suit.

"Miss Keller, my name is Thomas Aquinas."

"Bullshit. Like the Italian philosopher?"

"Yes."

"How random. Please, continue."

He clasps his hands behind his back and strolls over to the metal desk, which he perches on, swinging a leg back and forth. It's a very unmanly posture, and does nothing to raise my nonexistent level of fear.

"Miss Keller, we're aware of your involvement with the Russian Bratva. We're also aware of your involvement with the Irish Mob. These are indisputable facts, and well-documented, so please do me the kindness of dispensing with your ploy of innocence."

I admire his vocabulary. That rabid-dog smile, however, I could do without.

He continues like he's a pompous university professor giving a lecture that all his students are sleeping through. "According to the Patriot Act, I have the authority to keep you here indefinitely. As a terrorist operative and enemy combatant, you have no rights. Your entire future rests solely in my hands. Please consider all that carefully before you respond to my questions."

He pauses to give me some time to decide if I'd like to start crying and begging.

I yawn instead.

"How did you become involved with Declan O'Donnell?"

"I have no idea who that is."

His expression sours. It's a feat, considering he's got a face like a toilet bowl. He snaps his fingers, and two enormous men enter the room.

They're both dressed in military fatigues and combat boots. They're both the size of mountains. One of them carries a manila folder in his meaty hand, which he gives to the suit. Then they flank the mirrored glass, spread their legs, clasp their hands over their crotches, and look at me.

The one on the right licks his lips.

I bet he's the one who does the waterboarding.

From the manila folder, the suit removes an eight-by-ten photograph. He holds it up for me to see. It's a black-and-white shot of me and Declan getting into his giant helicopter.

"This is you."

"Are you kidding? I'd never wear those jeans. Totally last season."

He holds out another picture, this one of Declan and me in the kitchen the night of the ill-conceived poker party. Declan is holding my face in his hands. It looks like he's shouting, which he was.

How creepy that they've been watching us. Photographing us together. It gives me chills.

Oh god. Did we have the drapes open when we had sex?

"This is you."

"No. But whoever that poor girl is, I feel sorry for her. That guy is screaming right into her face. Looks like a lunatic, if you ask me."

"Oh, he's undoubtedly a lunatic," agrees the suit, nodding. "To the best of our knowledge, he's killed more than thirty-five men. And those are the ones we know about."

He looks at me expectantly.

I say, "Sounds like he's got a lot of unresolved issues. I suggest anger management classes."

He sets the folder and photographs aside. He folds his hands in his lap. He says calmly, "Your father is a patriot. Exceptional man. Exceptional military career. It would be such a pity if he were stripped of all his honors and thrown into prison for aiding and abetting a terrorist."

My dislike for this guy takes an elevator down to pure hatred, where it disembarks and settles in. I stare at him, all traces of humor vanished.

"Threatening my family isn't going to work."

"No? So you'd like your little sister, Riley, to spend some quality time with my associate here, Lance Corporal McAllister?" He gestures to the lip licker, who produces a lascivious grin.

Lance. Of course he had to be a *lance* corporal, the fucking asshole.

When I don't respond, the suit says, "Or how about your older brother, Drew? Perhaps his law practice needs a review from the state bar. I understand his ethics are what you'd call lacking. Something about sex with clients? Embezzling money? Bribing jurors?"

"Nice try. My brother's ethics are pristine."

He smiles his rabid-dog smile. "I'm sure we can manufacture something convincing."

"I'm sure you could. Government workers are always manufacturing some kind of bullshit to cover up their incompetence."

His smile grows wider. He knows I'm angry now. He smells blood in the air.

"And what about your friend, Natalie?" he says softly, eyes glittering. "How do you think she'd enjoy celebrating the rest of her birthdays inside a prison cell, thanks to you?"

I want to kill him. I want to kill him so much, I can almost hear his pathetic screams as he drowns in his own blood from the stab wound in his neck that I'll give him.

Take a deep breath and remember who the fuck you are.

I close my eyes, count to four, then decide I don't have time for the rest of the breathing exercise. I need to tell this guy to go fuck himself sooner than that.

Opening my eyes, I say calmly, "If you tried to put my friend in prison, her man would burn you alive. Then he'd burn Moose and Rocco here." I shoot a dismissive glance at the two burly, uniformed Marines. "Then he'd find your mothers and burn them alive, too. Your siblings, also. And your pets. And your houses, your cars, and the towns you grew up in. So I won't worry about her. She's covered.

"As for my sister, brother, and dad? Well, I can't control what happens to them. Life's a gamble, and I guess they rolled unlucky dice for being related to me. Besides, it really wouldn't be my fault. You're the douchebags who have the control. Whatever nasty thing happened would be on your conscience, not mine. So do what you have to do. Leave me chained to this chair forever. Lock me up and throw away the key."

After a calculated pause, the suit says, "There are worse things we could do to you than imprison you, Miss Keller. I'm sure you can imagine what they are."

Lance Corporal McAllister steps forward. He gazes down at me with a small, evil smile.

I almost laugh. Instead I heave a heavy sigh and nod my head. "I actually don't have to imagine. I'm very familiar with the particular brand of savagery that useless, worthless, dickless males enjoy. Go ahead, guys. Do your worst. I still don't know who Declan fucking O'Donnell is."

Nothing happens for several moments. Then a tinny male voice crackles over a hidden speaker in the ceiling.

"Put her in C-9."

The suit stands. Lance Corporal Fuckface walks behind me and unfastens my handcuffs from the chair. He hauls me to my feet with fingers like steel claws that dig into my biceps.

The suit says, "Have it your way, Miss Keller. The worst it is."

They drag me from the room.

I manage to kick the suit in the kneecap on the way out. He falls to the floor, howling.

What a sissy.

THIRTY-SIX

DECLAN

Three and a half days later

Where is she?" I roar, bursting through the conference room doors. *"Where the fuck is she?"*

"Easy, big guy," says Grayson, rising from his chair at the long mahogany table. He's got his hands up and an apologetic smile on his face. There are ten other men seated around the table, several of whom I recognize, a few I don't.

But I spot that ugly fuck, Thomas Aquinas, the head of the High Value Detainee Interrogation Group, right away.

Grayson jumps in front of me as I lunge in his direction, snarling. "Declan! Chill the fuck out!"

He's trying to get me to slow down, shoving and pushing me back with every ounce of his considerable strength, but I've got the demon of fury in my veins, thirsting for blood. Nothing on this earth is going to stop me from getting it.

I shove Grayson aside and punch Thomas in the face.

He topples backward in his chair with a cry, feet flying. He hits the conference room floor with a thud, rolls to one side, and starts flailing, trying to clamber to his hands and knees to crawl away. The fucking cockroach.

Before I can kick him in the gut, three men tackle me.

They take me down to the floor. I'm up within seconds, headed back to kick the life out of their boss.

I stop short when the remaining men at the table—now all on their feet—pull pistols from the holsters under their suit jackets and point them at me.

"Everybody calm down!" commands Grayson, holding his hands out. "He's a friendly! Put your weapons away! That's an order!"

Reluctantly, the men obey him. They glower and grumble, but obey.

Always the fucking peacemaker, this guy.

Breathing hard from rage, I point at him. "I'm holding you responsible for this. If there's even a tiny fucking scratch on her, if there's one minuscule bruise, I'll kill you *and* your piece-of-shite boss."

The man in question is still struggling to get to his feet. He's gripping the edge of the conference table like it's a life preserver and staring at me with all the whites of his eyes showing, holding his bleeding nose.

"I'll put you in prison, you maniac!" he screeches. "You can't come in here and assault members of the federal government!"

"I can and I did, and if you don't shut your piehole, I'll do even worse. Where is she?"

"She's in a holding cell," says Grayson in a tone meant to be soothing. It's fingernails down a chalkboard instead.

"A holding cell?" I thunder, infuriated. *You put my woman in a bloody holding cell?*

"She's fine. In fact, right now, she's sleeping. Okay? Take it easy, brother. Take it easy."

"Don't give me that bloody 'brother' shite, you traitorous fuck.

What the hell were you thinking by picking her up? I've been going out of my bloody head!"

"I know, and I'm sorry. But this was the only way we could vet her. We couldn't tell you about it in advance. You know the ropes."

Vet her? Oh, Jesus fucking Christ. "I said I potentially wanted to make her an asset! *Potentially!* I never gave you the green light!"

He shrugs, looking sheepish. "I told you I had to run it up the flagpole. This is what the top brass wanted. And now we know."

Sucking hard breaths into my lungs, I curl my hands into fists and try to contain the homicidal urges making me want to stab him repeatedly in the face until he's as unrecognizable as a pound of hamburger meat. "What do you know? What are you talking about?"

"He's talking about your little girlfriend!" shrieks Thomas, still kneeling on the floor. "She's as crazy as you are!"

I point at him, blood pulsing in my vision. "Say that again. Go ahead. Call her crazy one more time."

"What he means," says Grayson soothingly, putting a hand on my outstretched arm, "is that she passed with flying colors."

I lower my arm. When I only stare at him, he nods. "She re-fused to admit she knew you at all, even when we showed her the pictures."

"The *pictures*?"

"Don't get your hackles up. You know how this works. Would you like me to tell you more, or would you prefer to continue the rampaging-gorilla routine?"

"You can tell me on the way to where you're holding her. And so help me, God—"

"I know," he says drily. "If she's got even a minuscule bruise, you'll kill me. Copy that."

He heads to the door, knowing I'll follow him. On the way out of the room, I notice one of the men who pulled a gun on me has two black eyes and a white strip of medical tape across the swollen bridge of his nose.

Oh, baby. My fierce little lion. Hold on a bit longer, here I come.

We walk through a labyrinth of passageways, our footsteps echoing on the floor. Marines in fatigues nod at us as we pass. There's an elevator ride down, then we exit into a small room overlooking the cargo hold of the vessel.

It's a vast space. Three stories of steel-enforced walls the length of a football field. Metal shipping containers fill the main part of the floor, painted on the top and sides with a letter and a number in white.

"She's in C-9," says Grayson, pointing to a windowless red metal container.

"I'll kill you for this."

"Man, you know I don't call the shots. You start talking about making someone an asset, wheels start to turn."

"Why did you wait almost four bloody days to tell me where you were keeping her?"

"Standard operating procedure. Most people cave during the intake interview. The ones who pass that have to be isolated without food or water for seventy-two hours to see if that'll break them. Which it almost always does."

"Without food or water?"

He turns to me with a half smile. "You're focusing on the wrong shit, here, Dec. She's legit. Fucking hard core. She didn't even wobble."

"I could've told you that, you bloody wanker."

He chuckles. "She broke Cliff's nose on her way in. Took Aquinas down with a kick to the kneecap during her interview, too. The deputy director is impressed."

He picks up the receiver of a phone hanging on the wall and presses a number. "Discharge on C-9. Paperwork's been processed." He listens a moment, then says, "Copy that," and hangs up.

He turns to me. "It's gonna be a while. They'll clean her up, debrief her, and give her something to eat. After that, she's all yours."

I look out over the graveyard of shipping containers with a feeling like a hundred pounds of sandbags are on my chest. "She'll never forgive me for this."

"Yeah, she will."

He sounds confident. I shoot him a querying look. He smiles.

"No woman backs a man like she did you unless it's true love, brother. Just give her some space when you get her home. She'll get over it."

I mutter, "Enough with the 'brother' shite," but what I'm really thinking about are the two words he said right before that one.

One thing's for sure. If she doesn't love me, I'll find out fast.

The minute she buries a knife in my chest.

THIRTY-SEVEN

SLOANE

I'm asleep when the door to my cage opens.

"Miss Keller. Follow me, please."

A woman stands in the doorway. I can't see her face. She's just a dark figure backlit by light so bright, it makes me wince.

Sitting up on the thin mattress on the cold steel floor that passes for my bed, I raise a hand to shade my eyes against the glare. "Follow you where?"

My voice is a rasp. Dry and cracked, like my lips and throat. These bastards haven't given me any water.

"You're being discharged." She steps away, leaving the door open.

Discharged? Maybe that's a government term for "executed."

I debate with myself for a minute about whether or not to just go back to sleep. If they're going to kill me, they should have to come in here to do it. Why should I make it easier for them?

But nobody rushes in with a gun. No evil doctor with a syringe full of poison creeps in, leering. So curiosity eventually wins. I stand, holding my hands out for balance when the room starts to spin.

I haven't been without food this long since fat camp. I'm weak

and dizzy. My stomach is gnawing on itself. I have a new empathy
for supermodels, who probably feel like this all the time.

I shuffle out of the shipping container, past the big plastic bucket
I've been using as a toilet because otherwise I'd have to pee on the
floor. Aside from the mattress, bucket, and the black eye of a camera
on the ceiling, the space is empty. There are no mirrors, no lights,
no television, no furniture, no shower, no sink. They didn't even give
me a pillow.

I knew guys in college dorms who lived like this, but I like
things a little more luxurious.

The soldier who told me I'm being discharged waits patiently
for me a few yards away, standing in the narrow opening between
two tall rows of identical shipping containers. She's dressed in fatigues and combat boots. Her brown hair is wound into a tidy bun
at her nape. She's holding a clipboard.

"Are you the welcome committee? Because, boy, do I have some
complaints to lodge with you. This place is a *dump*."

"Compared to my last assignment, it's a palace."

I scoff. "Really? Where were you, Guantanamo?"

"Yes. Follow me, please." She turns and walks away.

Some people have no sense of humor.

I follow her past dozens of containers identical to the one I was
thrown in. Most are eerily silent, but from within maybe five or six
comes the sound of music. Though the walls of the containers are
made of thick steel, the music isn't muffled. It's so loud, it thumps.

It's the Meow Mix commercial theme song, a mind-numbing
chorus of *meow-meow-MEOW-meow* performed by a singing cat set
to a ragtime piano score.

I'm glad they didn't subject me to that. I definitely would've
cracked.

The woman stops in front of a metal door. She enters an impos-
sibly long code into a keypad on the wall, and the door unlocks.
She pushes it open, stands back, and gestures for me to go inside.

"Is this where you keep the gas showers and the ovens?"

Without a trace of emotion, she says, "This is the United States. There are no gas showers. We kill people in civilized ways."

When I arch my brows, she says, "By raising them on high-fructose corn syrup and fast food."

I think I'm starting to like this lady.

"Amen, sister." I walk past her into a long, narrow passageway lined on both sides with closed doors.

"We'll be going into number six. It's just down here, on the right."

She passes me, walking briskly to the door numbered six. Without waiting for me, she opens the door and disappears inside.

Okay. I'm game. I walk into the room and am hit with the mouth-watering scent of bacon.

I knew it. Now the real torture starts.

But I could be wrong. This room is very different from the one I left. It has comfy-looking chairs and a sofa on one side, and a long table draped in linens on the other. It's a mini buffet, with platters of food, both cold and hot.

There's also a first aid station with a blood pressure machine, a glass cabinet full of medical supplies, and—ominously—a defibrillator, one of those electrical devices that give jolts of electricity to restart a stopped heart.

The soldier indicates a chair in front of the first aid station that she wants me to sit in. I oblige her, fighting my instinct to lunge for the bacon. She takes my blood pressure, then my temperature, then opens a small fridge and hands me a bottle of cold water.

I'm too weak to twist off the plastic cap, so she does it for me.

"Small sips, or you'll throw it right back up because you're dehydrated. Your electrolytes are imbalanced enough as it is. I don't want you passing out on me."

So now she's Mother Teresa.

"When do I get my lollipop?"

A hint of a smile lifts her lips. Her voice low, she says, "I thought you'd do well. The guys had their money on Gray getting you to crack in under two minutes, but you struck me as someone who digs in her heels."

"Really? How could you tell?"

"I saw them bring you aboard. What a shit show. You managed to make eight trained Marines look like circus clowns."

I say drily, "Apparently, I do my best fighting when I'm under the influence of mind-altering drugs. I don't remember a thing about getting here. Which isn't exactly reassuring considering I had a brain bleed recently."

"I don't know about your brain, but there's nothing wrong with your fine motor skills, that's for sure."

She sounds like she's proud of me.

I'm curious about her until she says, "Let's get you some food," and she's instantly dead to me. All I can think about is stuffing my face.

She makes me a plate, sets it on the coffee table by the sofa, then exits the room. I wobble over to the food and fall on it like a farm animal at the trough.

When I'm finished, I collapse back onto the sofa and close my eyes. I lie there listening to my disgruntled stomach grumble and groan as it tries to digest the first food it's had in days, and wonder what's happening. Wonder why I've been let out of the cage.

Wonder what they're really going to do with me.

Because I know it won't be as simple as letting me walk away scot-free. Everything involving the government comes with a catch and miles of red tape.

"Declan O'Donnell is one of our finest espionage agents."

I open my eyes to see a middle-aged man with shoe-polish-black hair in a navy blue pinstripe suit sitting across from me in one of the chairs. I didn't hear him come in. Did I fall asleep? Or did he simply appear from thin air, like Dracula?

And what the hell did he just say about Declan?

Confused, I repeat, "Espionage?"

"It's another word for 'spy.'"

"No shit. I don't like you already."

"I was trying to be concise, not condescending."

"You failed."

He purses his lips and frowns at me. "Perhaps you'd like to sit up so we can talk more comfortably."

Talk. Here comes that catch. "I'm perfectly comfortable where I am, thank you."

He crosses his legs, plucking at a piece of nonexistent lint on his suit jacket.

I'm annoying him. Good.

As if I hadn't interrupted him at all, he continues from the beginning.

"Declan has been an invaluable asset to us for more than twenty years. One of our longest serving. I know him as a man of impeccable integrity, unfailing loyalty, and," he chuckles, "though his methods are sometimes crude, exceptional abilities."

Declan is a spy? Is that what he's saying? That can't be right. My brain isn't working.

Just go with it. He's waiting for you to say something.

"Meaning this Declan kills people well."

"Indeed. He's the Leonardo da Vinci of killers. Utterly efficient, utterly ruthless. As evolved to kill without remorse as a crocodile." Behind his wire-rimmed glasses and practiced demeanor of a friendly advertising executive, his gaze is a vulture's. "So imagine my surprise when I found out about you."

"I already told you guys. I don't know a Declan. Thanks for the food, though. Will I be going back to my cage now?"

He waves a hand like I'm being ridiculous. "You've passed the test. No need to continue the charade."

Sitting up is a struggle, but I eventually get there. *"Test?"*

"Did you think we'd let one of our most valued agents get romantically entangled without a vetting process?"

"Is that a rhetorical question? Because I have some feelings to share with you if it is."

"The answer is no. We would not. We don't take those kinds of risks. So you were brought here for evaluation."

I say nothing. I'm still dizzy and nauseated, and I might smell like pee. It's hard to concentrate on what this suit is saying, or what he wants from me, because a disbelieving chorus of *Declan is a spy?* is running through my head like a song on repeat.

Gazing at me with an odd expression, the suit says, "I didn't expect you to perform so well."

I realize that his weird expression is admiration and get a bad feeling about where he's going with this. "Um . . . thanks?"

"We'd like you to work for us."

I have to take a moment to let that ridiculous statement sink through my throbbing skull. "I already have a job, but I appreciate the offer."

He chuckles. "Not as a yoga instructor. In intelligence gathering."

"In other words, spying."

"Correct."

To buy some time for my brain to recover from that newest shock, I say, "Who's we?"

"The United States government."

"You mean the CIA?"

"The particular branch is immaterial."

"I'd like to know who I'd be working for."

"You'd report to a handler who'd give you your assignments. That's all you need to know at this point."

"Would I still have to pay taxes?"

"Yes."

"So what's the upside?"

"You'd be serving your country."

"I consider myself a citizen of the multiverse."

"I'm not joking, Miss Keller."

"Neither am I. I'd be a bad investment. When the aliens land, I'll be the first one to volunteer to head off with them to Mars."

He pauses to gather his fraying patience. "I'm not making myself clear. This isn't an offer. It's an order."

I smile condescendingly at him. "Too bad you're not the boss of me."

His expression sours. "If you refuse, you'll be administered an injection of potassium chloride that will induce cardiac arrest within seven minutes. It will be fatal. It will also be an excruciating seven minutes. Then we'll wrap your body in a biodegradable shroud enhanced with shark attractant and dump you into the sea. No part of you will ever be found."

"Wow. And here I thought we were getting along so well."

"You're exceptionally stubborn. I like that. I also like your spirit. In twenty-five years on this job, I've had thousands of enemy combatants pass through the various facilities I oversee. Ninety-one percent of them give us the information we're looking for within one day of arrival. Another four percent make it two days before they give in. You can see why I'm impressed."

"What about the other five percent?"

He smiles.

"Sleeping with the fishes, huh?"

"Such a quaint expression to describe something so unspeakably violent. Before you make your decision, there are two things I'd like you to keep in mind. First, refusal equals certain death."

"You already mentioned that."

"I thought it important enough to restate. Second, you're not the only one that applies to."

He lets that hang there for a moment, just to make sure I understand what he's threatening.

"You said Declan was one of your finest agents."

"And now he's one of our finest agents with a weakness. You."

I can tell he's serious. If I don't cooperate, both Declan and I will die.

Fucking bureaucrats.

"Oh, one other item. You'll end things between the two of you."

My pulse goes haywire. My hands turn clammy. My stomach clenches into a horrid little knot. We stare at each other for what feels like a long time in total silence interrupted only by the occasional rumble of my stomach.

Finally, I say, "The hell I will."

"I can't have one of my best agents distracted. Your relationship is a liability."

My voice rises. "I won't end it."

"You will, and you'll make up something that won't make him suspect we had this conversation. Perhaps that you did a lot of thinking while you were locked up and realized he wasn't the man for you."

Panic grips me. I'm both hot and cold, frozen in place but shaking violently. My voice shakes, too, when I say, "He won't believe it. He's too smart for me to pull it off convincingly."

"I have the utmost confidence in your ability to be convincing. After all, Declan's life is at stake." He smiles. "And it does seem as though you're quite taken with him, considering you'd rather starve to death alone in a shipping container than admit you'd ever met. I so admire that kind of loyalty. I know you'll do well for us."

He rises. His footsteps are whisper quiet against the floor. At the door, he pauses. I feel him looking back at me, but I can't tear my gaze away from the empty plate of food on the coffee table. I can't focus. I can hardly breathe.

Declan is a spy. I'm going to be a spy. And I have to end it between us. Convincingly.

Or he dies.

Maybe I'm still in the hospital with that brain clot, hallucinating everything.

"I'll give you some time to get it sorted. Don't take long, though. Best to rip off the Band-Aid quickly. I'll be in touch once it's done. And remember, we never spoke. Don't try to get creative and tell him about this conversation in some silly way like writing him a note. I'll know if you do."

Feeling sick, I say, "How would you know?"

"The same way I know the name of the boy who pushed you down the steps of the quad in school when you were fourteen and made you miscarry. It's my job. Welcome aboard, Miss Keller."

The door swings open and closed.

He's gone before he can see me vomit all over the floor.

THIRTY-EIGHT

DECLAN

I wait for her in another room down the hall from the first. In almost two hours of pacing, I manage to convince myself that I'll let her go when she asks me to.

Because she *will* ask me to. That's a given. There's no way in hell she can ever trust me again, not after this.

I can't let myself think about what she might have been through in the past few days. Deprived of food and water, thrown into a cold, black, windowless cell, threatened with who knows what . . . I can't think about how she must've suffered.

How she must hate me.

I just have to focus on getting her off this bloody ship and safely onto dry land.

A door finally opens. I spin around and see her standing in the open doorway. Our eyes lock. My heart stops dead in my chest.

She's barefoot. Wearing jeans and a red sweater, both wrinkled and stained. Her hair is a mess of snarls. Her face is pale and drawn.

Her gaze is haunted. She looks like she might have recently been crying.

My heart starts up again, beating painfully hard. I cross the room in a few long strides and swing her up into my arms. Without a word, she buries her face in my neck, shivering.

We take an elevator up to the flight deck. Neither of us speaks. I walk down a short passageway, then we're out in the cold ocean air.

I cross the flight deck to where the bird awaits. I help her in, buckle the safety harness around her, and put the headphones over her ears.

She closes her eyes and tilts her face toward the sun.

The flight back to the house seems endless. Mile after mile of ocean stretches beneath us before the shoreline finally comes into view. I land on the helipad and barely take the time to shut everything down before I've got her in my arms again.

I pass a shell-shocked-looking Kieran and Spider on my way into the house.

Kieran says in Gaelic, "How is the wee lass?"

"Alive," I answer curtly.

I leave them behind, wondering. They won't ask more, and I won't offer any other information. They think it was one of our enemies who rose from the sea to take her. They think I made a deal to get her back.

They can never find out otherwise.

Oh, what tangled webs we weave.

In the master bedroom, I ease Sloane onto the bed. She lies there looking up at me with those haunted eyes.

Why isn't she talking? Why won't she say anything? How the fuck did I let it come to this?

I sit on the edge of the bed beside her and carefully take her cold hand. "Are you hurt?"

She's silent for so long it scares me.

"They tried to make me talk about you."

I've never heard her sound like this. Weak. Hollow. Defeated.

"I know," I say, stroking a strand of hair off her forehead. "I'm so sorry. There's a lot I need to explain."

I have no idea where to start, though. Maybe it would help if I knew what they told her in the debrief. Or maybe I should stop worrying about myself for a change.

"Do you want to talk about this now? Do you need food? Should I let you rest?"

"I'm not hungry. I am tired, though. And I think it might be best if we didn't talk about it at all."

I say vehemently, "If they hurt you, I'll kill every one of them."

She closes her eyes and inhales slowly. Then she turns her head to the windows and gently pulls her hand from mine.

It feels like a kick to the chest.

"Sloane. Baby. Please talk to me."

She moistens her cracked lips. Sounding a thousand years old, she says, "I can't right now. I'm . . . I don't know what I am. Mainly tired. I really need to sleep."

All the breath in my lungs leaves in a rush. "Bloody hell. I'm so sorry. I had no idea they'd do this. I—"

"Stop."

I clench my jaw and sit stiffly, waiting. It's one of the most difficult things I've ever done.

After a fraught pause, she opens her eyes and looks at the ceiling. She says flatly, "I've had some quality thinking time over the past few days."

The tone of her voice makes my stomach roll over.

She's ending it.

"Sloane—"

"Just let me get it out."

"I can explain everything—"

"There's nothing to explain. If we stay together, I'll always be a target for stuff like this. First, it was MS-13. Now, it's the government. Someone will always be trying to get to me because of you."

"Hold on. Just tell me what they told you."

Her voice rises. "They threatened my dad and my siblings. And Nat, Declan. They threatened Nat. I can't risk their safety. And I won't go through something like that again."

She stops to take a breath. "So I'm going to take you up on that promise you made that you'd let me leave if I asked you to."

The floor drops out from under me. My entire body goes cold. When I speak, my voice is rough with pain. "Just like that?"

"It's like that Sun Tzu quote you told me when you found me watching TV after you were gone for three days. 'The wise warrior avoids the battle.' I'm gonna sit this whole battle out."

She turns her head and looks me square in the eye. Looks at me with piercing intensity.

My heart skips a beat. The cold in my body thaws, then turns boiling.

That wasn't the quote I told her. I know it. She knows it, too.

She's trying to tell me something.

But I need more information to understand what it is. I need to ask her more questions.

"Where will you go?"

"To see Nat first. After that, I'll go back home to Tahoe." A flicker of laughter shines in her eyes, but her face remains impassive. "It's time for me to settle down with a real boyfriend, not one of you mafia types. Someone a little more boring."

Boyfriend? Boring? She hates both those words. What the bloody hell is going on?

She sees my confusion. Moving casually, she encircles her right wrist with the thumb and index finger of her left hand. The other three fingers she spreads out like a fan.

I recognize the sign instantly. It's a tactical signal members of the military use to communicate silently with each other.

She's making the sign for enemy.

When my gaze flashes up to meet hers, she tugs on her left earlobe.

I put it together: an enemy is listening.

Then I remember Grayson telling me that the deputy director was impressed with her, and it all clicks.

That bloody cunt tried to make my woman turn on me.

But he doesn't know my lion like I do. He doesn't know how much she hates to be told what to do. How strong or fearless she is. How impossible it is to make her bend to your will.

She only bends willingly. Even then, she's still holding a sword.

Adrenaline floods my veins. My clever, clever girl. I want to laugh out loud, but that urge is cancelled by the rage I feel when I think of what I'm going to do to that son of a bitch.

Only, I have to be careful. I have to assume he's got ears everywhere. Maybe eyes, too. Kieran did a full security sweep before we moved in, but I don't know if he's been doing them every day, as he should. Over the past few days, I haven't exactly been on top of my game.

The only thing I could think of was Sloane.

Playing along, I say solemnly, "If that's what you really want."

When she exhales a slow, relieved breath, I know she can tell I understood her. She says, "It is."

"All right. I'll make the arrangements."

I stand, lean down and kiss her cheek, then whisper gruffly into her ear, "I adore you."

I leave the room without looking back. I go into my office, lock the door, and remove a small radio-frequency detector from a bottom drawer in my desk. I take my time sweeping the room for bugs. When I'm satisfied the space is clear, I take my cell phone from my pocket and dial a number I've memorized.

When the line is answered, I say, "Hello, Kazimir. This is Declan. I have a proposition for you."

THIRTY-NINE

SLOANE

*A*lmost a day passes before I see Declan again.

In the meantime, I sleep. I shower. I dress. I eat the food Kieran delivers. We don't speak to each other, I simply open the door to his knock and watch as he sets the tray on the coffee table. He leaves without meeting my eyes.

I have no idea what's happening, except that Declan is taking care of whatever needs to be taken care of. I know the message I was trying to transmit was received loud and clear.

If it wasn't, he never would've agreed to let me go so quickly. There would have been a fight, long and loud.

Because he's as stubborn as I am, the beautiful bastard.

On the morning of the second day, he appears in the doorway to the bedroom after a light knock. Dressed in his customary black Armani suit, he looks somber and so handsome it hurts.

"The flight to New York leaves in ninety minutes. We need to leave here within fifteen."

"I'm ready. I packed a bag. I hope it's all right that I'm taking some of the clothes you bought me. I left all the jewelry."

His eyes flash. They flash again when I tuck a strand of hair behind my ear and the diamond tennis bracelet he gave me sparkles on my wrist. I smile and pull the sleeve of my sweater down to hide it.

"It's fine," he says, his voice tranquil. "Shall we go?"

"Let's."

I don't know who we're playing this polite pantomime for, or if the black-haired man telling me he'd know if I told Declan about our conversation was only a hollow threat. But every game has its rules. I'm sure the spy game has plenty that involve covert surveillance. Better to play the part to a tee than be caught unprepared.

We take the helicopter to the private terminal at the airport. Declan's jet waits on the tarmac, the engines already running. He whisks me from one to the other with emotionless efficiency, like he's delivering a package for UPS.

At the bottom of the airstairs of his jet, he kisses me formally on both cheeks.

"Goodbye, Sloane."

He turns and walks away without a glance.

Pretending his cool demeanor doesn't hurt, even though it's a ruse, I trudge up the airstairs and take a seat in one of the big captain's chairs in front near the galley. On the table between the chairs is a book.

The Prophet, by Kahlil Gibran. One of the pages is dog-eared. When I turn to it, a single passage is highlighted.

Love knows not its own depth until the hour of separation.

My throat constricted, I whisper, "Me, too, gangster. Me, too."

The cabin door closes. The plane takes off. I buckle my lap belt, close my eyes, and do box breathing until I realize that stupid shit never works.

Then I raid the booze cabinet in the galley and get drunk on a five-hundred-dollar bottle of champagne, because I miss him already.

FORTY

NAT

*K*age refused to let me go to LaGuardia to pick up Sloane. He wouldn't go, either. He said it was too dangerous. Said everything was too volatile right now, and until it all settled down, I wasn't leaving his sight.

I put up a fight, of course. She's my best friend, I said. She needs me.

He said the only thing Sloane needs is a container big enough to keep all the broken hearts she collects.

Then I realized it could be a trap. Declan has already killed off every other mafia boss Stateside over the last few weeks. Drawing Kage out into the open would be the perfect way to get the last one standing.

I only agreed not to go because of that. Because the thought of losing Kage is as terrifying to me as the thought of losing Sloane.

He finally had to delete the security video of her abduction from the parking garage. I watched it so many times, I nearly wore out my tear ducts.

By the time Kage's driver calls to say he's en route from the airport with Sloane, I'm having a panic attack.

"Did he say how long it would be?" I demand, wringing my hands as I pace back and forth in front of the big executive chair in the office.

"Take it easy, baby," he says softly, watching me with those sharp dark eyes that never miss anything. "Come sit on my lap."

"I can't sit. I'm freaking out. What if she's hurt?"

"She's not hurt."

"But how do you *know*?"

"Because she's indestructible, like Styrofoam peanuts."

"Or your ego."

His eyes grow heated. "Is that sass I hear?"

"Don't act like you don't love it."

In a throaty voice, he says, "Come here and let me show you how much."

Sighing, I turn and pace the other direction. "Later. Sorry. I'm too distracted. This is the longest I've gone without talking to her since I was five years old, and I feel like I'm missing a limb. She sounded okay when we talked on the phone—like her usual self—but that feels like a million years ago. And what if it was an act? What if he was *forcing* her to sound happy? What if—"

Kage reaches out, pulls me down onto his lap, and wraps his hand around my jaw. Gazing into my eyes, he says, "She's fine, baby."

He kisses me deeply. I instantly relax, melting against his big hard body, loving the feel of his mouth.

"Better?" he whispers when we come up for air.

I hide my face in his neck. "Better. If he hurt her, will you please kill him?"

He exhales. "I can see there won't be any peace around here if I don't."

On his desk, his cell phone rings. My heart starts pounding. I jump off his lap and stare at the phone with my hands on either side of my face, biting my lip.

Shaking his head, Kage swings the chair around and reaches for it. He answers without saying anything, which is a weird thing he does, then listens for a moment. Then he hangs up and looks at me.

"She's on her way up."

I make a little noise of joy and terror and tear out of the room to the elevator landing.

The front door is a bank of elevators. We're on the top floor of a high-rise building.

From his position sprawled on the living room floor, Mojo lifts his head and looks at me. He woofs in solidarity, then promptly falls back asleep.

I hold my breath as the elevator slows to a stop. The doors slide open, and there she is.

Looking like she's returning from a yoga retreat in hell.

It isn't her outfit, which is a beautiful cream cashmere sweater, designer skinny jeans, and sky-high heels, or her face, which is as pretty as ever. Though maybe thinner.

It's her eyes.

Her normally clear green eyes—her normally *dry* clear green eyes—are welling with some kind of strange watery substance that if I didn't know her better would think is tears.

My heart flip-flops. I say hesitantly, "Sloane?"

Her face crumples. She drops the bag she's carrying. She hiccups, says loudly, "How the fuck are you, sis?" and throws her arms around me.

I smell alcohol and am swamped with relief.

She's only drunk, not crying. Crying would mean it's the end of the world.

I blurt, "I'm good, I was so worried, I can't believe that bastard took you, Kage will kill him if he hurt you, oh my god, I missed you so much, *are you okay?*"

"Great. I'm *great,* babe, simply *marvelous.*" She laughs. It sounds crazed.

I pull away and hold her at arm's length. Inspecting her expression, I say, "You're giving me the willies."

"Girl," she hiccups, "same."

Frantic again, I look her up and down. "Sloane, talk to me! Are you hurt?"

She nods vigorously. "It feels like all my skin has been peeled off, and I've been thrown into boiling water, and there's a live wire in there, too, so I'm getting electrocuted *while* I'm being boiled alive. No. No, no, that's not it. It feels like I'm being suffocated and roasted over hot coals and pushed off a very tall building, all at the same time. It's awful. It's the worst! How the hell do you deal with it?"

Now I'm totally confused. "Deal with what, honey? What the heck are you talking about?"

From behind me, Kage says, "Sounds to me like she's talking about being in love."

We both look at him. Then we look at each other. Then Sloane says wearily, "Oh, fuck."

I shout, "Shut the front door! *You're in love with your kidnapper?*"

She makes a face. "I mean . . . maybe? How do you know if it's really love?"

Kage folds his arms over his chest. "It's only love if you're willing to die for him."

Her moan is faint, miserable, and even more alarming than the almost-but-not tears.

"Oh, no. Sloane, you *don't* have feelings for him. This is a thing that happens to kidnapped people sometimes. They develop sympathy for their captors. It's called Stockholm syndrome, and it's . . . Why are you laughing?"

"Long story. Can someone please get me a drink? I think I'd like to spend the next several days in a coma."

She walks past me into the living room and throws herself face-down onto the sofa. I look helplessly at Kage, who somehow doesn't seem surprised by this turn of events.

"Better look after that," he says with a chin jerk in her direction. "I'll get you girls some whiskeys. Look like you could use it."

He kisses me on the forehead, then ambles off toward the kitchen. I hurry over to Sloane, kneel beside her on the floor next to the sofa, and pet her hair.

She turns her head and looks at me. She sniffles. "You know what the worst part is?"

"What?"

"I *like* him. He's smart. And funny. Oh my god, that dry sense of humor. It's exactly like mine! And he's as stubborn as me, too. More. You wouldn't believe how stubborn the man is. He's practically a mule."

Her face screws up again. She whimpers. "Like one of those mules they take tourists to the bottom of the Grand Canyon on."

I'm not sure what's happening, but there's no way she's in love with her kidnapper. She doesn't fall in love. It's simply not something she does. And not with *him*.

I wonder if this is some kind of decompression thing that happens after a traumatic event? I have no idea what to say, so I just make a soothing noise and continue petting her hair.

She rolls onto her back and flings an arm over her eyes. "And he smells good. When he's not smoking, that is. And he's generous. God, you should've seen the jewelry! Here, look at this."

She thrusts her arm at me, displaying a fat diamond tennis bracelet I wouldn't wear outside for fear of being mugged.

"He bought you that?"

"Yes. And clothes. So many clothes. La Perla lingerie. Cashmere sweaters in every color. Thirteen-hundred-dollar jeans, for fuck's sake. Who does that for their captive? And he protected me from MS-13! He saved my life!" She groans. "And when I was in the hospital—"

"Hospital?" I repeat, alarmed. She ignores me.

"—he stayed with me and told me a bedtime story, and even though he said I looked like a camel, he didn't really mean it. And when the nurse said I was pregnant—"

"Pregnant?"

"—he called Stavros to come get me. He didn't want to, but he did, because he thought Stavros was the baby daddy and it was the right thing to do, but when he found out Stavros wasn't the baby daddy, he kidnapped me *again*!"

I shout, *"Who's the baby daddy?"*

She bypasses that and continues nonstop with the litany of Declan's positive attributes until she exhausts herself—it takes a while—and falls silent.

I sit there stunned.

A lot has happened since she's been gone.

And, quite clearly, she's been having sex with Declan. *Emotional* sex.

The kind she never has.

"Holy shit," I say quietly. "You *are* in love with him."

After a thoughtful moment, she becomes completely calm. "Yes. How awful. Do you have any cyanide in the house, by chance? If this is what love feels like, I'd like to kill myself immediately."

I wave that off because she's only being dramatic, and drama is her middle name. "But, if you're in love with him . . . why are you here?"

Her silence seems oddly fraught. "What did Kage tell you?"

"Only that Declan called and said he was bringing you back. I was too busy having a mental breakdown to get into the particulars. Why?"

She sits up abruptly and looks at me. "You know I love you, right?"

I blink. "Okay, you're really starting to freak me out now."

She takes my hands and squeezes them. "Just listen for a sec." She draws a breath, releases it slowly, closes her eyes. "This thing . . ." She pauses for a hiccup, then starts over. "This thing with me and Declan is complicated. His life is complicated."

I say drily, "Tell me about it. Loving a criminal isn't exactly a walk in the park. The amount of gunfire you have to get used to is ridiculous."

Sloane opens her eyes and gives me the strangest look. One I've never seen before, like she's trying to decide what to say.

Or what not to say.

"No matter what happens, I want you to know that you're my best friend, and I love you. No one and nothing will ever come between us."

I wrinkle my forehead. "Is this about the baby?"

"There's no baby."

"You're not pregnant?"

"No."

"I'm very confused."

"I'm here because Declan needed to take care of some business, and it wasn't safe for me to be around him while he did."

With a deep sense of surprise, I realize what she's saying. "But he thought you'd be safe with Kage?"

"Yes. Well, sort of." She winces. "Like I said, it's complicated."

"So uncomplicate it for me."

She exhales a slow breath, then murmurs regretfully, "I can't."

Now I'm even more confused. "Did he give you an ultimatum? Like it was him or me or something?"

"No. He said he'd never make me choose." She looks down at our hands. Her voice softens. "But he thought you might."

I say vehemently, "No way."

When she glances up at me, I insist, "No damn way, Sloane. I don't care whose dick you're sucking, you'll always be my best friend."

After a beat of silence, she drops her head to our joined hands and dissolves into laughter.

I make a face at the top of her head. "I'm glad one of us thinks this is funny."

She raises her head and grins at me. "If I didn't laugh, babe, I'd have to shoot myself."

Kage returns from the kitchen with two tumblers of whiskey. When he hands them to us, I say, "Honey, what did Declan tell you when he called you about why he was bringing Sloane back?"

He answers without hesitation. "That he had to take care of some business, and it wasn't safe for her to be around."

I narrow my eyes at him. "Why didn't you tell me that before?"

"You were already climbing the walls with worry. Wasn't gonna add to that."

I glance at Sloane, who looks oddly guilty, then back at Kage. "What else did he say that you didn't tell me?"

He folds his arms over his massive chest and says in a disapproving tone, "That your Styrofoam-peanut girlfriend is the love of his life."

My mouth drops open. "Wait. Are you guys *friends* now?"

"No. But he did me a huge favor, so we agreed on a truce for the time being."

"What?" I leap to my feet, dropping the glass of whiskey. *"You're not at war anymore?"*

"Not for the moment. We'll see how long that lasts." With a dark look in Sloane's direction, he says, "He's a wily one, that Irish bugger. Got lots of tricks up his sleeves."

The smile that lifts Sloane's lips is small and mysterious.

Aghast, I look back and forth between them. "You guys are keeping secrets from me!"

Kage pulls me into his arms. "I don't keep secrets from you, baby. You want me to tell you exactly what he said, I'll repeat it word for word."

"You're damn straight you will," I say forcefully, winding my arms around his neck. Even when I'm mad at him, he's irresistible.

He kisses me softly, but it quickly turns passionate. I stand on my tiptoes to get closer. He reaches down and grips my ass with his big hands, pulling me against his crotch. A growl of pleasure rumbles through his chest.

Sloane says drily, "I'm still here, kids. Just so you know."

I break away from Kage, grinning, and look at her. "That reminds me. What do you think of blush for the color of your maid of honor dress?"

Sloane's mouth drops open. Her eyes go wide. "You're getting *married*?"

Kage frowns. "You didn't notice the rock? I told you it was too small, baby."

"It's ten carats, honey. Any more and I'd need a wrist brace."

Sloane rises from the sofa, grabs my hand, and gapes at my platinum-and-diamond engagement ring. She says loudly, "I thought it was a fucking cocktail ring!"

"That's it," says Kage, bristling. "I'm getting you something bigger."

Sloane is still staring in shock at my hand. She looks up at me, eyes wide.

"Speaking of complicated . . . my plus-one for the wedding might present a small problem for the rest of your guests."

"Don't worry. We'll make everyone check their guns at the door."

Sloane's eyes shine. "I love you, sis."

"I love you, too. Now let's sit back down. I want you to tell me everything that's happened since you've been gone, including what the hell the deal is with this baby of yours."

Kage says loudly, "Baby? What *baby*?"

Sloane and I look at each other and smile.

FORTY-ONE

SLOANE

A week goes by. I don't hear from Declan. I try not to worry about him, but fail spectacularly. Meanwhile, Nat and I are like a couple of sorority girls, staying up late watching movies, drinking wine, and obsessing over boys.

Except our boys are dangerous grown men who do bad things for a living.

On day eight, I'm watching the ten o'clock news on TV in the guest bedroom when a report comes on about the sudden death of the deputy director of the FBI. At only forty-eight years old, he succumbed to a fatal heart attack at his home in Virginia.

They found him in bed. His housekeeper said she thought he was sleeping late and left him alone when she arrived to clean in the morning.

The picture on the screen is of the black-haired man who offered me the job as a spy.

I sit bolt upright in bed, spilling my wine all over the comforter.

I know it's Declan's doing. I just don't know how.

Ten minutes later, Kage knocks on my bedroom door. "You up?"

Wearing one of Natalie's nightgowns, I yank open the door and stare at him.

"Your man called. He wants you ready to leave in thirty. I told him to make it in the morning, but he said he couldn't wait that long."

My heart beats so hard, I have to press a hand over my chest. "I'll be ready. Is he coming here?"

"Unbelievably, yes."

"Why is that unbelievable?"

He simply looks at me.

"Oh. You could kill him."

"Yes."

"But you won't."

"No, I won't."

We look at each other for a moment, until I say, "Thank you."

He huffs out an aggravated breath. "Do you have any idea what would happen to me if I harmed him now?"

"Yes. Nat would surgically remove your balls."

"Correct." He pauses. His dark eyes grow darker. "But my men aren't held to the same standard."

"Understood. Honestly, I think he'd be disappointed in you if it were too easy."

He nods thoughtfully. "Tell him I said I'd love to know how he came by the information he gave me."

"What information?"

"That the FBI had been compiling a file on me going back a dozen years with the goal of putting me in prison. He sent me everything. Apparently, they were getting damn close. But somehow, all that information is gone now. Wiped clean like it never existed in the first place."

His dark eyes drill into mine. "You know anything about that?"

"No," I say without hesitation, not flinching under his penetrating gaze. "I don't know anything about that."

After a moment, he says drily, "And even if you did, you wouldn't tell me."

I say softly, "It's not out of disrespect for you."

"I know what it is. And I gotta say, I didn't think you had it in you."

"You and me both."

He smiles, shaking his head. "All right. Get your things together and say goodbye to Nat."

When he turns to leave, I say, "Kage?"

He turns back, waiting.

"How can you be sure all the information about you is gone now?"

His smile is small, so small it's almost nonexistent. "Your Irishman isn't the only one with a contact inside the bureau."

He knows someone who works inside the FBI? Oh shit. What does that mean? Does he know Declan's a spy?

Panic makes my heart beat like thunder. It's difficult to keep my expression perfectly neutral, but I think I manage it.

Kage's smile grows wider. "When I told him that, there was this weird pause on the other end of the line. He was probably wearing the same expression you're wearing right now."

I wait until he's out of sight before I collapse against the wall.

Down in the parking garage of the building, Nat and I stand beside each other, holding hands behind a line of armed Russians. Kage stands in front of his men, arms crossed over his chest.

When a big black Escalade pulls in, the men raise their rifles and point them at the car.

Picturing Declan dying in a hail of bullets right in front of me, I smother a gasp and squeeze Nat's hand tighter.

The SUV pulls to a stop. Declan opens the driver's door and gets out. His eyes find mine. The hunger in them is palpable.

Beside me, Nat murmurs, "Whoa. His eyes are so blue."

Kage shoots her a sour look over his shoulder.

Declan walks slowly around the front of the SUV, adjusting his tie and licking his lips as he looks straight at me, ignoring everyone else and their guns.

"That's far enough," orders Kage.

Declan stops. The two men assess each other for a moment. Kage's men are restless, fingers on triggers, itching to pull. The tension in the air is so thick, I want to scream. Nat's hand in mine trembles.

Only Declan and Kage remain calm.

Maintaining eye contact with Kage, Declan says, "Say goodbye to your girlfriend, baby."

His voice is smooth and untroubled, but I hear the need underneath. It fills me with something buoyant and expansive, like helium.

Nat and I throw our arms around each other and hug.

She whispers into my ear, "Holy cow, he's intense."

"Tell me about it."

"Are you sure this is what you want?"

"More sure than I've ever been of anything."

"Because the only time I talked to him, he was threatening to dump your mutilated body on our doorstep."

"He's the only person I've ever met who's more dramatic than me. But he's actually a pussycat. I promise."

She sighs. "Call me the minute you get settled."

"I will. I love you."

"I love you, too."

I give her a final squeeze, then let her go and turn to Kage. "Take care of her for me."

"You know I will."

"And thank you."

He glances back at Declan, and his voice gains a dark edge. "Don't thank me yet. This isn't over."

Nat warns softly, "Honey."

I kiss his rough cheek and try not to smile. Declan opens the passenger door for me, and I hop in.

"Seat belt," he says gruffly, his eyes locked on mine.

I missed you, too.

We pull away without a shot being fired. I watch Nat and Kage receding in the side mirror and wonder how this tale of friends, lovers, and enemies will play out without one of us eventually getting hurt.

Honestly, I don't think it's possible.

In a story as twisted as ours, someone always dies in the end.

FORTY-TWO

DECLAN

On the ride to the airport, neither of us speaks. I watch her from the corner of my eye as she looks out the window at the city lights passing by, but I don't press her to talk. She's in her head, working on knots. I know better than to interrupt her.

The moment we're in the cabin of my jet, I pull her into my arms and kiss her deeply.

She responds by making a small sound of relief and sagging against me, as if her knees are giving out.

I fist a hand in her hair. She clings to my shoulders. We kiss in hot desperation until the airstairs fold up and the cabin door closes. Then she opens her eyes and stares deep into mine.

In a breathy voice, she says, "So you're a spy for the U.S. government."

"No. I'm a spy for the Irish government."

She takes a moment to digest that, blinking slowly in surprise. "A double agent?"

"More like a free agent. Nobody knows what I'm really up to."

After an astonished pause, she exhales a slow breath, shaking her head. "That explains a lot."

"So it's settled, then."

"What is?"

"We're getting married."

After a beat, she hides her face in my chest and dissolves into laughter.

I caress her hair and smile. "Where should we go on our honeymoon?"

"Where's the closest insane asylum?"

"I'm being serious."

"So am I."

I say firmly, "It's not up for discussion."

"You have no idea how women work, do you?"

"You're not the typical woman."

"There's zero chance we're getting married."

"Why, you want a three-year courtship followed by the fluffy white wedding dress and the white picket fence?"

"Fuck no."

"I didn't think so. It's settled."

"Declan!"

"Enough for one night, woman. You can yell at me about it later."

When she remains stiff and resistant in my arms, I add softly, "Please."

"Oh, you're *evil*."

"You have no idea."

She says drily, "I think I have a clue."

I kiss her again, this time even harder.

It's not altitude that makes me feel like I'm flying, because we're not even up in the air yet.

FORTY-THREE

SLOANE

When we get back to the beach house on Martha's Vineyard, it's very late. Or very early, depending how you look at it. Spider and Kieran are at the front gate, rifles in hand.

I give them a little wave. Spider smiles and tips up his chin. Kieran sends me a jaunty salute, grinning.

"They seem like they're in good moods," I note as we drive through the gate.

Declan says, "That's because their fearless leader has returned."

"Aw. It must be a good feeling for you to have such loyal men."

His voice turns dry. "I wasn't talking about me."

That makes me smile.

We park in the circular driveway. In front of the entrance to the house, ten more armed men await. One of them opens the passenger door before Declan is even out of the driver's seat and helps me from the car.

I recognize him. He was one of the men in the kitchen the night I almost cut off my pinkie to save Spider's.

Inclining his head, he says something in Gaelic.

I ask Declan what it was once we're inside.

His smile is amused. "Roughly translated, 'Welcome home, my queen.'"

"Really? How fantastic. Can you tell all the guys to call me that?"

"No."

"Okay. I'll have Kieran tell them for me."

He chuckles, then takes my hand and tugs me along, headed for the master bedroom. Just to tease him, I yawn. "I think I'll take a nice long bath before bed."

"You can take it after."

I ask innocently, "After what?"

He throws me a smoldering look. "After I show you why you want to be my wife."

Pushing open the bedroom door, he pulls me inside, then kicks the door shut behind him. He doesn't bother with any other explanation, he simply grabs me and kisses me, hard.

I break away, breathlessly laughing. "Did someone miss me?"

Holding my head in his hands, he says gruffly, "Aye. You and that smart mouth and that perfect arse of yours. I almost went bloody mad. I never want to be apart from you that long again."

My heart pounds with happiness. I look up into his beautiful blue eyes, so full of adoration, and can't help the stupid smile that takes over my face. "I think that can be arranged . . . sir."

His lids lower. A muscle flexes in his jaw. He licks his lips then kisses me again, holding my head as I wrap my arms around his waist. He drinks deep from my mouth, making a masculine sound of pleasure in his throat.

When the kiss ends, we're both breathing raggedly.

"I have a homecoming present for you," he whispers.

"Oh, good. How many carats is it?"

He cocks a brow. "How many carats do you want for your ring?"

"I wasn't talking about a ring. There are plenty of other pieces of jewelry besides rings." I smile sweetly. "Like tiaras, for instance. Have you seen the one the Duchess of Cambridge wore for her wedding to Prince William?"

He's trying not to smile, but not managing it. "Aye."

"Like that. Only bigger."

"So a crown."

"Now you're getting the picture."

"I knew from the second I laid eyes on you that you were high-maintenance. Come over here."

Taking my hand again, he leads me over to the bed. Then he stands silently, watching my face as I look at the carefully lined-up display on the silk duvet cover.

A flush of heat blooming over my chest, I say faintly, "That's quite the collection."

He slides his hand slowly up my spine and grips the back of my neck. Bending close to my ear, he says, "Choose your favorite."

My nipples tighten. My mouth goes dry. Between my legs, a pulse of heat blooms to match the one heating my upper body. *Oh god. I'm going to pass out.*

I don't want to miss all the fun, though, so I force myself to take slow breaths as I look over the whips, floggers, riding crops, and paddles lined up from one edge of the mattress to the other.

I point at one in red-and-black leather with a braided handle and long leather tassels dangling from the end.

Massaging my neck, Declan makes a low sound of approval. "I like that one, too. Take off your clothes."

He stands back, folds his arms over his chest, and gazes hotly at me.

Waiting.

Holy cheese and rice, this man knows how to welcome a girl home properly.

I slip off my coat and let it fall to the floor. My hands shaking, I unbutton my blouse. It's long-sleeved white silk, one that I brought with me to New York when I first went to visit Nat, what feels like a lifetime ago. All my clothes were packed in the trunk of the Bentley that I was taken from, and Nat kept them for me at their house.

I make a mental note to ask Declan later what happened to the Betsey Johnson pink tulle skirt I was wearing that night, then clear my head of all thoughts and slip the blouse off my shoulders.

My bra follows it to the floor.

Declan stares at me with avid eyes as I unbutton the fly of my jeans and pull the zipper down. Licking his lips, he watches as I take them off. When I shimmy out of my panties and kick them aside, he does nothing for a long moment but stare at my naked body.

Then he walks an excruciatingly slow circle around me.

From behind, he brushes my hair off my neck. He kisses the nape, then moves his mouth to the side of my throat and gently bites me there, sliding his other hand around my front and down between my legs.

Standing behind me, he growls hotly into my ear, "This is mine. Say it."

His big hand covers my sex and squeezes.

Breathing hard in anticipation, I whisper, "It's yours."

I get a light slap between the legs for my omission.

I jump and blurt, "It's yours, *sir*."

"Aye, baby. Mine. And these."

He slides his hand up my belly to my left breast, which he also squeezes, then the right, thumbing over my nipples until they're aching for his mouth.

"Yes, sir. They're yours."

A low, pleased growl rumbles through his chest. He slides his hand up to the middle of my sternum, pressing it flat over my throbbing heart.

"And this," he whispers, nuzzling my neck. "Is this mine, too, baby?"

I inhale a hitching breath and close my eyes, leaning back against his chest. My entire body thrums with electricity. Emotion courses through my veins like fire. My skin is so sensitized, I think I can feel every fiber of his suit jacket against my shoulder blades.

"Yes, sir. All of me, sir. All of me is yours."

He exhales a rough breath against my skin. Fisting one hand into my hair and winding the other around my throat, he pulls my head back and kisses me.

I open my mouth and let him take and take and take, feeling his erection jut into my ass, knowing that soon he'll give me what I need and barely being able to contain myself from begging for it.

When he breaks the kiss, he says, "Don't move, or you'll be punished."

He walks around to the dresser on the left side of the bed and opens a drawer. He leans down and removes something from it. Turning back to me, he's holding a pair of handcuffs in one hand and a black velvet blindfold in the other.

"On your knees."

His voice is so hot and dark it makes a shiver run through me. It's his alpha voice, the dominant one. I react to it like Pavlov's dog and start salivating as I sink to the floor.

He strolls over to me, taking his time, knowing the longer he makes me wait, the more my need will grow. I don't understand how no one before him, not a single man, ever understood this about me. I didn't even understand it about myself.

He's unlocked doors inside me I didn't realize were closed or were there in the first place.

"Give me your hands."

I lift my arms and present my hands, wrists together. He snaps the handcuffs around them, cinching them tight. Then he bends down and slides the blindfold over my eyes, adjusting the elastic in the back so it's snug and I can't see a thing.

He steps away, leaving me shivering on my knees, swallowing convulsively, blinded.

"Perfect," he murmurs.

Between my legs, I'm soaking wet. I want to reach down and touch my clit to see if it's as swollen as it feels, but he hasn't given me permission to, so I simply wait and tremble, feeling gloriously alive.

I hear the slither of fabric. The *zizz* of a zipper being drawn down. He's taking off his clothes. It's taking him forever.

I'm so turned on, I'm in danger of exploding.

Then his voice is near my ear. "I'm going to fuck you while you're bound and blindfolded, sweet girl. But first I'm going to eat your pussy and turn that perfect arse of yours bright red."

My exhalation is a moan.

"If you come before I allow it, I won't be pleased. Do you want to please me?"

I blurt something. Babble it, more like. I think it's an affirmative, but I honestly couldn't say for sure until Declan replies, "Good girl."

How those two simple words make me shake. How they make emotion expand inside my chest until it's painful.

He smooths a hand over my hair. Kisses me softly on the forehead. Tweaks my hard nipples until I'm panting. Then he pulls me to my feet and helps me over to the bed. He pushes me flat on top of the collection of sex toys and holds me down with a hand pressed against the middle of my back.

His voice rough with emotion, he says, "You own me, Sloane. Every corner of my worthless black soul. Every piece of my corrupt black heart. You own it all, and you always will. I'm your slave, not the other way around. Never forget it."

Then he gives me such a forceful whack with the leather whip, I scream.

"Tell me if you want me to stop," he says through gritted teeth, and whips me again.

My moan is loud and broken. My ass burns and my pussy throbs. My nipples are tight and tingling. "More," I beg. "Please, sir. Again."

He says something in Gaelic, something that sounds like praise. I get another blow, and another. Pain sears along my backside, followed by heat, followed by a powerful pulse of pleasure.

I might be able to come with this and nothing else but his words.

He rolls me roughly to my back, forces my thighs apart, and shoves his face between my legs, latching on to my engorged clit with his greedy mouth and sucking.

Arching, I groan and bury my hands into his hair.

He slides a big finger inside me and fucks me with it while he eats me and I writhe helplessly against the bed.

"So fucking beautiful," he growls, pausing to bite the tender flesh on the inside of my thigh. "My beautiful girl. Say you need me to fuck you."

"I need you to fuck me, sir. Please, please, please."

He goes back to licking and sucking my clit, reaching up to pinch my nipples as he does. It feels so good, I cry out his name.

He rolls me back over to my belly and whips my ass again. The slim leather straps crack over my skin with a sharp, whistling noise that sounds like the most beautiful music I've ever heard.

Desperate for relief, I break and start to grind against the bed.

Abandoning the whip to the floor, Declan drags me up to my knees and spanks my ass and upper thighs with his bare palm. He stops only to fondle my drenched pussy and tweak my clit before spanking me again.

I'm sobbing. Begging. Crying out deliriously, trying so hard to be good and not come. Trying to please him because at this moment, it's all that matters to me in the world.

He's my world, and everything in it.

The bed dips with his weight. He grips my hip in one hand and guides his hard cock to my entrance with the other.

Breathing hard, he commands, "Ask your master nicely to let you come, sweet girl."

I whisper brokenly, "Please let me come on your beautiful hard cock, sir. Master—master—please—"

He shoves inside me with a grateful groan and starts to fuck me fast and deep, pulling me back into his cock with every hard thrust of his hips. It sends shock waves of pleasure through my body, starting in my pussy and spreading everywhere, fast. I'm breathing in short gasps, my face buried in the duvet and my breasts swinging. His grunts of pleasure ring in my ears.

When he starts to spank me as he's fucking me, I climax.

Bucking and crying out, I come so hard, he curses. He reaches around and strokes my clit, making me convulse even harder around his cock. He's buried so deep inside me, he feels every pulse and squeeze. He groans, dropping his forehead to my spine as he continues to fuck me through my orgasm.

Then he's coming, too, bent over me, driving into me with chest-deep grunts, propped up on his elbows with his hands tangled in my hair.

Shuddering, he gasps my name.

And it's like a dam breaks inside me. A lifetime of built-up emotion just cracks through my ribs and blows me apart.

I burst into tears.

"Angel," he says, panting and alarmed. "Baby, why are you crying?"

I wail, "I'm crying because I love you!"

Incredibly, the man starts to laugh.

It's a soft chuckle at first, but it quickly builds to genuine, chest-shaking laughter. Laughter that just might get him killed.

He withdraws, rolls me to my back, and settles himself between my thighs. He pushes inside me again with a low moan. Then he pulls the blindfold off my face and kisses the tip of my nose.

Gazing deep into my watering eyes, he says, "That's the first bloody thing you've said that makes any sense."

Then he kisses me and tells me he loves me, too, and I cry even harder.

FORTY-FOUR

SLOANE

When I open my eyes, it's morning.

I'm on my side, facing the windows. The curtains are drawn, but a sliver of light peeks beneath, spreading golden sunbeams across the floor. Declan slumbers behind me, his breaths deep and slow, one arm thrown over my waist. His nose is buried in my hair.

I'm not a particularly religious person, but I do believe in miracles. I know there are so many things we cannot understand, but that have the power to move us regardless. Mysterious things. Wondrous things. Things of great beauty that speak to the soul.

Things that heal us in places that have been broken so long, we thought they were lost forever.

Lying in this warm bed in this quiet room with this beautiful man, I feel miracles all around me.

Declan stirs, stretching his legs. His arm tightens around my waist. His lips find my nape, and he gently kisses me there.

His voice thick with sleep, he says, "You camels snore something wicked."

I start to laugh.

"It's not funny. I barely got a wink of sleep."

"You'll live."

I roll over in his arms and smile at him. He returns it, smoothing my hair from my face.

He murmurs, "Good morning."

"Good morning to you."

Adjusting his head on the pillow, he lets his gaze travel all over my face. He sighs softly in contentment. "Thank goodness I didn't become a priest."

I arch my brows. "Yes, that would have been a poor career choice, considering your tendency to shoot people."

"I almost did, though. I planned on pursuing my master's in Divinity, but went into the military instead."

I stare at him, certain he's joking. "Really? You?"

He chuckles. "Aye. I wasn't always a hard-ass. Once upon a time, I was very much the romantic." A cloud passes over his eyes. "But life disabused me of all my romantic notions early on."

I reach up and caress his rough cheek, instinctively knowing there's a story there. A story of loss and pain.

A man with a big, black *Vengeance Is Mine* tattoo inked into his chest has some seriously heavy baggage.

I take a shot in the dark and guess at what it might be. "You were in love?"

His lips curl. It's a smile, but a bitter one. "If only it were that simple. No, what led me away from god is how my entire family was murdered, one by one, and no one was ever held accountable for it. None of their killers ever paid a price."

His voice drops. "Until I decided to make them pay. And pay they did."

I stare at him with my heart beating fast and my stomach twisting. "Who killed your family?"

In his pause, I sense an ocean of misery.

"There were bloody gang wars in Ireland then. Every day, there was more violence. My parents were caught in the crossfire of a shootout at a café. They were celebrating their wedding anniversary. My older brother, Finn, died in an explosion at a pub. My younger brother, Mac, was killed in a collision with a lorry driven by two IRA members on their way to blow up a bank. And my sister, Cecilia, was in a nightclub that was set on fire by a gang who wanted to intimidate its owner into paying protection. It didn't work, because he died of smoke inhalation along with twenty-three others, including my sister. The doors had been barricaded. Emergency personnel didn't get there soon enough to get everyone out."

I rest my cheek against his chest, close my eyes, and snuggle closer to him. There's nothing I can say to make it better, so I don't even try.

"I had nothing and no one left, including my faith, so I joined the Air Corps. From there, I was recruited to the Directorate of Military Intelligence, Ireland's version of the CIA. And I learned to kill people. Bad people. Threats to national security and the like. I did it so well, I kept getting promoted. Then our family's priest, who'd emigrated to the States before my parents died, contacted me. Said he'd heard of my reputation. Said he didn't agree with my choices, but he'd made some contacts here I might find useful."

His tone turns dry. "For a price, of course. The church looks the other way for sinners whose pockets are deep enough.

"Anyway, it got me to thinking that I needed to expand my base of operations. There were evil men all over the world who weren't being held accountable for their deeds. So I came here, where no one but the priest knew what had happened to my family, joined the Mob, and worked my way up."

"You're good with navigating male-dominated hierarchies."

He exhales heavily. "'Keep your friends close and your enemies closer.' There's no better way to destabilize a system than from the inside."

"So you're a Trojan horse."

"Aye. The goal is checks and balances. There's only so much official legal systems can do. They need a helping hand."

I think about that for a while. Counterterrorism, counterespionage, whacking bad guys while pretending to be friends . . . He's got a lot on his plate.

No wonder he's always so crabby.

"Now that all the heads of the other families are gone, what will happen?"

"They'll regroup. It'll take a while, but there's always a new snake to replace the old one. But you're not in danger anymore of being used as a bargaining chip for them to try to get Kage to reopen their shipping routes."

"Because . . . ?"

"The word's out. You're mine. Anyone who dares to do so much as breathe in your direction dies."

I groan. "I'm sick."

"How so?"

"That made me fall for you even harder."

"If that turns you on, you're definitely spy material. It takes a certain kind of personality to excel in my line of work." He pauses. "Which is why I thought you might be interested."

I look up at him, aghast. "In murdering people for a living? I'm sorry, but no matter how evil they are, I couldn't do it. I don't even like to kill spiders."

"There are many other ways to be useful as a spy."

I furrow my brow. "So it was *your* idea that those assholes on the ship interrogate me?"

"No," he says firmly. "My idea was that I'd be your handler. *Potentially.* But they ran with it and decided to do a trial by fire."

"Handler? What's that?"

"The person who gives you assignments."

I think for a moment. "Except for the killing-people part and you being my boss, it does have a certain glamorous appeal."

Eyes alight, he murmurs, "We'd be like Mr. and Mrs. Smith."

"You really like that idea, don't you?"

"Don't you?"

"What about the yoga studio I'm planning to start? I'd have to change the name to Fit for a Queen—When We're Not Out Spying."

"You could still have your studio. Most people who work in spycraft lead completely normal-looking lives on the outside."

"Spycraft," I repeat, trying out the word. "Ooh."

He chuckles. "See? You like the idea, too."

I quirk my lips. "Let's table this discussion for after breakfast."

He smiles like he's already got it in the bag.

"Changing the subject: how long do you think this truce between you and Kage will last?"

Declan rolls onto his back and tucks me under his arm. I slide my leg over his and wind my foot under his ankle.

"Dunno. I'm still Irish, like his family's killers. He won't be able to look past that for long."

"So you were planning to put him in prison?"

"No, that was the FBI's plan. He was on my hit list, until you asked me not to hurt him. But now he owes me a favor, the bastard."

"Is he really that bad?"

He huffs a short, hard breath out his nose.

I take that as a yes. Nat and I are going to have to put our heads together about how to handle the guest list at her wedding. The rehearsal dinner could be a bloodbath.

Which is the last thing the poor girl needs, considering her first fiancé never showed up for theirs.

Declan turns his head and looks at me with a hard glint in his eye. "Speaking of people I should've killed when I had the chance, did you see Stavros while you were in New York?"

"I haven't seen him since you tried to ship me off to him like you were returning a sofa."

The hard glint fades from his eyes. It's replaced by a tender shine. "You were so angry with me over that."

"I still am. You're not the only one who can hold a grudge."

He rolls over, pressing me against the mattress, and grasps my jaw. "Any way I can make it up to you?"

His tone is suggestive. His eyes are hot. And that big pistol he's packing between his legs is nudging my thigh, hoping for playtime.

I press the smile from my lips and answer him somberly. "Yes. Address me as Your Royal Highness from now on."

Gazing into my eyes, he murmurs, "Anything you want, my queen. Anything and everything, no matter what it is."

Then he kisses me, and in his lips I taste forever.

EPILOGUE

KAGE

*H*e stalks back and forth in front of me like a man possessed, his eyes wild and his energy thermonuclear.

I've never seen him like this. Compared to the rest of my men, Stavros is a mouse.

Then again, love can turn even the sanest man into a raging beast. I should know.

"How could you let him have her?" he shouts, red-faced. "She's mine!"

His words echo off the bare cement walls, rising up to the rafters high above and scattering like pigeons startled into flight.

It's a good thing we're alone in this warehouse. Otherwise, he'd already be bleeding for disrespecting me like that.

"Take a tone like that with me again, and you'll regret it."

He stops short and looks at me, wide-eyed. Wringing his hands, he whispers, "I'm sorry. I'm so sorry, I didn't mean . . . I just . . . I can't live without her. Sloane is my life."

I have no idea how that woman brainwashes men into falling at her feet like slobbering fools, but it's a gift, I have to give it to her. If she ever decided to organize her own syndicate, the rest of the bosses would be in dire trouble. A crooked finger from her, and all our soldiers would desert us in ten seconds flat.

"Take a breath, Stavros. Have a seat." I jerk my chin at a nearby chair.

He collapses into it and props his elbows on his knees. Dropping his head into his hands, he groans. "The Irishman. The *Irishman*. I hate him so much!"

I say drily, "You're not alone in that sentiment."

He lifts his head and looks at me beseechingly. "Why can't you just kill him?"

"Politics."

That's one way to describe it. Another is that my manhood would be chopped off and thrown into a blender by my woman, then fed to stray dogs. But I'm not about to tell him that.

Besides, there are ways around it.

"That's not to say it won't happen. Just not at the moment. And it can't be by me."

His expression turns hopeful. "So I could do it? *I* could kill him, and it would be okay?"

The thought of him getting close enough to lay a finger on that wily Irish bastard is laughable, but I don't want to discourage this kind of enthusiasm.

"Not only would it be okay, I'd give you a year off from tithing."

Energized, he leaps to his feet.

"But not a word to anyone that you received permission," I warn, gazing at him steadily, the threat of violence in my eyes. "Disobey me on that, and you're done."

He babbles his thanks, rushing over to kiss my hand.

I want to swat him away, but I don't have the heart to kick him when he's down.

Falling in love has made me fucking mushy.

We exchange a few more words, then he leaves, looking like he's floating on cloud nine. Had I known he'd be so eager to shed Irish blood, I would've had assignments for him far sooner.

When he's gone, I lock all the doors and turn off all the lights. Then I head to the back of the warehouse to the hidden stairway.

A button recessed in the floor operates a swinging door disguised as a section of brick wall. The door swings slowly open on silent hinges, revealing inky blackness beyond. I walk forward a few steps, feeling around on the wall for the button to close the door.

I hit it. The door swings shut behind me. I'm plunged into darkness.

I hit another switch, and a bare bulb dangling from the ceiling illuminates the staircase landing. I'm surrounded by unpainted drywall on three sides. The fourth side is open, with a pine staircase descending into more darkness.

I trudge down the stairs, flick on the light at the lower landing, and head over to the metal cage.

It's not big, but it is strong, made of reinforced steel bars sunk into concrete top and bottom. Inside the cage is a toilet. On the floor sits a plastic gallon jug of water and an empty plate. On the thin mattress, a man lies on his back.

He turns his head toward me, squinting against the light. He's a young Latino male, just shy of thirty, who the rest of the world thinks is dead.

He might as well be.

I lean a shoulder against his cage and smile down at him.

"Hello, Diego. I understand your friend and former second-in-command, Declan O'Donnell, is a spy. I have a proposition for you."

AUTHOR'S NOTE

Of all the novels I've written, Sloane and Declan are two of my favorite characters. I've heard the same from many readers. I had so much fun with them while writing *Carnal Urges* that I ended up with an entire file of outtakes and deleted scenes, a few of which are included here.

These scenes take place between the end of *Ruthless Creatures* and the start of *Carnal Urges,* after Sloane has been kidnapped by Declan in the parking garage of Kage and Natalie's high-rise building. I played around with how Sloane would react to being kidnapped and came up with a few different scenarios, all of which she kicked ass in either physically or figuratively.

Because as we've seen, Sloane Keller is a fighter and a survivor at heart.

I knew from the get-go that I wanted her to be tougher than her captors, who she'd eventually win over and wrap around her pinkie finger. I just wasn't sure at the start how much to show of the logistics of her being taken. While in the final published version, she wakes up on Declan's plane, in these deleted scenes, Declan doesn't get off quite as easily.

A few other details were changed for the final version, but all of the banter and chemistry remain.

I hope you enjoy the wee camel and her besotted gangster king.

DELETED SCENE #1

SLOANE

Never one to spend time agonizing over decisions, I quickly conclude three things as the SUV rockets down the rain-slicked street at top speed with an army of enraged Russian gangsters in hot pursuit.

First: this will be my one and only trip to New York City. I'm pretty much up for any kind of adventure, but kidnapping is a little over-the-top, even for me.

Second: I'm always going to carry the gun I stole from Stavros. I can't believe I packed almost every item of clothing I own to visit Nat for a week but left the .357 behind in Lake Tahoe. I'm so disappointed in myself.

Third: as soon as I get out of this car, someone is getting his ass kicked.

And by "someone," I mean the blue-eyed bastard who grabbed me and tossed me in here like a sack of rocks.

My kidnapper.

Declan.

I can't wait to see the look on his face when he discovers his captive isn't as defenseless as she looks. Even without Stavros's handy little pistol, I know half a dozen ways to incapacitate a man.

I'm distracted by the pleasing image of my fist crushing Declan's balls when I realize I'm handcuffed. I stare down in astonishment at the cold metal rings encircling my wrists and huff out a disbelieving laugh.

They handcuffed me! The nerve!

"She's awake."

The gruff voice comes from my left.

On the seat next to me in the back of the SUV sits a man large enough to need his own zip code. He's dressed in a black suit with a white shirt and black tie, the standard gangster uniform. Tense and scowling, he glares at me with narrowed eyes and thinned lips, thunderclouds roiling over his head.

I smile at him. "Hi there. I'd ask your name, but considering you'll be dead in a few minutes, it doesn't really matter."

He blinks. He wasn't expecting that.

"Unless you'd like to use what little smarts I suspect lurk in that weirdly giant skull of yours and let me out of the car right now. In that case, you *might* survive. I'll put in a good word. I can't guarantee anything, mind you, but your odds would be better than they are right now. Because when Kage catches up with you . . ."

Still smiling pleasantly, I make a slicing motion across my throat.

Big Brute looks vaguely unnerved. I guess it's less the threat itself and more about how I'm acting. Most kidnapping victims probably aren't quite so composed.

Most kidnapping victims haven't spent as much time as I have around gangsters, either.

Besides, I already know they're not going to kill me. Declan flat-out told me so himself. That was right after he snatched me out of Kage's Bentley, dropped me onto the asphalt of the parking garage, and threw me into this car . . .

Wait. I'm missing something.

I don't remember the time between when we left the parking garage in a thundering roar of squealing tires, revving engines, and gunfire, and right now, speeding down the street toward who knows where with Kage's men on our tail.

And how did I get these handcuffs on?

Did I black out?

The missing time and painfully throbbing spot on the back of my head would indicate a yes.

A cold sense of unease creeps over me. A head injury jarring enough to cause unconsciousness isn't good. At best, it's a concussion. At worst . . .

Well, at worst, I've got bigger problems than being kidnapped by a bunch of Irish gangsters.

As we careen around a corner at top speed, tires squealing, I demand of no one in particular, "You need to take me to a hospital."

I have to shout to be heard over the sound of the engine. It doesn't matter, anyway, because my captors ignore me.

The driver, another Irishman in a black suit, says through gritted teeth, "These bloody Russians are right up my arse!"

He takes another corner too fast, throwing me against the door and making Big Brute brace his feet against the floormats so he doesn't fly across the seat and crush me.

Then, from the front passenger seat, Declan says, "Run the red light."

He sounds utterly calm, as if we're out for a pleasure cruise and not involved in a high-speed chase through busy city streets. At night. In the rain.

While people shoot at us.

The driver doesn't look thrilled by the idea that we play chicken with cross-traffic but doesn't question it. He simply grits his teeth and stomps on the gas pedal.

In the fraction of a second before the SUV lurches forward and the force of it slams me back against the seat, I see Declan's reflection in the passenger side mirror of the car.

He's smiling.

Looking out into the rain, his lips curved into a small, secret smile, he looks as if he's thoroughly enjoying himself.

As we enter the intersection and the headlights of an oncoming car harshly illuminate the hard angles of his face, he smiles wider.

Horn blaring, the oncoming car narrowly misses hitting us, blasting by inches from the rear bumper.

Breathless, I twist around in my seat to look.

More cars slam on their brakes, fishtailing, and the entire intersection becomes blocked within seconds.

When I turn around again and glimpse Declan's face in the mirror, he's yawning.

Yawning.

The man's got balls of steel. I get the feeling it takes something much more dramatic than a high-speed chase to ruffle his feathers.

I don't have time to dwell on what it might be, because I'm probably dying of a brain hemorrhage.

"Excuse me, guys? I hate to break up the party, but unless you want a corpse on your hands, you need to take me to a hospital."

Crickets. Everyone's too focused on being intense and murdery to pay any attention to me. Except for Declan, who's yawning again.

This guy needs a nap.

I say louder, "I'm no use to anybody if I'm dead."

In his lilting Irish brogue that I'm sure he thinks is charming but isn't, Declan says casually, "Oh, I don't know about that. There are plenty of uses for a dead woman. Isn't that right, Kieran?"

Big Brute leers at me and says gruffly, "Aye."

Disgusted, I make a face. "Okay, first of all? Gross. You need professional therapy. Second of all, I'm not joking. Head injuries are extremely serious and can be life-threatening. The risk of a subdural hematoma or traumatic brain injury caused by a fall is real."

The driver glances at Declan and mutters, "What the bloody hell is she on about?"

Declan says, "Brain injury. Sounds like she's got one."

Big Brute pipes up, "Didn't Muhammad Ali die of a traumatic brain injury?"

"Parkinson's," corrects Declan.

"Ach. Tragedy, that. What an athlete. He was my idol when I was a wee chiseler."

Speeding around another corner, the driver says, "I bet David Beckham's got a brain injury. You ever heard that welter talk? I don't think he's the full shilling."

I have no idea what language these people are speaking, but it's not English.

"Hello?" I say, exasperated. "Anybody?"

"We heard you, lass," says Declan, sounding bored. "I'll have the doc take a gander when we land in Boston. Now quit running your mouth. You're about to give *me* a traumatic brain injury."

His two goon buddies chortle while I look back and forth between them in disbelief.

What I wouldn't give for that damn gun.

I'm distracted from thoughts of playing target practice with Declan's face by a sharp stabbing pain in my temple. Wincing, I close my eyes and rub the spot. *Damn, that hurts.*

When I open my eyes again, Declan's looking at me in the side mirror. He's not smiling anymore.

That gives me an idea.

The next corner we speed around, I slump against the door and squeeze my eyes shut, groaning faintly and trying to look as pathetic as possible.

Declan says drily, "You'll never win an Academy Award for Best Actress lass, that's for sure."

I really dislike this guy.

Stavros would've had the decency to fall for my damsel in distress act. He would've made his driver pull over, leapt from the car, and taken me into his arms, clucking and cooing with worry.

This Declan bastard's heart is as icy cold as his blue eyes.

I decide Russian gangsters have better manners than Irish ones. Men who can't be manipulated with feminine wiles are uncivilized.

"Ten minutes to the airport," says the driver.

"Make it five," answers Declan. "We need to be gone before they can get their shit together and try to stop us before we're in the air."

Situation recap: I've been kidnapped.

Handcuffed.

Possibly mentally compromised.

I'm being driven to an airport by a trio of lunatics, one of whom might have a kink for doing bad things to dead women, another who drives like a kindergartener on crack cocaine, and a third so desensitized to violence he doesn't break a sweat under heavy gunfire, high-speed car chases, or narrowly avoiding being crushed to death by an oncoming vehicle.

I'm going to be put on a plane headed for Boston where I'm to meet the head of the Irish mafia to answer some questions about how I may or may not have started a war between his family and the Russians . . . and everyone else.

And my only hope of salvation lies miles behind me in an intersection in a tangled mess of crumpled steel.

I'm in it knee deep, and no knight in shining armor is coming to save me.

Conclusion: this princess is gonna have to save herself.

What the hell. Won't be the first time. Won't be the last.

I wait until we slow slightly for a corner, then take a deep breath, throw open the car door, and jump out.

DELETED SCENE #2

DECLAN

I had a bad feeling when I woke up this morning that today would be a shit show, and I was right.

Kidnapping a woman shouldn't be this fucking hard.

She sails through the air in slow motion like a trapeze artist, arms outstretched, hair flying, a look of intense concentration on her face. I have only a split second to admire her lithe form in the side mirror as she launches herself from the car into the rainy night, graceful as a cat, then she's gone, and I'm hollering.

"Stop the bloody car! She's out! She's out!"

Sean slams on the brakes. The SUV fishtails, then straightens. As soon as we slow enough, I'm out of the car and running after her.

What kind of woman jumps from a moving vehicle?

While handcuffed?

She's either an idiot, a daredevil, or more goddamn trouble than she's worth.

It's not like she's exactly incognito, either. Dressed all in white, she stands out like a candle. She's fifty meters in front of me, running barefoot down the middle of the street.

Running bloody *fast*. This girl is really moving.

I stifle another flash of admiration and run harder, pumping my arms and legs, dodging oncoming traffic and ignoring the blaring horns. Within moments, I've almost got her.

I'm also soaking wet.

And extremely fucking aggravated.

She glances over her shoulder and sees me close behind. She's trapped. We both know it. Parked cars line both sides of the street, packed together bumper to bumper as they always are in this part of the city. If she slows to squeeze between them, I'll have her.

Then she veers sharply right and does something so unexpected I almost stumble.

In one long leaping stride, she jumps up onto the hood of a parked car and uses it as a springboard to launch herself to the sidewalk beyond.

It's effortless. It looks professional, like she spends her days jumping on and off large wet objects in her bare feet while fleeing her kidnappers.

Another flash of admiration is followed by the uncomfortable sense that I might be dealing with more than I bargained for.

She lands in a crouch, pops right back up, and disappears around a corner.

The rain and the traffic noise must be messing with my hearing, because I could swear I hear her laughing as she goes.

DELETED SCENE #3

DECLAN

Whether it's opening a business, starting a relationship, or going to war with your sworn enemy after he killed a few of your men, the beginning of any new venture is the most important time. What happens at the start sets the tone for everything that follows.

My point is that when things begin badly, they have a tendency to stay that way.

Which, considering my current situation, is concerning.

Kidnapping a woman shouldn't be this fucking hard.

"Go get her, Kieran."

He snorts. "I like my balls where they are, boss."

"It wasn't a request."

He looks at Sean, curled into a ball on the wet ground, his eyes squeezed shut in pain, cupping his groin and weakly groaning. Then Kieran looks at the woman standing over him in the street.

Chin up, fists clenched, eyes blazing. A defiant set to her mouth. Bathed in the glow of the streetlights, her dark hair glimmering with droplets of evening rain, she's undeniably beautiful.

But her beauty isn't that of a princess or a butterfly, delicate and sweet.

It's that of a samurai sword, all deadly curves and sharp edges.

Sloane. It's Irish for "raider."

Should be Irish for "giant pain in the ass."

From the second she regained consciousness in the back seat of the car, she's done nothing but mouth off and fight. I've met rabid dogs who were more agreeable.

Kieran makes an impatient gesture with his hand in the dangerous beauty's direction. "Oy. Lass. Get over here and get your arse back in the Escalade before I lose my temper."

Her smile is grim. "You want me? Come and get me. Fifty bucks says I'll make you cry even louder than your friend."

Staggering as he tries to rise from the ground, Sean grunts. "Bitch."

She looks at him down her nose and tosses her hair over her shoulder. "That's Queen Bitch to you, fuckboy."

I don't understand this woman. Why isn't she crying? Sobbing? Pleading for her life? She's alone, unarmed, and surrounded by ten gun-toting men. She's standing in the middle of a dark, rainy street, with no way to escape and nowhere to go if she did.

She's been fucking kidnapped!

There must be something mentally wrong with her. That bump she took to the head when Kieran accidentally dropped her onto the asphalt back in the parking garage where we snatched her knocked something loose in her pretty skull.

Whatever the reason, I don't have time for this shit.

I say coldly, "You have five seconds to get back in the car."

She looks me up and down, green eyes assessing. "Or what? You'll shoot me?"

"In three more seconds, you'll find out."

"If I'm dead, I'm useless to you."

I drop my voice an octave and hold her gaze. "There are plenty of uses for a dead woman. Isn't that right, Kieran?"

"Aye, boss. Plenty of uses." Licking his lips, he lets his gaze travel the length of her body, head to feet and back again.

Instead of putting the fear of God into her as I expected, it lights a fuse of fury under her ass.

Her nostrils flare. Her cheeks turn red. Her eyes burn two holes straight through me.

She folds her arms across her chest and snaps, "That's sick, dude. You need help. The professional kind. Seriously, just . . . ew."

After a beat, Kieran turns and looks at me. "Did she just call you *dude*?"

He's trying not to laugh, the son of a bitch.

Keeping my gaze on Sloane, I answer through gritted teeth. "She did. And if you don't lock the fucking doors this time when I get her back into the car, I'll let this crazy bird kick your balls even harder than she did Sean's."

Without waiting for an answer, I walk closer to where Sloane stands. She's about fifteen feet away from the SUV she escaped from, taking advantage of the slowed speed when the car braked for a corner to leap out and run.

I realize I should've had Sean cuff her, but she was blacked out at the time, slumped against the door in the back seat and looking all kinds of defenseless and pathetic.

Two things I now know she's not.

How long she was awake and pretending not to be, timing her escape attempt, is anyone's guess.

I take my time approaching her and stop a few feet away. Far enough to be out of reach from that vicious kick of hers that took Sean down. Despite wearing heels and a skirt, she adopts a fighting stance, balancing her weight on the balls of her feet and raising her fists to eye level.

She's ready to defend herself. To physically fight me.

Me, a man twice her size and weight with years of military background, weapons training, and hand-to-hand combat experience.

It's ridiculous, but also oddly appealing.

Examining my expression, she says, "You think I'm funny? Take two more steps closer and you'll never be able to have kids."

"I don't have time for this nonsense. Get back in the car."

"Why, are you afraid to fight me? You should be. Even though I'm smaller than you, I'll win."

"I see you've taken the David and Goliath story to heart, but Biblical parables aside, there's no universe in which we fight and you win."

"I can break your jaw without breaking a fingernail."

I want to sigh deeply, but don't. "This is pointless. Get back in the car. *Now*."

"You won't think it's pointless when I'm through with you. I'm a black belt, asshole."

Looking at her trendy outfit, expensive haircut, and meticulous makeup, I lift my brows. "Really? In what, online shopping? Makeup tutorial videos? Savage celebrity takedowns in internet chat rooms?"

Her eyes glittering, she says softly, "Shōrin-ryū, you smug prick. And you won't be the first man to underestimate me and find out fast he wishes he didn't. Just because I'm girly doesn't mean I'm a little girl."

I'm aware of the men staring at us, and of the rain drumming softly on the roofs of the SUVs, and of my own impatience, a hot and prickly sensation inside my chest and on the back of my neck.

I'm also aware of her bare legs, full lips, and tits.

But more than all that, I'm aware that this defiance and self-confidence of hers is a strange, unexpected, and very powerful turn-on.

Fuck.

I decide to ignore that for the moment and try a different approach. Otherwise, we could be standing out in the cold all night.

"Okay. You're a black belt in Sho-whatever. I apologize for insulting you."

Sloane narrows her eyes at me. She doesn't lower her fists.

"I have no intention of harming you. Neither do my men. My instructions are only to take you to see my boss. He wants to talk, nothing more. If you cooperate, this will be over very quickly. I'll take you wherever you want to go, and you'll never see me again."

I pause for a moment to let that sink in. Then, staring straight into her eyes, I add quietly, "If you don't cooperate, however, I'll hurt you in ways you can't imagine and won't recover from. I say that not as a threat, but as a statement of fact."

She swallows hard, the first and only sign of fear she's shown so far.

"So you have no problem hurting a woman, huh, big guy?"

"You're the ones who're so adamant about equality, lass. You've gotta take the bad with the good. Now please put your fists down and get back into the fucking car before I'm forced to do something I don't want to do."

I step aside and hold out my arm toward the SUV.

She looks me over, taking her time, her jaw working, anger and ambivalence flashing in her eyes. Then she exhales, lowers her arms to her sides, and pulls back her shoulders.

"Fine," she says tightly, not looking at me. "But only because you said please."

With that, she walks past me, head held high, and climbs back into the SUV, slamming the door shut behind her.

PLAYLIST

"Good Time Girl" Sofi Tukker

"Flames" R3hab, Zayn, and Jungleboi

"Up" Cardi B

"Take It" Dom Dolla

"Wildside" Claptone

"Hey Lion" Sofi Tukker

"Let Me Touch Your Fire" Arizona

"Medicine" James Arthur

"Cuz I Love You" Lizzo

ACKNOWLEDGMENTS

. . . and the twists keep a'comin'. I love writing good guy/bad guy characters because you never know what they're going to do next!

(If you haven't yet read the *Beautifully Cruel* mafia duet, you might want to go back and read that to get an introduction to Diego and Declan. That's where they first show up.)

Thank you to Linda Ingmanson for being a great editor. Fantastic job fixing stuff!

Thanks to my girl at Social Butterfly PR, Sarah Ferguson, for always being on top of it, even when it hasn't been easy. You're a rock star.

Shannon Smith at SS Media Co, I heart you. How long has it been now? Twenty years? Amazing work. Amazing responsiveness. So much appreciation for all you and Scott have done for me.

Thanks to Letitia Hasser at RBA Designs for doing my covers, putting up with my anal retentiveness, and only saying, "You're killin' me, Smalls!" once since we've been working together. I deserved it way more times.

Thank you to my wonderful, amazing, beautiful readers, who tolerate my love for multiple adjectives to describe things and are probably better people than I am. It depends on how much wine I've had to drink when I think about it. I spend my days with fictional characters I make up in my head to entertain *you*. Hopefully, it works once in a while.

Thank you to my husband of twenty-one years, Jay, the most competent and thoroughly badass human I've ever met.

Mom and Dad, I miss you and think of you every day. I hope you're proud of me.

ABOUT THE AUTHOR

J.T. Geissinger is a #1 international and Amazon Charts bestselling author. Ranging from funny, feisty rom-coms to intense, erotic thrillers, her books have sold more than fifteen million copies worldwide and have been translated into more than twenty languages.

She is a three-time finalist in both contemporary and paranormal romance for the RITA Award, the highest distinction in romance fiction from the Romance Writers of America. She is also a recipient of the PRISM Award for Best First Book, the Golden Quill Award for Best Paranormal/Urban Fantasy, and the HOLT Medallion for Best Erotic Romance.

Find her online at www.jtgeissinger.com.